Hearts on the Table

Julia Fisher

For the perfectionists, the quiet ones, the ones carrying the weight of the world.

And for Cynthia, who called me a writer before I ever imagined I could be one. She could walk a man like a dog without breaking a sweat. This first one's for you.

Chapter 1

Lainey

Time was standing still. Or maybe it had just slowed down dramatically, like in the movies when someone leaps over a table to fling themselves in front of a bullet, yelling a long, distorted, "*NooOoooOooOooooo!*"

At least, that's what it felt like. It was hard to gauge, considering everyone around me had stopped moving, too. You could hear a pin drop in the Cardiovascular ICU. The shiny, pristine floors and mirrored windows all reflected my frozen face back at me.

Across the heads of my residents, my favorite nurse practitioner, Rija, widened her eyes at me. That, too, seemed to happen underwater.

The man before me wasn't helping. Most days, I didn't mind talking to Dr. Samuel Reese. His slow, methodical demeanor could be a pleasant change of pace to the hustle and bustle of the cardiac unit. Usually, interactions with him felt like pumping the brakes. Today, it was more like running into a brick wall.

"Sorry, could you repeat that?" Surely, I had misheard him.

Golden lashes lowered in the slowest blink known to humanity. The residents around us held their breath as Reese responded with: "Collaborate with Jones and come back to me with some different options."

"*What the fuck?*" someone whispered from the back of the group. To my left, I could practically feel the smug satisfaction radiating off of Dr. Robert Jones, the other fellow in my year. I did my best to ignore him.

"I…" I faltered. Having never been denied an OR before, I wasn't sure how to proceed. "The patient's repeated episodes of angina make her a strong candidate for a bypass."

Reese continued studying me, expressionless. I bit my tongue to stop from filling the silence with more details that Reese probably didn't even need. I'd already reported everything on the patient, her comorbidities, and all the justifications for her surgery. Maybe he didn't fully comprehend what I said. The man was a solid surgeon, but for all the reaction he was giving me, I might as well have been speaking to a bowl of oatmeal.

"I understand." Reese paused here, blinking again. He tipped his head towards my colleague. "Jones recently had a similar case. He can help. Hold that OR till you consult with him."

My turn to blink. Surely I was having some sort of end-of-shift, oatmeal-induced hallucination. In my three years as a fellow at Chicago's Cedar Hospital, and five years as a resident here before that, no one had ever denied me an operating room. Ever. Certainly not Reese.

Dr. Whitaker may have been the hospital's educational program director, but Reese, who was just a few years older than me, had taken on a lion's share of voluntary resident and fellow responsibilities. Working at a teaching hospital like Cedar, everyone was expected to educate the next wave of doctors. Reese took it to a whole new level, personally shepherding the baby residents until they got their sea legs. Over the last few years, he'd taken more and more duties over from Whitaker, too.

He was basically the unofficial resident dad, at this point. I didn't have a problem with him or his general slowness, since he usually signed off on my cases and approved every surgical procedure I recommended.

Until now.

One bracing breath later, I was about to calmly, and frickin' politely, ask Reese where he got off. But the porridge wasn't done.

"I also rescheduled you off that EVLP with Cooper next week. You'll scrub in with Mitchell on a quad bypass, instead. Jones, you're scrubbing in with Cooper."

Jones sucked in a breath right as mine whooshed out. Sucker punched.

"I...I...You mean the Ex Vivo Lung Perfusion and transplant?" I asked, just in case there was another super cool and amazingly rare and complicated surgery Dr. Gabriel Cooper was performing next week, also called an EVLP...and I was just confused. "Dr. Cooper specifically asked for me on that case, sir."

Because Dr. Cooper *always* requested me for his cases. Especially the cool ones. Only five years out of his own fellowship, and he'd made a name for himself by pushing the boundaries of surgical innovation. Almost daily, he dealt with complex, cutting-edge procedures, and I geeked out on them as much as he did. I was his freaking *protégé*. Reese couldn't just take me off the case.

"I'm aware. We'll make it work next time. Jones, get with Cooper to review the patient files." After one last expressionless look, Reese nodded, then turned to trudge down the hallway.

"Next time?" I muttered through gritted teeth. There wouldn't be a next time for years. It was an advanced procedure, and Cooper had been putting all the pieces in place for this surgery for *months*. And I was one of those pieces, darn it.

Around me, the residents scattered, as we always did after evening rounds. A few patted me on the back, or muttered apologies. Some of them looked as shocked as I felt. I could only imagine what was going through their heads. *"Carmichael got taken off a case? Now I've seen everything…"*

Jenkins, a first-year resident, placed a Snickers bar on my tablet. "Maybe you need this more than me," he whispered before scuttling away. I'd slid it into his pocket not even an hour ago, after word had made it around that he'd gotten kicked out of an OR this afternoon for failing to exhaustively list the various causes of sepsis.

Residency was brutal, and we'd all had those crushingly bad days. I'd hoped the chocolate, and a little support, would give him a boost. *"It's Reese on rounds tonight. You know he'll go easy on you,"* I'd told Jenkins. More the fool, me.

"I'm assuming now would be a bad time to gloat?" Jones' grin could have lit up the whole surgical ward.

"Yeah. Probably."

"Don't take it so hard, Lainey. I'm sure there's a good reason," he cajoled as he followed me down the hall, undeterred by my stomping feet.

"Yeah. I'm sure it wasn't personal," I muttered, ducking into the break room. Rija leaned against the quartz countertop, waiting for her coffee to brew. Her big brown eyes widened as she pointed towards the main floor, where I'd just smacked face-first into failure.

"Um, what the fuck was that?"

"Reese denied her OR request for Mrs. Marquett until she could consult me on it. And I'm on the EVLP now."

For a self-professed "friend" of mine, Jones didn't have to sound so smug about it all. Not that I was surprised. As the only cardiothoracic surgery fellows of our year, we were constantly paired together. Despite working so closely, I'd never grown accustomed to his smarmy vibes.

"We can salvage this, though. Let's grab some drinks and talk about the Marquett case." He tousled his chestnut-brown, prince charming hair, eyes scraping up the front of my scrubs.

Exhibit A.

"Jones, you little shit, I wasn't talking to you. You're not helping anything, and she doesn't want to go out with you. Especially not after she just got bitch-slapped during rounds by an attending." Rija scowled, and I once again thanked God for her existence. I was in no mood to deal with Jones tonight.

Everyone else tip-toed around him, hesitant to piss off the grandson of the head of Cedar's surgical quality board. He made it a point to remind everyone, as often as possible, that his grandaddy, Robert Sturmond, had almost single-handedly made the shiny new hospital I stood in a reality.

Thankfully, when everyone else walked on eggshells around him, Rija didn't hesitate to verbally smack him around a little bit.

"Double whammy, huh?" Rija reached out to rub my shoulder as Jones shuffled out the door. I felt bad enough that I let her console me for a few seconds before I crossed to the coffee bar. Her hand fell.

"I don't even want to talk about the EVLP. I'm going to have to get with Cooper to see if he can pull rank. And when I asked about the OR for Marquett, Reese told me to get *Jones's* input on it. As if I didn't just conduct that successful bypass graft two weeks ago by myself? Frack that. I should have just waited and asked Cooper when he's on call tomorrow."

Cooper would have given me OR priority in a heartbeat, as long as he'd be able to make some cuts. Nearing the end of my fellowship, with interviews just around the corner for an open attending surgeon position at Cedar, I was desperate enough for surgical time that I'd hand him the scalpel myself.

She nodded, considering me. "I know you don't cuss, so I'll go ahead and say it for you: what the hell, Reese? Fuck off!"

"Thank you!" One of the great things about Rija—she had a mouth like a sailor and I always appreciated the assist. Sometimes, telling someone to "frack off" just wasn't as effective.

"Any time. Sending you to Jones was a low blow. You're perfectly capable."

"Thank you," I breathed while I grabbed a tea bag. The familiar habit of filling my beat-up insulated mug with hot water soothed a modicum of the rage swirling inside me. "Stupid Reese. What does he know, anyway?"

"Well..." Rija quibbled, fiddling with a few buttons on the fancy chrome espresso machine.

"What?" My voice was as flat as Reese's, which was an accomplishment. Just thinking about his slow, bland take down in front of the residents boiled my blood. "Talking to him is like trying to speak to a bowl of oatmeal. How did he even get a job here?"

"Ouch," Rija sputtered out a laugh, eyes darting around the empty black leather couches and pristine white tables of the lounge. "Pull those punches a little, lady. He's not a bad surgeon."

I scowled at the hot water in my cup. So, maybe he wasn't the worst surgeon on the floor. But I was too caught up in my feels to admit that, yes, Reese was in fact a very competent doctor. He'd have to be to end up here, at one of the most prominent cardiac programs in the country.

"I mean, maybe he's not the most exciting guy in the world. But he takes care of the baby residents. It's that 'Northwestern' in him; the teaching hospital DNA. The residents learn more from him than all the other attendings, combined."

Ok, fine. Reese was also a good teacher. And he had a habit of pointing us in the right direction and letting us figure things out for ourselves, which I usually enjoyed. But right now, in this moment, he'd humiliated me in front of freakin' Jones *and* my residents, and that made me want to key his car.

"Aaaand..." Rija handed me a cup of ice, leaning back like I would bite.

"What." I anticipated betrayal.

Rija flung her hands up to her shoulders. "I'm just saying Jones is an ass, but he isn't a complete dummy, either. He just had two CAD cases last month. Let him look at the files. Can't hurt, you know?"

I sipped my tea. Apparently, there were *two* cars to key tonight.

Rija steered me out of the room. "Listen. You've been here since five a.m. and were supposed to go home an hour ago. Let Jones look at the files, chat with Cooper in the morning, and let the anger go. Be the bigger person. Even the great Lainey Carmichael can take an L every once in a while."

She gave me a little push towards the staff locker rooms. I glared at her, knowing somewhere deep, deep, *deep* down that maybe she was right. Maybe.

"Jones still sucks, though," I growled. She patted my head.

"Yes he does, sweetie. I'll tell him to fuck off again when I see him next."

I slumped into the lockers to grab my stuff. Keying two cars in my current state would have been too much work, anyway.

***

I slept poorly. Even though I didn't have to be at work until eight (practically afternoon, in the surgical world), I swung out of bed as soon as my alarm rang at five-thirty. I'd spent the night tossing and turning, beating myself up, and was eager to pound something else into the ground.

I yanked on a workout set from a pile of unfolded laundry in my closet before padding across the apartment to start water for tea. I'd lived in this unit for three years now, upgrading to the shiny new building as a reward to myself for bagging the Cedar fellowship.

The tall ceilings and fake-wood floors might have seemed homey, if I'd bothered to decorate. But I didn't spend enough time here to invest much in hanging pictures, or whatever.

That could come after I was an attending, perhaps, and had some more time and money on my hands. For now, I had a gray Ikea couch and a few chairs if I needed a place to sit. A dining room table from Target I'd only used once. The most color in the place was in the corner where I'd set up my desk, which was covered in Post-it notes, index cards, and medical journals. When I wasn't at the hospital, I was usually there, working on research.

While the kettle warmed, I brushed my teeth and flicked through emails. Jones had already sent over his thoughts on the case. The notes were thoughtful, his recommendations sound, despite the strong whiff of superiority practically oozing from my screen. Jones also didn't recommend surgery. *Frack.* I flicked to my other emails, vowing to think on it later when I didn't feel so crabby.

A night spent thinking about Reese and the case and the patient had given me some distance from the roaring anger I'd felt last night, but my ego still sported a dent. It would take me some more time to fully get over it.

I glossed over a few notes from a research partner at UCLA who was working with me on a paper, a note from my mother reminding me about the upcoming reception for a regional cardiology association, and...

I froze, toothpaste dripping down my chin, staring at the name I'd have sworn I'd never see in my inbox again.

From: Kate.McDaniels@HoustPresbyterian.com
Subject: DON'T DELETE - CHI JOB - PLEASE READ!!

Blood froze in my veins before blazing through my body. A thrumming sound filled my ears and my eyes narrowed, tunnel vision burning a laser beam into the email that I wanted to print out just so I could shred.

Seeing her name obliterated any semblance of calm I'd cultivated last night. The anger sprang back to life, hot and illogical.

I slammed the sink on, slurping water and flinging my toothbrush into its cup, nearly shattering the ceramic. My reflection in the mirror looked wild; normally unruly brown curls spiked in crazy disarray from my restless night. Freckles were stark against my usually tan skin, bleached now by outrage and something that felt uncomfortably close to fear. Beneath arched, disbelieving brows, my brown eyes were wide open. *What did she think she was doing?*

I swiped to delete Katie's message without opening it and fled my apartment, water droplets still sluicing down my face. I needed to pound something sooner rather than later.

My building was conveniently located between Cedar's new hospital and my gym. Work five minutes in one direction, work-out fifteen minutes in the other. When embroiled in a tumultuous fury, the gym commute was closer to ten. Gravel spewed as I pulled into the parking lot behind the building.

R^3 had opened just last year and ticked all my boxes: It was new, clean, well-equipped, and it didn't hurt that since I'd been coming here for the last few weeks, I'd struck up something of a flirtation with the gym's hot owner, Will. His brother, Conner (also hot, but sporting a wedding band), ruled over the other half of the business, a high-tech physical therapy practice specializing in athletic recovery.

The prospect of working off some steam and getting a little shameless flirting in was appealing. Maybe Will would wear me out and charm me senseless so I could stop feeling like I wanted to strangle someone. I didn't want to think about Katie and her email, so my brain helpfully supplied the next best person for me to imagine pounding into the gym mats. *Reese.* The oatmeal, himself.

Rija's words bounced around my head. *"He's a good teacher."* He was, darn it, and the interns and residents universally favored him. All that boring translated into boundless patience, which meant he didn't lose his crap when we messed up. It would also be just like him to send me to Jones to make me work on my collaboration with other doctors or whatever. Or to help me see for myself if I was making a wrong call, so that I could self-correct before he stepped in.

But that didn't mean that for the next hour, I had to like him. *"Be the better person,"* Rija had said. Well, sure. I could do that. But only after I imagined my punching bag was his face for a while.

"There's my favorite regular!" Despite my mood, I couldn't help but return Will's smile as I walked through the doors. He was standing at the reception desk, talking to a tall man while the rest of the class spread out by the mats. "Hey, I'm not sure if you've met my other brother, Sam? You're usually a morning person and he's mostly here at night."

My smile froze.

"Dr. Reese?" I sounded out the syllables of his name through gritted teeth.

"Lainey." He nodded at me. I was so caught off guard seeing him here, in my inner sanctum, I almost didn't notice that he'd called me by my first name. Not Doctor, or Carmichael. *Lainey.* The familiarity grated.

"I didn't know you worked out here." Translation: *What the frickity-frack are you doing at my gym?!*

His head tilted ever-so-slightly towards Will. "Brother."

Right. That made sense. Looking between the two of them now, I could kind of see the resemblance. Though Will was clean-shaven with brown hair, they had the same blue eyes. The same big, tall build and, if I thought about it, the same thoughtful, focused way of moving. Even Conner lumbered around like that. Reese gave the same patient encouragement to freaked out residents as Will did when people in class were almost ready to give up.

I felt stupid that I hadn't seen these similarities before, or bothered to look up Will's last name. It took some of the wind out of my sails. If it was his brothers' gym, this place had been Sam's long before it had been mine. Maybe this was *his* inner sanctum? Though that didn't quite compute.

Considering he was the most boring man alive, I hadn't given any thought to Reese's extracurricular activities. I just assumed he'd left work, driven his boring car to his boring house, and stared at the wall till it was time for work again. Like a surgical robot.

But now, suddenly, he was here in *my* gym, wearing something other than scrubs. Without an OR scrub cap, his dark blond hair was thick and wavy, like he'd run his fingers through it a few times. It matched a short beard that was a little more unkempt than I was used to seeing it. Clear blue eyes seemed sharper here than they did within the hospital walls.

The quick-dry fabric of his t-shirt clung to his muscles. I'd never seen those before. I knew he was tall, but all at once I realized he was jacked. Jacked like he worked out all the time. Jacked like his brother owned a gym. Like he wasn't such a robot after all.

Frack.

"So, you two know each other?"

"Yeah." I tried my best to fix my falling smile. It wasn't Will's fault that his brother was on my "cars to key later" list. "We work together at Cedar. Dr. Reese is...just...great..." I swear I heard something pop in my jaw from all the grinding.

Dr. Reese, as usual, didn't even put in the effort to respond verbally. He opted to nod his head a few times and call it a day. It made me want to howl. Why couldn't he just *speak*? Why did he and his oatmealness have to crash my OR dreams *and* my gym?

Well, you know what? Fine. If I could be a bigger person with Jones, I could be a bigger person with Reese. I'd been hoping to burn off my ire with some serious circuit training. So now, I'd just have to do that while he was in the room with me. Whatever.

"Well, I'm going to go warm up." I gave them both a tight smile.

"Sure thing! We'll start in a few."

I gave Will a thumbs up over my shoulder without looking back.

Whatever.

Fine.

Oatmeal.

Chapter 2

Sam

"You're sure that's the one?"

My gaze trailed Lainey Carmichael's back from head-to-heels. That familiar, curly ponytail swung as she walked over to the rubber mats. Her profile reflected in the mirrors was as familiar as my own. Pouty lips, cheekbones sprinkled with freckles. The tick in her jaw from clenching her teeth.

Oh, yes. "That's the one."

She smiled at a guy in a red shirt as she plopped down to stretch. They struck up a conversation. It never ceased to amaze me how comfortable Lainey was talking to strangers. Even when I knew she wanted to punch something (like me, right now), she still managed to work a room without breaking a sweat. It was one of the things that had first drawn me to her. Years later, watching her shine still hadn't gotten old.

Beside me, Will cursed. "I was really hoping."

"Hmm." I dragged my attention away from Lainey to frown at him. "And how many Lainey Carmichaels do you think work in my department?"

"I don't know, man. Stranger things have happened." Will and I both turned to sneak a glance at where Lainey was rolling her shoulders, mixing among the handful of people ambitious enough to make it to the gym at six a.m. on a Saturday morning. "Well, I'll back off."

I grimaced. Conner and I had given him shit for weeks when he'd started talking about a new member at the gym who had caught his eye. Even with his policy not to mix business with pleasure, he'd seemed interested enough to make an exception with Lainey. Once he'd learned she worked at Cedar, he'd begged me to come see if it was *my* Lainey. Just in case.

Well, case closed. She was. But that didn't mean I had any claim on her. "Dibs is for the last slice of pizza, William." Not for people, and definitely not for her.

"Sam." My brother lowered his voice and leveled a penetrating stare in my direction. "You've been in love with her for years. I'm not going after her."

I shrugged, even though my stomach pitched at the idea of Will "going after" Lainey. Where I was quiet enough to cross the line into awkward, Will had personality in spades. Everyone loved him. If he set his sights on her, it would be game over for me. Not that the game had ever really gotten started to begin with.

"I've hardly even spoken to her outside of work. She doesn't know..." that I'd already named our hypothetical future children. All three of them.

Will waved a hand in the air. "Doesn't matter, bro. I'm not going after your girl. You've been mooning over her for long enough that she's practically already a member of the family."

"You make me sound like a loser," I muttered, bending to retrieve the towel and water bottle from my bag. Yes, maybe I'd been aware of—even attracted to—Lainey for a long time. But my brother didn't have to make it sound like I was pining after her.

"Not a loser. Can't date residents or fellows. I get that." Will gave me a sideways look. "Might be for the best right now. She didn't seem happy to see you."

"She's not." Lainey hadn't outright glared at me when she'd walked in, but the smile had slipped right off her face. In Lainey's world, that was as good as a middle finger. Yeah, I'd known she'd be pissed about me sending her to Jones, but she hadn't been in the mood to listen to me, anyway. And the EVLP wasn't even my gig. I was just the messenger.

"What'd you do?" Will waved at a few stragglers jogging in before the class started.

"Gave her some work she won't enjoy. Had to pull her off a big surgery."

"Seems like you should apologize. Something like, 'Hey, sorry about that thing. But I see your face in my dreams and I want to build you a house like in *The Notebook* and fill it with our babies.'"

"William—"

"Besides, isn't her program almost done? Surely this close to the finish line, the attending/fellow dating rule doesn't apply."

Yes, in fact, her program was almost done. Only two months and she'd be fair game. We had two open attending roles and one of them was practically hers for the taking. Then, once she had settled into her new job, maybe I would start thinking about ways to work *The Notebook* into our conversations. If she ever let me speak to her again.

"A few weeks won't matter, bro. Ask her out." Will clapped me on the back, then turned to the rest of the room. "Hey! Let's have some fun today. Not many people brave the elements this early on a Saturday, so let's make it count!" Will called to the five other attendees for today's class.

"Let's start on the bags for a treat. Pair off for me, Lainey and Sam, Erica and John..."

I carefully schooled my face to stop from glowering at my brother. Lainey's expression turned sour for a heartbeat before she rose from the floor and stationed herself by a bag. She paid unnecessarily close attention as Will explained the warm up—a simple kick box combo that we'd switch back and forth. She fiddled with her hair and tied her shoe. Frowned down at her gloves as she pulled them on. Anything to avoid looking at me.

Finally, when she took a test punch at the bag, I stepped forward to stabilize it. My face was only a few inches from her fist. She couldn't avoid me now.

"You're mad."

Punch, punch, kick. "No."

I sighed, watching her execute a near-perfect combo again. "You're upset about the EVLP."

"I'd prefer"—*kick*—"not to speak about work things"—*punch*—"while I'm not at work." *Punch.*

"Switch!" Will called. Lainey shook her hands out and took her spot behind the bag. I lobbed a few punches at it.

"It might help if you didn't consider me your attending right now," I offered. She laughed out loud. *Yeah, right.* I threw a few more combinations at the bag as she watched my feet in silence.

"Switch!"

She moved to the front and paused, swiping a small curl off her forehead. Some hairs had gotten stuck in her long, brown eyelashes. I held my breath, but she threw another punch without saying a word. Again, and again, and again. After a few rounds of that quiet, focused repetition, she started laying down a real beating. The next kick to the bag would have sent me staggering to the side if I hadn't readjusted my hold.

"Aim a little higher. You can pretend it's my head."

A huff of laughter burst out of her lips even as she scowled. I wanted to make her angry-laugh until the day I died.

"I don't...want to kick you..." she panted, throwing more combinations and mixing in a few new kicks, too. Sweat shone on her forehead, her cheeks glowing from the exertion.

"Arguable," I muttered when her sneaker landed mere centimeters from my nose. Another huff, then more silence.

"Switch!"

Something about making her laugh made me bold. "Take my turn. You have more aggression to work out."

"Reese..." she hissed, pacing away with her hands on her hips. She grimaced before throwing a few more punches.

"I'm sorry about the EVLP. And Jones," I started once she got back into a rhythm. She cut me off before I could get any momentum going on a real apology.

"Jones is a buttface."

I wasn't going to touch that one. Jones was an entitled brat, but it didn't mean he was a bad doctor. "I just went through this same thing with him a few months ago. Surgery isn't always the answer. Check out his notes and you'll see for yourself."

I stumbled when she slammed a kick into the side of the bag. Her roundhouse made me want to fall to my knees and weep. *Gorgeous.*

"You could have"—*punch*—"just told me"—*punch*—"that." *Kick.*

"You'd just have gone to Cooper."

She scowled again, which told me I'd hit on the truth. The guy would have approved her surgery in a heartbeat. "A bypass might feel like the right move now, but it won't fix the underlying issue."

"Switch!"

We ignored my brother's command. Lainey aimed a halfhearted jab at the bag. "Okay, maybe...you're right."

I'm not sure what my face betrayed, but I was exactly right and we both knew it. Her scowl deepened. I wanted to trace the little lines between her brows with my finger.

"Fine. But"—*punch, punch, punch, punch*—" my freaking EVLP?!"

"Orders from above. Don't shoot the messenger."

"You're practically in charge of the fellowship program. You could have pushed back." She wouldn't be glaring at me so much if she knew just how much I'd pushed back on that mandate from the board.

Jones' grandfather had pitched an everloving fit when he noticed Lainey got better surgical cases than his grandson did, and he'd put Lainey directly in his sights. After sitting through his winding, half-hearted speech about equal learning opportunities, I'd kicked up enough of a racket that the director of the program had pulled me aside.

"Your points are valid, Reese. We can't let the quality board choose the people in the room with the patients. We can't do anything about it now. Let me handle the next one."

It was nice to know the director had my back. But that didn't do shit to help Lainey now.

"I was integral"—*punch*—"to that"—*punch*—"case. And you humiliated me"—*punch*—" with frickin' Jones." *Kick.*

"I tried to get them to change their mind. When that didn't work, I got you a quad bypass. It won't be a walk in the park. And Jones isn't half bad, either," I offered. She didn't even deign to look at me, scowl or not. And I hated that. "Come on, Carmichael. Don't get a God complex on me now."

She wasn't. She wouldn't. She was a helluva doctor. I'd gotten about four requests for her to assist with surgeries next week within hours of the EVLP clearing from her calendar. The bypass had been the most complicated, the only bone I could throw to her.

She paced away again, resting her gloved hands on her head. That little curl had escaped again. Will strolled into my line of sight and gave me a *what is happening here?* look. I ignored him, as I did, often.

"I am sorry that I compared you to oatmeal. It was unkind and I regret it. It was undeserved."

"Excuse me?" I wasn't sure what threw me most: that she'd chosen this moment to make eye contact with me for the first time all morning, or the words she'd blurted. "Oatmeal?"

She swallowed, eyes round. Contrite. "I was angry yesterday. And I compared you to oatmeal, which is inexcusable and unprofessional. So I apologize."

"For...comparing me to oatmeal?"

"Switch!"

"Yes. Kind of, you know...bland." She had the decency to look away as she said this. All the better, because she'd just round-house-kicked me right in the proverbial nuts.

"Ouch." Bland. It was just another word for boring. Or shy or uninteresting. Things that people had been calling me my whole life. It rarely bothered me anymore. I knew I wasn't oatmeal, so to speak. But I'd hoped that maybe Lainey, who I'd worked with for several years, might have seen that, too. "Are the residents going to give me a new nickname now?"

Her shoulders bunched up to her ears. "No, I only said it to Rija. I was just venting. Listen, I'm really sorry. But this is maybe the longest actual conversation we've ever had with each other, like, ever. And I'm realizing just now that I haven't given you enough credit. I tend to be fairly single-minded."

I already knew that. Sometimes I shuffled a little closer to her in the OR just to make sure she was still breathing. She got so caught up in the procedure she nearly forgot about basic vital functions. "Single-minded" was putting it lightly.

"But you're being really honest and you're right. You're right about all of it, with Jones and the collaborating and all the things. Insulting you is childish and if you're being honest, I will be honest, too." She bit her lip, looking up at me. "Again, I'm sorry. I hope this doesn't affect our working relationship."

"Break! Sam, you decide you're not participating today?" I held my hand up to Will. I didn't want him intruding on whatever was happening in this moment with Lainey. Oatmeal aside, she was standing there with her hip cocked, staring right at me. And something about it felt new. She'd looked at me almost every day for the past three years, but right now, right this second, was the first time she'd ever *seen* me.

"Oatmeal is pretty brutal."

She hid her face in the gloves. "I know. I'm so sorry. I really hope we can move past this. I wasn't myself yesterday."

So many things ran through my head, mostly some variation of "you can make it up to me over drinks later." But I wasn't that guy. Never had been.

"I'll forget the oatmeal if you don't hold the EVLP against me."

"Deal," she answered without hesitation, which made me smile. I stuck my glove out for her to tap. She smiled, too. Her eyes sparkled and despite never being that guy, something about this moment felt pretty ideal. I opened my mouth to say...I don't know. How beautiful she was or how her sutures were impeccable and that made me want to buy her flowers on a weekly basis, or that she was warm and kind and everything I wanted in my life. Or maybe just to ask her to grab that drink with me.

"Sammy, what the hell? Burpees, dude. Now. Not even my big brother gets to slack off during warmup." Will punched me in the shoulder hard enough to hurt, pointing to the mats in the other corner like he was sending a puppy to its crate.

"William—"

"No excuses. You've taken enough of the good doctor's time. And you"—he turned to Lainey, giving me his back—"gorgeous form. You done a lot of kickboxing before? Tell me about it while you're on the battle ropes."

I wanted to wrangle my brother into a headlock, but Lainey shot a smile at me from over her shoulder. It didn't matter how many burpees I did, I still felt lighter than I had in ages.

Chapter 3

Sam

"You can express your gratitude by taking this out to my car so I can drop it at the laundry place." Will shook a trash bag filled with used sweat towels in my direction.

"Gratitude for...?" I asked, re-racking the last of the weights. Nearly everyone had cleared out, with only a few people lingering around, chatting by the water fountain or leaving the locker rooms. Lainey had ducked out the door a few minutes ago with a little wave in our direction. I was still riding the high of that look from earlier, that smile she'd given me.

Will's eyebrows bounced on his forehead. He looked so smug, it was ridiculous. "I saw you two hitting it off once she finished whaling on that bag. Thanks to me."

"Thanks to you?" I eyed him as I walked back to the front. "In what fucking world?"

"Who paired you two up? Who told you to get the ball rolling and ask her out? All me, bro."

"No." This morning was all me. No way Will was taking the credit.

Somehow, a single, honest conversation had done more to improve our relationship than three years of working together had accomplished. By the end of class, she looked like she actually *wanted* to talk with me or share a smile when Will said something completely ridiculous. Considering where we'd started when she'd walked in this morning, it was a miracle.

Except for the oatmeal thing. I'd be nursing that wound for a while. But once we'd gotten over that, she'd stuck around my vicinity for most of my workout. Oatmeal aside, a win was a win.

It was enough to make me rethink my strategy of hanging back and waiting for her fellowship to be over. Maybe I needed to get on her radar now. Lay the foundation a little, so when I did ask her out, it wasn't coming out of nowhere.

"Yes," Will insisted, launching the trash bag at my head after I pulled my duffel onto my shoulder. Of course, Will *had* been the one to force us together this morning. But that didn't mean I had to admit it to him.

"Goodbye, William." I grabbed the trash bag and headed for the door.

"Car's unlocked," he called as I stepped into the sunlight. He raised his voice as he continued, yelling, "And do yourself a favor. Grow a pair and ask Lainey out!"

I turned my head to yell back at him, but stalled out halfway there. Lainey stood by her car, only a few feet from the door, staring at me with wide, *"holy crap"* eyes. A hole opened up underneath me and my stomach dove into it.

Shit. How much of that had she heard? The door swung shut behind me, the soft click more like a sonic boom.

She pointed to her chest. "Ask *me* out?" she squeaked. Her eyes flashed around my face, taking in the heat I could feel flooding my cheeks. "I wasn't supposed to hear that."

"No," I grunted in agreement, the only sound I could make at the moment. Embarrassment clawed up my neck, dragging my galloping pulse with it. This was bad. Very bad. And I was just standing here, staring at her, beet-red, probably making it worse.

"Sorry, I was talking to that new guy, Jackson. I guess you thought I was already gone...I'm sorry," she babbled, looking at me like she also wanted to be swallowed up by whatever massive sinkhole my vital organs had dropped into. Her apology somehow made everything worse, and the burning crept up to my ears.

Fuck.

"You have nothing to be sorry for." I pinched the bridge of my nose, closing my eyes and willing myself to breathe, to think for a second, instead of clamming up from the raw mortification currently flooding my system. Looking at her wasn't helping me figure out what to say next. Her face was pained, like my humiliation had flooded the parking lot and she was absorbing some of it, secondhand.

This was all wrong. Sudden and out of the blue; I didn't know what to say. I'd formulated a plan: play the long game. Get closer to her when her fellowship was done. Once we've had a few conversations that didn't include someone's ventricles, ask her out.

It had been a solid plan, but this? This was not good. My thundering heartbeat was at odds with my sluggish, halting thoughts. I didn't know what to *say*, dammit. What words could take that stricken look off her face and smooth out some of the astronomical levels of embarrassment swirling around us?

I blinked my eyes open. She was still there, grimacing, like she didn't know what to do, either. I took a steadying breath. Another one. And I vocalized the only complete thought my brain could supply right now.

"I'm sorry you heard that." I was. *Very* sorry. Like, would have sold about ten years of my life to go back in time and keep the damn door closed for three extra seconds.

"Should we...pretend I didn't?" She looked like she wasn't sure that was the best course of action.

I grunted, taking a few seconds to consider while I stomped to Will's car and jerked the door open. It was a tempting, easy solution. She'd go her way, I'd go mine, and we'd just forget this ever happened. Except that look on her face would haunt me—Distress, surprise, unease. None of the things you want a girl to feel when she learns you're interested.

I ripped the plastic bag open and dumped the towels directly into the passenger's seat. *Fuck you, Will.*

I could see how it would go down. We'd ignore the moment, now, but what would happen if I saw her at work on Monday? She'd awkwardly avoid my gaze? Paste on a polite, impersonal smile whenever she saw me, pretending everything was fine when in reality it was super weird? Worst-case scenario, it got so uncomfortable that she avoided me completely?

I cursed under my breath. No, that wouldn't work. I had to do this right, and just do it now. The thought made my throat tight. I wished, not for the first time, I was more like my brother. Someone who said the perfect thing at the perfect time, without having to think about it for a while.

But I didn't have that skill. All I had right now was the truth. It had been working for me so far this morning. I might as well grow a pair, as Will advised. *Fucking Will*.

Lainey bit her lip, waiting. My whole body felt like it was burning now. Best to just rip off the bandaid. "Will said that because he knows I like—that is...I'm attracted to you. I have been for a while."

Her mouth popped open, like she was surprised I'd actually said it out loud, instead of letting her walk away. "You—oh."

I cleared my throat, gave a tight smile. "Yeah. I was planning to tell you. Not now, obviously. Fellows and attendings...we're not really supposed to mix. Romantically."

"Right." She nodded, brow furrowing. "Hospital policy."

"I also didn't want to make you feel uncomfortable." I paused, sizing her up. Her surprise looked troubled now. Baffled. Like I'd only explained half of a surgical procedure, then asked her to complete the rest without me. It didn't seem like a good sign.

"I...right. I'm not. Uncomfortable, that is." She frowned deeper, like she was feeling the words out as she said them. Checking in on how she *really* felt. My bet was on completely dumbfounded. Before this morning, we'd never had a single non-work-related conversation. Now I was telling her I liked her? Bizarre.

"Well, great. That's one of us, because I'd like to throw myself in front of a car."

My response actually surprised a laugh out of her. A real one, not a you-just-told-me-you're-attracted-to-me, and-I-think-you're-a-bowl-of-oatmeal, so-here's-a-pity-laugh, laugh. Despite the ridiculous awkwardness of this conversation, it broke some of the tension crackling between us.

Her chuckled ended on a strained groan, and she put her hands over her face. Definitely secondhand humiliation. "I'm so sorry, this is just really unexpected and really—"

"Awkward. This is really fucking awkward. Don't worry, I'm going to kill Will later." She smiled again and I latched onto it.

My brain was picking across the undercurrent of the conversation, teetering precariously from one sentence to the next. I felt like at any minute I'd miss something and drown in the demoralization of it all.

I cleared my throat, trying to put my finger on the next best thing to say. The next truth. The only thing that came to mind was an echo of what she'd said earlier. "I hope this doesn't affect our working relationship." I made a face. This time, her laugh sounded strangled.

Her eyes darted around the parking lot, like she was looking for answers. "Ah...I don't think it will?" Even though she was smiling, working to gloss over the uncomfortable situation, I didn't like the hesitation in her voice.

The strained, impersonal smiles and workplace avoidance were still a distinct possibility. It was the last thing I wanted, and I felt the need to reassure her I wasn't going to make it weird. I'd heard her tell Jones she didn't date people from work. I hated the thought of her being on edge around me, thinking I was going to hound her like he did.

"I'm cool if you're cool," I offered. I could be cool. I'd been cool this whole time. Playing it cool, keeping my cool. So fucking cool. *Alright, stop thinking about the word cool.*

"Yeah, I'm...cool." Now, only half her mouth tilted up, like only part of her was committed to it. I'd take it. This shitshow of a conversation had gone on long enough. I wanted to get out of here.

I didn't need to hear her tell me she was *so flattered, but she'd just never thought of me like that before*, or something. It had been written all over her face the second I'd walked out that door. She wasn't into it. I didn't need to drag any of this out.

Time to regroup. Far away from here. Take the world's longest shower and plot my brother's demise and try not to think about how such a great morning had gone south so fast.

"Then, we're good." I swallowed. We were good. This was fine. Just fine. "Good workout today, Dr. Carmichael." I turned away before I could second-guess myself and her and this entire conversation. She was still standing where I'd left her as I drove away.

***

"I swear, Reese, it's freaking Grey's Anatomy out there!" Director Caplan nodded out his interior window, where it overlooked the lobby of the cardiac unit. It was Monday, and I'd worked up the nerve to come to work after cringing for two days straight every time I thought of my conversation with Lainey.

I'm attracted to you. Caplan was right. That was some Grey's Anatomy shit.

"So, she's suing?" I took a bite of my sandwich, telling myself to stay on track. Caplan had invited me here to talk about my new proposal for the residency program, but he'd gone off on a tangent. A love triangle gone wrong between a cardiac attending and two anesthesiologists.

Caplan scowled. "She's saying it's a toxic work environment now that she has to work with both of them. The board is tied up in knots over it. It's the third time this year some office romance bullshit has threatened the organization."

I shoved another bite into my mouth, trying not to think about how close I'd come to proposing my own office romance bullshit to Caplan's favorite fellow.

"Anyway. They're working it out with legal. They're talking about some new policy to report relationships up to HR, as if it'll help anyone keep it in their pants. At least it takes some liability off of the hospital. Sturmond's been beating his quality standards drum. I think he's doing most of the work to push it through."

"Hmm." Not many people could discern how I felt at any given moment. I was tight-lipped at the best of times and downright silent for the rest. But I'd been working with Caplan long enough that he was getting the picture, especially since I'd started taking over responsibilities with the residents, even if it was only in an unofficial capacity.

"Yeah, yeah. I know you're no fan of Sturmond's right now. Or the quality board." An understatement, and we both knew it. "But we wouldn't be sitting here if he hadn't convinced the hospital board to open up this new campus."

The sleek glass and steel around us was a testament to the man's hard work; I'd give him that. Our cardiac center was no longer crammed back behind the main hospital campus across town. The new building was the jewel of the row of hospitals known as Chicago's medical district.

The tall glass exterior glittered. Everywhere you looked in here, it was all gleaming white tile and shining chrome fixtures—and that was just in the patient-facing areas. The ORs, the staff lounges, conference rooms, and offices were crammed with the latest amenities and medical gadgets. Yeah, Sturmond was an ass, but he knew how to build a damn hospital.

"He's feeling overly proprietary about everything. The whole advisory board is. I give it another year before they get bored or turn their members over and we can go back to business as usual."

Caplan wasn't a bad man, and he wasn't even a bad director, but he rolled over for the board. First, the hospital board, when they'd announced they were putting Sturmond in charge of the new quality board. Now, he lacked a spine when that same quality board marched in and stomped all over our clinical proceedings. I wasn't sure why, exactly, Sturmond felt it was his right to intrude on our surgical cases, but the man certainly loved playing king of the castle.

I kept those thoughts to myself. Caplan shifted, pulling a file closer to him. "Let's talk about better stuff, huh? This is great work. I like the approach—take surgical time from the attendings and focus it on the residents. Give the residents more time in the OR. No one else is doing it quite like this." Caplan tapped on the folder containing my proposal for the new resident teaching structure. I'd been thinking about it for months, and it had been on his desk for three weeks. It was gratifying, at least, that he had read it.

I hoped that the hiring committee for the new resident program director would be equally as impressed as Caplan. I was early in my career, only three years out of my own training, and it was rare for someone with that little experience to head a program like this. But I wanted it more than anyone else at Cedar, and every little bit would help to sway the committee into taking me seriously.

"You'll have to get the surgeons to buy into it, though." He flipped through the pages. "Usually, we have to pry them out of the OR. Not sure how many will want to trade a surgical day to babysit the residents."

"I've had several surgeons express interest." After some convincing, of course. I was a man of few words, but what I lacked in quantity, I liked to think I made up for in quality. Every surgeon I'd discussed the plan with had eventually admitted its merits, and even told me they'd be interested in trying it. At its core, Cedar was a teaching hospital. If we lost that foundation, we weren't anything but a money-making factory that happened to stitch people up.

"Be that as it may, I'm running it by a few people on the executive team. It's an unorthodox concept, but you have a way with the residents, so you must know what you're talking about." The folder flipped closed. "Carmichael okay when you broke the news about the EVLP? How'd she seem when you saw her last?"

When I saw her last? In those leggings, with the post-workout glow, looking bewildered in a parking lot while I confessed my feelings to her? Something told me that wasn't the version of the story Caplan wanted to hear.

"She was upset, but she'll come around. It didn't help that I denied her OR request the same day."

"Ah, that CAD patient? It was the right call. She's getting close to the end of her fellowship. She's antsy to prove herself. We've all been there." Caplan took a bite of his roast beef on rye, not bothering to cover his mouth as he continued, "Besides, the job is hers in a few months. If anyone's earned it, it's her. You hear about the research she's working on with UCLA? Incredible."

Yes. She was incredible. She may have come to Cedar under less-than-conventional circumstances, but she'd more than proved herself. And she only had a few more weeks before her dream of working here became a reality.

After our conversation this weekend, I knew I didn't have to waste my breath to see if she was interested. We could both just live our lives, crossing paths occasionally when a case needed another set of eyes or specific expertise. And that was for the best. Really.

Until then, I'd just stay out of her way as much as I could.

Chapter 4

Lainey

I thought more about Samuel Reese over the next few days than I had the last three years of working with him combined.

After replaying our conversation, I convinced myself that I'd made it all up. Or maybe it had all been some sort of weird practical joke. Only, he wasn't really the joking type. And then I thought about all the times we'd led rounds together, or stood side-by-side in an OR, and wondered *he liked me that whole time?* Then, in an effort to mine more information from our limited conversation, I replayed it in my mind again. The cycle was vicious and unstoppable.

Worse, nothing really changed, at least not externally. I still went to work and took care of patients. I sidestepped Jones as much as I could. Went to the gym. Read the American Journal of Medicine before bed each night. But somewhere in the squishy place behind my lungs, I felt an unexpected shift. I was curious about Dr. Reese. Who was this man who claimed to be attracted to me?

Now, I wasn't just rounding; I was looking for Dr. Reese around every corner. I went to R³ hoping to run into him there, too, and barely even noticed Will's banter. That article on new techniques in mitral valve replacement did nothing to calm my brain. Not when I was stuck in The Reese Cycle.

Attendings usually traded off leading daily rounds, and by the middle of the following week, I'd yet to catch even a glimpse of him. I started to think he was avoiding me on purpose, but I genuinely couldn't remember how often I usually saw Reese day-to-day. Was it all the time? Never? As much as I wracked my brain, I couldn't put my finger on it, and it bugged me. I should have *noticed* something like that, right?

On Wednesday, the fates and scheduling Gods aligned, and I found myself leading rounds with Dr. Reese. I'd done this a million times: strolling along this familiar path; the residents following like little ducklings and Reese guiding the way. The sound of his black sneakers on the linoleum and the scratch of the stylus on his tablet were unnervingly familiar.

Yet, it was all different now.

I'd never noticed before, but he had an impeccable set of sturdy, rolling shoulders underneath that hospital-issued white coat. Now that I'd seen him work his way around a set of weights, my mind helpfully supplied images of all the lovely muscles attached to those shoulders. The fingers holding that stylus were long and precise, but stronger than I'd expect from someone who spent their days interfacing with one of the most delicate organs in the human body. Today, my brain decided that the sound of his voice wasn't flat, but rather contemplative.

With all these new, somewhat inappropriate thoughts churning in my head, I stumbled through my patient reports, fumbling an update on an aortic aneurysm repair so hard Jones gave me the side-eye. Reese barely looked up from his notes when I spoke, as if it were any other day. By the end of rounds, I had to thank whatever deity was listening that he didn't seem bothered by my gawking. Because if I hadn't paid such close attention, I would have missed the most important observation of all.

Reese wasn't just quiet. He *listened*. He was a *listener*. And it was hot.

Jones was jabbering on about some latest research on bypass techniques. In the past, I'd assumed the blank look on Reese's face was something akin to a loading screen. I'd thought when a person was that quiet, it took effort to form the five words required to reciprocate a conversation. I wanted to go back in time and shake past Lainey by the shoulders.

The more I watched, the more I realized how seriously he was taking it all. Reese listened attentively to everything, from our routine questions to a patient's complaints about stomach pain, as though he were trying to commit every word to memory.

So when he finally answered, each word counted. I hung onto every syllable he gave up, fiercely curious about what he'd say. How could someone who listened that closely *not* consider every single thing coming out of their mouth? He was practically doing everyone a courtesy: paying near microscopic attention to them, then only giving them exactly what they needed. No more, no less.

By the time he'd dispatched an intern to fetch a GI doc for the patient—"*Get Holloway; room eight.*"—and directed Jones to what I assumed would be a brilliant and relevant commentary on the current state of bypass innovations—"*Check out Haas and Dresden's latest.*"—I'd started sweating.

"He's hot, right?" I blurted after rounds, parking my laptop on the nurse's station next to Rija's and just barely containing the urge to flap my scrubs against my overheated body.

"Who?" She peered around before catching my gaze as it followed my attending down the hall. "Oh, Daddy Reese. Obviously."

"Daddy?" I nearly choked on my tongue.

"Oh, hell yeah. How have we never talked about this? Tara and I wax poetic about his pecs weekly." Rija flagged Tara down as she walked by with her cart. Tara fell into the same category where I'd placed Rija: a more-than-colleague, not-quite friend. She frequently joined me on breaks and gave me a heads up when we got a new shipment of the good gloves. "Yo. Haven't we talked to Lainey before about Reese's chest?"

"If not, we've been doing you a disservice. It might not be morally appropriate to ogle other people, but *damn,* those calves. Oh, Daddy Reese," Tara breathed as she passed by on her way to a patient's room.

"He's a sleeper. Creeps up on ya." Rija nodded sagely before peering at me. "Are you only just now realizing this? I mean, he's not in-your-face hot like Morris up in Urology, but after you notice his muscles, it's all downhill from there."

"Right. Yes." I nodded sagely back, unsure how I felt about some of my closest colleagues ogling the man who'd professed his crush to me mere days ago. Regardless of my personal feelings on the oddness of it all, she had a point. "Yes. It's just one thing and then…then you notice *all* the things."

My eyes flicked back down the hall.

"Don't worry, babe. You'll grow out of it." She steered me by the elbow to the break room.

"Yeah?" I wasn't sure that was accurate. My neck felt hot, and now that I'd opened the door to all the *noticing* I was doing, it didn't feel like I'd ever stop. We had only been in the same proximity for a few hours, and I felt overwhelmed by the avalanche of things I was noticing. One movement of his hand led to the flex of his forearm and the bend of his elbow and…and…and…it all grew exponentially until I was lost, staring at him and trying not to drool.

"Oh, sure. We've all had a crush on him at one point or another. After a bit you realize he's too serious for his own good and still kind of, you know"—she glanced around the break room, but we were alone—"boring."

I frowned, choosing to withhold my newfound knowledge of Reese's covert listening and considering. I wasn't sure I was ready to share it, yet.

"Enough about him, though. Are you coming to my party this weekend?" She grabbed me a cup of ice as I started up the hot water.

"Oh! That was this weekend? I'm sorry, I'm on deadline for that paper I'm writing. Shoot, I thought it was next week." Not true, but a little white lie wouldn't hurt anyone. People often told me I was married to my job, which was accurate enough. It just wasn't the reason I usually avoided people's birthday parties or housewarmings, baby showers, etcetera.

"Fuck, seriously? My roommate's brother is going to be in town. I wanted to introduce you. He's a total smoke show."

"Well, maybe you should introduce him to yourself." I waggled eyebrows at her before she shoved my face away.

"He already knows me, dummy. He'd be hot for *you*, not for me."

Although I appreciated the gesture, my hormones had suddenly perked up and become fixated on one man. I had mixed feelings about it, but I didn't think they would focus on anyone else for a while.

"My roommate wants to meet you, anyway. We've given Samantha a place of honor in an armchair in our apartment. We're obsessed with her. We got her some new outfits from eBay. Thank you for that, again."

"Again, don't mention it." I stared into my tea. When Rija had told me her childhood dream of owning one of the Samantha American Girl dolls, it had taken me less than five minutes to have my mother's house manager track mine down from storage, package it, and send it over. I'm pretty sure I played with the thing—part of the full set—less than five times. Rija's happiness when she opened the box far outstripped any I'd gotten out of my time with it. "Tell me about the party, though."

I didn't care to linger on the gift too much. Her frequent mentions made me anxious that something had shifted between us. Our working relationship was cordial and close, and I was perfectly content with it. I wasn't looking for anything like a soul sister or a BFF.

My deflection worked, and I listened to Rija chat about the cocktail she was whipping up and the karaoke machine they were renting. I tried not to think about Reese and his forearms and all his considering.

I didn't succeed.

Chapter 5

Lainey

Any clinician in the world will tell you that the worst part of their job is notes. Give me a spurting aorta all day long. Necrotic tissue? No sweat. But *documentation*? I'd rather pitch myself off the roof.

Unfortunately for me, my chosen profession required a lot of documentation, and all of it had to be completed before my butt left the hospital. People developed their own coping mechanisms for inputting notes. I'd watched every attendings' habits like a good little worker bee and found that I did best when I could devote the last bit of my day to some serious, godforsaken note taking.

I didn't always accomplish it. Emergency surgeries and declining patient cases took priority over an hour of peace at the end of my shift. When I could, though, I escaped from the unit to find a quiet conference room or empty office on the administrative side of our floor.

Oddly enough, today was the first day I realized I'd adopted this particular habit from Dr. Reese. Which is why I shouldn't have been surprised when I found him hunched over the conference table in meeting room B.

"Oh! Shoot. I'm sorry. I didn't realize anyone was in here...I can..." I jabbed a thumb over my shoulder at the hallway. The movement set off a chain reaction that bobbled my laptop and caused my phone and tablet to slide precariously across the protective plastic case. I made an undignified squeaking noise as I clapped my hand back over the whole technological mess. My neck heated again.

The on-call board said he was supposed to leave at six today, and I'd breathed a sigh of relief when the clock hit 6:01. I'd spent the last few days looking for him around every corner, equally anticipating and anxious that I'd run into him. It was exhausting.

But lo-and-behold, here he was, still in the building. Staring at me with raised brows while I flushed and squeaked in his direction.

"Stay."

I froze, halfway out the door. "Oh, ah, I don't want to interrupt your—" My belongings shifted again as I flailed my hand towards his computer.

"I'm almost done. Besides, I'm pretty sure I'm responsible for intervening when hospital property is endangered." He pointed a look at the wobbling pile of devices in my hands. Across the table from him, one of the rolling chairs shot backwards, kicked out by his sneakered foot.

"Thank you." I cleared my throat, lowering myself into the chair and spreading my various gadgets around me. "I can't chart without some quiet."

"Mmm." Reese's eyes met mine for a split second before lowering to his computer screen. Just long enough for me to perceive very clearly that he had already, in fact, known this about me.

My throat worked as I tapped my way through the log-in screen to the electronic health record portal. I'd start with Mrs. Johnson and the post-op I'd gone through this morning.

"I'm attracted to you. I have been for a while."

His words from this weekend lingered in my mind as I navigated through her chart, entering the codes and notes. Just how much *did* he know about me? As my attending, it was normal that he knew my preferred charting environment, right? I knew his, after all.

I didn't realize I'd stopped typing to stare at the man across from me until his blue eyes connected with mine. His eyebrow twitched, and I wondered how, seemingly overnight, I could interpret those little ticks and twitches. In this case, something along the lines of *"You good?"*

"Sorry. Long day." I shrugged, slipping lower in my chair in an unsuccessful attempt to hide behind my computer screen. He was so *tall*, and I wasn't sure what to do with him now that I knew he had feelings for me; at least, he claimed he did. His behavior didn't reveal anything out of the ordinary. I was the one being a doof.

"Any issues with that valve repair this afternoon?"

"Nope, all good. Patient is stable." I tip-tapped away, trying not to draw attention to the flush slowly crawling up my face.

He paused. I could still *feel* his eyes on me. I frowned at my computer, hopefully doing a decent job of imitating someone actually working. He nodded once and then focused on his own screens, fingers running over his beard.

I managed to get through three more patient files before my gaze strayed again. His eyes met mine for an instant before he returned to his notes. Unfazed.

"What are you working on?" The question tumbled out of me before I could stop myself. It didn't feel right that I was suddenly so preoccupied with his existence and he was so unaffected by mine. I remembered how intensely he'd focused on me at the gym. His unwavering honesty in the parking lot. The entire experience had been so different from my normal interactions with him. It was distractingly enigmatic.

Like he always did, he paused, studying me. "I'm working with a patient right now that I'd consider a fringe case. I may recommend an ablation, but I'm not sure she's the right candidate."

"An atrial fibrillation ablation?" I gasped. The corner of his mouth twitched. Something about it felt like a win.

"Yes."

"You're performing an atrial fibrillation ablation in this hospital? Like, soon?"

"Maybe." The twitch turned into something deeper. Not quite a smile, but not quite *not* a smile.

"Do you need an assist?"

A full-blown grin slipped across his face. Something fluttered in the vicinity of my gastrointestinal system. He leaned forward slowly, tenting his elbows on either side of his computer. "Doctor

Carmichael. If I move forward with the procedure, would you like to assist in the operating room?"

"Yes!" My voice sounded squeaky again. How could it not, when one hundred percent of this man's attention rested squarely on my face? But I didn't care. I'd just nabbed a potential assist for a very cool surgery. "I've never seen one before. Not live, that is. Only videos."

He nodded, considering me. "Alright. I'll request you if I go down that road."

Our eyes were locked. I couldn't tear my gaze away. Though the table seated twelve, the room was getting smaller by the second. I swallowed. His eyes didn't waver from my face.

"You could give it to Jones, you know. I don't want you to feel like..." I trailed off, not sure how to finish that sentence. *I don't want you to feel like you have to give me the cool surgical case just because you have the hots for me?*

He shrugged. "You asked first."

"Right, right." My head bobbed up and down. Another few seconds of silence descended on our little staring competition. I broke it again, succumbing to the intrusive thought that maybe he *was* only giving me the cool surgical case because he was attracted to me.

"I just mean...I wouldn't want any special treatment be-cause...because...of what you said earlier. In the parking lot. This weekend." *Shut up, Lainey!* As if he needed to be reminded of the particulars of the conversation. Or, heck, maybe he did. Maybe he ran around in all his spare time talking about long-term unrequited crushes with everyone he knew.

"It hasn't been a problem so far."

His face was as expressionless as ever, but something about it seemed amused. Well, he had every right to be amused. I was being ridiculous. I'd been ridiculous all day long, with all my staring. And here I was, still doing it.

I couldn't decide if it was better or worse now that he was staring back at me.

"Is this weird for you?" I whispered.

A pause. "Not weird, no."

Ah, well. Just me then.

"I'm attracted to you. I have been for a while." Despite the tension in the air and the weight of his eyes on me, something about his bare honesty this weekend gave me enough courage to lay my own confession on the table between us.

"I've been staring at you a lot today."

"Yes." He nodded. So, he *had* noticed.

"I can't help it. Ever since this weekend and what...what you said. I can't look at you the same."

He scowled. It was possibly the most movement I'd ever seen on his face. "I didn't intend to make you uncomfortable or to change anything between us. I apologize if—"

"No, no." I waved my hand like I could swat his apology out of the air. "No, it's not you. It's totally me. I hadn't thought of you like that before and now...now it's like you're a totally new person."

It felt like I'd spent the last three years going about my life and then someone had pointed out there was a bear in the corner of the room I'd never noticed before. It was shocking. And I couldn't stop staring at it. Or, you know, *him*.

"Hmm." His thumb traced back and forth over the edge of his laptop. The movement hypnotized me. "You said that before. You'd never thought of me that way."

"No. Never."

"Oof."

"I didn't mean that you're not—" A smile cracked across his face before my horrified gasp was complete.

"I'm kidding, Lainey." His fingers flickered through the air before returning to the edge of his keyboard. *Back and forth and back and forth.* "I'm not the most outgoing guy in the world. There aren't a lot of reasons for you to think of me that way."

"More than you'd think," I muttered before leaning in like we were conspirators. "Some people on our floor call you 'Daddy Reese.'"

"Jesus," he stuttered. Finally, *finally*, his eyes slid away. His cheeks started working on a flush of their own. Something in my competitive little brain cheered. A reaction. *Yes.*

"I'm serious. Someone told me that everyone has had a crush on you at some point. *Everyone*," I repeated when his incredulous gaze swung to mine. He maintained eye contact even as his blush deepened.

"I'll have to ask Whitaker next time I see him." His fingers ran over his beard again, like he was seriously considering it.

A cackling laugh burst out of me at the thought of him asking the oldest, most curmudgeonly surgeon in the hospital if the old guy had a crush on him. The sound echoed in the big, empty room. His flush burned bright now, but so did his grin, and yet his eyes never left mine. That gastrointestinal flutter became a full on stampede.

"It's a slippery slope," I warned. "Once you know Whitaker's into you, you can't close that Pandora's box. Next time you're in the same office with him, you're going to look over and suddenly notice how nice his hands are, or his shoes...or something."

He blinked at me, golden eyelashes brushing slowly across his cheekbones. "Is that why you've been staring? You realize you like my shoes?"

The smile slid off my face. It was easier for me to talk about all the noticing I'd been doing today if I projected it onto someone else. It was harder to swallow when I confronted my own feelings head-on. Even more so because I still wasn't sure exactly *what* I felt. I was confused and intrigued and, dare I say, a little bit interested? That gave me pause.

But he'd been honest with me at a vulnerable moment. I owed him the same.

"Yes. That's what happened." My eyes fluttered down, unseeing, to the screensaver bouncing around my laptop. Just because I owed him some honesty didn't mean I had to stare at him while I talked. "I do like your shoes. And the way you talk to patients. And lead rounds. I like..." *You.*

But that felt like a bridge too far right at this moment. Right when I was still in the noticing part.

"I liked working out with you."

When I finally dragged my eyes back to his, I expected to see confusion, maybe exasperation at my obvious cop-out. Instead, I got that steady, straightforward gaze. A slight deepening at the corners of his mouth. "I liked that, too."

"I know I'm a fellow and you're an attending so we can't...But you should know that I don't like to date guys from work, anyway." This was important for him to know. And important for me to remind myself. My formerly staid, oatmeal-esque feelings for this man had been diverted, like a train hopping off a track. If I didn't apply some brakes, I wasn't sure what would happen. "Entangling my professional life with my personal—it's too much."

He nodded, still studying me seriously. "I've heard you mention that to Jones."

"It's not just lip service to get him off my back. I do really want to keep those aspects of my life separate." Been there, done that, got the t-shirt and wept a river of tears. I wasn't interested in a repeat. But..."But maybe we could hit the gym again. Together."

That was acceptable for two colleagues who attended the same gym, right? It just made sense that we'd chat if we happened to see each other there. Surely that was safe? It felt like a good step, at least, when I felt like I needed to know him much better than I currently did.

"I'd like that."

The corners of his eyes crinkled up like he found this whole conversation amusing, and I was telling myself again and again not to blush. It was only a loose commitment to work out. Not a date.

"I work out in the mornings, when I can," I offered.

That dang corner of his mouth deepened ever so slightly again as he closed his computer and gathered up his things. "Yes." Another lingering second of eye contact. Another reminder that the man knew my schedule and, somehow, also knew my recreational fitness habits.

"Have a good night, Carmichael."

It was on the tip of my tongue to respond with something equally bland. A nice "see you around" or "have a good one", perhaps. But his quiet, unruffled demeanor was throwing me off. Now that he was standing, his presence filled the room, choking out any of the air or logic I had left. I babbled, "This weekend, you said you'd...you said you'd felt this way for a while. How long is a while?"

For the last few days, all I could think about was the fact that he'd been into me and I'd barely noticed his existence. It didn't seem right. I'd been in this man's orbit for nearly three years now. That was a long time. Although to some people, six months was a long time. Which was it for him? Surely I'd have picked up on something if he'd flipped head over heels for me the moment we'd met. Right?

He paused, fingers on the door handle, seconds from slipping down the hall. I wanted to know what he was thinking. I wanted to hack his brain and watch all his thoughts circling in real-time. I wanted to understand how he listened and watched and cared so much and then how he distilled that all into...

"Night, Lainey," he tossed over his shoulder, avoiding the question—and looking at me—altogether.

Chapter 6

Lainey

I knew the second Reese entered the gym, even though the room was packed with legging-clad bodies. It was mystifying, really, to think that I'd never been aware of him like this before. He was huge; towering as he waded across the sea of women. Something warmed in my chest when I realized he was making a beeline for me.

I'd spent the entire night reliving my conference room confessional and calling myself all sorts of idiot for being so weird with him. Hours ago, as I glared up at the dark ceiling, cringing at my parting question, it had been easy to convince myself that I was going to stop staring at him whenever he was in the room. And that I'd stop asking weird and inappropriate questions.

Now that he was in front of me, though, I had a feeling sticking to those commitments was going to be harder than I'd thought. I already had to remind myself to look somewhere else as he crossed the crowded floor.

"I thought you were scheduled today?" He was. At least he had been when I'd left the hospital last night. Not that I'd been looking at the board or anything.

His only response was a shrug. I pursed my lips, watching him watch me. I couldn't believe I'd never noticed before what the weight of his gaze did to my body. I felt all buzzy—light and heavy at the same time.

I was about to ask whether he'd switched his schedule this morning just so he could take a workout class with me when Will trotted over. Thank God. I was pretty sure that would have fallen under the "asking inappropriate questions" category.

"Shit, it's packed. We've had fifty people register for this session, alone. The rest of the week is getting wrecked." He ran his hands through his hair and looked warily around the milling crowd. It was mostly women with a few hardcore looking gym bros sprinkled in. "I had to put limits on class sizes for the rest of the month."

"You're telling me I should register now before everything fills up?"

Will grinned. "Aw, Lainey, you know I'll always find a spot for you."

A week ago, his comment would have made my day. Now, I just laughed it off, glancing around. "I've never seen this place so crowded before."

"A TV station was doing a piece on new local businesses. I did a quick interview that aired yesterday." Will looked a little helpless. "I didn't expect all this. Who even watches the news anymore?"

Suddenly, the female majority made more sense. "New gym in a cool area... hot trainer... It's a workout girlie's dream."

Reese's eyebrow twitched. Without a peep, he conveyed his dissatisfaction with my response.

"What? It's the objective truth." I gestured at Will, who was looking adorable and flustered as a few more spandex-clad people trickled through the gym doors.

"Favorite regular, I told you!" Will grinned at his brother before winking at me.

"What's your plan here?" Reese interrupted, his eyes flicking between me and his brother and then back to me.

"Fuuuuuck, I don't know, man." Will gazed around, mentally calculating. "I'll have to split them up and rotate through the circuits to fit everyone in. I could use your help, if you're game."

"I'll take this section." It could have been unintentional, the way Reese gestured to a group of about a dozen of us standing towards the back of the room. He herded me a little, almost knocking me into the two Lululemon ladies behind us. The move was so smooth, so casual, I assumed he gestured randomly to the closest side of the room.

Until Will rolled his eyes. "Sure you will, bro. So generous of you to take *this group right here.*" His hands circled over my head.

Teeth flashed white beneath Reese's beard. He clapped Will on the back and steered him to the edge of the floor where their other brother, Conner, stood with a clipboard.

I shuffled forward to give the women behind me some more space. "Sorry," I muttered.

"No worries. Is this your first time, too?" One of the Lulus behind me piped up. I wrenched my eyes away from the other side of the room, reminding myself again to *not stare at your attending, Lainey*, before facing them. The one who addressed me was taller, the cream color of her matching workout set making her dark skin glow. Her friend was shorter, standing close with her arms crossed. Her eyes peeked from behind blonde hair with purple streaks.

"Nah, I've been coming here for a while. You?"

"First time. We saw the owner's interview on Facebook." She nodded to where Will and his brothers were talking through some sort of chart on the clipboard. "Someone posted his interview on one of the Chicago workout groups. It's gone a little viral. I'm Sameera, by the way."

"Lainey." I offered my hand. The blonde girl's name was Tess. She barely met my eyes when we shook.

"How intense is this going to be? Tess and I are new to the HIIT thing. We're nervous." Sameera gave Tess a warm smile.

"Meery's not nervous. She's just here for emotional support." Tess sighed. "It's important to try new things outside of my comfort zone." She droned like she was reciting something. Her arms clenched around her waist.

"It's not too bad. Will's good at modifying and giving options for people who want to take it slow."

"Will? That's the Viking one?" Meery looked back at the guys. I glanced over at Reese. Now that the three of them stood together, it was easy to see their resemblance, but he had a few inches on his brothers. And now that she mentioned it, that big, blocky build and light hair did give off solid Viking vibes.

"That's Sam. I actually haven't seen him teach a class before, but we work together. He's got the patience of a saint. You'll love him."

All true. He was a good attending. A good person. Had I always admired him this way? Or had I only realized it now that I was in close proximity to his impressive shoulder circumference?

"Hey everyone! We're about to get started here. We've got a full house today, so we're going to split up into a few groups!" Will corralled us into three groups so he, Connor, and Reese could lead us through the exercises. We shuffled together as we got sectioned off.

"Actually, does that look a little uneven? Lainey, you want to come over here with me?" Will sported a downright wicked grin.

Before I moved a muscle, Reese's hand landed between my shoulder blades, steering me deeper into his section without so much as a backwards glance at his brother.

"No? You guys good over there?"

"All good," Reese called, still not looking back. Meery raised her eyebrows. The shaky smile I gave her turned into a gulp as Reese's hand slid several inches down my spine before falling away. I rubbed at the goosebumps on my arms.

"Morning. I'm Sam. I'm helping Will out today. We'll rotate through circuits to avoid the other teams. Start with a few laps to warm up, then we're heading over to the tires, then kettlebells—"

"We're going to kick your asses!" Will jogged by with his group on the way to the rack of exercise bands in the corner. Some people trailing him laughed and gave us *bring it on* gestures. I grinned.

"You'll have to catch us first, team Will!" I called back. *Oohs* sounded at my back, along with a few other catcalls from team Sam. I glanced back at my attending. "We have to win, now."

I got one of those slow blinks. For a split-second, I felt silly.

"Then you'd best get started, Carmichael." He nodded to the track around the perimeter of the room. "Give me ten. Smoke 'em."

Behind me, Meery whooped and started jogging. The rest of our group followed suit, calling out good-natured jibes to the other teams across the room. Reese gestured with his chin for me to follow them. A challenge.

I grinned, throwing a backwards glance at my attending as I fell in with the group. His eyes tracked me as he set his clipboard on a bench and followed.

***

As far as competitions went, this one was sketchy on the rules. Will and Connor started yelling ridiculous estimations of their teams' accomplishments, including an exaggerated count of their group's burpees and a highly inaccurate average speed for laps. Reese was a little more specific.

"Eight thousand pounds?! You're full of it!" Will crowed while his team sprinted past. Reese didn't bother responding, but the figure checked out with some quick mental math.

"We had...at least...nine thousand!" Connor huffed from the burpee corner.

"Another set!" a girl in my group cheered. Forty-five minutes into the most competitive workout of my life, I would have expected groans and denials from the rest of the team. Instead, we rallied. Next to me, Tess huffed, smiling, as she hefted the five-pound weight Reese handed her.

Another set, then another. My butt was killing me. All around, my teammates dropped like flies. Meery was dowsing herself in water from her bottle. A man in a blue shirt sprawled on the mats with his discarded kettle bell. I wasn't far behind him.

"Give me three more."

Reese's voice came out of nowhere, rumbling right next to my ear. I jerked, kettlebell swinging wildly. When had he snuck up behind me?

"You got it. Keep your core engaged." His chest radiated warmth to my back.

My whole freakin' body *engaged* when his fingertips pressed lightly on my ribcage. I chanced a glance behind my shoulder to find him peering down at my form. My body moved without my permission. Maybe I was just used to following his direction. Maybe that gruff, assured command was so different from his gentle recommendations in the OR, I *wanted* to do as he said. I gulped a breath on my way down, forcing my mind away from that particular train of thought.

Reese followed me down, keeping that light, steady pressure on my ribs.

"Good."

I squatted again, squeezing my eyes shut against the sudden flutter his praise sent ricocheting through me.

"One more."

Breath burst from my lips at the feeling of his chest brushing against my back. I was sweaty and panting and about to fall over from exhaustion. I shouldn't have had the capacity to get turned on right now. Yet...

"Perfect," he murmured in my ear as I rose from my final rep. Those fingertips pressed ever-so-slightly where they rested against my ribcage before he released me to walk back to his clipboard. A shudder vibrated through my body that had nothing to do with muscle fatigue.

"Well, damn. How do I get a hands-on assist like that?" Meery sidled up next to me, toweling off. Tess raised her brows. All I could do was gulp down my water, still not completely sure what had just happened. When they turned away, my hand ghosted over the ridges of my ribs, still feeling the heat from where his fingers had rested.

I had an inkling that I'd be able to feel it for a very, very long time.

Chapter 7

Sam

"I guess I didn't realize we were competing over who could get the most gropey during class today."

The glare I sent my brother should have shut him up for the next week. Will was still on thin ice. Instead, he kept grinning.

"Yeah, this is a nice place, Sammy. We'll lose our customers if you start feeling everyone up," Conner chimed in.

Most of the class was packing up or already heading towards the doors and Lainey had disappeared into the locker room a few minutes ago. Thank fuck. When Will and Connor started riffing off each other, they were insufferable. Especially when it was directed at me.

"I didn't grope her."

I had groped her.

Maybe it didn't count as groping in the traditional sense, but I'd gone three years without so much as brushing past her in the hallway. My fingers on Lainey's body had felt indecent.

It didn't matter that I'd barely touched her or that I'd kept everything above the waist and completely professional. Her ass had been about two inches away from my dick and she'd been sweating. The simple connection of my fingertips with her torso had nearly sent me over the edge. It all had made me think much too deeply about other ways I wanted to be behind her while she panted and I told her she was perfect.

Shit. What had I been thinking? I avoided my reflection as I wiped down the medicine balls. I knew *exactly* what I'd been thinking.

That the last time I'd taken a risk and opened up to her, it hadn't crashed and burned as badly as I thought it would. I'd been thinking about how gorgeous she was and how she'd asked yesterday if it was weird that she'd been staring at me during rounds.

It hadn't been weird. It had been glorious. Demoralizing, really, how much I'd liked it. But I cut myself some slack. Ever since we'd met, I'd been the one to sneak furtive looks in her direction. It was nice to be on the receiving end for once.

By the time she'd hinted that she would be open to working out together again, I'd been ready to buy this whole place out from under my brother's nose and gift it to her as a token of my affection. I sighed, tossing a towel into the laundry baskets by the front desk. Being around her did stupid things to me to begin with. Now that I had her attention? I was certifiable.

Didn't matter, I told myself, finally squaring a stern look in the mirror. We weren't dating. That wasn't even on the table. I needed to keep my hands to myself.

"Hey, great workout today!" The woman Lainey had been talking to earlier—Meery, I think—exited the locker room with Lainey and the blonde on her heels. I hadn't caught her name.

"You put in some nice work. The vibes in here were on point today." Will nodded to Lainey. "I think I've got you to thank for that."

"I take no responsibility for the vibes. You should just know for future reference that my competitive streak cannot be silenced. No challenge can go unmet."

I nearly grinned. I'd seen that competitive streak in action every day since I'd met her. The rivalry between her and Jones was like something out of a Shakesperean tragedy. I'd caught her practicing her stitches in an empty OR once, hours after a nurse had complimented Jones on his needlework. She'd cranked out nearly five hundred sutures before her hand had cramped up.

"Noted for next time." Will winked as he grabbed a pack of gum off the counter. I wanted to punch him in the face. I settled for leaning over and pinching the shit out of his arm under the desk until he gave me a piece.

"Fuck's sake, Sam," he muttered, shuffling over a few feet. He'd felt like shit when I told him Lainey had overheard his comment about asking her out. So guilty, he'd been my first call last night after Lainey had asked to work out together again. I think he'd been as relieved as I was at the turn of events. He was still on my shit list, though, and he'd have to rein in the flirting if he wanted to get off it anytime soon.

"Don't be so modest! You have a gift." Meery looked at him with unfiltered interest. "Do you do any private sessions?"

Will's face transformed from genial to distant in a second. "Sorry, no. Groups only. We don't get into the personal side of personal training."

"That doesn't seem to be stopping them." Meery's head tilted to where Lainey leaned on the counter in front of me. Far enough away to be civil, close enough to be...distracting.

I froze, but Will jumped in before I could fumble something up too badly. "He doesn't work here. He was just helping out during the rush today."

I cleared my throat. Now I felt bad about pinching him.

"They can get up to whatever they want."

Nevermind.

"You don't work here? Are you a trainer somewhere else?" the one with the purple in her hair asked softly.

"I work at Cedar."

She blinked, seeming to expect more, but I wasn't sure what more there was for her to know.

"The hospital?" she prodded.

"Yes. We work together in the cardiac unit," Lainey chimed in. "Reese is one of the best educators in our program."

I blinked down at her. I didn't know she felt that way.

"But you did pretty well today," she continued. "I didn't realize you're such a fitness buff."

"I—"

Conner butted in. "He is. Worked as a trainer through college. Studied kinesiology before he went to the dark side with the heart thing."

Lainey whirled on me. The movement whipped her ponytail around, wafting the scent of her floral shampoo into my face.

"Kinesiology? Not pre-med? Or Biochem or something?" She continued listing common medical majors, apparently not satisfied with my nod.

"It's actually a good story. You should tell her over coffee, Sammy," Connor butted in. "Molido has the best cold brew in town. Definitely worth the walk across the parking lot."

"There's always a crazy line," the purple-haired one whispered, peering to look at the café that shared R³'s lot.

"Right? I tried to go there once after work and they said they were out of milk. I was gutted." Lainey eyed the people waiting outside. "I've always wanted to go, though."

"Sam can get you in, no line," Will offered. No doubt payback for the pinch earlier. Asshole. He was barking up the wrong tree, anyway. Lainey didn't do coffee. Or relationships. But despite these things, she looked up at me with those brown eyes, brows quirked.

"Can you?" She seemed...intrigued. Was she? Being a heart surgeon was usually enough to snag someone's interest at a bar if I was out with friends and open to some company. That obviously wouldn't fly with Lainey. But somehow, having an in at the coffee shop next door seemed to do the trick.

"Sure." I pulled out my phone and nodded at the group around us before tapping it to life. Lainey's goodbyes took slightly longer as she and the blonde talked quietly about seeing each other at the next Thursday class. I batted out a text while I pointedly ignored my brothers and their barely hidden smirks.

I followed Lainey out of the gym, both happy and tortured with the way her ass looked in her leggings. Habit made me look back at my brothers as I headed out the door, and I immediately wished I hadn't. Will was air humping to some rhythm only he could hear while Connor flexed his arms, silent-screaming in a spot-on imitation of some pumped up wrestler entering the ring. I flipped them off as Meery burst into a fit of giggles and her friend blushed.

"Like I said, line out the door." Lainey looked back at me, so sweetly unaware of the jackassery being conducted at her expense just a few feet away. I hustled her a little faster to ensure she didn't see any of it. "I've been wanting to try this place forever. I have heard the cold brew here is insane. I swear, every time I open my Instagram I see a Molido cup with, like, a maple bacon cream latte or something. Have you had anything like that from here yet?"

"Hmm." I shook my head, unable to put into words how little a maple bacon cream anything appealed to me. Despite my affection for this place, I had my limits. My phone buzzed in my hand. Thank God. It gave me something to focus on while she dropped her gym bag into the trunk of her car. She bent down—God help me—to pluck her phone and wallet out of the outer pocket.

"It must be good if it's so popular. I was hoping they'd be able to do something crazy with a cold foam tea latte or something."

I tapped out a response and pocketed the device. "We'll see in a minute," I muttered, stopping at the back of the line. It snaked around the parking lot. Lainey snorted.

"It'll take more than a minute," she shrugged, shielding her eyes from the sun. I stepped to the left to cast her in shadow. "It's okay. I don't have anywhere to be today."

Not until her shift started later tonight. But revealing I knew that information qualified as creepy in most contiguous U.S . states, so I refrained. Something about her assertion nettled. "You don't think I can get us in?"

She had the grace to look guilty. She probably thought it was far-fetched for her oatmeal attending to have a hookup at the most viral coffee shop in the city. My eyes narrowed.

"I can get us in."

"It's really okay. I'm sure you—"

"You're not the only one who's competitive, Lainey."

Surprise registered on her face. I relished being the one to put it there, especially when it morphed into consideration. That feeling crept up on me again—that she was really seeing me, instead of just looking through me. "Are you?"

"Just because I don't jostle for first dibs at an OR doesn't mean I'm not competitive." Lainey had a renowned reputation for jostling. Or bribing. Or doing pretty much anything she need-ed to get into whatever procedure she wanted. That wasn't really my style, but growing up with two brothers and limited resources had made me plenty competitive. Slow and steady just happened to work for me more often.

Case in point, I was standing in the longest line imaginable with Lainey Carmichael, and she seemed genuinely interested in what I had to say. Miracle of miracles.

"Samuel Rodriguez Reese! What the fuck are you doing in line?"

Lainey, and everyone else in the parking lot, turned to see Santiago standing on the porch of the cafe, hands on his hips and scowling.

"Just come inside, for fuck's sake. I don't have time to chase you around the parking lot, you inconsiderate ass!"

"I didn't want to assume." My hand on Lainey's back propelled her forward with me amid a mix of curious glances and frowns. People didn't really look kindly on the fact that I could skip to the front while they stood for over thirty minutes in the sun.

He ushered us through the doors to a tiny table by the pastry case. The scent of coffee and melted butter greeted us the second we stepped in.

"Tiago, we could have just grabbed something to go—"

"Literally shut all the fuck up. You think you can just come to *mi café* and wait outside in the elements like a common peasant? And with a lady friend, no less? I'm ashamed of you. Sit."

He bent down to swipe a kiss across my cheek when I complied. My best friend was a touchy-feely kind of guy. It still didn't stop me from giving him shit.

"My middle name is not Rodriguez. And you shouldn't seat us here with all those people waiting outside."

"Of course I can! You're family, you ass! I'm done with you now. You're not even going to introduce us, you fucking Neanderthal." He pivoted to smile at Lainey, curly hair falling across his forehead. "I'm Santiago."

"I'm Lainey. It's nice to meet you."

Anyone else would have missed the split-second when he froze, his long, black-polish-tipped fingers barely twitching when their hands clasped. Lainey likely didn't catch the quick flicker of his eyes to my face, then back to hers. But I did. I met his eyes again when he looked at me, silently pleading for him to be cool.

His teeth glinted. "Sit. Stay." He swept away. As soon as Lainey's back was turned, his head whipped around and he mouthed *holy shit, holy shit, what the fuck* at me. I ignored him, opting instead to watch Lainey gawk at the shop.

I'd been coming here since before it opened, and sometimes even I was still impressed. Colorful paper and bronze lanterns crowded together on the ceiling. White stars and moons swirled across the indigo walls. Tiago had spent several very late nights informing me exactly what all the various runes and astrological bullshit were, but I didn't remember them now. Once I'd painted one, I just moved onto the next.

Outside, colorful umbrellas strung together to make a massive, whimsical patio cover. Jordan and I had nearly come to blows over that one. Believe it or not, umbrellas aren't the most ideal material if you're trying to build a sustainable roof structure.

"This place lives up to the hype." Lainey swept her eyes around the pastry case, stuffed with a dizzying array of Cuban, French, and American confections. "Does he own it?"

"Yes."

Her eyes widened. "When you said you could get us in here, I didn't think it'd be because you know the owner. Dang. They even know your order."

Tiago's hand appeared, placing a cup and saucer in front of me. He scoffed. "Of course I do. Not that it's hard to remember."

"Coffee. Black. Pretty standard for a doctor." Lainey rolled her eyes along with Santiago. She knew my coffee order, too. I took a sip to hide my smile.

"He takes it with sugar here. Classic Café Cubano."

"Not like I'm allowed to have anything else," I grumbled.

"Anything except plain black, *Amor*. You need to spice things up. You"—he swiveled on his way to the back, pointing at Lainey—"little miss decaf iced tea and 'something cool with cold foam.' You good with spice?"

"Ah, yes?"

He clapped twice and whirled through the beaded curtain to the kitchen. I sipped my drink, savoring.

"You gave him my drink order?"

"Are you impressed yet?" Our eyes met. Held. Warmth spread in my chest and turned molten. The table between us was the size of a postage stamp. Our knees bumped underneath it.

"Yes." A thousand thoughts rattled around in the back of my head. Like how we'd just endured the workout of the year and I probably smelled like the men's locker room. That she was most likely starving, like me. I was wondering whether or not Tiago was going to play it cool now that he knew exactly who sat across from me. But it faded to the background; her eyes like a tether, reeling me in closer and closer the longer she looked at me.

"Pardon," Jordan's voice rumbled somewhere above us. His arm descended over the top of the pastry case to deposit a plate of baked goods. He gave Lainey a slow smile. "I'm Jordan. Tell me what you think of these two." He pointed to two pastries on top of the pile before ducking back behind the case.

I leaned back in my chair, not entirely sure when I'd moved towards her. Lainey likewise pushed her shoulders back in her seat, looking lost and staring at the plate before us. A faint flush touched her cheeks. "They drop pastry out of the sky here? Is this heaven?"

"Jordan runs the kitchen."

"He talks as much as you do." Her nose wrinkled at me, teasing.

"It's my curse to be surrounded by large, silent men. I have to carry on all the conversations around here." Santiago managed to Tetris the plates to make room for—I'm not kidding—a whole fucking platter of iced tea drinks. He presented them to Lainey like she was a queen. "For you, a flight. We've got the floral Rooibos with the dreamsicle cold foam. Lavender hibiscus with the honey foam. Decaf earl gray with coconut caramel. And chai with habanero brown sugar."

Tiago smirked at me, batting his eyelashes. I shrugged. "You lost me at dreamsicle."

"You have flights of tea here?" Lainey gaped at the colorful glasses as if he'd offered her a selection of jewels.

"We don't. But you're a VIP."

Lainey bit her lip, looking up at Santiago with stars in her eyes. "I think I'm in love with you."

"Oh, Honey, that's sweet, but I'm taken. My friend's single, though." He patted my shoulder and swept off to buss a table. It was a challenge to stop myself from glaring after him. Thankfully, Lainey seemed too entranced by her tea to have noticed his wing-manning.

"Okay. I'm impressed now."

Chapter 8

Sam

You couldn't have paid me to go near the purple concoction on Lainey's tea flight, but her groan of delight made me want to reconsider. And buy her a lifetime supply.

"How do you know Santiago? No offense, but it's hard to imagine you as friends. You seem so different."

Her eyes rolled in her head as she sampled another drink. I shifted in my seat, undecided on whether this was amazing or horrible. I frowned down at my coffee, seeking a distraction from the foreplay Lainey was having with her cold foam across the table. "I've known him since middle school. He's practically a brother."

"And does *he* know why you became a surgeon? That's what we're supposed to be doing, you know. Talking about your origin story."

I swallowed, watching her rub a glass straw across her lip and trying not to become hypnotized. "It's not that good of a story. Or a long one."

"Conner said it was a good story." Lainey widened her eyes, palm pressing to her chest. "Or are you telling me he had some sort of ulterior motive for forcing you to take me out for a coffee?"

"He didn't force me."

Her lips tilted up. Something about my response had pleased her.

"Regardless, embellish a little. It's going to take me a while to get through these." Ice clinked in her glass. All at once, I felt edgy. My origin story, as she'd call it, wasn't dramatic or flashy. But, like most people in medicine, it was important to me. It had never occurred to me until now that sharing it was like sharing a part of myself.

I picked at a pastry. "The short story is my dad died of a heart attack when I was six."

She offered a customary apology for my loss. I had very few memories of him. Mostly, all I remembered was how hard my mom had worked to keep a roof over our heads. I took a bite and hummed my approval, clapping Jordan on the back as he passed by. He gave me a nod, then a sly grin as he passed Lainey's chair. *God.*

"What's the long version?"

Stalling, I took another bite and followed it up with more coffee. "I saved someone's life once."

"I've seen you in the OR. I think that number is higher than one."

Her nose wrinkled when I gave her a flat look over the rim of my cup. "In college, before I was a surgeon, I worked at a gym near my university as a trainer. One of my clients was an older guy. Had a heart attack right on the bench."

"Jesus."

"Yeah, it was a bad day. I started CPR while someone called an ambulance. And he lived. Came back a few months later to thank me. The CPR had saved his life." I plucked at the folds of my napkin. "We didn't have much growing up. Single mom, three boys running around. I'd always assumed the gym was the best I could do. I liked helping people. It was good work. But that day...I just spent hours staring down at my hands. I'd saved someone's life. Everything else felt like a waste of time after that."

I shoved the rest of the coconut thing unceremoniously down my throat, nearly draining the rest of my cup at the same time.

"That's a legitimately good origin story, Reese." Her use of my last name killed me a little, but the feeling went away when I saw the look on her face. Surprise and something close to awe. More than I deserved for a story about administering CPR. Not when I knew what she could do.

"What about you?"

She set her cup back on the tray, choosing a croissant with some sort of sausage inside. "You know my story. *Everyone* knows my story. Mom's a doctor, dad's a medical engineer. They meet and have a baby. It's incredible. It's ingenious. It's a pioneer in cardiac medicine."

She wiggled her fingers like she was putting on a show. I propped my elbows on the table as she chewed. I'd never discussed this part of her life with her before. Her background—*her* origin story. She was correct. Everyone in our field already knew it.

Her parents were young when they'd paired up on the research project that cemented their names in medical history forever. The

Carmichael-Davis stent had been a new category of medical device, including a new, specialized approach to insertion that had nearly doubled the rate of patient success and reduced scarring by 50%. The two had launched the stent, raked in the cash from the patents, and then gone their separate ways. Somewhere in there, Lainey had made her appearance as well.

"Was it hard to grow up in the shadow of Carmichael-Davis?"

She nearly choked on the last bite of croissant, smirking. "No one's put it like that before. 'The shadow of Carmichael-Davis.' Sounds kind of ominous." Despite her grin, she placed another pastry onto her plate, peeling off a few of the layers, one by one. Santiago swapped my cup for a fresh one while I watched her fidget. "I guess so, yes. But you know my mom." She pulled more pastry apart until she hit the chocolate filling in the middle.

"I've met her before, yes."

Her eyes rolled, tongue darting out to lick the sugar from her thumb. I nearly missed what she said next. "You and everyone else. She's the most famous heart surgeon in the world and she hasn't stepped foot in an OR in over twenty years. I grew up with an anatomically labeled heart poster above my bed. Ending up a surgeon was practically destiny."

Following her success with the stent, Dr. Rebecca Carmichael had made a name for herself, lecturing passionately about patient-centered care and surgical innovation. Her career transitioned from practicing medicine to speaking on the circuit. She was on a few boards and had founded a nonprofit helping underserved patients receive life-saving heart care. Years ago, I'd heard a rumor that Dr. Carmichael was being considered for the surgeon general's office. Somewhere around that same time she'd appeared on Oprah.

But that didn't tell me how Lainey had ended up here, far from her home in Texas, talking with me. And I really, really wanted to know what cosmic whateverthefuck had aligned to make all this happen. "That's her origin story. Not yours."

Silence settled again on our table. Around us, customers bustled in and out. The milk steamer screamed. Tiago shouted for another chair from the back. Lainey frowned, but the pouty downturn of her mouth only made her more beautiful.

"I've lived a very privileged life. I had the nannies and the chauffeurs and everything. But people out there are suffering. There's not enough food or money or...*love*. I've never struggled once in my life. It feels like I shouldn't waste that opportunity, you know? Not everyone has my advantages, but we all have hearts. And I know hearts. If I can use that knowledge to help someone live a better life or have more time on this earth, I have an obligation to do so." She stared down at her plate, visibly uncomfortable.

"I don't know. Maybe that's a stupid reason to get into this. I'm good at it. I like it. I like that I can help improve the world, even if it's just one artery at a time. Your story is better." She polished off the last of the chocolate thing.

"I like your story." I *loved* her story. It was honest, and she was self-aware enough to understand it. I got the feeling that, like me, she wasn't used to sharing this facet of her past with people, and I loved that she trusted me with it.

"Yours didn't have a butler." She huffed, crossing her arms as she sat back.

"A butler?" I whistled. A freaking butler. And I'd grown up scrubbing the mold off the walls with just my little brothers to help. We were worlds apart. And yet, not really.

"Two. Divorced parents, right? Everything is duplicated."

"So, you left the butlers behind and went to med school in Texas. How'd you end up in Chicago?"

A burning question, often hotly debated at Cedar. According to the rumor mill, she'd matched with Houston Presbyterian for her residency and switched to Cedar at the last minute. Something normal people couldn't really do, but Lainey came with the advantage of a hefty medical legacy. Having the favor of someone like Dr. Carmichael could open major doors for an organization.

All Caplan would say on the matter, when someone had asked him about it once, was that they wanted the best at Cedar, and they'd opened up a spot for her when she'd requested a transfer. I'd still been at Northwestern at that point, but the story of her irregular entrance into the program still popped up every once in a while, so I was familiar with it. Sometimes people dredged it up when she and Cooper did something particularly brilliant in the OR.

Whatever the naysayers muttered about didn't matter, though. Lainey had entered the program and promptly blown everyone away. She knew hearts in-and-out. But I'd always been curious about the actual story of how she got here.

As she stiffened, her gaze shooting down to the empty cups around her, I immediately knew the question was unwelcome.

"Another round?" Santiago plucked up the tray, cutting off whatever I'd just opened my mouth to say. An apology, perhaps. Lainey gave him a small smile. Strained.

"I couldn't. It was all amazing. The dreamsicle? A literal dream."

"A literal dream. It's going on the menu board. I told you!" Tiago snapped his fingers in my face. I smacked his hand away. "What did you think of the coconut pastelitos? Jordan has been agonizing over them. He thinks there's too much salt, even though he's wrong." He glared at his partner, who ambled over to listen in on Lainey's response.

"The coconut things? Ohmigod, don't change a thing. I want to eat this until I die. And then I want to be embalmed in whatever glaze you have going on here. And then stuff me in my casket with as many of these as you can fit." She thawed as she talked, conversation melting away the awkward freeze from when I'd mentioned Texas.

Or maybe she was just that good at faking it.

Despite her insistence otherwise, Tiago handed her a decaf matcha something or other with some sort of ginger whip on top, and handed me another cup as well. When my friends drifted away to see to other customers, we fiddled with our drinks in awkward silence. For maybe the first time in my life, I felt compelled to fill it.

"Embalming, huh?" I surprised a laugh out of her, which was gratifying.

"Hey, those things were good! I'd be rich and well-fed in the afterlife."

"Hmm. More of a cremation guy, myself."

A week ago, if you'd told me I'd sit across from Lainey Carmichael, trying to distract her by talking about our post-mortem preferences, I would have called the psych ward. Now? Her smile lit up the whole fucking room.

"Tell me more about that."

I smiled back.

Chapter 9

Sam

Shiny plastic and metal chairs filled conference room C, and I was currently planning to burn them all to the ground. They creaked. Every one of them. Fuck conference room C.

Cooper shifted beside me, tugging his sleeve to check his watch again. As he moved, the metal frame of his chair squealed, and I decided I'd burn his first. I'd allow him to vacate it before I started, of course. Considering how he was crossing and re-crossing his legs, he might even help me with the lighter fluid.

We weren't the only ones agitated. Groans sounded at Caplan's announcement that there were "Just a few more things before we close out."

Almost all of us—nearly thirty attending cardiac surgeons at Cedar—squeezed into the space. I didn't have any issues with conference room C, aside from the shrieking chairs. Like the rest of the hospital, it was clean and modern: Gray and white striped carpet, whiteboards on the walls. Big projector screen that lowered with a press of a button. The room itself was fine.

It was the quarterly department meetings, held in conference room fucking C, that made me want to grab a lighter. The agendas usually consisted of arduous hashing and rehashing of new quality standards initiatives, HR programs, and patient outcomes metrics. Caplan claimed they were an integral component of our surgical team morale. Everyone else thought they were fucking boring.

"If I don't get out of here soon, I'm going to go crazy. You going to the thing tonight?" Cooper whispered.

I nodded, keeping my eyes on Caplan, as if the force of my attention could hurry things along.

"Alright, seriously, give me five more minutes, people. We'll be sipping watered down drinks in no time."

The Eastern chapter of the Regional Cardiologists Association had commandeered a hotel ballroom a few miles away to kick off their annual conference. Most of us had the night off since Cedar wanted a good showing when one of the biggest trade associations came through our hometown. Especially when our favorite fellow's mother was the keynote speaker.

That was possibly another reason I was itching to get the hell out of this room. Lainey and I had gone our separate ways after our coffee...date? *No,* not date. Meeting?

Whatever it was, I couldn't stop thinking about it. And since I specifically avoided consulting Lainey's on-call rotation when I made my schedule every month, we'd been like ships in the night all week. I'd had rounds with her once, yesterday, before she'd rushed off to surgery. I was stuck waiting for tonight, when I knew for a fact we'd be in the same room.

Pathetic. Maybe that was pissing me off, too. I didn't know what the hell was going on with us. Not that there was even an "us." We couldn't date. And Lainey didn't date people from work, anyway. She'd told Jones many times, and I wouldn't push that boundary. I respected her too much for that. I kept coming back to...friends. Friendly colleagues. So, we'd keep working together. And maybe grab coffee after a workout every once in a while. And that would be great. Better than what we'd had before, which was a politely cordial working relationship.

Great.

"We're sad to say goodbye to Dr. Randall, whose last day was Tuesday. We wish him the best."

The room stirred, this time in interest instead of irritation. Cooper leaned over to me. "You know about Randall?"

I shook my head. I'd known he was a key player in that love triangle with the two anesthesiologists, but I hadn't known about his departure. Surely there was a connection there.

"With that in mind, we're opening up a new attending spot as soon as possible to replace him. We'll be hiring three new permanent roles. Thankfully, the timing coincides with the graduation of our current class of fellows. Let us know your recommendations there. If we can keep the good ones in-house, we'll do what we can to make it happen."

"Can we just put Carmichael's name in three times?" Everyone chuckled at the suggestion from the front of the room.

"Carmichael's a given. Shoot me an email if you know anyone else looking for a job. Speaking of personnel changes, HR has been working with the board to enact a new policy on interpersonal relationships. There's some new paperwork involved to disclose any romantic relationships with a colleague. I know, I know"—Caplan held his hands out, trying to placate a few grumbles around the room—"it's just a few forms to limit liability for the hospital."

"What constitutes a romantic relationship?" someone piped up. The director shuffled a few papers and read from one of them. "Any reciprocated romantic interest or relationship must be disclosed to HR. Following submission and processing of documentation, the department will take action to maintain the professional working environment which we pride ourselves on."

"So, if we start something up, we won't work with that person anymore?" Cooper asked. Caplan nodded.

"That's the plan. Separation of church and state and all that. I think we all agree that a lovers' spat is the last thing we need causing tension in the OR. The board is breathing down our necks too much as it is. Go to HR if you get the hots for anyone and we'll take it from there." He clapped, dismissing us. "Not too painful today, I hope. Go have some appetizers. Make us look good. Gold star to anyone who can get Dr. Carmichael to write a check to the department."

Chuckles and chatter followed me into the hall as we all booked it to the physician's lounge. I'd stuffed a tux in my locker and was considering whether to change here or at the hotel when Cooper loped up next to me.

"Well, there goes my plans with Carmichael."

"Hmm?" His comment came at me with no context. I rifled through my bag to find a pair of nicer socks.

"The new HR bullshit. I was planning on asking her out when she finished her fellowship. Guess that's out. She's too valuable in the OR."

I froze, fingers clenching the black cotton. "You and Carmichael?" *Shit.* They were a dynamic fucking duo around here—everyone knew Cooper and Carmichael and the mind-blowing procedures they took on.

Obviously, I'd considered before that I probably wasn't the only one who'd noticed Lainey. It had even crossed my mind that there may be something more happening between her and Cooper, but I'd told myself again and again I was being paranoid. I'd gotten the feeling that their relationship thrived more on professional compatibility than any romantic sparks. Maybe not.

"Haven't we all thought about it? She's gorgeous. Talented." He shrugged, unaware that he was causing me serious palpitations. I convinced my body to move again, pulling the garment bag from my locker. "But she knows me too well. I practically can't operate without her."

He grabbed his own garment bag, humming in consideration. "Maybe it'd be worth it, though. She's one of a kind, you know?"

"Yeah." I knew.

Cooper strolled away. I sighed. The rush of air leaving my lungs felt good, so I sucked in a breath and sighed again. So Cooper had a thing for Lainey. Apparently, we all did. I headed to the bathroom to change, trying to find equilibrium after that mindfuck of a conversation. I wasn't the only one waiting in the wings to make a move after Lainey finished up her fellowship. It made me feel like we were all vultures circling around her.

I tugged on my suit, reminding myself that I'd *known* people were probably interested in her. But now I had solid proof of that. Right now, when she'd started looking at me as more than just her attending, the concept put a sick feeling in my gut. *Dammit.*

I fiddled with my bowtie in the mirror, trying to convince myself that it didn't matter because Lainey didn't date people she worked with. Even if she made an exception, she certainly wouldn't date *me*. Not with Cooper on the hook. He was an outstanding surgeon. Best in our field, many might argue. Bright, well-connected, and good looking. Me? I was...quiet.

I cursed, jerking at the tie, starting over when it wouldn't stay straight.

Right. This was fine. Great. *Great.*

***

The ballroom was packed. And Lainey was short. It should have taken me much longer than it did to find her, but I apparently came pre-built with some sort of radar where she was concerned. That, and she was standing next to her mother. People flocked to the woman like moths to flame.

Their little corner of the ballroom buzzed with activity. People circled the fancy red-and-gold carpet, trying to get closer to them. Chandeliers glittered overhead, their dim light encouraging a sense of intimacy in the cavernous space. A jazz band played softly on stage across the room, where tables and chairs were set up for dinner.

Too captivated by Lainey looking like *that* in a dress like *that,* I hardly noticed anything else. I knew the general shape of her body, I'd just never seen it outlined so damn clearly before. The black fabric of her dress hugged every curve, clinging to her torso and hips before flaring out below her knees. I didn't know much about dresses. I'm sure there were words to describe what she was wearing, but the only ones that came to mind were *holy shit.*

I snuck peeks while I stood in line at the bar. She smiled at something her mother said and engaged in conversation with the man next to her. Her laugh tinkled over the heads of the crowd. Another woman approached her and they hugged. She was good at this. The schmoozing.

Not surprising. Lainey charmed the pants off of everyone she met. Given her upbringing and her mother's celebrity, it made sense for her to be well-versed in the art of working a crowd. And damn, she worked it. As people orbited her mother, desperate for some of her attention, Lainey circled the fringes, attentive and engaged, not taking up too much of anyone's time. Everyone she talked to left the conversation with a smile, and she caused more than one riot of laughter.

"Your eyes will dry out if you don't blink soon."

"Fuck off." I dragged my eyes away from her at Blake's warning. My old friend clapped me on the back as I scowled.

"Any chance you'll introduce me?"

"Fuck. Off." I ordered him another drink, along with mine. Under no circumstances would I introduce Blake Dresden to Lainey Carmichael. If she charmed the pants off people, he *actually* got the pants off people. My friend hadn't changed his M.O. since we were roommates in med school, and he didn't show any signs of slowing down his bachelor lifestyle. After the conversation I'd just had with Cooper, the idea of him and Lainey hitting it off felt too raw to consider.

"Not the little one. Mama Carmichael. We could use the good vibes. Think she'd take pity on a poor, struggling cardiac department?"

"Probably. Not yours, though." Blake glowered, knowing I was right. Mercy Midwest Hospital was just down the street from Cedar and currently an absolute dumpster fire. They'd practically cleaned house last year when it had come out that the previous director was working with the board to embezzle funds and report false patient data to CMS. Not a good look. Blake was young for the director position, but he was one of the few willing to take on the challenge. Now he and the Mercy cardiac staff were still recovering, trying to restore a semblance of stability. "What are you doing here, anyway?"

"Recruiting, mostly. Getting people drunk and begging them to come work for me. Hello." A shit-eating grin stretched across Blake's face, aimed at someone behind me.

"Hi. Sorry, I got stuck over there." I turned at Lainey's voice. She fanned her face and set an empty champagne flute down. "It's a madhouse. I've been dry for over an hour."

Speechless, I pushed my glass in her direction, watching as she smiled and took a sip. Had she come over here for me? Wrestled through the crowd of adoring fans and department heads who wanted to snap her up now that her fellowship was ending? I smiled at the thought.

"Seemed like you were having fun." I watched her drain my drink. That made me smile, too. Something beastly and proprietary growled in my chest, adoring the sight of this girl, walking over to me, taking my drink without fear.

Her shoulder bobbed as she swallowed. "Daughterly duties and all that. I think my obligation is fulfilled, though. I'd rather hang out over here than with my mom's fan club."

"I'm Blake." He stuck his hand out, practically leaping over the table to get to her. I gave him a warning look that he didn't see, too engrossed with her.

"Lainey. Nice to meet you." Her eyes widened when she read his nametag. "Mercy, huh? Wait. Blake Dresden? As in the new director over there? You might need this more than me." She slid the near-empty glass across the table. Blake laughed.

Pants. Charmed. *Dammit.*

"You're probably right. Hey, any chance you want to ditch a brand-new, state-of-the-art facility and come slum it with my scrappy crew? We'll name an OR after you."

"Don't poach my fellow," I muttered. This time, he spotted my warning glare and shrugged.

"I have to try, dude."

Lainey laughed, craning her neck towards the bar and the long, snaking line. "I don't know. I'm fond of the attendings over there. Hard to beat good, hands-on instruction these days."

She pointedly evaded eye contact with me when she spoke, which somehow made it even more clear that I was the attending she was referring to. Blake's eyebrows jumped, gaze darting between the two of us while we avoided looking at each other. I struggled to wrench my mind away from picturing the kinds of hands-on I could get with her, if she would give me a chance.

"Well, sure. Reese has always been the best. Helping people is his love language." Blake leaned in, propping up on the table. "He used to organize study groups for the first years in med school. President of our class year three and four."

Lainey glanced at me. "Really?"

"Really. No wonder Cedar poached him. You know Northwestern recruited him *hard*." Lainey looked impressed. As impressed as someone could be when they, themselves, had been heavily recruited by literally every hospital in the country before she'd finished med school. Blake continued laying it on thick. "Are you going to his lecture tomorrow?"

"You're doing a lecture?" She turned to face me. I hailed a passing server with a tray of water.

"Oh, yeah. ERCA holds a standing spot for him on the conference agenda. What is this, the fourth year you've done the interactive overview?"

"Hmm." I nudged the water towards Lainey. "Want something stronger?"

Before she could answer, a frazzled-looking woman in an aggressively slick bun squeezed through the crowd and shoved a glass of wine into Lainey's hand. "Sorry, I lost you back there. I noticed your glass was empty, so I went to get a new one, but they stopped serving champagne at six, so I tried to track some more down and—"

"Oh my gosh, Jessica, you didn't have to do that! That's so sweet. This is perfectly fine. Why don't you take the rest of the night and enjoy yourself? You don't have to wait on us hand and foot, you know." Lainey squeezed the woman's arm. Despite her attempts to soothe, a hectic air clung to the woman. "Blake, Sam, this is Jessica. My mother's assistant. She keeps all our trains running. We'd be lost without her."

"Well, thank you. I appreciate that. Especially when I'm trying to..." Her gaze sharpened, honing in on Blake and me. Suddenly, that frazzled energy turned focused. Hawk-like. "Where are you two sitting? For dinner."

"Uh—" Blake started, checking around the ballroom for the tables currently being set for dinner.

"The McCrareys' flight was delayed, so we have three open seats at our table, right up front. If we don't fill it, it'll be a disaster." Jessica grabbed onto Lainey's arm, imploring. "Do you know these people? Do they want to sit with you?"

"Want an upgrade, fellas?" Lainey glanced at us, laughter shining in her eyes. As we agreed, easing some of the tension from poor Jessica's shoulders, Cooper edged his way around her to stand by Lainey.

"There you are. I need friendly faces. Everyone here only wants to talk about AI diagnostics and that last transplant I did."

Jessica clicked her fingers. "Dr. Cooper. Perfect. You're number three. Problem solved."

She gave Lainey a smile, then whirled back into the crowd.

"I...what?" Cooper stared after her, bewildered.

"You're sitting with us now. Primo seats. Front row." Lainey patted his arm.

"Sweet." They smiled at each other, then looked away at the same time. Cooper to survey the crowd around us and Lainey to glance up at me. I tried my hardest not to over analyze if they were standing too closely, or if that smile had been a little too friendly.

"Tell me about your session tomorrow." Lainey leaned closer so I could hear her. The soft fabric of her dress dragged against my pants. Before I could respond, someone else popped out of the crowd.

"Lainey? Hi." The woman was short by most standards. About an inch taller than Lainey. Blonde. She wore a soft smile on her face and a gauzy pink dress that hugged a small, unmistakable baby bump. Nothing about her seemed off or wrong, but Lainey's spine stiffened as if the woman held a gun to her head.

A man walked over, putting his arm around the blonde woman's shoulders. "Lainey, hey. Long time, no see. How you been?"

His smile didn't quite meet his eyes. Lainey tensed even more, if that was possible. Her eyes widened a fraction before all expression left her face completely. "Excuse me," she murmured, then walked away. I watched as she wove her way through the crowd.

The man cleared his throat, smiling at us without watching her leave. "Nathan McDaniels. It's nice to meet you, Dr. Cooper. And Dr. Reese. I was hoping our paths would cross tonight. Word has it you have a few attending positions opening up."

I tracked Lainey's progress through the crowd and out the door. Her wine sat abandoned in front of me. Where was that glittering smile and charisma? The blonde was still watching her, too, looking at the door long after Lainey had disappeared through it. The man rubbed her arm. Her husband, I assumed, since they were both wearing rings.

"How do you know Dr. Carmichael?" I interjected, as the man was listing out some credential or other at Cooper. He paused, face tightening for just a second.

"We, ah, used to go to school with Lainey. At UT." His smile looked more like a grimace. "I was always jealous she ended up here. My grandfather was head of surgery, back in the day. It was always my goal to end up at Cedar, too."

Nathan's name tag listed him working at Houston Presbyterian. So did the blonde's—Kate McDaniels. The same institution Lainey had matched with before she'd ended up here for her residency. He was prattling on about something to Cooper, only marginally attempting to include Blake in the discussion.

"Anyway, I'm glad I got a chance to introduce myself. When those resumes come in, I'd appreciate it if you'd keep an eye out for mine." He flashed a winning smile at us. He was average height and blandly handsome in that way people looked when they had some money: Styled hair and good skin.

"We have two very talented fellows who will also submit their names for the job." My statement sounded like a warning when it left my mouth. And maybe it was. I wasn't sure. All I knew was I didn't like the way Lainey had reacted to these people. I didn't want this guy anywhere near her.

"Um, yes, obviously," Mr. Average stuttered, grimacing with another smile. "I know Lainey is exceptiona—"

"*Dr. Carmichael,*" I interrupted, unable to help myself. Hearing this stranger say Lainey's name like he knew her...it didn't sit right.

He cleared his throat, chancing a smile at Cooper, hoping for backup. My colleague gave me an odd look, but didn't otherwise chime in on our exchange.

"Of course. She—Dr. Carmichael is brilliant. Anyway, please do get in touch if you have...any questions..." He trailed off, offering another pained smile before guiding his wife away.

"That was weird." Cooper frowned as I watched them cross the room. They didn't head towards the door Lainey had just used to disappear and I relaxed a bit.

"Yeah," I agreed. Cooper gave me one last look before shrugging and turning to Blake to ask something about Mercy's new surgical initiative. I kept my eyes on the door, but Lainey didn't come back through it.

***

"Why do these places only give you one tomato?"

Lainey plopped into the seat next to me just after the servers brought out sad looking salads with, in fact, a single cherry tomato perched on top. Cooper sat on her other side, bracketed by Jessica, who hadn't stopped moving or tapping on her phone since we'd sat down. Next to me, Blake laughed too loudly at a joke from the man across the table. Apparently, he was some bigwig investor. Blake was probably angling for a donation. *Good luck.*

"You good?"

Lainey reached for the ranch dressing without meeting my eyes. "Of course. Line to the bathroom was out the door. Oh, it's starting!" She finished settling in her seat just as her mother strolled onto the stage. Almost as if she'd planned it that way.

Sitting as we were—on the side of the table, all angled to watch Dr. Carmichael's keynote—it was easy for me to keep a close eye on Lainey. She nodded when appropriate. Applauded salient points. Murmured appreciatively at the right moments, yet didn't seem to listen to the speech at all. I wondered how many times she'd heard it, or some iteration of it.

Throughout the talk, her back remained ramrod straight. She chased her tomato around the plate, never touching a bite. I refilled her water twice from the pitcher at the table. She didn't seem aware of the fresh glass of wine by her left hand. She deigned to pick at a roll, popping minute crumbs into her mouth and chewing on them longer than necessary.

By the time her mother had finished and descended to sit, I'd managed to sneak my roll onto her plate and snag Blake's just in case.

"Dr. Cooper! The man of the hour. Word on the street is that the Clinical Innovation award is coming home with you after the ceremony tomorrow." Dr. Rebecca Carmichael was very good at her job. She knew every player in the space who was worth knowing, and used them to her advantage—sometimes ruthlessly. It didn't surprise me that Cooper was on her radar. Not when someone had recently called him "cardio's bad boy" in an association forum and the nickname had stuck.

"And Dr. Reese! So glad you could join us, as well. Jessica reminded me a little while ago how active you are with the foundation. What was it, fifteen pro bono surgeries last year for people in need? An inspiration! I'm hearing good things about your bid for resident director."

"Fifteen?!" Lainey hissed, quiet enough that no one around us could hear her. She stared down at her napkin, like she hadn't meant for me to hear her, either. Jessica nodded and smiled, likely having pulled a dossier on every single person at this table so Dr. Carmichael could mingle most effectively.

"Of course, Elaina is also active in our work." She smiled fondly at her daughter. "I can't wait for her to engage more once her fellowship is complete. Dr. Dresden, how is it going over at Mercy? I hear you're working on righting that ship. Awful stuff."

Blake leapt at the chance to capitalize on her attention. Around the table, heads swiveled to listen. Mercy was everyone's favorite drama these days.

"Fifteen pro bono cases in one year. That's more than one a month!" Lainey whispered.

"Yes. You're sure you're okay?"

"Y-yes," she stuttered, making eye contact for the first time since she had sat down. "Sorry about that. Old enemies. I wasn't thrilled to see them."

"Not too late to put a laxative in their cheesecake." My response set Lainey laughing—a real one, not a fake, cocktail party laugh I heard so often at these things. I was dying to know what had set her off. Who were those enemies of hers? What had they done and did we ride at dawn?

But her petrified face was still too fresh in my mind. The same one she'd worn back at Molido when I'd asked her about Texas.

"I don't want to talk about them. I want to talk about you. And those fifteen surgeries. And that session tomorrow." She accepted her wine glass when I pushed it closer, looking surprised to find it there. And simultaneously, seemed to find something surprising about *me* being there, too. "I mean, who the heck are you?"

"Name's Sam. Nice to meet you." I offered her my hand. She took it with a smile, shoulders relaxing a bit when she laughed.

For the rest of the night, we chatted about my session, the association, and her mother's next speaking tour. Eventually, Cooper left the table to find a bar and didn't come back. Blake took his spot and Lainey didn't make any move to follow when her mother left.

By the end of the night, it was just the two of us, lost in conversation as the staff started cleaning up around us. And I loved it. Or at least would have loved it if not for the niggling feeling that she was still on edge, keeping a wary eye out for that blonde and her husband.

Chapter 10

Lainey

"Any guesses what I'm looking at right now?" Dr. Reese asked, clicking the slides to a close-up image of a heart. Since he'd taken the stage, the room had been silent. Now, hands shot into the air. "It's interactive, people. No hands. Shout it out."

And so we began. Over the course of the hour, he came alive as he led the room through a rare case, making us collaborate on the disease, possible comorbidities, and treatment options. His smile was nearly blinding. When he didn't get a correct answer, he skillfully redirected the crowd, coaxing us to the right conclusion. People started teaming up, competing to see who could answer his questions fastest. Me, Blake, and a few of the Mercy folks I'd sat with ended up giving the people around us a run for their money.

Though there was no discernible demographic of the room, younger residents and attendings, like me, crowded towards the front while older professionals watched from the back or shouted out from their seats.

It was unlike any presentation I'd ever seen before. By the end, when he walked us through the patient's real diagnosis and treatment (we'd gotten pretty darn close), there was a feeling of camaraderie in the air, fresh and energizing, and I wasn't the only one who thought so.

I lingered by a coffee cart as people lined up to talk with Sam when the session was over. Crowd members stuck around instead of rushing over to the lunch buffet. All of it was as remarkable as it was embarrassing.

Just a couple of weeks ago, I'd compared this man to oatmeal, for God's sake. Now here he was, leading one of the hottest sessions at the biggest cardiac conference on the East Coast, and side-hustling as a personal trainer when he wasn't hanging out with his BFF, who owned the hottest coffee shop in the city?

I'd been a freaking idiot—blind idiot, at that—and now, all I wanted was a little more of his time. Me and the rest of the room.

"Lainey."

I jerked, water spilling from the cup in my hand when I seized up at the familiar voice. I'd been trying to rig up an iced tea situation with a bottle of water and a crumpled tea bag. Katie gave me an apologetic wince. I nearly growled, but I didn't want to give her the satisfaction of knowing she'd gotten a rise out of me.

I stepped around her, trying to escape.

"Wait! No, please, I need to talk to you. Just…just two minutes, please." She grabbed at my arm, but I yanked it back. Her pleas drew the attention of a few people around us. My heart pounded in my throat as I looked around, considering what to do. Part of me was screaming for me to turn and walk away. But I couldn't risk any public attention with Katie. I'd done my best to keep it all quiet, but cardiothoracic surgery was a small specialty. I wouldn't be surprised to find a few UT grads in the room today, if I looked hard enough.

I nodded towards the door, motioning for her to follow me out into the hall. We wandered for a few feet until I found a quiet alcove tucked away from the prying eyes of the conference attendees. I didn't know what the heck this was about, but I didn't care for any witnesses to the conversation. Especially if I gave into my baser instincts and strangled her on the spot.

"What?" She flinched as I spat out the word.

"Did you read my email?" she whispered, rubbing her hands nervously across her belly. *Pregnant.* She was freaking pregnant. The sight had nearly made me pass out yesterday. Looking at her now still incited a queasy feeling in my stomach.

"Obviously not."

She slumped. "I specifically put in the subject line—"

"And I specifically deleted it as soon as your name darkened my inbox, *Doctor McDaniels.* What are you even doing here? You're an OB, not a cardiologist."

A flash of something crossed her face, maybe pain or grief. In a blink, it was gone. "I accepted a position here. And I had time between jobs, so I came with Nathan."

A whining screech filled my ears. The world shivered slightly, like a mirage. "You...What did you just say?"

"I got a job here. In Cedar's OB department." She gulped when I didn't respond. My mouth had dried up. Maybe my brain had, too. "They got a massive research grant for pediatric neuro..."

"Yeah." I remembered hearing about the grant—the one funding research for Katie's specialty—and then immediately dismissing it as something totally unrelated to me. Because surely this woman wasn't sadistic enough to accept a job at my hospital. Absolutely not.

"Well, my advisor back at Texas is in charge of the research team, and she called me. It all happened so fast. It's such a great opportunity."

"But you work at Presbyterian. Both of you." I waved my hands towards the windows flanking the hallway, somewhat sure that the direction faced south, where their existence had continued while I'd holed myself up in this city. Now my walls were getting breached.

"He put in his application for an attending spot here." Katie wrung her hands, shifting her weight from foot to foot like she needed to pee. But she was just nervous. I hated how I knew that.

"You know he's always wanted Cedar. And when this opportunity came up, I couldn't let it pass. It was too perfect."

"Perfect," I repeated. I wanted to puke.

"Lainey, I promise you, I never thought we'd end up here. But when the attending interviews opened up right after I got my offer...There's a new OB director at Presbyterian and it's been really hard lately—"

"Oh, my God. It's been hard for you? Well, gee, Katie, why didn't you just say so? Was it so hard in your hometown? With your friends? In your house with your husband? Working at your first-choice hospital? Was it just so fucking hard for you?" I held my hand up when she opened her mouth. Rage shook my fingers. "No, please. Please tell me about it. What it's like to get literally everything you ever wanted, and it still not be enough."

I stared at the ceiling, shaking my head. If I looked at her for a single moment longer, I was going to lose it.

"I didn't want it to go like this," Katie whispered, swiping her fingertips under her eyes.

A bitter laugh cracked out of me. "How did you think this would go?"

"Listen, if you both get a job at Cedar, I know it might be uncomfortable to work with Nate after everything that...happened..."

"You think this is about Nate? Screw Nate. This is about you. You were my person, Katie. And you took everything from me."

"You were my person, too," she hiccuped, uneven.

"I wasn't. I would have picked you every day of the week over him. And I *loved* him. So much. But I loved you more." I slapped at the tickling underneath my eye. Must be a breeze in here, or something. "But you know what? It's fine. We all ended up where we needed to. You loved him more, I guess. Good job. Have him, the condo, Presbyterian, all of it. But now, just as I'm getting my own freaking life together again, you want to come here and steal that, too? How did you think this would go, Katie? That I'd just say good luck, welcome to Chicago?"

"I-I'm so...so sorry," she wheezed, tears filling her eyes. "You were my person. You were. And I couldn't imagine life without you. So, when Nate and I...started falling for each other, I convinced myself...that you would be okay with it after a while. I know that sounds so stupid, but I thought we could be stronger than all that. And maybe I still think that now. It's been so long, Lainey. And I miss you so much. I still miss you all the time."

"You chose that. You made your decisions, and I am allowed to make mine."

I recoiled as she reached her hands out. "I know that. You have no clue how much I know that. But...maybe after all this time...It's been years, Lainey. I thought maybe if you'd found someone else, and had moved on a little, we could have a fresh start."

"We can't."

"R-right. I understand. Of course." Her head was spring-loaded, bobbing up and down. She ignored the tears running down her face. "Listen, I have no right to a-ask you this, but you're a-already pissed. Do people here know about...what happened between you and Nate? Between all three of us?"

"How many years later and you still can't say it, Katie? That you fucked my boyfriend for months right under my nose?"

She hiccuped, trying to control a sob rising in her chest. The movement jostled her top, highlighting her belly. *Pregnant.*

"Y-yes. That we cheated, and that's the reason you left your spot at Presbyterian. How many people know besides Dr. Reese?" She sniffed, swiping her wrist across her cheekbone.

"He doesn't know. No one knows. I left Texas back in Texas." Where it belonged.

"You weren't there last night. Reese was so cold to Nathan. Now he's terrified he'll never get a chance at Cedar because everyone knows what happened. We can't commit to moving here if he doesn't at least have a chance."

My palm flew to my forehead. "Oh, God. How horrible! You mean he might actually have to face the consequences of his own actions? God forbid." More tears leaked down her chin. "Well, don't worry about it. No one knows. I don't know why Reese was weird with you last night." *Maybe because you acted like a psycho and fled as soon as your ex and ex-best friend crashed the party?* Yeah. Maybe.

"Really? Dr. Reese doesn't know?"

"Yes, really. Nate will have a fair playing field, just like the rest of us." I kicked at the carpet. *Dr. Reese.* I didn't know whether to laugh or give into the prickling behind my eyes or claw her eyes out because I hated hearing her say his name. I hated that she even knew he existed to begin with.

"Thank you. Lainey, thank you so much. That's...thank you."

"I hate you." Katie recoiled at the force of the words. Good. Maybe she'd back away all the freakin' way to Texas. But I knew that wouldn't happen, not when she'd already accepted the position here. "I hate you for doing this to me again," I hissed, staring up at the ceiling once more, this time to keep the traitorous tears from sliding down. "What am I supposed to do now? Where am I supposed to go again? Are you going to chase me around the country or something? Just pick up and move and ruin my life every few years?"

"Lainey, I'm so sorry. Of course not, it was never our intention—"

"Lainey?"

Sam's low timbre cut through the high-pitched frequency of my distress. Suddenly, I realized I was only partially obscured from my colleagues—those whom my mother needed to impress...those whom I needed to impress.

"You good?" Sam took another step into the little alcove that had become more like a fighting ring. I'd been taking punches since I walked in here.

"Sorry, I'm sorry." I didn't know why I was apologizing. But one thing became crystal clear. "I need to get out of here."

"I'll drive."

"Lainey!" Katie whispered after me. Her voice held universes—grief, hope, anger, despair, familiarity. I let Reese's warm hand on my back lead me out of the hotel.

Chapter 11

Lainey

After a few minutes of blindly riding around in the passenger seat of his car, it occurred to me that Sam deserved some sort of explanation. We'd been sitting in silence since exiting the parking garage, when he'd reminded me to buckle my seatbelt.

He hadn't asked me why I'd been crying in an alcove with my arch-nemesis. My usually stoic attending was true to form, navigating around the crowded Chicago streets like he was un-bothered by the panicking colleague currently riding shotgun.

"She's..." I cleared my throat, needing to try again. "She used to be my best friend. Her husband, Nate? He used to be my boyfriend. They...got together while I was still with him."

There. That was a fairly cut-and-dry explanation of what had gone down. No need for more waterworks. No extra drama. Just cold, hard facts.

"He cheated on you?"

"Yes."

"With the blonde."

"With Katie, yes." I toyed with the hem of my dress. It was pretty, made with flowy material and a tiered skirt. I'd felt nice when I picked it out for the conference; demure enough to suit my mother and still fun enough to be me. Now I just felt cold.

"You don't have to talk about it if you don't want to." For some reason, his quiet assurance made me want to tell him. He looked at me as we slowed to a stop at a red light.

"I didn't have many friends growing up." He looked hesitant to tear his eyes away, but gave me his profile when our car inched forward. "I traveled with Mom, or stayed with the nanny while she was away. Hard to make friends when you're not around a lot, you know? I met Katie Sophomore year of high school. It was like an instant connection. Her parents are so great. I think I spent more time at her house than mine. So obviously we roomed together during college. Mom wanted me to go somewhere fancy, like Harvard or something, but Katie had her heart set on Texas and I couldn't just leave her. She was family, you know?" Sam nodded. I swallowed, studying my skirt once more.

"We were both pre-med and ended up at med school together. That's where I met Nate. First week of classes during First Year, he walked up to me in the lecture hall and told me he thought I was beautiful." My laugh echoed in the car, a surround-sound of bitterness. "Then it was the three of us, together through med school. And I was so happy and in love and everything was perfect."

Out the window, buildings rolled by. I cleared my throat again, wishing I'd had the wherewithal to salvage the tea I'd been making after Sam's session. "He started acting weird towards the end of fourth year. The three of us were so focused on studying for exams and matching into residency together, but I noticed. I told Katie

I thought he was going to propose." My stomach twisted at the memory. I dropped my head to the headrest.

"She'd been acting weird, too. I thought she was just in on it, you know? She was my best friend. Surely she'd know if my boyfriend was about to propose to me." Another dry chuckle huffed out of my lips. "He did not propose. They sat me down the night we all matched with Presbyterian. Like a divorce talk from my parents or something. I'd thought we were all just busy with studying, but they were, like, building a life together behind my back."

I stared out the windshield, my gaze unfocused, as I grappled with a storm of emotions and lingering betrayal. The pit in my stomach reminded me why I never talked about this. I'm sure a mental health professional would tell me it was a bad idea to bottle up the grief and anger, duct tape them in a dark place somewhere in my brain, and leave them there to fester. I didn't know if it was good news or bad news that the same feelings were always still there on the rare occasions I checked on them. I didn't know what to do with them. So I usually just got some more mental duct tape and packed it all up again.

"Were they sorry for what they'd done?"

I'd been monologuing and lost in the past for too long. I hadn't expected Sam to actually engage, figuring he'd let me word-vomit all over his car and then drop me off at my apartment.

"Oh, yes. Don't worry, they were very apologetic and logical about it all."

"Logical?"

I smiled at the disbelief that tinged the single word out of his mouth. "Logical. Yeah. Like, they'd waited until after exams to tell me, because they didn't want it to affect my scores. And how it didn't *change anything*. We could still all live together in that two-bedroom condo next year during residency like we'd planned. And they were so sorry, but it had *just happened*. And it was love so, what could they do? They assured me it was okay for me to be upset."

At some point, the landscape outside the window had transformed from business buildings to houses. Trees and neighborhood parks rolled by. I unfocused my eyes until they filled with the memories of that absolute cluster of a day. "That was one of the worst things, honestly. They were just so...superior. Since they thought they were more in love with each other than I was with Nate, that somehow gave them the moral high ground. Like it made it alright for them to *do* all of this behind my back. They assumed I'd see that, I guess, and accept it."

"You didn't end up at Houston Presbyterian."

I snorted. "No. Nate had always had his heart set on Cedar. He has, like, some family legacy or something. I'd assumed he'd wanted to match in Texas to stay with me. Really, it was her. Katie's the one who didn't want to leave."

I hesitated because this part was hard, too. I didn't like this about myself, and I certainly didn't want to go spilling my deepest secret to my colleague and...guy I kept noticing. My eyes focused ahead again. It was easier if I didn't look at him.

"I know it's not ethical, necessarily, but I couldn't commit to that program, with them living their life together like everything was fine. I just couldn't," I whispered.

"Of course not." His soft words encouraged me to keep going. A brick building rolled into my line of sight as the car slowed.

"My mom liked to brag back then about how many hospitals had wanted to match with me. She knows all the directors and stuff, so she knew who wanted me. The only reason I'd matched with Presbyterian is because I'd wanted to. So, I, ah, backed out. And I told my mom everything, obviously. And...And..." I became captivated by the crack running along the wall. "All it took was one call to Cedar. And I was in. I don't even know if I bumped someone from their spot. I just packed my bags and left."

I traced the crack again more slowly. I'd somehow arranged it all in less than forty-eight hours. Or my mother had. An hour after Katie and Nate had broken the news, I was in a hotel, staring numbly at the TV. The next day, my dad showed up with movers and I got the call that I was heading to Chicago.

It had been nice, in a way, to realize that my parents could take care of me. They'd delegated the task to nannies and tutors and coaches for so long, but they'd been there when I needed them. Despite hardly speaking to each other since their divorce, they'd sat with me against the wall of my new apartment that night, a Chicago-style pizza between the three of us, and for a little while it hadn't felt like my whole world was ending.

"You didn't."

"Huh?" I looked back at Sam. I'd lost track of my ramblings.

"You didn't take someone's spot. Someone asked Caplan about it once, in front of me. He said they'd opened up an extra spot for you. You didn't bump anyone from residency that year."

"Oh." My hand rested on my chest, feeling the pounding of my heart. Despite all the ick swirling around in there, something lightened. "I've always been worried about that. And was afraid to ask," I whispered, feeling small.

"You should have asked. You didn't have to live with that." He looked at me with such gentle compassion, I wasn't sure I could take it.

"I don't like to bring it up too often. Nepotism isn't a great look."

"You were the best resident in the program. No one can argue that you belong here."

I pressed my palm a little harder to my sternum, trying to trap the warmth that flooded there at his words. "Well, thank you for saying that. And for, uh, listening to my little sob story. And for taking me..."

Now that I'd purged the whole sordid tale from my soul, I became aware of our surroundings for the first time. The crack in the painted cinder block wall continued for a few feet before it ran behind a row of gardening tools on a hanging rack. A mountain bike leaned next to a door. Out of the corner of my eye, I spied some workout equipment on the other side of the garage.

My mouth dropped open. "Dr. Reese. Are we at your *house* right now?" I glanced around the garage again, letting the surprise crowd out the sad cobwebs sticking around my chest cavity.

"Please call me Sam. I can take you home, if you want. This was just close and...private." He cleared his throat. "You seemed like you needed to get away from people for a while. I can take you home," he repeated himself.

A warm rush of an entirely different sort flooded my veins at the thought of being somewhere private with *Sam*. It felt kind of illicit and giddy, nice on the tail end of the grief that was weighing me down. Besides, if I returned to my apartment now, I was afraid the sadness tsunami would crash over me again.

I also remembered the energy—that buzz from his session at the conference—and how much I'd wanted to spend more time with him; not reliving my past trauma.

I rolled my lips between my teeth, studying him and trying to will the last shreds of sad out of my system. If Katie and Nate were moving to Chicago, that was future Lainey's problem. After the gala last night, I had wasted too much time emotionally spiraling about them, and I had no intention of dedicating any more of my time to them today.

"You're just going to dump me at home? In my fragile state? It's not very 'white knight' of you. The least you could do is ask me up, Dr. Reese." His brow furrowed when I used his last name, like it got under his skin. I discovered in that exact moment that I liked getting under his skin.

"White knight?"

"Oh, yeah. Saving me from an awkward conversation with Katie. Listening to my sob story. The ride." I smiled as I ticked all his good deeds of the day off on my fingers, hoping the ring of smudged mascara probably sitting under my eyes didn't ruin my flirty tone. "You've come this far, doc. Take it home."

Those little indentations at the corner of his mouth deepened, and I knew I had him.

"Alright. Let's go."

***

He looked over his shoulder at me, hesitation radiating from every line of his body. It shouldn't have been adorable.

"I'm just now realizing I haven't cleaned up in here recently."

I didn't bother hiding the grin that lit my face. No matter how quiet or contemplative he was, Reese...Sam, was always solid. He had the sort of slow and thoughtful demeanor that made him seem sure of everything, never second-guessing himself. Witnessing this little bout of self-conscious hesitation on my account was a thrill.

"Well, now I have to see." I ducked under his arm before he could stop me. The move brushed me against his side. I made the mistake of looking back at him as I stepped into a dark hallway. Something equally dark and hot flashed across his face.

My lips parted on a gasp when he pulled me suddenly against his chest. His eyes traced my cupid's bow before he blinked, nodding down at my feet. A discarded gym bag and a pair of sneakers lay heaped in a pile inside the door, right where I'd nearly stepped.

"Nice save," I whispered. His hand curved around my hip. We were just inches from each other in the dim doorway. *Private*, he'd said. "Is the rest of your place this dangerous?"

"Hope not." His fingers slid across the fabric of my dress, like they had to be convinced to let go. I caught my breath when he turned to lead me up a few steps into his living room. Despite his concern, it wasn't a disaster. There were a few odds and ends scattered around. A Kindle rested on the table. A t-shirt draped across the back of a chair.

But he didn't have to worry about any of that. The other side of the room beckoned me through an open kitchen with a small breakfast table. And beyond...

"Holy crap." I stumbled towards the sliding glass doors.

"Holy crap? That's practically an F-bomb coming from you."

"It's...you have...Holy crap." He slid the door open so I could step out onto the covered porch. Sam possessed that mythical urban dream: *outdoor space*. Like many houses in Chicago, the back held a private garden area away from the street. But Reese's little garden area was extra special. The porch held a massive picnic table and grill, surrounded by gorgeously blooming flower beds. A little gate opened into a courtyard roughly the size of a tennis court. Sunlight reflected off the bright green grass. For Chicago standards, it was ginormous.

Sam muttered something about drinks and disappeared behind the sliding door. I took the opportunity to gape. Townhomes like Sam's surrounded the courtyard. I counted eight little gardens in all. Eight little porches and gates, all overlooking their own miniature park.

"This is amazing." I felt like Alice falling down the rabbit hole. True, I hadn't exactly noticed any of the houses' exteriors, but I also didn't know anything like this existed within a few minutes' drive from the hospital.

"Mostly my mother's doing."

Sam set a bag of chips and two glasses of water on the table before rummaging in a mini fridge next to the grill.

"Your mother?"

I sank into the chair he pulled away from the table, accepting the beer he offered. I held it steady while he popped the top off. Our fingers overlapped on the bottleneck. Warm.

"She's a gardener. Started with Conner's, moved to mine. Now she knows everyone in the units and does all the beds."

"Conner lives here?" I grasped onto the information like a lifeline. Anything to keep pulling my attention away from the fact that Nate and Katie had just dropped an A-bomb on my life and I wasn't sure what to do about it except cry. *Future Lainey problem*, I reminded myself.

Sam tipped his bottle to a unit across the yard. I spotted a child's soccer goal resting against their gate. "I didn't know Conner had a kid!" I called after him as he disappeared into his kitchen again.

"One and a half. His wife is due in a few weeks." A container of guacamole and a bowl of mixed nuts joined the chips on the table. He was taking the white knight thing pretty seriously.

"I guess I don't know much about them. Your brothers, I mean. Or, your family." *You*, I thought. "It feels unfair. You know about my parents. And now about my tragic backstory."

"What do you want to know?" The glass bottle made a satisfying *thud* as it landed on the teak table. I tented my fingers in front of my face. This was the distraction I needed. "Everything."

Chapter 12

Lainey

It turns out his brothers had always been the sort of lovable goof-balls they were now. Sam wasn't shy about rolling out some of their more embarrassing stories, like the time a snake bit Will on the butt cheek during a camping trip. Or how Conner had drunk-enly proposed to his now-wife, blacked out, and then forgotten about it until he saw the ring on her finger the next morning.

He looked kind of indulgent whenever he talked about his mom, which made me melt a bit. Over the course of our conver-sation, he thumbed open the top two buttons of his shirt, and I had to roll the beer between my palms to keep cool.

"I can't imagine it. Three kids on a landscaper's salary. And living in the city, too."

Sam smiled softly. "She's amazing. She had to travel to the suburbs a lot. When we got a little older, I took care of Will and Connor. She made it work. None of us are in jail, at least."

"You're all incredible."

The sides of his mouth perked up as he surveyed the courtyard. "You think?"

"Absolutely! You're a heart surgeon, for God's sake. Look where you live. And Will and Connor own the gym and the physical therapy business. She won the jackpot with you guys. Three for three."

His attention shifted from the yard. Every time I thought I was getting used to that heavy, focused consideration, I realized how wrong I was. I could practically hear it between us, the question on his face. Did I think they were all *equally* incredible? Did one brother stick out a little more than the others? The lift of his lips told me he'd already guessed the answer. I gripped the bottle tighter.

"Tammy!!!" A child's scream cut through the moment. I turned to see a toddler running full-tilt through the grass. He fell twice, a floppy pile of flailing limbs, before picking himself back up and resuming his sprint to Sam's garden gate. Sam was already there, opening it to scoop the boy into his arms.

"Hey, bugle-boy." He gave the curly-haired boy a big, smacking kiss on his cheek. Something in my heart wobbled, which could not have been correct, or medically accurate.

"Eli! I told you to wait!" A woman trudged across the grass, chest heaving. She cupped an arm around her belly.

Pregnant.

I sipped my beer.

"I've got him, Jas," Sam assured. She huffed, hands planted on her hips.

"Doesn't matter. I told him to *wait*." She shook her head at her son, braids swinging together. He grinned and clung to Sam's neck.

"You should sit," Sam muttered as she followed her son inside the gate.

"YOU should sit. I've been sitting all day and I can't sit at home because it's a wreck in there and we're out of the lime seltz—Oh. Hi."

Up close and personal, this woman was absolutely knock-out gorgeous. Even swollen and waddling up the porch stairs (where she'd frozen as soon as she saw me), she was a snack.

I wiggled my fingers at her, pretending I hadn't just surreptitiously swiped under my eyes just in case there was any leftover mascara streakage. "Hi."

"Eli, we gotta leave Tam—Uncle Sammy alone. He has a friend over." The boy shrieked when she reached to pull him away. Sam's face twisted. His big hand dwarfed the toddler's back where he patted it.

"No, stay." Maybe my ovaries weren't ready to relinquish the image of Sam cradling a small child in his tree trunk arms. Or maybe I was greedy to collect new pieces of him, even if that meant squeezing them out of his family members.

"No, I really, *really* don't want to intrude. Come on, E, we can do bubbles at our house."

"I'd actually appreciate it. Sam's given me tons of stories about his brothers. Haven't heard one about him, yet."

She paused, cocking her head at Sam before trudging up the final two stairs.

"You've been holding out on her, Tammy. I'm Jasmine, Conner's wife." She offered her hand before collapsing into one of the patio chairs.

"I figured. I'm Lainey."

"I figured."

Sam murmured something as he set a green can of seltzer in front of her. It sounded like a warning, which she promptly ignored. She popped the top. "Let's start with the college years."

***

Eli loved bubbles. Sam set up a machine that kept a constant stream of them blowing, and if the solution ran out before we could refill it, Eli's screams became so loud they could quake the bricks of Sam's house and his neighbors'. Even with six gallons of the stuff in the weatherproof cabinet on Sam's deck, I worried we'd run out.

We kept a close eye on the bubble levels as we chatted. Sam mostly played with Eli, or sat quietly and listened to Jasmine's increasingly outrageous stories of the three brothers. She'd been with Connor since high school, so she had more than enough material to satisfy my curiosity and fill in some blanks about my attending. Sam provided a spattering of commentary.

The time Will crashed his car and Sam helped him get it fixed before their mother came home ("He crashed it again three weeks later, idiot."). When Connor had gotten pre-wedding jitters and

Sam had attended six weeks of ballroom dance classes with him in secret ("He wouldn't let me lead.").

When they'd all chipped in to pay off the mortgage on their mother's home. He hadn't added much to that one.

Jasmine herself was delightful. A financial analyst at a major firm in town, she had her sights on a big promotion after the baby was born. Another boy, she lamented a few times, smiling. Yoga and Pilates interested her more than her husband's circuit gym. She expressed her thoughts openly and showered her son with love without letting him run around completely unchecked. I loved her.

At some point in the evening, she whipped out her phone, claiming the guacamole was making her crave Mexican food. Conner magically appeared twenty minutes later with three massive takeout bags full of tacos.

Sam's fingers on my forearm stopped me when I got up to leave them to it. The four of them—Eli included—convinced me to stay for dinner. I shivered at the feeling of those fingertips dragging across my shoulder, Sam's eyes asking wordlessly if I wanted another beer.

Crowded around the table, tubs of queso and taco wrappers strewn around, I felt more and more like I really had fallen into Wonderland. Underneath the smell of grease and jalapenos, the scent of gardenias wafted from where they grew against Sam's fence. The breeze cooled as the sun sank. Porch lights flickered on around us. We talked about the gym, how insane it was to be a heart surgeon, that new Netflix show that was getting good reviews, and Will's ridiculous dating escapades.

Jasmine and I shook our heads and rolled our eyes at each other when Sam and Connor argued over who would take the bags of trash out to the curb. Sam won when he pointed out that someone had to carry Eli home, since he was nodding off in Jasmine's arms.

"Please come back. I like you so much." Jas surprised me into a hug before they departed across the yard.

I laughed, tucking a strand of hair behind my ear. "You don't like the other girls Sam brings home?"

"Lainey." Jas slid her hands to my shoulders. Jiggled. "There are no other girls, girl. You get what I'm saying?"

I did. I flicked through my phone apps, calling a rideshare while she waddled across the lawn, catcalling Conner. That done, I gathered the few remaining bottles and empty water glasses from the table.

"I can take care of those." Sam plucked them out of my hands before I could insist.

"You're very polite," I accused, watching him set the glasses in the sink and toss the bottles in a recycling bin. He recycled. I wasn't sure why that was hot, but it was.

"My mother's doing."

"I had fun tonight. I like your brothers. And Jasmine."

"She's great."

"Hmm." At some point, he'd folded the sleeves of his button down to his elbows. Watching him load the dishwasher was tendon porn. I had to rip my eyes away when I felt his gaze on me, lest he catch me mentally undressing him.

"What."

"What, what?"

He crossed his arms, settling against the sink. "You're being quiet. Is it about earlier with...?"

"No." The truth was, I'd hardly thought of Katie at all once Jasmine and Eli had shown up. His family *had* been fun. Their closeness was intriguing, even if I didn't really understand it. In addition to the industrial-sized bubble solution on his deck, Sam kept a folding booster chair in his hallway closet. Maybe it was normal to make space like that for the members of your family, and I was just out of practice. I didn't have a room in my mother's apartment in New York, let alone any designated closet space.

Something to think about another time. For now, Jasmine's words stirred in my brain. I felt like I was circling around something, hesitant to fully grasp it. *"You should have asked,"* he'd told me earlier. I bit my lip, wondering if I could take his advice to heart.

He waited for me to decide. Patient. The way he looked at me made me think he was willing to stand here like this, with me, for days, simply because he was interested in what I had to say. That, more than the bubble machine or the forearms or the recycling, loosened my tongue.

"Jasmine says you're not seeing anyone. At least, not right now. Or maybe not for a while."

"Hmm." His eyes flicked out the window to his brother's house. I wondered if Jas was going to get an earful later, or as much of an earful as Sam could deliver. Maybe a full sentence or two.

"Is that..." I flushed, feeling like an egomaniac. But I had to know. I knew he liked me, just not to what extent, and it was becoming increasingly critical that I know how deep his attraction went. "Is that because of me? You said you'd been attracted to me for a while. I mean...do you like me? Or do you, like, *like* like me?"

I took a page out of Sam's book and shut my mouth after that masterpiece of grammatical tomfoolery. It didn't get any easier to stand there feeling like an idiot when it took Sam an extra-long time to answer, even by his standards. Once, he opened his mouth, sucked in a breath, then closed it. He stared at the ceiling, measuring every word in his head.

"I've dated women since I've known you." He paused. "I like you more than I liked them. Not that they weren't lovely." Another pause. While I waited, I tried to reconcile the sharp prickling in my brain at the thought of him with other "lovely" women.

"I have found it hard recently to..." Pause. He rubbed at his forehead. "To have feelings for you and pursue other relationships."

"Feelings for me." That didn't sound like just attraction.

"Hmm."

"Took a long time for you to come up with an answer that didn't really answer my question."

The kitchen was dark, only the oven light and the twinkle lights on the porch illuminating us. His smile flashed in the gloom. "Probably best if I filter a little bit."

"What if you took the filter out?"

"You'd run for the hills."

No, he hadn't directly answered my question, but that didn't matter anymore, because for the last two weeks, I'd been grasping at straws with him, trying to uncover every piece that I could. And he'd been hiding some of it. Or, as he put it, *filtering*. Eff that.

All my noticing and watching and thinking about him crystalized into an overwhelming need to know exactly what the man in front of me was like, unfiltered. I wanted to meet the real Sam. Listen to his slow words. Peel him apart until he was completely exposed to me.

I stepped closer. It wasn't smart, I reminded myself, to poke this particular bear. Not with The McDaniels hanging over my head. Not since hospital policy said we couldn't date, anyway. Not when the thought of tangling every area of my life again with one person made me want to pass out.

I'd already learned my lesson there. Once one thing went south, it all did. It was in my best interest to keep those aspects of my life separate. Except...Except I wanted to poke the freakin' bear! Even as it felt reckless and crazy, his quiet, measured patience with me felt safe. Sturdy.

"What would you do, Sam?" It drove him just as batty when I used his real name as when I called him Doctor. A real win-win for me. "What would you say if you didn't have to hold anything back?"

Something feral slashed across my mild-mannered attending's face. Just as fast, it was gone.

"Whoa." My breath sucked in.

He muttered a curse, rubbing his hands down his face, erasing any trace of the unfiltered hunger that had blazed there just a few seconds ago. "We shouldn't do this." His eyes weren't piercing. No, the blue of his eyes was softer. More tempered. Like him.

"I know. Hospital policy."

"Yes. And Lainey policy," he reminded me. It didn't stop me from taking another step closer.

"Right. That, too. It's a good policy." Except was it? Was it really? He was close enough for me to feel the heat of his body. It charged the air between us. It made me want to press up against him because I knew he'd wrap his arms around me tight. *I freaking knew.*

"I will not push that boundary with you." He sounded like he was trying to convince the both of us, which I appreciated. I told him so.

"But..." My eyes snagged on those top two buttons he'd undone earlier. I was close enough to see the threads running through the holes. "But what if I took that boundary out of the way? Would you still be...interested?"

His laugh barked. "Uh, yeah. But you have reasons for that line, Lainey. I understand it today better than ever. You have to be sure, if that's what you want."

Oh, I was sure. I was practically salivating, I was so sure. Still, a little voice in the back of my head piped up, reminding me that Katie and Nate were potentially about to become permanent fixtures in my life, so now maybe wasn't the best time to go throwing my long-held rules out the window.

But, geez, he smelled good. And he'd gotten a bunch of cardiac residents all fired up this afternoon. And this white knight stuff suited him. I remembered the gentle press of his fingertips to my ribs and I wanted more. All of it.

Stupid personal rules. Even if I made an exception (which that little voice was sternly warning me against), the stupid hospital rules would get in the way. What kind of organization had policies against two people dating, anyway? How would they even know in the first place?

I stilled, staring at the buttonholes and the dip of skin at the bottom of his throat. *How would they know?*

"What if..." The idea formed all at once in my head. The little voice started yelling, threatening. I talked over it. "What if we didn't date?"

"I...of course. That's your call. We can be friends." He shuffled backwards, as much as the counter would allow. I didn't remember him moving toward me while we talked. I lunged to bring him back.

"No! You don't understand." My fingers twisted in his shirt, pinky ending up between the buttons. His skin practically burned. "What if we just prepared to date? Like a trial period? But not the real thing."

When I said it out loud, it sounded crazy, but it didn't *feel* crazy. Not to me. Not right now when his skin was so close and I was getting high off his scent of laundry detergent and coffee.

"A trial?"

"Like Netflix!" I blurted the first subscription service that came to mind. "You know, you get thirty days free, no strings or whatever, to try it out." My eyes bored holes into his, clutching his shirt and willing him to come even closer, to huff whatever fumes I was on. "I'm only a few weeks away from finishing my fellowship. Whether or not I get the job at Cedar, we'll still be in the clear from a hospital standpoint."

"Lainey, you'll get the job."

"And in the meantime, it'll give me some time to adjust, too. We can ease into it, right? Just try it out. No strings. We can see how that feels. All the boundaries and policies will remain intact."

His hands clenched and unclenched at his sides. I got the impression that he wanted to put them on me, somewhere (Yes, God, please anywhere!), but wasn't sure he should. "So, we try a relationship before we commit to…a relationship."

"Yes." He was getting it. "Exactly!"

"Hmm." He scratched at his beard. The sound made me wonder what the hairs would feel like under my hands, too. "What does that look like? I mean, would we go on dates?"

"Yes."

"Mmm." He liked that answer. His hand ghosted along the side of my body, resting on my hip. "And kissing. Do people who are only trial-dating kiss?"

"Oh, well, of course. I think they'd have to, don't you?" My throat was dry or clogged or something, and my heart had migrated to the base of my larynx. I felt all fluttery, and it was challenging to breathe correctly.

"Absolutely. To ensure they're physically compatible." He put zero emphasis on the last two words, but my brain emphasized them anyway, leaping straight to the conclusion I hoped he was aiming for. Yes! Compatibility! Take your clothes off, Sam. We can get compatible right here on the counter.

I swallowed, attempting to move my heart down to its normal position in my chest. "That seems wise."

"It kind of feels like we get all the perks of dating without actually dating." He slid a hand down my back, making me shiver.

"Genius."

"Truly," he murmured, pulling me in closer. "You're sure? You want this?" He growled my name when I nodded. He felt hot; palms searing through the thin fabric of my dress. I felt that heat spread right between my legs. By the time his lips brushed against mine, I was a goner.

Some awful, pained whimper fluttered out of my throat, but I didn't care because it matched what I was thinking. *Not enough.* I pulled him closer at the same moment he rocked me forward, plastering our bodies together. When I gasped, his tongue darted in, teasing. His beard whispered across my skin, rough where his lips were so smooth and warm.

He groaned my name again, backing me against the counter, hands threading through my hair to tip my head exactly how he wanted me. I moaned when he kissed me deeper, invading now, taking everything he wanted.

Zzzz. Zzzz. Zzzz.

We froze, gasping the same air. My phone vibrated on the counter. I took a breath, blinking down at it. It was hard to concentrate with his lips still a whisper away from mine, blowing warm, panting breaths across my skin.

Another look and my brain reengaged. "It's my Uber."

I reached up, feeling his beard again and lifting my head for another kiss. Two. Three.

"I could have taken you home."

"I didn't want to impose," I whispered, closing my eyes when his thumbs brushed slow circles across my belly.

"It would be a bad idea for me to ask you to stay, right?" His mouth skimmed against my jaw. One of his hands crept slowly around to my back, heading towards my ass.

"I, um. Yes."

Sam froze, pulling away just a few inches. "Yes? Bad idea?"

"Yes. Yeah," I repeated, shuffling further away. The modicum of space between us opened the floodgates to the irate, protective voice in my head that had been muffled by his lips. It was reiterating—rightly so—that I'd had a major shock seeing Katie today and I'd only just agreed to not-date this man and even if I'd known him for years, it was entirely too soon to get compatible with him on his kitchen floor, no matter how tempting that sounded.

He followed me to the front. We stared at each other in the doorway as a black sedan idled on the curb. "Thank you, Sam, for today. For everything today. The tacos and the rescue and...all of it." Now that I was breathing in the fresh night air, thanking him for kissing the crap out of me seemed a little too desperate.

"You're welcome. For all of it." The car beeped from the curb. He stopped me when I turned to go. "Wait. One more, please."

I grinned so wide our teeth clashed together, but something about even that was still sexy. My driver honked louder this time, and I broke away, panting. "Not dating."

"Not even a little."

He watched me check the plates of the car before I hopped in. He was still watching as I rolled away.

Chapter 13

Lainey

Did the trial start yesterday? Today?

I'd call yesterday a pre-trial trial.

You're angling for an extra day.

Yes.

Feels like a wasted trial day if I don't get to see you. Where even are you right now?

10th floor. Leadership meetings. Resident reviews.

Gross.

Samuel Reese

They can't all be OR days.

Lainey Carmichael

Sad but true.

Since you're doing reviews, someone mentioned to me that Carmichael lady is sharp as a tack.

You know…In case you'd like to enter that officially into the record somewhere.

Samuel Reese

I would, but your attending colleagues have been much more colorful with their praise.

Lainey Carmichael

Praise, you say? Care to share… :)

Samuel Reese

This would probably be where that HR policy comes into play.

Lainey Carmichael

Right, right. Can't play favorites or what-ever.

But I am your favorite, right?

Right?

Samuel Reese

Maybe I'll tell you next Saturday.

Lainey Carmichael

I'm not working on Saturday.

Samuel Reese

Correct.

Lainey Carmichael

Are you working Saturday?

Samuel Reese

No.

Lainey Carmichael

Did you just ask me out and I missed it?

Samuel Reese

Sharp as a tack, huh?

Lainey Carmichael

Crap.

Samuel Reese

I'll have to be more direct next time.

I'll pick you up a little before 6.

Lainey Carmichael

PM?

Samuel Reese

We both have the whole day free. You think I'm waiting around until dinner?

Lainey Carmichael

No, sir.

Samuel Reese

Get ready to sweat.

Lainey Carmichael

Yes, Doctor.

For a non-date, it was really pathetic how much I thought about it for the rest of the week. Somehow, our schedules never seemed to align, which meant unless we were grabbing a quick bite in the lounge or chatting between surgeries, we were stuck texting if we wanted to have any sort of substantive communication.

At least, I was. Sam wasn't super talkative to begin with. I was hoping he'd be easier to engage over text. I discovered that while he was down to flirt and happy to banter, he waited for me to initiate our conversations.

And thank God I did. Otherwise, I wouldn't have known what to wear (gym clothes, then stuff for walking around) or what to expect (hit the gym, then walk around).

Bright and early Saturday morning, I met him in front of my building wearing a matching workout set that I'd spent too much time deciding on. I'd stuffed my duffel with a cute little romper and my makeup bag, which had never even seen the inside of a gym before.

He put his emergency lights on when he hopped out to open the door for me, despite there being only a few cars on the road. The butterflies in my stomach rioted, which was ridiculous. I'd known this man for years. Walked shoulder to shoulder with him down the hospital halls countless times. But the simple brush of his hand against my shoulder made me want to wiggle.

The shimmer in my stomach didn't go away, especially after he handed me an insulated mug of iced peppermint tea after sliding back behind the wheel. He looked good in his athletic shirt that stretched across his chest perfectly and dark gray workout shorts that hugged his thighs. It wasn't anything special, but dang was it attractive.

After a few pleasantries, we lapsed into silence. The quiet drive felt cozy and charged. I could feel the potential energy building up between us.

"I guess I thought you'd be chattier on a non-date."

Sam's eyes flickered over to me. "You look incredible today."

"In my workout clothes?" I laughed. Maybe I had spent a little extra time putting some bounce in my ponytail and swiping on a layer of mascara (both ridiculous because they'd fall the second I started to sweat), but I wasn't sure I looked any better today than I usually did.

"Yes." Sam's response was quick and emphatic. "The leggings."

"The leggings. Booty guy, are you?"

"With you, everything guy."

I nearly inhaled my tea. "I'm flattered."

"Well, you know—hmm." He pulled his car into a spot by the gym, eying the lime green Jeep next to us. "I didn't know she'd be here."

"She?"

"My mother."

"Seems a little early in our non-relationship to meet the parents," I commented after he popped my door open.

He frowned, kicking at one of the back tires on the Jeep. "I was talking to yours just last week."

"Ah, well, nevermind."

"Ma," Sam chided, holding the gym door open for me. The woman behind the desk looked up. His mother had a shock of hair dyed a bright, boxed-copper shade. Freckles and wrinkles lined her tan skin.

"The fucking screen is frozen on the inventory page again. And we don't even sell any fucking inventory here, so why does this fucking screen even exist? Sorry, Dear." She smiled at me as Sam began clicking around on the computer. "Just one moment and I can sign you in. Technology and I don't mix."

"Try that." Sam swiped the barcode on his keychain and tapped a few buttons. "There you go."

"Well, thank fuck. I thought I was going to get fired on my first day." She winked at me. "Alright, Sugar, you give it a try."

Sam's mother pumped her arms when I swiped without incident. "Hell yes! Oh, and look at that. Your name's Elaina? I have a dear, dear friend named Elaine. Moved down to Florida a few years ago. Couldn't take the cold, you know." She leaned in closer. "Started dating some younger man. Not even in his fifties."

"Get it, Elaine." I grinned. Sam gave me a look, warning me not to encourage her.

"Oh, Sugar, that's what I said! Anyway, I'll let you two get to your workout. I'm June, by the way, Honey. I'm helping Will out a bit. Let me know if you need anything while you're here!"

"Nice to meet you, June."

"You, too!" She waved as Sam led me further into the gym.

"Your mother curses like a sailor."

"I really didn't know she'd be here today." Sam glared as Will strolled up. "A little warning would have been nice." Will shrugged.

"We needed the help. I've been going crazy."

"Yeah, about that," I scowled. "I tried to register for a class on Tuesday and the system said it was full. I thought I was your favorite regular?"

"You are, obviously. Text me next time and I can just write you in. Always a spot for you." Will winked.

"Stop flirting." Something about Sam's growly voice really worked for me.

"She started it!"

"She's allowed."

Will's jaw dropped. "Bullshit. She gets preferential treatment over your own brother?" He scowled when Sam didn't answer. "Right. Okay, you're going to pay for that. You'll all pay for it!" He clapped his hands before ordering us into a brutal set of sprints.

I took a quick shower after the workout. When I stepped out of the locker room, Sam waited for me across the gym, showered and dressed in a cotton t-shirt and khaki shorts. He was in deep conversation with Will and Connor, but his attention snapped to me as soon as I stepped into the gym. My skin tingled where his eyes scanned me from head to toe.

"You ready?"

"Wait, we haven't worked this out. I've got clients all day. I don't have time to take it down to the shop." Conner nodded a greeting at me as I sidled up to them.

"It's a slow leak. It needs a patch, not a trip to the mechanic," Will scoffed.

Sam clapped his brothers on the back. "I'm out. If our mother gets a flat later, it's on you." He stepped away. From the groans and choruses of denial from his brothers, you'd have thought he had told them to cheer for the White Sox. He grunted in annoyance.

"Everything alright?" I asked, waving to June as he led me back outside.

"Mom's tire pressure is low again. They're whining about who's going to fix it."

"Let me guess, that's usually more your thing." He squinted as I ducked into the passenger seat, holding the door open with one hand, the other braced on the hood of his car. I'd caught him off guard.

"Maybe." He looked at me for another moment. "You like croissants?"

I reared back as if slapped. "What kind of question even is that? Obviously, I do."

Sam smiled that quiet smile of his. "Good."

***

He claimed we could find the best croissants in the city on the fourteenth floor of an office building on the Loop. He was not wrong. As I marveled at the selection, trying to decide which I wanted, Sam was already ordering. Fruit-filled, chocolate-filled, brownie filled—he ordered six of them. I almost protested because surely between the two of us, we couldn't put away six pastries, but I remembered our breakfast at Molido, and how quickly we'd taken care of a full plate, so I remained silent. A wise choice, since they were all delicious.

This early, Chicago was still waking up. We had our pick of tables on the outdoor patio overlooking the river. Chicago's mercurial spring had turned chilly overnight and fog covered the city.

Before we'd parked, Sam had pulled on a thin quarter-zip and offered me his Cedar Patagonia. I had the same one at home, just about four or five sizes smaller. His swamped me and ruined the effect of my breezy, backless romper, but I was warm while I ate. It smelled good, too—like, superb—and I snuck sniffs while he wasn't looking.

We eased into our conversation, talking about the weather and how the Bears were looking this year. By unspoken agreement, we stayed away from work-related topics. I liked the idea of keeping my attending, Dr. Reese, separate from the guy I was kind of, not really, dating, Sam.

The more I got to know him, the more I understood he was top-tier boyfriend material: generous, smart, funny (when he wanted to speak). Even before our dating trial agreement, I'dbeen increasingly interested in him. It was becoming a problem.

"So, what's your deal?" I looked him up and down. He'd run his fingers through his hair a few times and it was sticking up on one side. Very cute.

"My deal?"

"Yeah. You know my deal. Tragic betrayal, absentee parents, perfectionist coping mechanisms, blah, blah, blah. I know why I'm still single. What's your excuse?"

"Being cheated on isn't an excuse, Lainey. That's trauma. You're allowed to process that."

"Yeah, well, I'm starting to think my processing phase has actually turned out to be more of an avoidance phase."

He nodded, looking me over. "I'd avoid people, too, if that guy and his stupid face had done that to me."

I laughed, surprised to find that talking about my ex didn't make me want to curl up in bed and wallow. "He does have a stupid face."

"I know." Sam shrugged.

"Katie said you were kind of mean to him at the reception. Cold, or something."

"I could tell you didn't like him. I knew there had to be a reason."

He was so, so cute...and big, barely squeezing into the bistro chair across from me. He split the croissants neatly down the middle so we each had an equal serving, but if one half ended up bigger than the other, he slipped the larger piece onto my side of the plate. To top it all off, when he'd met my stupid ex and seen how uncomfortable the guy made me, he'd immediately sided with me. No questions asked.

"How are you single? Seriously?"

"Dating usually requires conversation. Not my strong suit, if you haven't noticed. Plus, not many women outside the medical field understand how challenging it is to get through med school and residency."

"Not a ton of time for extracurriculars."

"Exactly. It's hard to have a life outside of work until you're an attending, and at that point, all a woman sees is a guy in his mid-thirties who doesn't talk and has never really had a serious relationship. It gives serial killer vibes."

I nearly spat out my tea, giggling. "You do not give serial killer vibes."

"You say that because you know me. Everyone else assumes there's something wrong with me."

"Is there?" I sat back in my chair. A breeze fluttered past, lacking the chill I'd felt when we'd sat down. Sam paused to think. Again, I was struck by how much I liked his quiet consideration. Most people on a first non-date would have brushed off the question or made a joke out of it.

"Probably. Everyone has something." He looked out over the city where the fog was beginning to burn off. "Hard to be the oldest kid in a single-parent home. My mom did her best, but I was responsible for Will and Con a lot. I resented it, sometimes."

"Hard to be a kid when you can't just be a kid," I commiserated. He nodded, glancing down at his coffee. "Do you resent it now? How much you help your family?"

His attention fixed on me, pensive. "I wouldn't say I help them more than the usual amount." My mind readily supplied multiple examples just from the last week that told a different story. Sam leading our workout at the gym when it was crowded, handing Jas her favorite drink and telling her to sit. That kick he'd aimed at his mother's back tire.

"I guess, since I grew up taking care of everyone, it's become a habit. I'm not good at putting myself first. That can be a problem. You are good at advocating for yourself with patients or other doctors. Will's that way, too. I wish I were better about asking for what I want."

I shrugged off the compliment. "Product of being an only child with busy parents. Kinda selfish, kinda bossy. I'm not sure what Will's excuse is. Sometimes I wish I were more introspective, though, or more considerate, like you."

"Considerate. Doormat. Same concept."

"That's not true. You got that one nurse fired."

"Well, he was lying about dosages."

"And you're a total ball-buster with the Fellows."

He shook his head. "You walk all over me."

"Oh, I'm sorry, mister 'OR request denied. Jones can take you down a few pegs till you remember patients are people, too.'"

Sam grimaced, gazing at the skyline again. "That's not how I meant that."

"That's exactly what you meant!" I laughed. Now that I had some distance from the moment, Sam's approach made sense to me. I'd lost sight of the patient. I was a surgeon, but I wasn't so egotistical that I couldn't see my own mistakes. "And it's fine, because you handled it like a total badass. You know how to get people's best out of them. You should be proud of that."

"A badass," he repeated, the sides of his mouth tilting up. The concept seemed novel to him, like he'd never considered himself that way before. "The resident stuff is fun. Teaching. And if it makes you feel better, I spent nearly half of my next meeting with Caplan talking about how amazing you are."

"Oh? Tell me more." I batted my eyes and swirled the ice in my cup.

"That surgery with Cooper last month? Incredible. All the nurses love you. *All* of them. Even the cranky ones." Sam mirrored me, sitting back with his mug. "Your sutures make me want to weep."

I clutched my chest, acting like the compliment had taken my breath away. It had. "No one's ever complimented my sutures on a date before."

"So clean. Minimal scarring. Perfect consistency." Sam's voice raked, raising goosebumps across my arms that had nothing to do with the chill still hanging in the air. I'd never considered discussing stitches to be a form of foreplay.

More. More of him. More of this.

"I hope you know I'll be thinking of this conversation the next time I have to stitch someone up."

Sam's grin chased away the last of the fog.

Chapter 14

Lainey

A few streets from the cafe, a park had opened up a seasonal market. Sam led me through the stalls, only dropping my hand when he sallied up to a local farm stand. Turns out Sam had a thing for organic produce.

It should have been boring to spend the better part of an hour discussing tomatoes, but this man continued to amaze. Getting him riled up about vegetables was the highlight of my week, and he humored me by creating an in-depth pro/con list for pesticides. (Virtually all cons, he informed me with a disappointed shake of his head, "Lainey, the *bees*.").

He waited patiently while I chatted with a woman selling hand-painted glassware after I noticed her sign said she was based out of Houston.

As we walked and the sun rose, he stowed our jackets in his backpack. It meant that when he brushed his fingers across my bare back to point at a painting, I felt it in every nerve in my body. When he gestured to the canvas, the backs of his fingers stroked up and down. I mumbled some sort of response. His hand dipped an inch or two lower when he directed me to the pop-up booth with the Molido logo splashed across it. Jordan pushed two mango lemonades and a box of cookies our way before shooing us off without taking Sam's card.

"I'm so jealous of that, you know."

He glanced at me as he took a cookie out of the wax paper. "My pastry supplier? They'd hook you up, too."

"Yes, because of *you*." I frowned down at the box, picking wisely. "You're beloved."

He grunted. "We're a close crew. You're beloved, too. You have more friends in the department than I've had in my life."

"Eh. I have people I'm friendly with. I'm good at my job and people like that." I shrugged. "I don't have anyone who'd notice my tire pressure is low, you know? Mmph thith ith amathing." I held up my half-eaten cookie for him to see. I washed it with some lemonade while he looked at me curiously. His cookie remained uneaten. "What?"

"That seems hard. Not having close people around."

I took another bite, squirming under the gaze that was suddenly too perceptive for comfort. "You're used to having the crew. I'm not, I guess."

He didn't let me squirm for much longer, cupping my wrist to get my attention. "You should have that. People you love, that you're close to."

I understood why he looked so distressed. For someone who'd spent their life building and maintaining healthy, long-term relationships, the way I kept things at surface-level might seem a little bewildering. Seeing as this was only our first non-date, it was challenging to explore this with him. A crippling fear of intimacy wasn't something you could drop casually into conversation.

Even if it was somewhat less terrifying when I was considering it with *him*.

"Close relationships," I hummed instead, squinting. "And I suppose you're going to tell me you're happy to apply for the job?"

He just bit into his cookie.

***

We made a second loop around the market. Then a third. I wasn't sure what the plan was for the rest of the day, but I couldn't bring myself to ask. The intimate little bubble that formed around us was too precious to pop. I was having more fun walking around with Sam than I ever did in the OR.

I paused over some interesting essential oil blends while he'd gotten sucked into a vintage book kiosk that boasted a significant section of wartime biographies. He got more riled up about his books than the produce.

"These people are going through hell. Literally. And they keep going. I might never know what it's like to be so dedicated to a cause." His vehemence made me bite my lip.

He left with three books, but didn't bat an eye when I confessed to being one of those cliché Americans who didn't read and instead filled my time binging Netflix and old reality TV shows.

He'd asked me just as many questions about my shows as I'd asked about his books. Maybe even more.

We were deep in conversation about a Korean drama that had recently consumed my life when my stomach started rumbling, awoken by the homesick smell of roasting meat.

"Mmm. Barbecue. Do you smell that?" Sam gave me a look I couldn't interpret. I tried to remember the details of his taco order from the other night and came up blank. "Oh, Lord, you're not a vegetarian, are you? I mean, it's fine if you are, but I'm going to get some pulled pork. If you have any ethical issues with eating meat, you're going to need to avert your eyes."

"No concerns."

"Where's the—oh." I realized that we were already standing in line for the food truck wafting the incredible smells my way. I was nearly close enough to feel the heat from the smoker. "We're getting barbecue?"

I squinted up at him, once more cursing the fact that I'd accidentally left my sunglasses at home.

"Yeah." He shifted, slipping his bulk in between me and the sun. "You're on a mission."

"I...Yes. I am."

Moving from Texas to Chicago had been a shock to the system in more ways than one. I found myself alone, cut off from my friends and family, and the world I'd always known, and in a new culture that took me a while to understand.

I was a full-fledged convert, and would argue about the best Chicago-style pizzeria with the enthusiasm of a local, but my little southern heart still yearned for good pit barbecue. I'd been on a quest for years to find a brisket that reminded me of home. So far, nothing had measured up.

"These guys are good," Sam assured as we shuffled forward.

"More than just good!" A woman in front of us turned around. "Best in the city. They're only at this market during the summer and they run out fast. I spent all week thinking about this. You're not really a vegetarian, are you?"

"No, ma'am," Sam replied, solemn. She sniffed and turned around. I realized that we'd actually been standing in line for quite some time, and that the queue of people stretching behind us was growing longer by the minute. I'd been too absorbed by him to notice.

When I couldn't decide what I wanted, Sam convinced me to split a sampler with him, complete with several sides and sweet tea that the cashier assured me was authentic. While we waited for our order, I surveyed the market, but my eyes flickered back to Sam again and again.

He didn't speak, as usual. My mind churned for another moment before I blurted, "Did you bring me here just for the barbecue?"

He paused for a split-second. "Yes." He looked down at me and I realized how close we were standing. "I thought you'd like it."

"Workout, breakfast, barbecue..." I frowned at him. "What else do you have planned?"

He shrugged, unconcerned about the lack of space between our bodies. "Walk along the lake. Go back to my place. Make pasta."

"Back to your place."

"Mmhm."

"To make pasta."

"Probably a salad, too. Wine."

If any other man had taken me on a non-date and told me we were going back to his house, I'd have assumed the agenda skewed more towards getting naked, rather than cooking dinner. I might not know Sam as well as he knew me, but I knew I could trust him if he said we were only going back to his place to make pasta. I was equally intrigued and disappointed that sex didn't seem to be on his itinerary today.

"Why? Why the pasta? Why any of this? No filter." I pointed at him, hooking my finger into his shirt to pull him an inch closer. He was happy to shuffle forward, a soft smile deepening the corner of his lips.

"You like to work out. You love barbecue. We spend all day cooped up in a hospital. I thought you might like to see the sun for a bit." He slipped his fingers along the skin of my arm. "You might also just want to sit on my couch with a glass of wine. I'm selfish enough to want you to do all that with me."

I *did* want that. All of it. The sunlight, the pastries, the conversation...to walk along the shore and then sit on the couch with a glass of wine. Even more urgently, I realized I wanted to sit on *his* couch—not just any couch—with a glass of wine. I wanted to recapture that cozy, comfortable feeling I'd gotten the night his family had fed me tacos while the sun went down. It all seemed perfect. With one exception.

"Would you kiss me?" I wasn't sure if it was a demand or a request, but I knew I wouldn't be able to stand this close to him much longer, on a day he'd specifically designed for me, without his lips on mine.

Sam didn't need to be asked twice. He gripped the bow of my romper where it tied between my shoulder blades, pressing me closer. The difference in our heights was laughable, but between his pulling and my tugging, we ended up exactly where we needed to be. He didn't tease as he pressed his lips firmly against mine.

When his other hand settled on my bare waist, I gasped. His tongue swept inside. Heat speared through me at the contact and I opened my mouth wider, silently begging him to do it again. He obliged.

He tasted like coffee and sugar and he kissed me like he'd been doing it for decades. Slow and methodical, in a way I didn't know men were capable of. His hand tightened on the fabric of my romper, twisting. In return, I clawed at his shirt and my fingers cupped his neck, straining to get him closer. His head tilted to take more and the slightest edge of his teeth caught my lower lip.

A low grunt answered my whimper. My hand slipped up his shirt to feel the stacked muscles of his abdomen. He gripped me tighter.

"...Sir?"

It took him a second to pull away. I was halfway up his shirt.

"Thanks." Sam's voice was rough. When he turned back to me, he held a tray of food between us, looking sheepish. My chest heaved while my lips tingled. I could still feel the rasp of his beard against my cheek. For a wild moment, I considered tossing the tray to the ground and jumping on him. He'd catch me.

He gave me a warning look, like my plans were clearly visible on my face. They probably were. I felt like my clothes were going to be singed off my body at any moment. He wielded the tray between us. "Meat."

I laughed and followed him to a picnic table without tackling him. I bit my lip when he sat close enough for our legs to press together. Groaned when the food actually lived up to the hype.

I tried to ignore that voice inside warning that I was treading on dangerous ground, along with the little smile on Sam's face that seemed to say he knew it, too.

Chapter 15

Lainey

Three days later, I was still smiling. This time, like an idiot over a Tupperware container. Not even Jones' waffling attempts at flattery and mansplaining could ruin my post-non-date-buzz.

After strolling around the market for a while longer, Sam had taken me back to his place. We'd made pasta and sat on his deck until long after the sun set. He'd pressed a container of leftovers into my hands before I left.

Something about him packing the dressing separately from the salad had made me want to drop the container and attack his face. Instead, we'd stuck to light, teasing touches while we made dinner, and a few chaste kisses that stopped well-short of qualifying as making out. Unfortunately.

I grinned like a fool down at my salad, remembering how the restraint had snapped when he dropped me at my apartment.

"Lainey. One more."

That *had* qualified as a make-out session, one that only stopped because the doorman knocked on the window of Sam's car to tell us we were blocking the flow of traffic in front of my building.

"What are you smiling about?" Rija set her plate down across from me. Jones, thankfully, beat a hasty retreat.

The lounge was relatively quiet, only a few of us scarfing down food between appointments. Despite our hectic schedules, I'd gotten used to sneaking coffee breaks or finding excuses to talk with Sam around the floor. I was quickly starting to miss him on days like today, when he was stuck in meetings, so I was glad to have Rija's company. She was a vast improvement over my smarmy fellow.

"Good mood, I guess." I shrugged. "How's your day going?"

"Lost a patient this morning."

"Crap. I'm sorry." I hesitated for a millisecond before I reached out to touch her arm. "You okay?"

It was a horrible, horrible truth: losing patients never got better. Ever. Some people learned how to shrug it off faster than others, or build up a thick skin, but it was all just coping mechanisms. When you lose someone under your care—which inevitably happens—the grief and the guilt stick with you, whether you pay attention to it or not.

A flicker of surprise crossed her face at my hand on her arm. "I'm better now...Thank you." Unease weighed on me at her reaction. I liked Rija a lot. She'd gone out of her way to be a friend to me and I had gone out of my way to avoid truly getting to know her.

"Would some tapas and wine make you feel better?" I offered. Sam's face flashed in my mind, along with the easy relationships he had with Santiago and his family.

"Wasn't tapas and wine invented to be an emotional cure-all?" A small smile curved her lips, though her body remained slumped over the table, bent by the weight of the loss.

"I've been wanting to try that place that just opened up a few streets over. Want me to bully a resident into switching on-calls with me tonight?"

Her eyes went round before she schooled her face. The suggestion, at least, had straightened her up in her chair. "Seriously? Are you sure?"

I tsk'd, spearing some more pasta. "Why would I joke about tapas?"

"Because you and Cooper have that surgery tomorrow morning. And you've never once hung out with anyone outside of work before."

It wasn't that I avoided my coworkers, necessarily, but it was just easier to keep things compartmentalized. I had work people and...well, not many other people. It was a depressing thought, especially when compared to Sam. He had good people. Checking tires people. I wanted that, darn it. Maybe it was time to put my big girl panties on and make some new friends, finally. I couldn't live in the shadow of Katie's betrayal forever.

I took my time chewing. Thinking. "It's sometimes hard for me to make friends." Rija's look told me she thought I was full of it. "I mean, close friends. I haven't had the best luck with relationships in the past, so I tend to push people away. But I think I need some people, you know?"

Rija's face softened. Now her hand wrapped around mine. "Aw, hun. I'll be your people. You're good people!"

There was a certain vulnerability in telling someone that you were socially celibate. Heat rose to my cheeks, but her immediate acceptance felt good, bolstering. "You're good people, too. Maybe we could be friends? Outside of work friends?"

"Fuck yeah, we're friends! We'll cement this new stage in our friendship together tonight over spicy octopus."

"Who could turn down an offer like that?"

"No one's ever turned down my spicy 'pus, Lainey. Don't be the first."

"Anyone seen Reese?" A nurse popped her head in the door.

"Dr. Reese has a meeting a few floors up. HR, I think." I pretended it was very chill and casual that I knew exactly where he was, even though today wasn't one of his clinic days. "What's up?"

"He's got some family here to see him, and they can't get a hold of him."

"I might be able to help." I stood, popping the top onto my container. "Is your spicy 'pus free at six?"

"I'm there. Thanks, Lainey, seriously." Rija's grateful smile followed me out the door and down the hall.

I stopped short when the patient check-in desk came into view. "Jasmine?"

"Hi. They said Sam's not here?" She rubbed a hand along her belly. Her eyes darted around the room.

"Yeah, sorry. Hey, what's up?" The closer I got, the more out of sorts she looked, pale and fidgeting. This was not the vibrant woman I'd shared tacos with two weeks ago.

"I...Shit. I was hoping he could come down to the maternal ward with me. My doctor sent me for some tests and Conner's stuck in traffic on the other side of town." Her hand ran across her forehead and she forced a smile. "It's okay. I can go by myself."

"I can page him again." I wasn't a super touchy-feely person, but I rested my hand on her arm. She looked like she could use shoring up. "Some tests, huh?"

"Yeah. My blood pressure is up? I've been having these headaches, and I didn't think anything of it but he said he's worried about preeclampsia which is just terrifying but it's okay. Right? It'll probably be fine." She stroked her stomach again, biting her lip. "Don't page him. I already texted him, and I'm sure it's nothing. Right?"

She repeated, looking around for assurance. Usually, I'd give her a pat on the back and ask Sam about her later. But something made me pause. Maybe it was the lost, scared look on her face—one I had seen on patients many, many times—or maybe I was still riding the high of my recent friendship proposal to Rija. It could also be the little voice in the back of my head whispering, "*Sam would do it in a heartbeat.*"

Whatever the case, I found myself saying, "I'll walk you down there. You want a ride?" I popped open a folded wheelchair by the elevator bay.

"Oh, no, you don't have to. I don't want to interrupt your day." She rubbed at her eyes, side-stepping me to get to the call button.

"I'm only on call. Nothing scheduled for the next few hours."

She took a breath, like she was about to tell me to take a hike, but she was one of Sam's people, even if I didn't know her well. It elevated her status in my head.

"Jasmine. You don't have to do this alone." I wheeled the chair back in her path, reaching out my hand. She studied me, only hesitating for a moment before she let me guide her into the chair. "If anyone asks, I'm down on six." The nurse at the desk nodded and watched as I wheeled Jasmine into the elevator.

"Thank you, Lainey," she muttered, reaching up to touch my hand where it rested on the chair handles.

"No sweat. We got this." I squeezed her hand. We stayed like that the whole ride down.

***

"Three hours?"

The nurse shrugged. "Sorry."

I breathed through my nose, telling myself it wasn't this nurse's fault that the maternal ward was understaffed and apparently busting at the seams with preggos. I made my way back to the waiting room as one waddled by. I'd left Jasmine with a promise that I'd "work some doctor magic" to see if I could get us a room. My magical white coat had failed me.

Her face fell when I shook my head. "They're not working with a full staff right now. I know they've hired some people, but everything's just taking a long time. I got a look at your records, though. This is a very mild concern. There's a reason they're not prioritizing you. That's a good thing."

Jas wilted. "You should go. Who knows how long this is going to take?"

"The nurse said it could be up to three hours before they're able to call you back."

"Three...?" Her eyes filled with tears and her forehead fell to her palm. "Oh, my God. What if something's really wrong and we're just sitting here *waiting* and something bad happens?"

"Hey." I stepped closer, fully about to tell her to frack this place and check into the hospital across the street. Mercy's cardiac ward was in shambles right now, but that didn't mean its OB department was. I could call in the referral myself and check their wait times while I was at it.

"Lainey?"

Blood drained from my face as Katie edged into my line of sight. She glanced between me and Jasmine. "Everything okay?"

I surveyed her coat and scrubs, the iPad she held in her hand. "I didn't realize you'd already started here."

"First week."

Jasmine tried to cover up a sniffle, and my attention whipped back to her. I glanced at Katie again. That little voice from earlier started peeping up. This time, I didn't want to listen. I whined back. *Do I have toooooo?*

Jas sniffed, and I caved. If anyone owed me, it was Katie. At one time in my life, she'd been the one I trusted to move heaven and earth if I needed it. Maybe that version of her was still in there. And if not, I would mercilessly make use of the fact that she'd ruined my life to cash in a favor.

I grabbed Jasmine's hand. "My friend's doctor has some concerns about preeclampsia. But she can't be seen for hours." I locked eyes with my former friend.

"I've got some time." Katie practically jumped at the opening. "Let's get you a room, Ms...?"

"Reese. Jasmine Reese," Jas snuffled. "I don't want any special treatment or anything. I just don't know what to think right now. The waiting is killing me."

Katie's turn to lock eyes with mine. *Reese.* She recognized the name. "Let me see if I can grab your file. Come this way and we'll get you sorted."

We followed Katie to the nurse's station. Jasmine dabbed at her eyes. "You know her?"

"We went to school together." I realized once the words were out of my mouth just how clipped and cold they sounded. Jas looked nervous, so I grudgingly added: "She's a good doctor. You'll like her."

Katie led us to an exam room tucked in the back of the hall. Jas assured us the whole way there that she was happy to wait, but her watery voice said otherwise.

"It's fine. It's my first week and my caseload is light. I've got some free time." Katie gestured inside the room. "We can set up in here. Hospital policy usually only allows family in the exam room..."

"She's family. She's going to be my sister-wife someday." Jas brought our joined hands to her chest. I could read the hesitation on Katie's face, but she smiled for Jas.

"You know, maybe I did see in your file that someone requested a cardiac consult, if anyone asks." She waved us in and gestured for Jas to get comfortable on the exam table. "How do y'all really know each other?"

I was impressed, despite myself. The Katie I knew would never have bent hospital policy, especially in her first week. Then again, the Katie I'd known also wouldn't have sex with my boyfriend for months and lie to me about it. People change and whatnot.

"Lainey works with my brother-in-law in the cardiothoracic department," Jas explained, easing onto the bed.

"Dr. Reese is your brother-in-law? I met him briefly at a cardiology event a couple of weeks ago. He seemed nice."

God, had it only been two weeks since she'd shown up and blasted my carefully manicured peace to smithereens? Despite the new thing I had going with Sam, late at night, it was easy to keep myself awake with increasingly outlandish, invented scenarios that involved running into one or both of the McDaniels in the hospital.

Oddly, now that it had actually happened, it wasn't going as poorly as my two a.m. brain had anticipated, even if she was fishing for information on Sam.

"Dr. Reese's brothers own the gym I go to. I'm friends with...their family." It felt odd saying it out loud, but I supposed that was the best way to describe it. I'd chased bubbles with Eli and I knew Jas liked spicy peppers on her tacos. Will and I harmlessly flirted whenever we saw each other. Was I...*friends* with Sam's family? Between the Reeses and Rija, I was wracking up quite the tally.

"Still doing the kickboxing thing?"

"No."

Her smile faltered, just a millimeter. "Too bad. I was hoping you'd be able to recommend a place."

"Nope. Sorry."

"I'm sure I'll find something. Mrs. Reese, let's get you changed into this gown and then we can see what the baby's up to in there, shall we?"

Katie closed the door on her way out.

"I can give you a minute, too," I offered, already reaching for the handle.

"Uh-uh. You stay right there." I stopped, frozen in place by Jas's Mom Voice. It was effective. "Spill the tea before doctor blonde lady comes back."

Jasmine rustled around with the gown as I kept my back turned. All the better for me to hide my wince. "What tea?"

"Why we hate her, obviously. It took me a second to pick up on it. I was too busy blubbering in the waiting room."

"You're allowed to blubber a little when you're in a hospital waiting room."

"You can turn around now. And tell me fast before she comes back. Why do we hate her?"

We. See, this happened when you started making friends with people and accompanying them into an exam room. Closeness. Camaraderie. *We.*

She was seated on the exam table when I turned, sporting a faded hospital-issue gown. "You do not need to hate her. I meant what I said earlier. She's a good doctor."

Jas pointed at me. "Your face did that thing when you said that before, too, like someone's pinching you. Come on. Let me in on the hot goss. It'll take my mind off...." She looked around the room, then back at me. Her puppy-dog eyes were a little *too* good.

I squinted at her, but she didn't budge.

"Come on. Tell ol' Jasmine why she's a bitch and when she comes back in here, I'll clothesline her with my giant stomach." She wiggled her fingers, drawing me closer to the bed. I studied the ultrasound machine in the corner.

"Fine." She clapped as I sighed. "Katie—Dr. McDaniels—was my best friend in high school. We roomed together in college. Went to med school together. And then"—I swallowed—"it turns out she was banging my boyfriend for several months behind my back just before we graduated med school."

Jasmine sucked in a breath. "What the fuck?!"

"Ha. Yeah. I thought he was going to propose. Nope. Just...in love with my best friend. They're married now."

"Shut up. She's carrying around a cheater baby under those scrubs?"

That surprised a laugh out of me, which gave me enough courage to look at Jas again. I didn't see any pity, just anger on my behalf.

"I don't think it qualifies as a cheater baby if they're married to each other."

"Mmm mmm. That's a cheater baby." Jas shook her head. "Once a cheater, always a cheater. Let's get out of here."

"Whoa! Absolutely not. We're getting you checked out so that you and your healthy baby can go about your day."

"We hate her. I'm out." Jas began inching off the exam table as quickly as her pregnant body would allow.

"You're not waiting for three hours." I pushed at her shoulders until she sat back down. "She owes me, obviously. If I can't shamelessly exploit her for my own uses, what was it all for?"

Reluctantly, Jasmine admitted I had a point and settled back on the table.

"Any progress on that promotion?" I asked. By the time Katie walked back into the room, Jas was laying back and regaling me with tales of her firm's all-white, all-male executive staff. Absolute bull crap.

"Alright. Let's take a look at you." Katie smiled as she approached.

Jasmine hummed, sizing Katie up from her seat on the bed. *Be nice,* my raised eyebrows said. *She's doing you a favor.*

Jas huffed, sitting up as Katie pulled a stethoscope from her neck. "Let's get this over with."

An hour later, Jas was hooked up to several machines, and had been poked and prodded within an inch of her life. But Katie was good at her job (ugh) and Jas continued to relax when all signs pointed to a mild preeclampsia diagnosis.

Katie was indulging Jas, giving her some extra screen time with the baby on the ultrasound monitor. He was awake, making us giggle over his kicks and flips. We were still waiting for a few tests to come back, but with every passing moment, I could feel Jas's tension fading.

A nurse knocked, sticking her head in. "Sorry to interrupt, Dr. McDaniels. Dr. Reese is here to see the patient?"

I grudgingly gave Katie credit when she didn't bat an eye at this news. "I don't mind a crowded exam room if you don't?" She looked to Jas, who nodded. "Let him in, please."

Sam's familiar frame filled the door. "Jasmine, what the hell?" He sighed, shaking his head at his sister-in-law like she'd purposefully ended up in the hospital. She threw up her hands.

"I know, I know. I just love the paper sheets on the beds so much. Listen to the crinkle." She rolled back and forth as Sam crossed the room.

"I'm Kate McDaniels. Nice to see you again, Dr. Reese." Katie stood from her stool and Sam shook her hand. I clenched every muscle in my body to stop myself from lunging across the room and pulling them apart.

Sam let go of her hand with barely an acknowledgment of her greeting, just a polite nod in her direction, before swiping Jas's file from the counter.

"I feel like that's a HIPAA violation," Jasmine grumbled, relaxing back on the table.

"I'm your emergency contact," he countered.

"He doesn't know what he's looking at," I whispered to her. "He's a cardiothoracic surgeon. Anything below the diaphragm is an utter mystery to us."

"I'm just going to step out for a moment to check on those tests." Katie smiled. Sam didn't look up from the file.

Jas sat up as soon as the door shut. "Hey. We hate her," she informed Sam.

"Yes. We do," he muttered, flipping through a few pages. "Her husband has a stupid face." I turned to frown at him.

"Yes!" Jasmine sat back again, satisfied that Sam was firmly on board the hatred train. "Yes, he *does* have a stupid face."

"You've never even seen him before." I scoffed. "Besides, I dated him for nearly four years. You're saying I have bad taste in men?" I glared pointedly at Sam. The look he exchanged with Jas was so quick, I almost missed it.

"Taste changes," she argued, crossing her arms.

"Mmm. It improves with maturity," Sam assured. "Like wine."

"Or like a beard?" I supplied. Nate was clean-shaven. He'd never been able to grow facial hair that wasn't patchy. Sam's grin nearly knocked me off my stool.

"Exactly."

"I should be upset that you're making heart eyes at each other during my very urgent prenatal check-up, but I can't find it in me." Jasmine clasped her hands to her heart. "I knew I was making the right choice in a sister-wife."

"Not the sister-wives thing, Jas. Come on!" Sam scowled at the files in his hands.

"Wait, you *knew* about the sister-wives thing?" I demanded. Sam's ears grew a truly delightful shade of pink just as Conner burst through the door, nearly mowing down the nurse who opened it.

"Jas, baby. What's happening? Have they done the tests?"

She smiled softly, reaching for him. "Come here, love. I think it's okay."

He cradled her, sweeping the hair back from her face. "Sam, what are you seeing?"

I backed out of the room as Sam gave his brother a surprisingly accurate and succinct rundown of Jas's condition and the monitoring we'd done this afternoon. There was something intimate about the three of them together, hunched over Jas's file. Family. Even if I'd started to call them friends, I felt like I was intruding.

In the hall, I took a moment to breathe. Jas and the baby were fine. And, hey, I'd just spent over an hour with freakin' Katie and the world hadn't melted. Was this what being an adult felt like?

I wasn't sure I liked it. Even if I was still standing, being around her and watching her be competent at her job was hard. She'd been the same old Katie, warm and disarming, cracking jokes that almost even made Jasmine forget that "we hated her."

"All good in there?"

I whirled. Speaking of the devil. We stood in the hallway, squared off. Tumbleweeds should have rolled past. I swallowed, thinking once again of how scared Jas had been a little while ago. How happy she was now. Calm.

"Fine. Her husband's here, so I figured I should pop back upstairs and see if the residents have burned it down yet."

"I thought I smelled smoke coming from the elevator..." She smiled at her weak joke. I couldn't find it in me to reciprocate, but I could still be an adult. (Ugh.)

"Thank you. For seeing her so last-minute. It means a lot to her...and me."

"It wasn't any trouble." The rows and rows of pregnant women in the waiting room would say otherwise. She was probably lying, but I didn't push it too hard.

We stood there awkwardly; her clutching her tablet while I tried to think if there was anything else to say here. I opened my mouth to tell her I was heading back when she blurted: "Reese, huh?"

I willed my muscles not to lock up, reminding myself I'd look defensive if I got defensive. And I had nothing to worry about.

"He's a friend."

She nodded, glancing around. "You seem close to his family. I mean, you accompanied his sister-in-law to an emergency medical appointment."

I shrugged. "Sam was in a meeting. I wasn't going to let her come down here by herself."

"Sam..." I realized my mistake when Katie repeated his name back to me. I'd said his name, not Reese. *Crap.* "Just be careful there, Lainey. He's an attending."

"I'm aware of that. We're just friends." Not true. Even if we slapped a "trial period" label on it, I knew what he tasted like, which went well beyond friend territory. "We're not dating." Also arguably not true, but I felt like I had to put it out there.

"I don't want you to get hurt. The hospital has all these crazy workplace relationship policies in place. Nathan and I had to do so much paperwork when he got accepted for an interview—"

"I know about this hospital's policies. I've worked here for almost five years," I snapped. I didn't want to hear anything about what she and *Nathan* had been getting up to. When I'd known them, they'd been Katie and Nate. But they were all grown up now. Kate and Nathan. Gross.

So much for being an adult.

She started to say something else, but halted when the door to Jas's room swung open. Sam and Conner stepped into the hall-way. I staggered when Conner wrapped me up in a hug without warning.

"Thank you," he whispered, tightening his grip around my shoulders. Haltingly, I patted his back. "Thank you for being here with her."

"I just brought her down in a wheelchair."

"You did more than that."

I read somewhere that the cast members at Disney World are trained not to break a hug with a fan until the kid breaks it first.

I gave Conner a few more pats while he cleared his throat. It took him a few more seconds to pull away. His voice was thick. "Next time we get tacos, it's on me."

"Didn't you pay last time?"

"I don't know what you're talking about." He turned to watch as Katie approached. His eyes flicked up and down. Surely the once-over was Jas's doing. Of all the Reeses, I knew Conner the least. But it seemed he, too, was ready and willing to ice out the doctor who was just doing her job, all because she'd wronged me years ago.

Sam's mouth curved into a smirk when he saw it, too. We shared a look before I tore my gaze away. Sharing *looks* with my attending right after Katie's not-so-veiled warnings would only fuel the fire. Once I made Conner promise to have Jas text me when the results were back, I spun on my heel and made my way to the bank of elevators.

It didn't matter that I'd barely seen Sam in days, and all I wanted to do was steal a few minutes of conversation with him on the ride back to our floor. I couldn't give Katie any more ammunition than she already had.

It didn't matter that something in my gut told me I could trust her. That feeling had let me down before, as had Katie. It was a vicious reminder of just why I didn't *do* this anymore. Any of it.

Chapter 16

Sam

"Guess I'm going to tell Carmichael the bad news." Cooper sighed, banging his fist lightly against an OSHA flyer hanging on the wall. They were everywhere on the executive level. He looked like he wanted to rip it down. "You want to come with? You can soften the blow, at least."

"Can't. I have the...thing."

Lainey had been avoiding me. I wasn't sure why, but ever since Jas's scare a few days ago, I'd only seen her once for rounds. That wasn't uncommon, but I missed how she'd recently found random excuses to seek me out. I knew she was busy, and I wouldn't have thought anything of it, except her texts had dried up, too.

Something had spooked her. I figured spending the afternoon with a woman who'd stolen her almost-fiancé was probably enough to do the trick, even if she hadn't seemed too weirded out when I'd made it down there. Whatever it was, I felt like she was running scared. I wasn't sure yet if it would be better to let her work it out on her own or push the issue by cornering her in a broom closet.

Every time I pulled out my phone to start a text, I remembered I was sort of her boss. Then I remembered her "no dating co-workers" policy. The last time she'd been serious with someone, it had crashed and burned so badly she'd self-isolated for years. Inevitably, I re-pocketed my phone.

"God. Good fucking luck. I can't be in that room for one more minute."

I glanced back down the hall at the conference room where a handful of the physician executives were still milling around, waiting for the next meeting. "It's not their fault."

Cooper snorted, jabbing the button for the elevator. "They're just rolling over and taking it. What's the point of a quality board if they're just going to steamroll everyone?"

"Isn't that exactly the point of a board?"

"Not in my OR." Cooper jabbed again. "*Too risky.* That woman will die without that surgery. Mark my fuckin' words."

Mrs. Harkness would likely die from her condition since the board had decided the LVAD was "too risky" for Cooper to undertake, not to mention the procedure was still considered fairly experimental. Implanting a mechanical pump into the patients left ventricle was not an everyday event. The board was only interested in nearly guaranteed successes.

In other words, they'd rather shove Mrs. Harkness out the doors with an apology than have her perish on our watch, even if the LVAD was her only hope.

It was a blow for everyone, including Cooper and Lainey, who'd been preparing for the surgery for weeks, but also for the rest of the department. This wasn't the first time in the last few months the board had voted down a procedure, but they'd never gone against their golden boy Cooper's recommendations. Now? No one was safe.

The elevator doors opened.

"Dr. Cooper. Dr. Reese. Great to see you again." Nathan Mc-Daniels stepped out. I hated him and his stupid face on a good day, but today…? Fuck him.

Still, I had responsibilities to uphold. Promises to keep. I offered my hand. "Dr. McDaniels."

I didn't have it in me to ask about the commute or lie and tell him it was good to see him again. Not after that clusterfuck of a meeting. The only salvageable thing that had come out of it was the green light on my ablation. That, at least, might make up for Lainey losing out on yet another surgery.

"I'm glad to be here. Can't wait to learn more about your organization. My wife raves about it already. She mentioned seeing you down there recently."

I jerked a nod to Cooper, who slumped, brooding in the elevator, and led McDaniels back down the hall to the conference room I'd just vacated.

"Just wrapped up another meeting. Let me see if everyone's ready." I nodded to the meeting room door, waving McDaniels into a plastic chair situated along the hallway wall.

"Oh. I was under the impression the first round interviews were just one-on-one."

"We work by committee." That, at least, the board hadn't been able to dictate. Thank God for the HR department.

"Take your time. I know I'm a little early." He eased into the chair, straightening his tie. I had to fight a sneer. *Stupid face.*

***

"You were supposed to go home hours ago."

"Stop. Touching. Me," Lainey gritted, slapping my hand away from where it hovered an inch from her back. I didn't bother to correct her. My day had started with that meeting from hell, continued with her ex, who insisted on a tour of the floor, and ended with two patients coding. Exhaustion dragged through every cell of my body. I wanted nothing more than to go home and fall asleep in my shower. Lainey had different plans.

I'd found her after I overheard LeeAnn, the nurse in charge of the floor tonight, warning the interns to stay away from Carmichael. "She's on a tear," she'd said.

I hadn't believed it until I'd seen her myself, ripping into a resident for failing to add a patient's new medication in the chart. I'd barely grabbed her before he'd teared up. Now, she was clinging to the doors of the locker room, doing everything she could to stay as far away from me as possible. Something panged in my chest.

If I'd had any doubt about her avoiding me, it was staring me in the face now.

"You can stop looking at me like that." I shuffled to my locker, entering the combination twice before it clicked open.

"What were you doing wandering the halls with Nate this afternoon?" She said it like *I* had been the one to fuck her best friend. The ultimate betrayal. I was so, so tired.

"It's standard procedure to give candidates a tour of the facility." I didn't want to be around the guy any more than she did, but it was part of the job, and I'd sworn that I'd be impartial.

"You knew he was going to be here."

"You knew he was applying for the position, Lainey. Did you want me to share the full interview schedule with you?"

"You should have told me he was coming in today." She jabbed me in the shoulder with a pointed finger. For someone who couldn't get away from me fast enough, she'd sure beat a path over here. That finger should be registered.

"I can't share information about candidates' interviews with other candidates." I scrounged in my bag for a protein bar. Took a bite without bothering to see what flavor it was.

"You didn't think to even give me a little warning?" *Jab.*

My palms dug into my eye sockets, easing some of the dryness. I should probably grab some more water on the way out. But before I went anywhere, I had to stem the flow of Lainey's meltdown. Or at least direct it some place other than me. "I wanted to tell you."

"Wanted?" *Jab.* "You wanted"—*jab*—"to tell"—*jab*—"me!" *Jab.* "I don't believe you." *Jab.*

Alright. Enough of that. I captured her hand. Thankfully, we were the only two people in the room. No one was around to see her outburst or how my fingers slid against her pulse to calm her down.

"Even if I wanted to, how could I? You've been avoiding me since Tuesday." She tried to pull her hand away, but I held tight. "Send a homing pigeon? Maybe that'd be able to track you down."

She pulled again, and I let her slide out of my grasp. We studied each other for a moment while I chomped another bite of my protein bar. I wanted to kiss away the angry wrinkle of her nose.

"I haven't been avoiding you."

I took another bite.

"I wasn't! And even if I was, it's not like you tried too hard to get in touch with me," she hissed, checking to make sure the room was still clear.

"Something spooked you last week. I didn't want to make it worse."

I launched the empty wrapper into a trashcan a few feet away. She glowered, looking exactly how I felt. Angry and tired. And under all that, maybe a little vulnerable.

"Listen. I know you've had a shit day with the LVAD getting canceled, and seeing your ex walk around probably didn't help things. But you can't get mad at me for giving you space when you seemed like you needed it."

She glanced at her feet, so I did, too. We both studied her neon green sneakers for several seconds. She'd added bright purple laces sometime in the last week. They were achingly adorable. Colorful and bright and so very Lainey.

"We had to tell her she was going to die." Her eyes flickered up, then back down again. "Me and Cooper. There's no reason we couldn't do the surgery."

"I know."

"It's less of a risk than a full transplant. She doesn't have enough time to wait for a donor heart."

"I know."

"Sam, she's a thirty-six-year-old woman with three kids, and I just delivered her death sentence."

"I know, Sweetheart." My chest squeezed. Losing a patient was never easy. Telling them you were going to lose them was worse.

She swallowed, rocking onto her heels without making eye contact with me. "You're right. I shouldn't have yelled at you. I'm sorry."

I checked the door before pulling her further into the row of lockers, out of sight, to wrap her in my arms. Something lightened from my shoulders when she collapsed against me, tucking her head under my chin like she was made to be there.

"It's okay."

Her ponytail tickled my chin as her head shook. "It's not. And I *have* been avoiding you. That's not okay, either."

"Yeah, what's that about?" I pressed my lips to the crown of her head because I couldn't help myself. Despite having been at the hospital for over twenty-four hours, she still smelled like vanilla. And antiseptic. Like Lainey.

She sighed, tilting her head to rest her chin on my chest. Her face was inches from mine. "Katie freaked me out. I think she suspects something's going on with us."

I grunted, thinking while my fingers slid through her ponytail. The curls were soft, wild. "You think it'll be a problem?"

"I don't know. It just made me jumpy. I'm sorry."

"You're forgiven." In another life, maybe I would have made her work for my acceptance. But I only had one life, and I only had this one girl. Dodging me for a few days wouldn't make me give up on her. I was here for the long haul. The sooner she realized it, the better.

She smiled at my quick response. "I probably don't deserve that." We were whispering, voices low so we could hear if someone walked in.

"You're not the only one who's had a bad day. I'm just happy to see you." Between the board and her ex and the patient crises, I was ready to call it and pull the covers over my head till morning, ideally with her in bed beside me, but I knew that couldn't happen. Not tonight.

Not only had she been avoiding me for the better part of a week, but she had an early on-call tomorrow morning, then prep for a surgery with Cooper, and her first interview for the attending role. As much as I wanted to take her home and drown both our sorrows between the sheets, today wasn't the day.

"You look tired." Her fingers traced underneath my eyes. I'm sure I looked like a warmed-over sack of shit, but it was nice of her to sugarcoat it.

"You, too. Walk out with me. You can go home and sleep."

Her brows pinched. This time, I indulged myself in smoothing the little wrinkle away, marveling at how easy this was, once we were on the same page. She felt right in my arms, leaning into my touch like she wanted more.

"I was just going to tough it out here tonight. I'm not on call but...I can't go home. I'll just toss and turn." The sadness lurking behind her eyes made me want to punch something.

"Grab your stuff." I stepped back, rummaging again through my bag and reminding myself to keep my hands off her when we were in public.

"I don't want to go home right now, Sam."

I handed her a protein bar. "We're not going home."

Chapter 17

Sam

"Now connected to device: Sam's a pussy."

"Will's handiwork, I assume?"

I sighed. It was nice that I had a key to my brother's gym, and he was cool with me coming in at weird hours between shifts. But it also meant he did dumb shit like label my phone under ridiculous names in the Bluetooth system. And, of course, it connected the instant Lainey walked out of the women's locker room.

My workout playlist filtered through the speakers as I patted the mat beside me. She dropped onto it, folding into a stretch that made my jaw clench. The Powerade and a second protein bar had brought me back from the brink of unconsciousness on the drive over here. But that didn't mean now was an ideal time to notice how deliciously bendy she was.

"This was a good idea. Do you do this often? Break in at odd hours?"

I nodded, thrilled to focus on something other than her forehead touching her shins, and the subsequent thoughts I had about seeing just how far she'd be able to bend with my cock inside of her. *Shit.* I flipped on my back to stare at the ceiling and stretch out my hamstrings. The last few days without her had made me feel deprived. Desperate. But she was going through something, dammit. And we'd both had shitty days. I needed to get looser, not harder.

"Often enough. Sometimes, if I don't come in the middle of the night, I don't get a workout."

She grunted in agreement. "I don't get to the gym nearly as much as I want, and I hate that. One time, a nanny told me I was 'excitable' if I didn't get enough exercise, which was just code for loud, I think."

"You're not loud."

She shifted on the mats beside me, changing sides. I did not look. "Take that up with Maria. She was Montessori-trained with a PhD in child development. If she said excitable, it was practically a diagnosis. It's why my parents got me so involved in sports when I was young. Now, if I don't hit the gym at least twice a week, I feel like I'm crawling out of my skin."

"Is she the one who taught you not to curse, too?"

"Ah, no. That would be Sister Mary Louise. Those catholic school nuns can put the fear of God into you."

I grunted, adding *do not think of Lainey in a catholic school uniform* to my list of things to avoid tonight. "I'm sure Will would give you the code to use every once in a while, if you asked. You're his favorite regular, after all."

Silence met my offer, and I could practically feel her walls coming back up, brick by brick. Dammit.

I rolled to a seat, peeking over to where she twisted on her back, staring blankly up at the ceiling. "Is this the part where you avoid me again?" I asked, teasing, but not.

"I...No. It's..." Her head rolled towards me on the mat. "It's stupid."

"I'd rather talk about something stupid now than not talk to you for another week."

"Oh, God." She shriveled up, a full-body grimace. Her hair hung in her eyes when she rolled up to face me. "I'm sorry. Katie freaked me out, and then, I don't know. Everything with Jas felt too real."

"Jas?" Throughout the past few days of wracking my brain, trying to figure out what I'd done wrong, my sister-in-law hadn't been on the list. They'd been thick as thieves after their time together. Jasmine was pestering me daily about when I was going to tie Lainey down.

Whenever the hell she'd let me, was the answer, but it was hard to snap at a woman recently released from the hospital. Jas's spirits were high, and she could work from home, but she'd needed something to take her mind off her diagnosis. She could fixate on me and Lainey, if that's what she needed.

"The only thing I'm good at is work, Sam. I've never been good at relationships."

"Sweetheart." I couldn't stop the endearment from rushing out. If I hadn't been sitting, those liquid brown eyes would have knocked me on my ass. She was so pretty and vibrant. Seeing her huddled on the mat, looking like she was confessing her deepest sin, tore at something inside me.

"No, really. I'm just not *good* at this. You don't get it because you are. You have all your family and your people. I don't have that." She bit her lip. "I grew up really sheltered, traveling around with my mom a lot or hanging out with my nannies. I didn't learn how to *do this*. I thought maybe I could, you know? I asked Rija out for tapas and then Jas needed someone in the exam room and Conner starts talking to me about tacos and Katie is standing *right there* making me remember how I've never had a successful relationship with anyone, ever."

Her hand shot out to wrap around my wrist. Those delicate fingers hardly closed around it. "This has *nothing* to do with you, Sam. I just got...overwhelmed, I guess. Maybe I tried to do too much too fast. I'm sorry."

Her skin looked good against mine. A few shades darker. Smoother. "Maybe you talk to me about it next time, instead of avoiding me in the hallways."

"I didn't *avoid* you." Her thumb brushed across my wrist.

"I'm pretty sure I saw you smack into the doorway of the physician's lounge you were trying to get away so quickly."

She smiled. It wasn't much, but after these days without her, it felt like the sun coming out after a storm. She grabbed my hand when I flexed it out to her. "You want to talk about it? The overwhelm?"

"No, thanks."

"So, I'll talk to you next week, I guess?"

Another smile, this one tinged with bitterness. "I really am sorry if I hurt you. It doesn't seem fair. You didn't sign up for all my baggage."

"I know exactly what I signed up for." I cupped her face when she looked away. "You're going to have to try harder than that if you want to scare me off. How am I supposed to get the full trial-dating experience if you don't give me the chance?"

As we moved through our sets, she cracked open, inch by inch. By the time we'd finished abs, she felt like Lainey again. No more avoiding my eyes or going weirdly, coldly silent.

Aside from a quick jog, I kept our exercises light. I wasn't trying to run us further into the ground. Her ongoing commentary on our reps kept me smiling. After our date last week, all I'd wanted was more of her. When she started avoiding me, I'd worried I wouldn't get a chance; not to hear her laugh, or feel her lips on mine again.

But as we moved our way around the gym, it started to feel like another shot with Lainey was a distinct possibility. As much as I was eying her, I could also feel her eyes on me. It was addicting. Especially when she dialed up the charm.

"Close out with squats?" She tapped a kettlebell with her toe. "Your favorite."

"Favorite?"

She met my gaze in the mirror, splaying her fingers across her ribs as she effected a low growl I assumed was supposed to sound like me. "Perfect." Her shoulders shuddered, eyes rolling back in her head.

My face warmed. She'd never brought up my little assist that day, and I told myself she hadn't noticed. It wasn't a big deal. I was equally pleased and mortified that she seemed to remember it just as well as I did. "Sorry about that. Couldn't help myself."

"Never apologize for feeding my praise kink." *Oh, fuck.* I was filing that one away for later. I could work with a praise kink, I really, really could. "Come on doc, my form needs correcting."

I wanted to go to her. Hell, I just plain wanted *her,* but I still had a few shreds of dignity left. Even though my dick was trying its hardest to convince me that dignity was for assholes and I should go shove my tongue down her throat.

No matter how much I wanted to, I was still coming down from that pins and needles feeling of her avoidance, and I wasn't keen to repeat it.

"You sure about that?"

"Oh, yes." She nodded solemnly. "I'm all over the place. Liable to hurt myself."

I smiled despite myself. I *liked* her. "Lainey, you have no idea how much I want to get my hands all over your form, but I'm not sure it's a good idea tonight."

Her face fell for a split-second, before she caught it and gave me a tight smile. "Right. That's fair. I haven't been very nice to you this week."

I caught her arm before she could back away. "Did you not hear me before? I'm still here for this. But I want to make sure you are, too." I stroked up and down her arm. "You said you're feeling overwhelmed. I don't want to add to that."

She bit her lip, looking down at the hand smoothing across her skin. I could hear her throat working as she swallowed.

"You're very close to people. Your family. Santiago."

"Hmm," I agreed. She'd mentioned this before, but I wasn't sure where she was going with it now.

"Being around you, seeing it all…I'm jealous." The concept was laughable. Lainey Carmichael, genius surgeon who grew up with two butlers, jealous of me? Yet the look on her face said she was serious. "I've been thinking about something Katie said when she told me she was moving here. She said she was hoping we could, like, bury the hatchet. She said that if I'd 'moved on,' maybe we could have a 'fresh start.'"

"Bullshit." I didn't need Lainey's air quotes to know exactly what part of that had been Katie's words.

Lainey's mouth hitched. "Maybe. But then the more I thought about it, the more I realized I haven't moved on at all." She stared, unfocused, at my throat. Her laugh sounded hollow. "It's kind of sad, really. I'm just existing here. I've been like that since I moved. I don't have any friends in Chicago. No family. Just work."

She shook her head, finally looking up at me. Pain flared in her eyes. "I don't have close people, and you have so many. It comes so naturally to you, and I can't even ask Rija out for tapas without it getting weird. I think they broke me."

"Of course."

Her lips pulled into a pout. "I didn't actually want you to agree with that."

"Lainey." She came willingly when I pulled her close. She fit against me like a dream, smelling of vanilla when I pressed a kiss to her forehead. "Of course they broke something inside you. You can't go through that and come out the other side completely intact."

Her head rocked against my sternum. "I don't know that I'm fully on the other side."

"That's okay."

"It's not. It's not okay. I've been stuck in the same place for years. You deserve someone who's unstuck." She put a few inches between us. "I want to be able to ask a friend out to dinner without it being weird or without freaking out that I'm getting too close to them."

"Alright. You should do that, then. Maybe not everything all at once, though." Her mouth trembled. My fingers glided down her cheek. "And in the meantime, don't worry about me." I'd waited this long to be with her. I could wait a while longer as she got her head on straight.

"Of course I'm going to worry about you. You're basically the whole reason this is happening." Her hands gripped my shirt, like she had in my kitchen that first night, and when we waited in line for barbecue. I liked it. It felt like she was sinking her hooks into me, worried I'd get away, and she couldn't stand the thought.

"This feels like something. Doesn't it?" Her hands clenched and unclenched in the fabric.

You have no idea, I wanted to tell her. *This feels like everything*. But I couldn't say that. She was still on edge and I wouldn't push her over. I settled for: "Yes."

"I know. And I'm tired of keeping people at arm's length." She searched my face. "You make it seem like it's worth the risk."

She *looked* tired. I pressed a kiss to the tip of her nose. "Sweetheart, you can keep me as close as you'd like."

She sighed my name, leaning her head into my palm. It felt like a surrender.

"I won't hurt you, Lainey. I *promise*."

My lips whispered over hers like I was sealing the vow. Breath mingled. The hairs stood up on the back of my neck.

I teased her, flicking my tongue across her bottom lip, staying there even when she opened for me instantly. I'd dreamed about her mouth. That pouty bottom lip drove me insane, and I owed it to myself to fully indulge.

She wasn't nearly as patient as me. Fisting hands tugged on my shirt until I pressed against her. Her frustrated little growl shot straight to my dick. I slipped between her teeth and the kiss turned a corner from teasing to full contact.

Fingernails scraped along my sides as she moaned. She tasted so sweet. Her tongue met mine, flicking across my lips in an echo of how I lapped at her. I didn't tolerate it nearly as well as she did. The move clenched me up, and I rocked into her without conscious thought.

She gasped when I rocked again, pulling on my neck to draw me closer. Absolutely impossible with how we were plastered against each other. But I was game to try if she was.

I moved, backing us to the wall a few feet away. She turned wild under my hands as her back met cinderblock, writhing against where I was getting harder, faster than I'd thought possible. The perfect weight of her breast was heavy in my palm. So soft.

"Christ, Lainey." I tore my mouth away from where I nipped along her jaw. Feeling wasn't enough. I had to *see* her arching into me. My thumb circled around and around, skirting the edges of the little budded nipple pushing against the fabric of her tank top.

"Sam. Please." I savored her whimper, hooking a hand behind her knee, boosting up at the same moment she wrapped her other leg around. We were practically choreographed. I thrust against her hard before I could control myself. Nails scraped up my neck and her fingers tangled in my hair. The pinch of pain where she gripped the strands only spurred me on.

"You like that, Honey?" My hips rolled into hers again and again. I echoed the movement with my mouth, tongue spearing through her lips as she panted, wide open for me, top and bottom. I clenched the fingers currently holding her ass to the wall. Her flesh was pliant under my hand. I slipped up into her spandex shorts. Gripped harder. She bit my lip in response.

I groaned. "Lainey, I—"

"No sex in the gym! I just cleaned the mats today, man."

Lainey froze, head jerking up to locate the source of Will's voice. I glared at the security camera in the corner, tilting my body to hide as much of Lainey as possible. We still had all our clothes on, but something feral in my chest growled at the prospect of someone else seeing her like this. Open and wet and *hot*.

"Go away."

"Bro, I woke up to take a piss and saw the security alerts on my phone going crazy. *You* go away."

"Oh, my God." Lainey buried her face in my chest and clenched her legs tighter around me, like she wanted to curl into a little ball and hide.

"William." I'd spent most my life practically co-raising my younger brothers. I liked to think I had netted some minimal authority over them.

"No sex, Sam! Lock up when you leave." The light on the camera blinked from green to red when he ended the livestream to his phone. Thank God.

My hands skated across Lainey's shoulders. Fucking Will. "Sorry about that."

She groaned, still tucked into my chest. "He's never going to let us hear the end of this."

Sighing, I stroked my hands across her skin again. She was probably right.

Chapter 18

Sam

My middle finger saluted the camera at the back door as I shepherded Lainey into the parking lot. I knew Will would review the footage in the morning, that dick.

It had been a Herculean effort to pull myself away, but hearing my brother's voice over a loudspeaker when I'd been about to dry-hump Lainey through a wall was as sobering as a bucket of cold water.

We'd both had shitty days, and she was reeling from all the stuff with her stupid ex. Not to mention she had an early surgery tomorrow. After all that, right on the tail of her confession that relationships made her overwhelmed, I'd manhandled her in a public place.

What had I been thinking? Obviously, I wasn't. I'd apparently outsourced that activity into my pants.

The lot was empty, same as it had been when we'd pulled up. Her arm brushed against mine when she opened her passenger door to drop her bag inside. Overhead, lights from a plane blinked in the sky. A breeze fluttered the shrubs my mom had planted last spring.

"Are there cameras out here?" She turned, those beautiful brown eyes gleaming.

"Just on the door. Not in the parking lot." I cleared my throat, rocking back on my heels to make my escape. She was too beautiful. Too distracting. Already, I was imagining the pep talk I'd have to give myself on the ride home.

Eyes on the road, brake with the left, accelerate with the right. Do. Not. Think about how you just had her ass in your hands. Don't.

But then she was grabbing for me again, clawing like she couldn't get to me fast enough. I groaned when her lips met mine. Fuck the pep talk. The edge of the car door jabbed into my hip when she pulled at my neck, and I didn't feel a damn thing. Nothing but her. I crushed her to me, lifting her up on her toes. Her mouth was hot and my brain felt like it was getting re-wired. I didn't need air anymore. Just Lainey.

"My place is closer," she panted, teeth nipping across my jaw. I hadn't had a hickey since I was sixteen, but all at once, I felt like I'd die without her sucking on my skin. I wanted her to take me into her mouth, her body, any way she could. The feel of sweet, sucking kisses damn near made my eyes cross. I grabbed her hips, grinding. She spread her legs and all that heat was *right there*. I thrust again, loving the feeling.

And suddenly she was gone. My hands on her hips had done nothing to stop her from tripping through the open door and plopping into the passenger seat with a thud.

There was a split-second pause when our breaths sucked in and hung in the air between us. She blinked up at me, panting and wide-eyed from the bucket seat.

"Shit. Are you okay?" I practically dove in, only registering her bubble of hysterical laughter once I was on my knees.

"Ohh-h-h! My God!" She pealed, clutching at her chest. I pried her hands off, sweeping palms across her back to make sure she was all in one piece.

"You good?" I repeated. She snorted. *Snorted*. And then, I was laughing, too, shaking with it. I'd dumped her ass into her car. My chest hurt I was laughing so hard, and a cramp clenched in my belly. Tears rolled down her face. I pressed my grin into her thigh.

"I'm s-so sorry," I wheezed. "Oh, shit. One minute you were there and the next-t..." I stuttered, losing myself to an all-consuming guffaw that set off a chain reaction of her snort-laughs.

"I-I'm o-kay!" She petted at my face, still trying to hold herself together. I hadn't laughed like that in a long time, and usually never with anyone aside from my brothers and Tiago. Maybe Blake.

"Really, I'm fine, I'm fine," she repeated, calming down. Our eyes met in the dim glow of the car's interior light. Gravel dug into my knees. And then, we both seemed to realize how close my face was to her pussy.

I couldn't help how my fingers grazed softly over the skin of her thighs, just below where her shorts ended. The spandex did absolutely nothing to deter me. I would rip it to shreds in seconds. Above me, Lainey's eyes darkened as if she knew it, too.

"My place is closer," she whispered. As she leaned forward to capture my lips, I realized she'd already said that, right before her topple. I was tempted, so damn tempted. I could still feel how she moved against me when I'd pressed her up against that wall. It was like a phantom limb. I'd never forget it.

"I...Sweetheart..." She peppered kisses across my cheeks. Goddammit. "Wait." I held her wrists. "You have surgery tomorrow. We can't do this now."

"Why don't you let me worry about the surgery tomorrow?" Her hands were in my hair, mouth on mine. My walls were nearly ready to crumble when she started reeling me into the car after her. "Or maybe I don't even want to wait till we get to my place."

But no. *No.* Not like this. I broke away, despite her hands in the collar of my shirt. "When I fuck you for the first time, I'm going to have a bed, and hours to spend on you."

"Sam—"

I shook my head, willing myself not to get caught up in the way she sighed my name like she'd die without me. "Our first time will not be in your car, Lainey. Not after everything else that's happened today."

"I—" She stopped herself, biting her lip even as her hand skimmed down my torso. She gripped the hem of my shirt, stretching the cotton.

"What, Sweetheart? Tell me." I didn't want this to be over, even though I knew it was. At least for tonight.

"I feel like...I need..." A little sound left her mouth. Frustration and something else. Her hand caught my wrist, sliding my fingers to the apex of her thighs. She gasped as soon as I made contact, head lifting like she was thanking the Gods.

She wasn't alone. "Fuck, Lainey."

She was soaked. So hot and wet, I could feel it through the flimsy fabric of her shorts. My thumb circled her and her hips swiveled on their own, like she couldn't stop herself. I rested my forehead on her leg once more, trying to get my head straight without letting up on the pressure and rhythm that had set her moaning.

"You need it, Honey?" I whispered, dragging my cheek against the delicate skin of her thigh. The muscle jerked and I couldn't help myself. My teeth sank into her, right where the stretchy fabric met miles and miles of tanned skin. She gasped and strained against me. No. *Towards me*. Like she wanted more. I licked around the indentations I'd made, wanting to preserve them forever. A flag planted in new territory. This one is *mine*.

"Sam, please, Sam," she chanted, gripping the short strands of my hair. She was getting even wetter, if that was possible, and my plans for a silent, strained drive back to my apartment, alone, were disappearing out the window.

No, I wouldn't fuck her here. The first time I was inside her, I wanted a mattress, not a stitch of clothing between us, and plenty of time to enjoy it. But there were a lot of shades of gray in between fucking her for hours and biting her leg in a parking lot.

Jesus, I was a dog. An absolute piece of trash. But, fuck me, she loved it, fingernails sinking into my wrist like she was planting a flag of her own, locking my fingers right between her legs.

"Come on." I urged her up and back between the front seats. She whined when my fingers left her, but I refused to do this hanging halfway out of the car. "Stretch out for me, Sweetheart." She finally got the message, scrambling to the back. I slammed the door, adjusting myself before opening the back door and climbing in after her. The air compressed when the door thudded shut.

"I've never had sex in a car before." She grinned, grabbing for me. She wouldn't today, either. At least not in the traditional sense, but my mouth was too occupied to tell her that. It was tight, but we managed to wedge ourselves in, propping her up in the corner with one of my legs hanging off the seat to brace on the floorboard. She gasped when I pressed against her, chest to chest.

Her hips arched into me, hardening my cock even more, which shouldn't have been possible. But I was crammed into the back seat of a car like a horny teenager, so my body might as well act like it. Enclosed with her here, without the threat of security cameras or interruptions, all the teasing and savoring I'd indulged in earlier evaporated. It smelled like her here: Lainey and sweat and sex. My mouth watered.

"Sam, God…" She sighed, hands dragging through my hair as I shifted my body against hers. Down, down, down. Her shorts peeled off quickly. No underwear. She was bare and smooth. Glistening.

"Look at you. Goddamn." I eased a finger between her folds. Her hips bucked. I wanted to make her make that noise again. That groaning plea that completely undid me. I circled her, fingers growing wet.

"Sam!" she screamed when I lapped at her, moaning at the taste. Sweet, wet, salt. Her legs threatened to close around my head as her hips churned. Her shrieks and moans filled the car, the only sounds I wanted to hear until the day I died. I speared my tongue into her over and over.

The way she moved made me want to shove my reservations out into the parking lot and bury myself in her. She was already begging for it, her sweet cries asking me again and again to get inside her, *now, please God, Sam.* I shifted, sucking on her little bud, shoving a finger inside. She was slick, ready. I added another, pumping in and out, holding on as she bucked.

She gasped, tightening. A rush of sweetness flooded my tongue. Fuck, it had only taken a few minutes. I hooked my fingers, desperate to feel her fall apart. She screamed as I kept up the pressure, sliding in and out. Again and again, as long as she needed me there.

She grabbed onto my shoulder, pulling me up. I resisted. Just a few more seconds of feeling her shake and sigh. Her taste was addicting. My fist cupped my dick, stroking.

My lips pressed against her again once, twice, before I crawled up her body, tugging her shirt up as I went. I wanted every inch of her I could get. Teeth scraped across her belly, tongue circling her navel. She tasted sweet here, too. The fragrance of Lainey and vanilla permeated the air around us. I gave into my baser instincts, biting and leaving marks while she clawed at me.

My hands dipped under her top as I moved further up, stretching it over her breasts. They were perfect. Her nipples dusky and tight, begging for my mouth. She pulled at my shorts, hand wrapping around my cock before I could stop her.

"Fuck. *Fuck.*"

"*Oh, my God.* You're so big. Jesus." She stroked, pushing the band of my pants down my thighs. Precum slickened her palm. The feeling of her hand almost undid me. I ducked my head to stare at where she held me. Pretty pink nails and long, lithe fingers working me up and down. I ran my hands across her skin, teasing her nipples and feeling the indentations of my teeth.

"Shit, Lainey, wait..."

"Come for me. Sam, please."

She reached her other hand down, cupping me against her wet pussy. She was still slick, my cock gliding up and down along her folds. So hot. For me. Her lips twitched, rolling when I rubbed her. Her mouth met mine. We panted together, moving in unison as the pleasure ratcheted higher and higher. She squeezed me, straining just as much as I was. The sight of my cock rubbing against her, so close to heaven, the sound of her, begging for it like my orgasm was her own, the feel of her. Everything crashed.

My groan filled the car as I came. She gripped me tighter, working her hands over the head of my cock again and again. I could practically feel it down to my toes. I shot all over her, the sight of my cum splashing across her stomach setting me off even more.

Her hands stilled as I came down from the high. My neck sagged, eyes dragging down her body, snagging on the sight of my seed sliding across the bite mark on her ribs. I shuddered. If she hadn't just wrung me dry, I'd have come all over again.

Our eyes met, leaving us both disoriented, breathing heavily. My hamstring started cramping from the uncomfortable position of my leg against the seats. Tomorrow, my back would most likely hurt too. One look at her, swollen lips and covered in me, made it all worth it.

"Next time. Bed. Hours," I grunted, still catching my breath and, honestly, questioning my ability to form full sentences. I'd been leveled. Flattened. I kissed her again because that, at least, I could do. She tasted like sex and she smiled when her tongue flicked my bottom lip.

We stayed like that for a few more minutes, lazy kisses soaking up whatever remained of our frenzy. Her eyes widened when I pulled my shirt off to wipe the mess from her stomach.

"Frack. We should have led with this." Her fingers spanned the tops of my shoulders, skimming down my obliques and back up. "Though, maybe not. I'd only have come faster. Which doesn't seem possible."

"We were both breaking records tonight. I can't believe how fast I just..." I shook my head, unable to articulate it. Not yet. Not while I was still wiping myself off of her skin.

"Secret's safe with me." We fell silent as I finished cleaning her up, saving that little bite mark for last. I circled it twice. "Do you think we'll be able to be cool about it tomorrow?"

"Tomorrow?" I ran my thumb over the mark on her thigh. Maybe I'd sucked on her, too, and not realized it.

"In my interview. Do you think we'll both be thinking about how fast you can make me come?"

My eyes lifted, locked on hers again.

God.

Dammit.

"Well, I will be now."

I kissed her again, just so I didn't have to see that sweet, satisfied smile she had on her face. The one that said she knew exactly where she had me—up against the ropes with no hope of recovery.

***

"Doctor Carmichael. Thanks for making the time."

"Oh, I was happy to come."

Lainey breezed into the conference room the next afternoon, tossing out innuendo in front of three other attendings and an executive director. No one batted an eye. Maybe it wasn't innuendo, when only two of you knew what was going on.

Our eyes snagged for an instant, but it felt like eternity. I could tell we were both thinking about it. How fast I'd gotten her off. How beautifully she'd come for me. Her back straightened, and she clasped her hands on the table in front of her, poised. I wanted to get her on her knees and fuck her from behind.

"Tell us about your time at Cedar, Dr. Carmichael. We'd love to hear your take on the progress you've made during your fellowship here."

I sounded normal, I think. She brightened as she talked. I could feel her love for her work all the way over here. On my left, Smithson—old codger that he was—smiled. So, I spent the next forty-five minutes staring at the woman I adored, imagining her coming on my cock in about twenty different positions, while she interviewed for a job that might make it impossible for us to work together. Only time and HR would tell.

Chapter 19

Lainey

Lainey Carmichael

Where are you?

Why is this place a maze?

Three different nurses have told me that they've seen you in three separate places.

Samuel Reese

Any reason you can't just page me?

Lainey Carmichael

Yes.

I laughed when Sam sent back an emoji of two eyes looking speculative. The day after my interview, I was on top of the world. The heady combination of nailing it with the interview panel, precluded by the best orgasm of my life, made me feel like I spewed rainbows every time I opened my mouth. It had been so hot. And unexpected.

Medical training took a long time, and Sam and I weren't even close to being in our twenties anymore. I wasn't sure what had compelled us to fold ourselves into my backseat and claw at each other like we were in heat, but I'd loved it. I wanted it again. I was so obsessed I could hardly even hear the worried voice in my head reprimanding me over what I was about to do.

Lainey Carmichael

I'm serious. I'm going to put a bell on your clipboard next time I see you.

An unfamiliar sound bleeped from my phone. *Samuel Reese wants to share his location with you.*

I stopped so fast a nurse nearly ran me over with a crash cart. I offered her a smile as I scooted to the side of the hallway, out of the flow of traffic. The little green notification pulsed on my screen.

Samuel Reese wants to share his location with you.

I swallowed, fingers stupidly unsteady when I clicked 'Accept' and shared my location back to him when prompted. The little screen loaded and there he was, a few yards away in one of the conference rooms.

Against my better judgment, I thought about Nate as I walked. I'd asked more than once for us to share locations, to make it easier to track each other down around campus and at the hospital. After a while, he'd snapped at me uncharacteristically, *"Jesus, Lainey, we're around each other all the time. Can't we get some space?"*

He'd apologized for it later and I'd forgiven him. Or maybe I hadn't, because here I was in a completely new city, walking towards a completely different man, still unable to forget every detail of the interaction. Maybe I'd known even then that something wasn't quite right.

Sam beckoned when I knocked on the door. I cracked it open, an excuse on my tongue for whoever he was meeting with, but he was alone. Smiling a little smile just for me.

Nate who?

"You're alone."

"I'm alone."

I glanced at his laptop. "You okay with some company?"

"Only if it's you."

I tried to suppress my smile. "Good, because we need to straighten this out once and for all." I plopped my laptop next to his and scooted a chair closer, showing him the screen for our schedule request portal.

"You want to sync our calendars."

I paused. When next month's schedule request had gone live an hour ago, this had seemed like a great idea. Maybe it was the orgasm talking, but I was no longer interested in just seeing him once a week for rounds or if our schedules opened up. I wanted every minute of his free time I could get, and even some of his professional time, too.

He'd already told me that the board had green-lit his ablation, and I'd be standing right next to him through the whole thing in two weeks. One surgery with him wasn't enough. I wanted to be a burr stuck to his side.

Only it had just now occurred to me he might not want that. Nate's stupid freaking face flashed in my head. "I mean. If you'd like to. We don't have to request every day off together. But it would be nice to see you more."

"Thank fuck."

I barely heard it, he whispered so low. "What?"

"Thank God," he said louder, self-correcting his curse. "I've wanted to do this for years."

"Years?" He nodded, guiding his cursor across his screen to the request portal. "Why didn't you?"

He hummed as the program opened. "Creepy."

"Ah, but consent can turn creepy into fun."

"Here, here."

His gruff admission reminded me of all the things he'd whispered to me in the backseat. No one had ever spoken to me like that before, in bed or out. Sex would never again be the same.

Even better, I didn't think he remembered it. Or maybe he did. When he told me while I jacked him off on my stomach that I was beautiful covered in his come and he wanted me to know I was his, maybe that was just his standard fare. It was not mine. But I wanted it to be.

Honestly, I'd gotten the impression at the end there that he hadn't been fully conscious of *what* he was saying, which made it all feel kind of precious and untouchable. Sam's *true* filterless thoughts revolved around how he wanted to come on my tits then go down on me for hours. His words, not mine.

It was the caveman stuff that I generally avoided like the plague, but for some reason, those words spilling out of the most quiet, thoughtful person I knew made me want more. Later, during my interview, it had been a miracle I'd been able to pull any coherent thoughts together. He'd sat there so normal and blasé, and I'd been squeezing my thighs together under the table.

We clicked through next month. I practically drooled at the amount of on call and off time he had. A dream. But it was all balanced out by the staggering number of non-clinical days he had to work. I'd seen other attendings' calendars, and it was nothing like this.

"How do you even function?" I pointed at the three days he'd blocked off in a row to prevent any surgeries from getting scheduled. "No wonder we never see each other."

"Teaching days, admin. Interviews. You have an admin day then, too." He pointed at the third day, enlarging it so I could see the title: Second Round Attending Interviews - Dr. Lainey Carmichael.

"I haven't gotten my interview date yet."

"You didn't hear it from me."

"Right."

We lined everything up as perfectly as we could for two surgeons who were also juggling other projects. My cursor hovered over the 'submit' button, checking one last time before I put in the request.

"You're sure no one will think this is weird?"

"For one month? No."

I clicked submit. "Even if anyone notices, it's not like we're doing anything wrong, right? Right?" I repeated it when he paused. His fingers scratched his beard. It was getting longer than he usually liked it. I wonder if he was planning on trimming it soon. Was it weird if I asked to watch?

"Right." He clicked submit, too.

"Because we're not dating."

"Mmhmm." He didn't look at me. If he did, I probably would have been able to see the words *"bullshit"* plastered across his forehead in big, flashing letters. But he didn't say anything else on the topic, allowing me to keep my no-strings, trial-dating illusion intact, at least for now.

***

We had another week before our beautifully coordinated schedule began. In the meantime, we tried to make due with hopefully inconspicuous chats during the day and ridiculously long phone conversations at night. And I tracked his location like it was my job. If he knew how often I checked his little dot, he'd revoke my access immediately. I was a fiend.

On my off night, his little dot still pulsed at the hospital when I walked into R^3.

Lainey Carmichael

> What are you still doing at work?

Samuel Reese

Resident planning.

Lainey Carmichael

When are they just going to give you the program, already? You're practically already their dad.

Some might even say daddy…

Samuel Reese

Oh, God. I'm literally sitting across the table from Whitaker.

Lainey Carmichael

I was hoping you'd stop by for a workout.

I snapped a picture of me in the R^3 parking lot, as close as I could get to the spot we'd practically melted the gravel down. He liked the image immediately.

Samuel Reese

I wish I could be there.

Lainey Carmichael

Would we even make it inside?

Samuel Reese

Well…I would.

"Holy crap!" I gasped, staring down at the text. Who the heck was this, and where was my oatmeal attending? I palmed flaming cheeks, glancing up to make sure no one was around, like somehow his text was lit up like a bat signal of impropriety above my head. Only a few folks trickled to the front of the building and none of them seemed to sense the aura of horniness around me. My phone buzzed again in my hand.

Samuel Reese

> That was inappropriate.

> Sorry.

I stumbled up the sidewalk, thumbs flying.

Lainey Carmichael

> It was.

> Would you call me a good girl if I asked you to say it again to my face? Slowly?

A hand whipped out to grip my arm. Jas shook me, looking frantic.

"Whoa. Hey, you okay?" After one night in the hospital and a minor preeclampsia diagnosis, Jas was on strict orders to check in with her doctor every week and "take it easy." For Jas, this equated to working from her home office and relying on "Gammy June" more than usual to look after Eli.

For Conner, that meant bed rest whenever possible, and hauling her to the gym the rest of the time to keep a close eye on her. She'd been texting me sporadically about Conner's ridiculous hovering ever since her hospital stay.

The texting had been nice. Low-key, though we got along well enough that she'd talked about going out for drinks or dinner after the baby came. But today was the first day she'd physically accosted me. She had crazy eyes, and I told her so.

"He'll hardly let me out of his sight to *pee*, Lainey. It was cute at first, but now I just want to have a minute to myself." Her fingernails bit lightly into my skin. "Last night, I went to bed at *seven thirty* to watch Bridgerton and he followed me. As if I wanted to watch the carriage scene with my husband right there!" she hissed, eyes darting around like Conner could pop out from the mats at any moment.

She shouldn't have worried. He was standing right behind her. I had clear sight lines to where he was instructing a patient to stretch their knee out, while he stared at us.

"Alright, Jail Break." I checked the clock on the wall. I had time for a quick stroll as long as Will was cool with me being a few minutes late. "How about a walk around the parking lot?"

That was about as far as I would travel with Jas, especially knowing that her helicopter husband wouldn't be far behind.

"Yes. *Yessss.* Tiago has been making me these adrenal mocktails. Let's have a drink. Omigod. Lainey, a drink! With a girl! Without a child hanging off me. Girl time!"

"Shit." Tess stomped out of the ladies' locker room. She was usually an early-bird like me, but when I'd texted to let her know I was taking a late class, she'd agreed without hesitation. After a few weeks of regular classes together, I liked her quiet, sharp wit. I'd never heard her curse before, and had definitely never seen her with that violent, bitter look on her face.

As she picked up the water bottle she had dropped, the top came off and water spilled onto her hands. She pelted it down onto the bamboo flooring, where it bounced and rolled to a stop at my feet. "*Shit!!*" she whisper-shrieked, grabbing at her ponytail.

Jas and I exchanged wide-eyed looks. "I'm not the only one who needs a girls' night," she muttered. "Hey! Tess, right? I need to get the fuck out of here. You coming with?"

It only took her a few minutes of prodding to get Tess and I to agree to skip our workouts and head over to Molido's, where apparently they turned off the espresso machines and transformed into a wine bar after five p.m. She sold me on the promise of cheese.

"And don't you dare just stand out here for the next hour while I'm in there. For fuck's sake, Conner, go do something that has nothing to do with me or the kids. Your mom is watching Eli for the night. Get wild!" Jas yelled across the parking lot. Conner paced along the line separating R^3's parking lot from Molido's, looking caged.

"It's not like I'm going to go hit up a strip club or something, Jas. I need to be here in case—"

"In case nothing! Go! Be free! Look at some titties!" She threw her hands up like she was at Mardi Gras, then ducked inside the packed cafe.

Conner ran hassled hands through his hair, then held them up to me, pleading. I gave him a thumb's up, following Tess up the stairs. "I'm on it. I'm a doctor!"

He was still pacing when the door closed behind us.

Chapter 20

Lainey

"I don't want to talk about me or children." Jas waved at her belly as Santiago rushed over to clean up the table she sat down at. Considering the scowling looks of some people standing in the corner, I had an inkling that she'd stolen someone's spot. Tess glanced at me uneasily, as if sharing the same concern. "Give me something good, ladies. I need intelligent conversation, where someone doesn't ask me twenty times in an hour if I need anything."

I studied the scarred wooden table Tiago wiped down. Usually, I was a wet blanket when it came to personal discussions. I had nothing going on except work stuff. But now...

"My ex best friend who cheated with my ex-boyfriend has moved to town and I might have to work with him in a month. And I think I'm emotionally stunted. And the board at my hospital has gone insane with power and I'm worried they are legitimately risking patient lives."

Jasmine pointed at me. "Yes. Great. We will get to that. You?"

Tess hesitated, her gaze flicking back and forth between us, before she blurted, "What happens when you get everything you've ever dreamed of and it actually sucks and you're scared you're just a trash human who will never be happy despite working your ass off for years to get this far?"

My eyes went wide. Tess's did, too, as if she hadn't meant to say any of that.

"You need wine," Santiago pronounced, nodding down at us. "And cheese. Carbs."

So, I sat with a glass of wine and a piece of brie, talking about work and ethics and happiness with two…friends? Yes, maybe these women were friends of mine. They were smart and kind and when Tess broke down into tears because her work as a creative director wasn't all she'd thought it would be, that was okay. And when Jas told us she was worried about what kind of mother she'd be to one son, let alone two, that was okay, too.

It was alright when I whispered, "I've worked all these years to become an attending at Cedar, but I don't know if I can work for those people." A truth I'd hardly even articulated, myself. Tess patted my hand, and Jas handed me another piece of gouda. Jordan dropped off a tray of brownie bites.

Was this what I had been missing ever since I'd closed the door to personal relationships? Growing up, I hadn't had anyone close enough to talk to like this. When Katie came along, it was like the heavens had opened up and sent an angel. *This is your person,* the universe had said. *This is your chance to have a real, true friend.*

Even though we'd jointly collected a few friends during college and med school, those relationships had fizzled when everything had fallen apart. I'd convinced myself I didn't need them. But maybe, just maybe, I did.

Eventually, Tess announced we needed to talk about something happy, and we both agreed. Jas's eyes narrowed at me.

"How goes it with Samuel?" She arched her eyebrows ominously. "Can't be too bad. Word has it you two were fornicating on the gym mats a few nights ago."

Tess choked on her brownie, and I thumped her back.

"We weren't *having sex*," I hissed, glancing around for Tiago. This would be the type of thing he'd eat up. Unless he already knew. Oh God. What if June had seen the security tapes? "We were just kissing."

"Hot kissing, by the sound of it. Relax." Jas swirled her cranberry-cherry juice in the wine glass Jordan had given her. "Will hasn't shown it to anyone. I think he only told Conner, but obviously Conner told me because he's legally obligated to."

"We don't have to talk about this," I told Tess, whose eyes were the size of the cheese plate. In my head, I begged her to please change the subject. I wasn't sure I was ready to talk about Sam to other people yet, especially not his sister-in-law. Unfortunately, Tess must have lacked the psychic powers I hoped she had.

"We've already gotten into vaginal tearing. We might as well just put it all out there."

Jas leaned forward as far as her belly would allow. "It's the different *degrees*, Tess. That's the terrifying part. But yes, let's talk about men now. I currently have no sex life. Let me live vicariously." Jas wiggled her fingers: *gimme.*

I bit my lip. "Listen. Technically, Sam and I aren't...anything. We're not supposed to date, and I have a lot of personal baggage that I'm trying to work through. He's been really patient and understanding. We're just..."

"Fucking," Jas supplied, spearing a gherkin.

"No, we haven't...well not fully..." Heat rose to my cheeks for the second time tonight. Tess and Jas swapped a look that had a lot of eyebrow action going on.

"I mean, yes, he's amazing. The chemistry is surprisingly great," I cut in, if only to stop the eyebrow situation from escalating. "He's so nice. And I love talking to him. And being around him. And his body is insane." They nodded, because no one could deny facts. "But we're not supposed to *be* anything right now."

"And you want more?" Tess asked.

"I want him to text me first!" My hand slapped on the table, rattling the cutlery. I hadn't realized how much this had been bothering me until just now. Maybe the wine and camaraderie had loosened me up, untangling some of my inhibitions so that I could clearly identify my issues. Now that I looked around, I realized there were two bottles on our table. One was empty and one was on its way there. With Jas sipping her mocktail, Tess and I had consumed more than I realized.

"He doesn't text you?" Jas frowned. "Well, he's a pretty quiet guy."

"No, that's the thing. He does text me. But only after I text him first. I mean, I've told him a few times that I want to take it slow. But we *are* kind of dating. Some proactive communication would be nice every once in a while, you know?"

My breath left my lungs and I shoved the rest of my brownie into my face.

"That's a deal breaker for me."

Jas and I both looked at Tess. I'd gotten used to her quiet musings so the steel in her words took me by surprise. "You think?"

She nodded, staring into her glass. "You deserve a man who will go out of his way to be with you. You're not just something that's *there*. Or *convenient*. If he's not willing to fight for it, it's not worth you fighting for, either."

I frowned. That didn't seem to be exactly what was happening with Sam. He was quiet to begin with, as Jas pointed out. Maybe he just wasn't as active a communicator as I was. My gut told me he wanted to be with me, though. All I had to do was think about those changed on-call shifts and that perfect non-date. The car orgasm. I didn't feel convenient, per se. But sometimes it felt like my minor obsession was one-sided.

"I hear you," Jas tapped her fingernail on Tess's plate. Tess blinked, like she was coming out of a stupor. "But I have to say—and I know I'm biased here because he's my brother-in-law—but I think you might wait a bit before kicking him to the curb."

Tess blushed and dropped her eyes, but Jas continued, contemplating her. "We all deserve to feel wanted, and I'm not saying you should keep giving him chance after chance." Her eyes flicked to me. "Have you talked to him about this?"

"No, because I've been pumping the brakes on us this whole time. Doesn't it send mixed signals? Especially when we're not even official?"

"Hun, you're official. Whether you want to put the label on it or not, that's the truth. Trust me, Sam would want to know you feel this way."

"You think?"

"I *know.*" She surveyed the slowly emptying cafe. I didn't even know what time it was. The vortex of supportive sharing and tapenade had me lost. "Listen, I'm not supposed to tell you this, but I've been hearing about 'Lainey from work' for like two years straight."

My jaw dropped.

"Don't freak out. It wasn't in a weird way, and he's dated other women since then, here and there. But he talks about your work, Lainey. How smart and charismatic you are. How you put the patients at ease. He likes you. A lot. He's wanted this for a while. Trust me, if you tell him you need something, he'll put in the work."

I drained the rest of my glass, not sure how to respond. Tess gulped hers as well.

"Yeah, ignore me. That doesn't sound anything like my situation. I mean, I was with a guy for *twelve years* and he probably never talked to his family about me like that." She buried her face in her hands, purple strands floating around her fingers. I thought I caught a whispered, *"Oh, God."*

I exchanged a look with Jas. "Maybe now we move on to *that*."

***

By ten p.m., Tess and I had worked our way through a good bit of our second bottle, and Sam and Conner arrived just in time to peel us all out of Molido's so the staff could close up. I kept telling myself that it was fine that I was a little drunk, because I didn't have surgery tomorrow, and it wasn't even that late.

I told that to myself, a lot. Also to Sam, who volunteered to take me home while Conner and Jas drove Tess.

"You're allowed to let loose," Sam agreed, which still didn't stop me from trying to justify my multiple glasses of wine. As someone who barely drank, splitting two bottles was out of my realm of experience. But it was so worth it. I babbled while Sam drove.

"...Can't believe he could do that to her, you know? Just forget about her like that. Or ignore her. And not how you ignore me, sometimes, you know? Ignore her like *he forgot her birthday, Sam.*"

"Hold on—"

"Which makes no sense. Because she's soooo pretty. Don't you think she's pretty?"

"Yes."

When I frowned over at Sam, he was frowning back at me. Matching.

"I bet you wouldn't say that if we were dating."

"What..." Sam swiped a hand down his face, trailing off. "What do you mean, I ignore you?"

"You never text me first. *Ever*. But that's probably since we're not dating."

"I'm sensing a trend."

"Would you text me first if we were really dating?" I asked, still twisted up like a pretzel in his front seat. He gazed out the windshield after throwing the car into park and shutting the garage door behind us. His frown didn't budge.

A moment or two of silence passed.

"Hello?" I'd gotten used to his unfiltered thoughts. The way he spoke to me now mirrored how he interacted with his brothers—easily and without too much forethought. Seeing him revert to his more contemplative state put me on edge.

He scoffed, mouth quirking in response to my impatience. "You know, if I could, I'd date the crap out of you, right?"

"Sounds unpleasant."

"You'd love it. The only reason we're doing this trial period is so you can ease in here."

I nodded. "And the plausible deniability."

He chuckled. "Lainey, no one at work is going to come after you for hanging out with me. You're too important to the department." His fingers stroked over my thigh. I cursed myself for wearing leggings today and not shorts, but I couldn't risk exposing the bite mark. It was fading, but it still had a few days to go. "You let me worry about the work stuff. As for the rest of it, I'm trying to respect your boundaries."

"My boundaries would appreciate a text every once in a while."

His teeth flashed. "Alright. Thank you for telling me that. Anything else?"

I leaned over the console, only to be stopped short by the seatbelt suddenly tightening across my chest. He rolled his lips under his teeth and reached over to untangle me, releasing the belt.

"My bites are fading," I pouted. He swallowed. "You should probably give me some new ones, just in case." Just in case of what, I didn't know, but it seemed like the right thing to say, especially when his eyes dropped to my mouth.

He reached out to stroke my bottom lip with his thumb. "You liked that?"

He had no idea. I wanted to get them permanently tattooed on my body. Evidence that I could drive Samuel Reese so crazy he lost all control.

"Mmmhmm."

"Then you'd better come in so I can take a closer look."

On the way up to his living room, I whirled, nearly crashing down the steps. He caught me around the waist and lifted me up the last few stairs to set me down on level ground. "Did I totally interrupt your night? I'm sorry."

"Don't apologize. I like you here." He fisted my ponytail gently to tip my head back and drop a kiss on my lips. It felt really nice. Natural. Like we were meant to be kissing in his living room, maybe forever? "I was going to grab a bite to eat and go to bed. Adding you to the equation drastically improves the next hour."

"Even though I'm a little wobbly?"

"I'll take you however I can." He squeezed my waist before heading into the kitchen to fill up two glasses of water. He moved like a boulder, slow and steady. It was oddly comforting to watch.

"So, about those bite marks..." I wandered to the kitchen island, hoping to seduce him into letting me spend the night. He pushed a glass in my direction and I gulped it down, attempting to quell the fire that started smoldering in my belly whenever he was around now. Again, I had to ask myself: *How had I not noticed him before?*

He looked tired as he rummaged through the fridge. It was past ten, and he'd put in a long day. If memory served (and it did, I had his schedule memorized), he had to be up early tomorrow for back-to-back morning surgeries.

"Are you sure this is okay? You probably need sleep."

"Really, I'm only planning on shoving some food in my face and then winding down. Please, stay."

Well, when he practically begged me... "Some food, huh?"

"Yeah."

"Like...pizza or something?"

"Yes." He didn't skip a beat, closing the fridge and pulling a pizza out of his freezer. I was usually a pizza snob—I had very specific crust preferences—but a few small cheese plates and brownie bites did not a dinner make, and my stomach was rumbling.

"You planning on eating the whole thing?"

His mouth tipped up into a smile. "I could be persuaded to leave a few pieces behind."

While it was baking, we talked about his day and his surgeries tomorrow and my wine night. He fed me pizza when it was ready. Later, he persuaded me into one of his massive shirts and told me in no uncertain terms that he would not be getting inside tonight. I yawned while I protested this. We went to sleep on soft cotton sheets, Sam's arm wrapped around my middle and my head pressed against his chest.

Chapter 21

Lainey

It was dark when he woke me.

"Hey. I'm heading into the hospital," he whispered, brushing a few hairs off my forehead. My brain felt a little fuzzy, but between the pizza and water Sam had poured into me, I was feeling better than expected after all the pinot.

"What time is it?" I was pretty sure I'd left my phone somewhere downstairs to fend for itself last night. Hopefully, it had enough battery for me to call a car.

"It's almost six. You should sleep in. Just didn't want you to worry when you woke up alone."

I smiled. It was warm under his covers, and smelled like Sam—like clean laundry and coffee and something else that I wanted to bathe in. And I got a few extra hours to wallow in it before I had to get up? Amazing. But...

"I can head out. I don't want to creep around your house."

He stroked my jaw, leaning in close. In the quiet darkness, with both of us whispering and the chill of early morning air teasing my nose, it felt like we were in our own personal bubble. A miniature snow globe that no one could intrude on.

"Feel free to creep. Your clothes are in the dryer. There's a pitcher of decaf breakfast tea in the fridge."

"You made me tea?" I'd stumbled into his house babbling like a tipsy wacko about him texting me more, and he repaid the favor by doing my laundry? The awe I was feeling must have leaked onto my face. He smiled down at me.

"I don't know if you know this, but I'm a surgeon. Putting some tea bags into a pitcher is well within my skill set."

"You have to add water, too."

"Damn. Knew I forgot something."

It wasn't even six a.m. and he'd already made me laugh. Plus, I was still riding the high from my cathartic drinks with Tess and Jasmine. Was this a dream? Did most people wake up feeling this cozy and content in the morning?

"Is there anything I can do before I leave? I can throw the sheets in the wash?"

"Don't worry about it."

"Well, if you insist. I'll just laze around here for a few hours enjoying my tea and snooping before I call an Uber."

"Your car's here."

I blinked at him. This was a dream. I'd left my car to sit cold and alone overnight in the R^3 parking lot. "What?"

Sam went sheepish. "I hope you don't mind. I gave Will your keys. He's driving it back here in a minute, and I'll take him over to the gym on my way to work."

"Who *are* you?" I should start calling him Super Sam. We should *all* start calling him Super Sam. He was amazing. For some unknown reason, he chose to spend all his selfless, amazing energy on me.

That soft smile made another appearance. He pressed a few kisses across my cheeks. "I'm Sam. Nice to meet you." Then he handed me my fully charged phone. I swooned.

After locking up with the code he'd given me (a code to someone's house wasn't equivalent to a key. Right? Maybe it was a temporary code that expired after a day, like one you could give to a house sitter.), I flicked through missed texts from last night.

Lainey Carmichael

> Would you call me a good girl if I asked you to say it again to my face? Slowly?

Samuel Reese

> Absofuckinglutely.

> Have a good workout.

> I told myself it was too late to ask you to meet me at Molido for a drink, but it turns out you're already there...

A screenshot of a picture Tiago had sent him accompanied the last message. I was leaning over the table, grasping Jas's arm and laughing. We were all smiling. My phone pinged, and I scrolled to a new message.

Samuel Reese

Did I forget to mention how much I enjoyed waking up with you in my bed today?

Lainey Carmichael

I don't believe you told me that, no.

Samuel Reese

A shame. Because I did.

Lainey Carmichael

Your bed is lovely. So is this tea. Is this the treatment I can expect every time I sleep over?

Samuel Reese

I'd do a lot more than make you tea if it got you in my bed again.

Lainey Carmichael

The tea is enough, trust me. You made, like, a gallon.

Samuel Reese

So you'll have to come back to drink the rest? Oh no...

Lainey Carmichael

Your sheets are in the dryer. I couldn't help myself. You needed some repayment for all that tea.

Samuel Reese

> Wish you hadn't.

> That pillow smelled like you.

Lainey Carmichael

> You mean I'll have to come back and sleep with you again? Oh no…

Samuel Reese

> I'd call you a good girl if you did.

Days later, the texts still made me blush. Aside from sitting down to plan out our upcoming ablation, Sam and I had barely gotten to see each other since that morning. We did a good job of acting professional, giving each other the same distant courtesy that we used to. Though, admittedly, it was hard for me to remember what we used to be like.

Even though it was only a few weeks ago, pre-Sam times seemed foggy to me, like he'd walked into my world and turned on a light.

"Doctor Carmichael? A moment?"

I refrained from grinning like an idiot when I saw him coming down the hall, instead dismissing the residents I'd just finished leading through rounds before I turned to face him.

"What can I do for you, Doctor Reese?"

His gaze flicked to mine. He continued to both love and hate when I called him Doctor.

"I wanted to check something with your calendar."

"Ah!" He smirked as I fumbled my laptop, ducking into the physician's lounge to grab a table. Next month's schedules came out today. As a senior fellow, I usually got my requests, but there were probably a few instances where Sam and my days wouldn't completely match. He looked over my shoulder as I pulled up my calendar. Our eyes flicked between his screen and mine, comparing.

I couldn't help smiling over my shoulder at him. All our off days lined up, as did most of our on-call and admin time. His gaze roamed my face, the corner of his mouth quirking.

"Sam," I whispered, checking to make sure no one was around. Two doctors sat at a table in the corner, too far away to hear us. "What are we going to do with all this time? I mean, look at that!"

Next Friday, our calendars were identical, color-coded blocks. My next attending interview in the morning, our ablation surgery in the afternoon, then an entire night and the next day off. After only snatching a few hours together here and there, the concept of a whole two days together—nearly thirty-six hours of free time, at that—seemed like an embarrassment of riches.

"I have some ideas," he murmured, pulling out his phone. I glanced through the rest of the month. My last as a fellow. My surgery schedule was packed, which was a good sign. Between standard procedures like stents, and more complicated ones like Sam's ablation and a few others with Cooper, I was fully booked. All the rest of the time...I'd probably be somewhere in Sam's vicinity. It felt too good to be true.

My phone chimed, and I glanced at the screen. *Samuel Reese has shared a calendar invite with you!*

A blue time block that simply said, "dinner", nestled into the blank space of my personal calendar next Saturday night.

"Oh my God, did you just ask me on a date via calendar invite?" I hissed, grinning as I hit "Accept."

"We're not dating." We shared a secret smile before I forced my attention back to my computer screen. There was only so much time we could spend smiling into each other's eyes before people took notice. I glanced at the following month and its appointment-free days. By that point, it wouldn't matter, would it? I'd be an attending and the trial period would be over. We'd be free to do this officially.

Honestly, if I could have slapped a title on him then and there, I would have. Despite a few bumps like my post-Katie freak out, I felt good about all of this. All those text exchanges and late-night phone calls and stolen, rushed lunches over the last few weeks had eased me into the concept of being with him, for real.

"Another surgery off the books." I jumped as Cooper slammed his bag down on the table. "This is getting out of control. Someone needs to talk to Caplan." He aimed a cutting look at Sam, who casually closed his laptop while he slid into a chair.

"Don't look at me."

"He listens to you. You're the most level-headed one out of all of us. If you say something, he'll do something."

Sam shrugged, sitting back. "He hasn't done anything yet."

"Damn, that's right. You almost blew a gasket when they switched Jones into that EVLP. Never seen you so worked up."

I nearly strained my neck to stare at him. "Is that right?"

Sam's eyebrows lifted. "It was bullshit."

"It *was* bullshit!" Cooper cut in before I could say anything. "Dude's grandfather is on a hell of a power trip."

"Can't we do anything about this? Go to others on the board?"

Cooper snorted. "You mean the other people who've been in Sturmond's pocket for the last fifteen years? Not likely. Hopefully, he's only freaking out because his baby boy is up for a permanent position here, and everything else will go back to normal once that settles itself out. Otherwise..." He trailed off, shaking his head.

"Otherwise, what?" I knew a lot about how hospitals worked, but the dynamics between physicians and leadership were still somewhat of a mystery to me.

"Otherwise, I'm out."

"What? You'd just leave?" My jaw was probably hanging open. I'd worked my whole life to be a surgical attending. It had never occurred to me that someone would just pack up and leave it. It didn't help that I got freaked at the thought of my favorite surgical partner abandoning me.

Cooper rolled his eyes. "It's not like it would be hard for me to find a job, Carmichael. I'm one of the most prominent figures in this field. No offense, Reese."

I was probably the only one who noticed Reese's mouth tipping subtly into a smirk. "No problem."

"I could write my own check somewhere. I won't stay here if they keep interfering," Cooper finished, eyeing the coffee machine.

"But Cedar is the best cardiac hospital in the country!" I protested. *We* were the best surgical team in the country. "Where else would you even go?"

"Won't be best for long if they keep roadblocking my fucking surgeries. I'd rather go somewhere where I have a chance at making a difference." Cooper tapped on the table, glancing at the two of us. "Like that ablation you two are working on? The simultaneous valve repair is going to make it tricky. You feel in over your head there? Want me to take the lead?"

He addressed Sam, but my hackles rose at the implication that he couldn't cut it. "Dr. Reese and I are perfectly capable of executing such a complex procedure."

"Whoa. I didn't mean it like that. I just want something interesting to think about before I fall asleep with a scalpel in my hand." Cooper rose. "I have to grab a cup before my next consult."

"Thanks for the backup." Sam smiled at me, opening his computer again to tap out a few notes.

"Anytime," I murmured, not totally sold on the innocence of Cooper's innocent comment. The man's inflated ego probably helped him keep his cool at the surgery table, but sometimes made him insufferable as a person. I'd gotten used to his little quirks. It helped that he seemed to hold me in some esteem, even if I was technically underneath him in the hospital hierarchy.

For better or worse, our stars had risen together over the last few years. Cooper and Carmichael: the cardio dream team. The thought of him leaving made me feel slightly queasy. "Do you think he'd really leave?"

"Maybe." Sam paused his typing to look at me, a flash of wariness in his eyes, before it cleared. "You seem upset by that."

"Maybe," I repeated, biting my lip and staring at the door. Cooper was a once-in-a-lifetime sort of surgeon. Smart and intuitive, focused without being a hard-ass. The two of us had a track record of success that I wanted to cling to with my own little egotistical claws. "We're a good team. It'd be hard to lose him."

"Professionally."

I snorted, navigating through patient notes. I loved these moments with him, stolen and innocuous. "Obviously, professionally. What else is there?"

His throat cleared. Something about it sounded off. I cut my eyes over in time to see him take a breath. "Personally."

This time, I snorted so hard I choked. "You think, me and Cooper?" I hacked, taking a sip of my tea. "Did you hit your head recently and forgot to mention it?"

"It's not as far-fetched as you'd think," he muttered, refusing to meet my eyes. His sudden bout of shyness baffled me. Was Sam *jealous* of Cooper?

"Um, hard pass. He's a surgeon."

"I'm a surgeon." The lines around his mouth canceled out the lightness of his tone.

"Yeah, but you're different."

He finally glanced over, working hard to suppress a smile. "Different how?"

"Well, Cooper didn't stand up for me to the board." I grinned. Sam grunted, gaze following the curve of my cheek. "He said you 'blew a gasket' when they pulled me out of that EVLP."

"Hmm," Sam grunted again, eyes on his computer. I got the impression he didn't really want to discuss this.

"Why didn't you tell me?"

"I told you I tried to change their decision."

It was so very Sam to go to bat for a co-worker and not say anything about it. "Telling me you tried isn't the same as telling me you freaked out on the board."

"I didn't freak out."

"Blew a gasket sounds like freaking out. How would you describe it?"

He shut his laptop before raising his eyebrow at me. He knew I was fishing. "I may have gotten frustrated."

"Did you yell?"

"No," he answered quickly. Too quickly. We eyed each other.

"Just what, exactly, does it look like when you get heated, Doctor Reese?"

"Maybe you come to my place after our surgery Friday and you can find out."

"Well, this looks cozy." Sam and I sprang apart when Jones dropped his lunch across the table. "Nothing like procedure planning on your lunch break."

"Right." Sam swept his computer up. "Carmichael, thanks for checking the schedule with me."

"Anytime." While I watched him walk out of the lounge, I counted to ten in my head. Stupid Jones. Now I'd never know what Sam was like when he got all fired up. At least, not until Friday. My heart fluttered.

"You two have been going hard on that ablation. Must suck to spend so much time with him. Talking to him is like pulling teeth."

"He's a great surgeon," I snapped.

"Whoa, damn, calm down. I'm just saying, it's like talking to a brick wall." I wanted to smack Jones's cocky smile. "You want some real stimulating conversation, you know where to find me."

"I don't date people from work," I reminded him for the hundredth time. Except for Saturday. I might be dating someone from work on Saturday. And...maybe Friday night, too.

Chapter 22

Lainey

An atrial fibrillation ablation was the kind of thing that made even me, an almost fully trained heart surgeon, go *"Whoa, what?"*

A catheter fed through an artery, a few electrical pulses and presto chango, we blocked abnormal signals to restore standard rhythm to the heart. Scientific wizardry. On top of all that, Reese was going to use the same catheter to repair a problem with the patient's mitral valve, which wasn't closing properly.

A delicate procedure, and a long one. But it flew.

After years of medical school, residency, and fellowship training, the OR was practically my second home. I was more comfortable here than in my apartment. But days like today, cases like this—*teams* like this—still gave me goosebumps. It was an honor to be here, and an absolute privilege.

Seven hours after entering the OR, I'd officially witnessed my first in-person ablation, and Sam had allowed me to personally implant the MitraClip to close the patient's malfunctioning valve. I couldn't keep the grin off my face as I scrubbed out next to Dr. West, the electrophysiologist who had come from Loyola to assist. Sam's surgery playlist still trickled through the speakers in the OR, *"Come and Get Your Love"* making its way into the scrub room.

"Great work today!" I called to two nurses wheeling a heart monitor out of the OR.

"You nailed it, Carmichael." Mary, one of the nurses, stopped to chat while I dried my hands. Dr. West shuffled by, humming along.

"It was flawless," I agreed, swaying my shoulders back and forth to the music. We'd been like a well-oiled machine. It was a kind of surgery magic that didn't happen very often. But when it did...I added a little hip wiggle and a few shuffles when the nurses joined, moving to the beat. Mary burst out laughing at something behind me.

My smile grew when I spotted Sam behind me, matching my shoulder sways move-for-move.

Our eyes met, and a different sort of magic swelled. My heart squeezed and my stomach felt weightless, like I was on a roller coaster. I grinned when he made his way closer, leaning back and forth with me to the music.

I wasn't sure if my face gave it away, or if he was just watching me *that closely*, but when I double-timed my shimmies to switch direction, he mirrored my every move on the beat. My laughter blended in with the nurses as they hooted and clapped, joining us in our impromptu dance party. Mary cackled when Sam did some sort of fancy footwork, reaching out to twirl me under his arm.

It felt like some sort of bizarre dream. My feet were killing me and I was exhausted, but the high of the successful surgery, performed side-by-side with this incredible man, was too much to ignore. Sam dropped my hand, dipping Mary when she shimmied past.

"Is this a Cedar thing? Surgical dance parties?" Dr. West grinned, reaching into his pocket to grab his phone. We all laughed. No. It wasn't a Cedar thing. It was just a happy thing. I got into some serious finger guns and arm rolling with Sheila, one of our surgical assistants. Cameron and Mary started to hip bump. We were all making fools out of ourselves, dancing in the scrub room. Through it all, Sam and I rocked together back and forth, perfectly matched, step for step.

***

It should have been seamless. Sam and I had planned this all week: We'd hand off Mrs. Singh to a resident for post-op, finish our documentation, do any last-minute patient checks, and then hightail it out the door to his place.

My bag was packed. I'd anticipated his hands on my body all week long. The patient was recovering nicely and my notes were done.

The only issue: I was so exhausted, I could barely sit up straight.

Even for the most seasoned surgeon, seven hours in the OR was a lot. You couldn't just sit around, either. You were on, mentally and physically, monitoring about seven different things at once. Oh, and also physically rearranging things underneath someone's skin.

So, despite all the anticipation and immaculate planning, hour fourteen at the hospital found me posted up outside of a patient's room. I was still on my feet, but barely. The wall was doing most of the work for me.

"Almost done. Give me one minute and we can go," Sam said, ducking into the room. I didn't have the energy to respond.

As much as I wanted to get up under his scrubs, I worried I wouldn't have it in me tonight. I liked him so much, but I was fried. I needed food and sleep. Then, maybe, I'd think about getting into his pants.

"Nice work today. Heard it was a success." The smile Jones gave me as he passed by probably qualified as more of a sneer. "Racking up those OR points just in time for your next interview."

"Fuck off, Jones! For God's sake, let her have her moment. There are plenty of scalpels to go around, you asshat." Rija took in my weak smile as she chased Jones away from me. "Don't let him get to you. You should be glowing. I heard the surgery went off without a hitch."

"Rija, it was so amazing. Such a cool procedure and the patient is doing great. Just a long day."

"Oof, I know. Long OR days are killer. You should go home and get some rest. Didn't your shift end a few hours ago?"

I hooked a thumb over my shoulder. "Have to talk with Dr. Reese about something before I head out." Vagueness was my friend. I didn't have the energy to come up with a lie right now.

Just then, Sam stepped out of the patient's room, closing the door softly. Rija swatted at him with her clipboard. "Congrats, Reese. I'm already hearing good things about that surgery."

He inclined his head to me. "Pays to have a good team. Dr. Carmichael handled the implant."

Rija whistled. "Look at you, fancy pants! We'll make a full surgeon out of you, yet!"

"Ah, he's just—" I stopped short, nearly about to tell Rija that he was biased. Oh, God, I was tired. "Being nice," I covered with a little shrug.

"Still. Big deal. We should celebrate. I'm off late tomorrow night?"

"Oh, ah, I can't tomorrow. Next week?" Heat rose to my cheeks.

"Let's do it! Great job again, you two. Have a good one!" She strode down the hall, leaving Reese and I to trudge towards the locker rooms. Together.

My sluggish mind raced, considering my dilemma from all angles. Maybe I could grab a Red Bull on the way out. Maybe I could power through and the sex would be great despite being nearly dead on my feet. Maybe I could just go home and meet him tomorrow, even though every fiber of my being insisted that I stay with him.

Caught up in my exhaustion, I didn't notice for several minutes that he was dragging, too. His forearm propped on the locker next to mine, while he rubbed tired eyes.

"Lainey, I'm so sorry..." He trailed off, shaking his head. My breath caught. So sorry, what? So sorry but I'm exhausted and can't hang out tonight? So sorry, but I'll need to chug an energy drink before I ravish you? Honestly, I couldn't decide which option I wanted more. "But I'm about to manipulate you."

"Ma...What?"

He had the grace to look remorseful. "I'm about to manipulate you. Hard."

Before I could ask him what, specifically, he meant by this (Physically? I'd let him manipulate me physically. I just needed that Red Bull first), a group of residents walked into the lockers. They made small talk, a few of them commenting on the surgery today. Sam accepted their praise and maneuvered us out the door at the same time.

The halls were empty. We had the elevator to ourselves, giving me ample space to corner him as the doors closed behind us. "I don't think it counts as manipulation if you give me forewarning."

He smiled. "You're not even going to see it coming."

"You're literally telling me it's—what do you want me to do with this?"

His head tipped back against the wall when I took the phone he'd thrust into my face. The screen was open to a food delivery app. My favorite Mexican place was already up. "Add your order."

"My order?"

"For dinner. Or whatever you call it when it's after nine p.m. and you're eating your second meal of the day." One eye cracked open. "If we order now, it'll be at my place a little after we get there."

I added my favorite burrito bowl—extra cheese, jalapenos, pico on the side. I glanced at him again as we walked into the empty parking garage, then added a small queso dip, too. He was a doctor. Surely he could afford some queso? Or, better yet, I'd just sneak my card info in here and I'd pay for dinner. He'd gotten breakfast the last time we were together. It was only fair.

But when I got to the checkout page, I found he'd not only added a large queso but also a large guacamole and churros. *Well, dang.*

He plucked the phone away before I'd had the chance to add my credit card number. "You ready?"

"Ah, I think I accidentally added another queso..." I watched him click the order button and preemptively leave a massive tip for the driver. My mouth snapped shut.

He stopped when we got to my car, one of the only vehicles parked on this level at this time of night. His was parked a few spots down from mine, which made me strangely happy. While we'd been inside together all day, our cars had been friends. Cute.

"I know I don't usually drink caffeine, but I might need some coffee when we get there." A yawn cracked my jaw.

"Coffee would be counterproductive for what I have in mind."

I frowned, opening my car door and slinging my bags inside without looking where they landed. "We don't need...a lot of energy for what you have planned?"

"Nope." He crowded me into my car a little. It made me think of him kneeling at my feet in the R^3 parking lot, except this time he towered above my head. It sent a thrill straight through me. A good, tingly kind of thrill that made me second-guess the need for coffee. "Here's my plan: Go home. Shower—separately," he qualified, correctly reading the alarm on my face. I was in no state for shower gymnastics.

His big hands skimmed down my arm. You know, the ones I'd personally witnessed save someone's life today? Those hands. "Clean clothes. Dinner. Maybe in bed? Then sleep."

I gulped in a breath, then another, eyes darting around the empty parking garage. "*That's* what you want to do in bed tonight? Eat cheese dip and sleep?" Hallelujah and praise the Lord. The plan had taken a sharp left from where I thought he'd been going, and I couldn't be happier about it.

"We can re-evaluate after a nap." He looked me up and down. I probably looked completely wrecked. No makeup, hair frizzing to the high heavens and in shapeless scrubs. He still seemed pretty interested. Another point in his favor.

"You ordered my favorite dinner, and now you're going to take me to your house to feed me and nap?"

"That's the plan, yes."

"You are so getting laid later," I whispered.

He smiled in the dim, flickering lights of the parking garage. When he leaned forward to press a kiss onto my cheekbone, he whispered, "Never saw it coming."

Chapter 23

Lainey

I woke up warm, blankets pulled up to my chin. Comfortable. I was one of those annoying fan sleepers who couldn't settle without the whir of air being pushed around the room. Sam had remembered this and turned on the ceiling fan without me asking.

After I'd luxuriated in his massive shower, we'd eaten queso in bed and watched an episode of a World War II docuseries. When I'd suggested it, he'd almost fallen over in shock.

"What?" I focused on the piece of avocado quivering precariously on my chip. "I saw a good review. I've already watched the first one, but I'd rewatch it with you."

"You watched a World War II docuseries? When?"

"I didn't see you a lot this week." I avoided his eyes, focused on my guac. "It reminded me of you."

He froze, a forkful of rice halfway to his mouth. "That's the hottest thing anyone's ever said to me."

It was a little intoxicating, doing something as mundane as watching a history documentary in bed. Spending a Friday night curled up with a bag of chips between us felt like playing house. I was being granted a sneak peek into what our future might be like if we hung onto this for the long-haul. Fun. Comfortable. Flirty.

So comfortable, in fact, it felt a little dangerous. This was only starting, even if it didn't necessarily feel like it. My trust issues screamed I was getting too attached too quickly. Apparently, I was getting better at tuning them out, though, because I'd slept like a baby.

Until the brush of calloused fingers across my stomach stirred me. Outside the curtains, it was still dark. At some point in the night, the t-shirt I'd stolen from Sam's drawer had ridden up, and he was capitalizing on it. He stroked a small patch of skin, back and forth. Every nerve ending in my body came alive.

A soft gasp escaped when his thumb dipped, charting a path to my navel

"Yes?" His breath was warm, beard tickling the back of my neck.

"Yes." The night was quiet and still. We were inside the bubble again. Any noise above a whisper would interrupt the heavy, heady air between us.

"I should have let you sleep." His fingers swept lower, bolder. He blazed a path across my stomach to the waistband of my underwear before traveling back up to my ribs. "But I couldn't help myself. You are so gorgeous laying in my bed, wearing my clothes. I had to feel you."

"I want you to. Feel me." *Please*. He maintained that steady rhythm of his hand. My thighs clenched.

"Tell me where. I want everything, Lainey. Tell me where to start."

I gulped. Everywhere sounded like an excellent place to start. I wanted to feel him all over me. My legs shifted restlessly, sliding against him.

"Where, Sweetheart? Higher?" His palms flowed over my skin, up, up, until the edge of his hand barely grazed the rise of my breast. I sucked in a breath.

"Yes. Higher."

"What about here? Lower?" He toyed with the lace of my panties, circling around and around where cloth met the skin between my hips. I arched against him, pressing into his hips to feel the hard length of his arousal.

His groan blended with mine. He was already hard. It went straight to my head. More heat flooded between my legs when I repeated the motion. He'd barely even touched me and I was already wet. Every moment we'd spent together for the last few weeks had just been an on-ramp; a build-up for what was about to happen. Even the fireworks in the R^3's parking lot had just been a precursor to this. In the quiet dark of his room, hearing his quickening breath in my ear, it felt different. Serious. Deeper.

His hand flattened, squeezing my hips back against him. "Feel so good right there, Honey. Soft and sweet." He grunted, digging his cock into me. "But you want me up here, is that right?"

I wanted to whimper when his hand moved, releasing his grip on my hip. His thumb swept once more up my chest, cupping me, his fingers never quite landing right where I wanted them. The ensuing ache between my thighs was nearly unbearable. He kissed a line down my neck. I actually *did* whimper when I felt his teeth graze my shoulder.

"Sam." My legs churned beneath the covers, scrambling to find some relief from the sweet heat rushing through me. I was burning up, and he wasn't where I needed him.

"Hmm?" He licked a spot near my throat lazily, like he had all night for this. I wasn't even sure I had ten more minutes before I was going to combust.

"Stop teasing. Please."

I unintentionally set something off with my desperate pleading. He moved so quickly my head spun. Rough hands pulled me onto my back and then he was over me, sinking his hips, lining us up right there.

Our mouths clashed, tongues tangling. I grabbed at him, scrambling to pull him closer. He thrust his hips. My head tilted back on the pillow, following the direction of his fingers in my hair. Mouths opened wider. I wanted to claw at him until our bodies melted together.

When he sucked my bottom lip into his mouth, my fingers pulled at the elastic of his waistband. He had the same idea I did, pushing at my shirt. Between the two of us, we flung it away somewhere into the dark of the room. His lips were wet against my throat, tongue lapping at my pulse point.

"Show me, Honey. Show me what you want. What you like. *Goddamn.*" He groaned against my skin when I bucked against him. The friction was so good and still so far from what I really wanted. I was hot for him, absolutely panting, still tugging on the cloth at his hips. He was rock hard, moving his hips mindlessly against mine.

A frustrated, animalistic noise ripped from his throat and he jerked away, propping up over me, fists on either side of my head. I groaned at the loss of his skin against mine.

"Touch yourself." He sounded gritty.

"Sam." His name a sigh, breathless as I tried to arch closer. I dragged one knee up his waist. He caught it, pinning it to his side to stroke my skin. A reminder that no matter how much the veins in his arms stood out or how urgently he pressed against me, he'd be gentle. He'd never treated me like glass, but sometimes he looked at me with a reverence I wasn't sure I deserved. Times like now.

His eyes roamed my body, bare except for a scrap of underwear. He looked like he was dreaming and didn't want to wake up. His dick strained against the front of his pants. Lips red from how I'd practically attacked him only seconds ago.

"Sam," I repeated his name, sounding dazed. I cupped my breasts, fingers pulling at my nipples like I needed him to. I rolled them, biting my lip to stop from groaning. Sam's throat worked as he watched. I didn't have the time or inclination to feel self-conscious about his stark appraisal. Not when he was looking at me like I was his dream come true.

He studied my pinching fingers like it was the most important thing in the world. He grunted when I tugged at them. His hips pulsed against mine involuntarily.

"I know you like it a little rough, Sweetheart. Show me how you get off." His words made me shake. He pressed my leg tighter to him, holding me open for those little rhythmic presses that did nothing to ease the heat between my thighs. He only drove me higher. "If it were my hands on those tits, my fingers working you over, what would you want me to do?"

I pinched harder, pulling my nipples with one hand while the other trailed down my stomach. What would I want his hands to be doing? This.

I dove beneath my waistband, driving my fingers through the drenched wetness I found there. Too slick. I couldn't find any sort of purchase. My finger pumped inside. I added another.

"Wait, baby, fuck, let me see." I hardly noticed when he ripped my panties off, baring all of me to him. I was lost, consumed by his words and his eyes on my body. Those whisper-soft strokes that had moved from my knee up my thigh.

"Sam! I need...I need...."

He grabbed my wrist, dragging my fingers to his mouth. Moaning at the taste. "I'm right here, Honey. God, the taste of you." He ducked down, nipping and biting along my ribcage as he sank down lower, muttering the whole way. "Haven't stopped thinking about it for a week. So sweet."

I turned molten when his teeth bit into the skin around my hipbone. He was still sinking, leaving a trail of stinging bites across my thighs and muttering obscene things into my pores. It filled me up, bubbling over until I couldn't stand it anymore. I needed him, all of him, right now.

"No. No, I need you." I tugged at his shoulders, fingernails digging. He looked at my face, eyes flickering between my desperate gaze and my breasts and my pussy.

"One taste. Just one..."

I cried out when he flicked his tongue against my swollen flesh. The feeling pulled taut inside me. My legs tightened on his shoulders. "No, no, please. Sam, I need you inside."

The words had no sooner left my lips than his hand was between my legs, dipping his fingers into me. He whispered about how wet I was. Moaned and sucked on me, pumping, telling me again and again how good I felt. Hot and slick and *his*.

A fierce orgasm spiraled from my core when his teeth scraped over me. The pain and the sweetness and the *Sam* of it all flung me into the stratosphere. Fireworks exploded behind my eyelids. I burned up. The whole time I gasped and pulsed and begged for more. He kept up his running monologue, driving me higher, somehow, when I should have been coming down.

I couldn't tell when the climax ended, or if it even did. I snatched at him, hands sliding on sweat-slicked skin. He scrambled up, capturing my mouth in deep, sucking kisses that at once made me feel like I was dying for air and breathing for the first time.

"...so beautiful, Lainey. Fuck, you're so perfect."

"Now, Sam. Now, I need you."

"Wait, Honey. Condom."

"No." He was too late. I'd already worked his shorts halfway down his thighs and now that I had him in my sights, it was game over. I gripped him. He was steel-hard, precum leaking from his tip. I swiped my thumb across it, using the slick liquid to ease the way as I pumped him in my fist. He shuddered, head dropping to the pillow beside mine. I craned my neck, pressing kisses to every inch of skin that I could: cheek, neck, beard. He tilted his head, lips capturing mine. More slickness against my hand.

"Stop. Shit, Lainey. I need a condom."

"I have an IUD. I'm clean."

"I..." His hand gripped my wrist, like he couldn't think with me holding him. I was well beyond thinking. My thinking brain would have told me it was irresponsible to have unprotected sex for the first time with a man I wasn't even sure I could call my boyfriend. But this was Sam, and I knew in my bones that he would rather throw himself in front of a moving vehicle than hurt me. "I'm clean. I swear."

I pulled him closer, stroking the head of his cock through my folds. It reminded me of that night in his car, when he'd exploded all over me. I wanted that again. But I wanted him inside me when it happened.

Breath hissed through his teeth. He scooped my leg up again, opening me. I liked the way he moved me to suit his desires. With anyone else, it might have made me feel lifeless or used, like a sex doll to be bent to his will. But with Sam, it felt desperate. Like I'd brought him to the brink and he could never get enough of me. I felt treasured and wanted. Maybe I wouldn't mind being his sex doll.

We were both grinding and sliding against each other. When I positioned his dick at my entrance, he met no resistance. My breath caught as his first few inches slid inside. I felt stretched. *Yes.*

There was that friction I'd been missing. Sam cursed violently, pushing my knee into the mattress, opening me up even more. He trapped my other hand against the pillow with his, while he stared down at where we were joined.

"Look at you." He pushed in a few inches more, holding me when my legs jerked at the feeling. "Taking my cock like a dream. You're made for it, Sweetheart. Made for me."

I nodded, biting my lip, trying to stem the flow of my needy, desperate cries. I felt like I was made for him. Or he was for me. I'd never fit with someone so perfectly before. Blackness fizzled around the edges of my vision by the time he pushed all the way inside.

"Breathe, Lainey. You with me?" I gasped an inhale just before his lips fell onto mine. Breathing. Yes. Oxygen. That was good. In and out. In and out. Just like how he was pumping back and forth inside. Stretching me, hitting the most perfect place. I was babbling, a mixture of his name and "please" and "oh my God" and "don't stop."

"Never. I'm going to fill you up. When you feel my cum leaking out of you tomorrow, you'll know you're mine. You want that, Sweetheart? I'll fuck you until you're full of me."

"Yes! Sam, I want it." Absolutely, God, yes, did I want it. Just like in my car, his words took on a stream-of-consciousness pattern, like his brain had disconnected a little and every word out of his mouth was the raw, unvarnished truth. It made me wild. I clutched at him, squeezing his fingers in mine, running my other hand down his flexing abdomen. His muscles were insane, popping while he thrust into me.

"Good. So good. Stay still. Right there." He dropped hectic, open-mouthed kisses on my face, sometimes landing on my mouth. The hand on my knee slid upwards, thumb teasing my clit as he shuttled in and out. "Come on my dick, baby. Fuck, the way you squeeze me." He kept talking, but I was gone. Eyes wide, head thrown back, weightless with a climax I could never have imagined. His praise, his dirty words, the way he touched me and moved with me...

Every muscle clenched. He groaned and told me how amazing I felt. So tight and hot and wet and then he was shouting, snapping his hips into mine as he came, saying how much he loved, loved, loved it. So good. And my name over and over and over.

He collapsed over me and we lay together like that, connected and panting. I stared up at the ceiling and tried to catch my breath. After a few moments, he raised up on his forearms, looking as stunned as I felt.

I didn't know what to say. Who had words for this kind of thing? My soul had left my body, and I wasn't sure when or if it would return. He swallowed, eyes searching my face.

He said my name again. Breathed it while the tips of his fingers trailed across my cheek. Hair. Forehead. Lips. I clutched him to me, threading my fingers through his hair. His forehead rested against mine.

When I finally returned to myself, stretching my toes and stroking up and down his spine, my body felt different. Or maybe it felt the same as always, and something else had shifted.

Either way, I felt changed, somehow. It didn't feel scary at all. It felt like I wanted to do it again.

Chapter 24

Sam

"You're never going to believe this."

"Hmm?" I looked up from flipping a grilled cheese. Lainey and I had stayed in bed well past noon. Both early risers, we'd kept commenting on it, how odd it was to still be horizontal after the sun was up. But inevitably, one of us would reach for the other and it would be another hour or so before we brought it up again.

Finally, we'd dragged ourselves downstairs for sustenance. I'd have kept her up there all day, but we were burning up a lot of calories. I had to feed her if I wanted her again later.

I'd suspected my crush on Lainey was intensifying the more time we'd spent together. Last night had blown straight past a crush and into let's go to a jewelry store and catch a flight to Vegas territory.

It wasn't just the sex—although, God Almighty the sex was phenomenal—it was the way she fit with me. Burrito bowls and workout sessions. How she looked in my t-shirts and did everything within her power to make me laugh.

I honestly felt a little too smug about it. The first time I'd ever seen her, our eyes had met over a patient's bed and she'd knocked my breath out.

That's the one, I'd thought to myself. *That's the one.* I'd been right.

So damned smug. The multiple orgasms and nail marks down my back only fueled the contented hum in my chest.

"My phone's blowing up. Is yours?" she asked, coming down the stairs in a pair of leggings. She'd stolen another one of my shirts. At this rate, I was going to have to buy more. *Worth it.*

"Mine's upstairs on silent. Something wrong?"

"Not wrong." She laughed, staring at her screen. "We're viral."

"What?" I tipped the sandwich onto a plate. I wasn't a viral type of guy.

"I'm serious, look!"

She peered over my shoulder while I watched the video of us and the nursing team dancing in the scrub room yesterday. Cedar had posted it on their Instagram channel. We were up to half a million views already.

"What..." I repeated.

She reached around me to press play again when the video stopped. In the second it took to reload, we racked up a few hundred more likes.

"This is..." I watched us two-step while the nurses did a little shuffle in the background. Video Sam spun Lainey. Video Lainey grinned.

"Crazy? I know! They're calling us the dancing doctors." She accepted her phone back, as well as the grilled cheese, still looking at the screen as she took a bite. "Who can blame them? You got mooooves, Reese. Where'd you learn to dance like that?"

"Lessons for my brother's wedding, remember?"

"Ah, right. He wouldn't let you lead. Bet you never thought they'd come in handy like this."

"It may have crossed my mind that women like dancing."

She hummed, looking up at me through her lashes. "Maybe with the right steps, you could convince said woman to come home with you. Hop into bed?"

"Nah." I leaned over to press a kiss into her cheekbone. "I don't watch documentaries with just anyone, you know."

We watched another episode while we ate. Got distracted during the next. Our phones lay, all but forgotten, on the counter. The more I had her to myself like this, the more I wanted. By the time dinnertime rolled around, I was completely enchanted, hanging on her every movement while she dabbed on makeup and swept her hair up. The sleeveless dress she had on showed off the freckled skin on the top of her shoulders.

I could barely keep my hands to myself on the drive to the restaurant, though my touch lingered on her back when I opened the door for her. The look she gave me told me to behave, while somehow also inviting me to come closer.

"Oh, my God! Aren't you the dancing doctors?" A voice snagged my attention away from Lainey's teasing eyes.

"Um..." I blinked, the woman in front of me whipping out her phone.

"Can I get a picture with you two? My friends and I have been texting about that video all day! Too cute." She held her phone up for a selfie, the screen showing her excited grin, my baffled face, and

Lainey's alarm-filled expression. I grabbed the phone, covering the camera with my palm as I lowered it.

"Sorry, not right now."

"Oh, I just—" The woman frowned, looking put out.

I didn't care if this woman wanted to take our photo, even though it was weird as fuck. She didn't know us, even if she had been texting about us with her friends. Also weird. If Lainey didn't want her picture taken, it wouldn't be.

"We'd like to keep a low profile, if you don't mind."

"We're, ah, here to discuss a patient case. HIPAA laws, you know?" Lainey chimed in. I frowned, not entirely sure what HIPAA had to do with our date, but it seemed to make sense to the woman, who nodded and went to sit back at her table after telling us to "keep up the good work and keep dancing!"

A few other patrons had turned to look at us while a dark-haired woman in an apron bustled to the front counter.

"Reese? Table for two?" she grabbed a pair of menus while surveying the restaurant. A few tables continued to stare. "I had you set up by the windows, but let me see if we can get you settled somewhere more private."

She led us to a booth in the back, partitioned off by a frosted glass panel. While I walked, I tried to wrap my brain around the fact that we needed any privacy to begin with. We had a viral video. How fucking bizarre.

"You two come and sit down now." She gathered a few plates and cups from the previous diners. "Just give me a second to get this out of your way."

"We're here to discuss a patient case," Lainey blurted, perching on the edge of the booth. The woman blinked, gathering a few napkins on top of the dishes she held.

She took in Lainey's dress and my sport coat, but didn't comment other than to say, "Discuss whatever you like. I'll be right back with some fresh waters for you."

"Oh my God," Lainey hissed, whipping her phone out and thumbing through apps. She buried her face in her hands, whispering, "Frack."

The video had ten million views. As her phone lay on the table, several texts and social media notifications pinged, mostly people congratulating her. She stared at it, forehead to palm, in horror, like it had turned into a snake. While I watched, a text from Jones popped up, asking her if she wanted to go out to celebrate.

"It's weird, but it'll be okay," I murmured, making a mental note to trip Jones the next time I saw him in the hallway. She flinched away when I raised my hand to stroke her arm.

"You cannot touch me in public." She went so far as to scoot a few inches over the booth. My hand dropped to my lap.

"Lainey, it's just a video on social media. It'll blow over." I didn't know this to be true, but it seemed right. Tomorrow, there'd be a video of a panda sneezing or something and everyone would go crazy over that.

She scoffed, falling silent the moment the dark-haired waitress reappeared with a basket of breadsticks and two waters. Lainey let out an audible breath when the woman left the booth.

"Hey," I coaxed, clenching my hands to stop myself from reaching for her. "Talk to me. What's going on?"

"It's not just a viral video. Rebecca Carmichael's daughter, the heart surgeon, going viral post-op won't just go away. Jesus, they're going to drag my mom into this..."

She crumbled, and the smug/happy/satisfied feeling I'd had all day deflated. I hadn't considered the implications of the video for her. Maybe she hadn't, either, until we'd been confronted head-on by a woman waving her camera in our faces.

"What if someone took a picture of us walking in here? What if it gets back to the hospital?"

I mentally retraced our steps from where I'd parked on the street into the building. I didn't recall anyone pointing a camera in our direction. Then again, I hadn't known to be on the lookout for something like that.

"I told you before, the hospital won't care."

"I'm a fellow. You practically run the fellowship program. You're leading the hiring committee for my next job. This will look awful."

I wasn't exactly in charge of the hiring committee anymore, but I hadn't decided when to bring that up with her, or how. Certainly not now. I glanced around the booth. Under any other circumstances it would have felt secluded. Cozy. Now, it felt like we were trapped.

"Could we ask them to take it down?" Something, anything to pump the brakes on some freak social media event that was spiraling quickly out of control.

"They have complete authority to use it. Our contracts have image and likeness clauses in them. My mom's lawyers fought to get them removed when I was a resident, but Cedar wouldn't budge."

"We could still ask."

"We can ask," she agreed, but she was shaking her head as if she didn't hold out much hope. I wasn't holding out much hope for the rest of my night with her, either. Her mother's face popped up on her phone, and I knew we were done.

"Crap. I have to take this. Do you mind getting the car?" Lainey lifted her phone with her fingertips, looking warily at her mother's face on the screen.

"You sure? You want to leave?" I didn't like the idea, but I hated her feeling uncomfortable even more.

"Yeah, sorry, I...yes...Hi, Mom, how are...no, I didn't see your calls, sorry. I was away from my phone."

I escaped the restaurant without much fanfare. When I pulled up to where she stood at the curb, she was still on her phone, looking distraught. She ducked into the car.

"Well, I don't appreciate you talking with my directors without my knowledge, Mom. No, I didn't intend for it to go viral. I didn't even take the video! One of the nurses must have sent it around and Cedar picked it up."

She nodded and muttered, "uh-huh" as I drove back to my place. I could hear snatches of her mother's voice coming through her speaker. Lainey crossed her legs and arms, clenched up.

"No, I don't need media training from your team again. This is going to blow over…Because I want it to blow over. I'm not making this any bigger than what it needs to be."

She shook her head, glaring out the window. "No. I'm not leaving the rest of my fellowship to do a media tour with you…Because it's my career and I want to finish what I started!" A massive sigh. "Taking me out of the OR would make me miserable…Well, tell Kathleen I'm not doing it. I'll give them a sound bite or a quote or something."

On and on her conversation went like that. She didn't make any moves to get out of the car when I pulled into the garage, so I sat with her while she tried to wind down the call. Her mom sounded excited. Lainey sounded like she'd rather drive a nail through her eye than contemplate more media exposure.

"Okay, that's fine. Have them email me whatever and I'll sign off on it…Yes, I'm sure. No interviews." Her mother's voice rose excitedly. I caught the words "Harvard" and "New York Presbyterian." Lainey's fingers clenched.

"No. My life is *here*. I don't want to move to the East Coast." She flung her hand out, dropping it into my lap. I wasn't sure she knew she'd done it, but I scooped her fingers up like they were a lifeline. Just a few hours ago she'd been wrapped around me, naked. Now I was just glad to have her hand. The night had taken a truly bizarre nosedive.

"I'm not leveraging a viral video that has nothing to do with my surgical training to get a job in a different state. I know I had help getting into Cedar the first time, but I can do this by myself now."

Her voice sounded steely. I couldn't really do anything for her except stroke my thumb over her hand, but I hoped it came across as supportive. I listened as she hurried her mom off the phone, promising to schedule a call with someone named Lawrence later tonight. She practically flung her phone into her bag when it was done.

"I feel like I should apologize." For what, I wasn't sure, but I knew for certain that the day was completely ruined and I'd had something to do with it.

"You have nothing to apologize for. Even whoever took that video and sent it to Cedar couldn't have foreseen this would happen." She leaned over the console, sliding her other hand up my leg.

"I'm sorry it ruined our date. I was looking forward to this all week. At least we had a good day together. Didn't we?" She fluttered her eyelashes. My gaze dropped to her mouth, remembering what she'd looked like on her knees...

"Yes." We'd had an excellent time together earlier today.

"I know *I* did." She smiled when our lips brushed. We'd been doing this almost nonstop for the better part of twenty-four hours. We'd gotten a rhythm down now. I knew when she wanted to tilt her head. She knew when I wanted to get deeper. It was heaven, kissing her.

"I was looking forward to an encore performance." I nodded towards the door, already planning how we'd salvage our night together. We'd start on the couch because I wasn't sure we'd make it to the bed, let alone the stairs.

"I wish I could," she groaned, giving me a few more pecking kisses. "But my mother's PR team is in a frenzy. I have to talk with her communications person to draft a statement they can give to the media. And NPR wants a sound bite in time for Morning Edition tomorrow. I'm just going to head home."

"NPR?"

She was already heading out of the car, checking her phone. I could see the screen lighting up with notifications all the way from here. Within minutes, she'd grabbed her bag from inside, loaded up her car, and was driving away.

I stood in my garage wondering what the fuck had just happened.

Chapter 25

Sam

There's nothing quite so ominous as getting called into your boss's office first thing on Monday after the girl of your dreams ghosted you over the weekend. It's even more nerve-wracking when you're stopped approximately every three feet by someone wanting to congratulate you or take a selfie. Our video hadn't just gone viral. We were everywhere. Global.

"Hey! Dancing Doctors!" An Ortho bro stopped to administer some complicated high-five, fist-bump combo I barely kept up with. A pair of nurses snapped a picture with me before I could stop them. I wasn't even at the elevator yet.

I opted for the stairs. I was sweating when I hit the tenth floor, but at least the trip had been quick, with limited interruptions.

"Reese! Man of the hour!" Caplan slid his phone into his suit pocket and clapped me on the back, steering me into his office, where I stopped short at the sight of Lainey's ghost-white face.

Another dozen faces also stared at me from Caplan's meeting table and the Zoom meeting projected on the large screen in his office. Lainey's mother grinned from one of the tiles, her face surrounded by people I'd never seen before.

"Dr. Reese! The other half of our dancing duo!" Caplan gestured around the table and up at the video call, listing out names or departments or affiliations. The people in the room seemed to represent the majority, if not the entire Cedar marketing department, while the folks on the call were all Dr. Carmichael's people. Sturmond, bafflingly, sat at the head of the table, overseeing the whole damned circus.

I practically fell into a chair, dazed, hardly able to take my eyes off of Lainey. It was the first time I'd seen her since she'd left me in my driveway. My texts yesterday had gone unanswered.

"Dr. Reese. Lovely to see you again! We were just putting a game plan together for how we can optimize this for both our benefits." Dr. Carmichael beamed, unaware that her daughter was about to toss her cookies onto the table.

"...our benefits?"

"We can hardly field all the media inquiries we're getting. CNN, The Times, MSNBC. We're swamped." One of the Cedar people across the table sounded like she was in ecstasy.

"CNN is calling you about the video?" I glanced around. That seemed unlikely, and I couldn't help but note that for a team overrun by media calls, we seemed to have a full house right fucking here, and no one was on the phone.

"Of course we're conducting some outreach on your behalf, to keep the conversations going." One of the Carmichael people smiled like a cat who got the canary.

"On my behalf?" I'd never met these people in my life. Based on the nods around the table, I wondered just how many calls these people had made.

A woman next to me shuffled some papers around in front of her. "You can imagine the opportunity this presents for Cedar. It's rare to get this kind of organic attention for our work. We all need to capitalize on it."

"The timing of this couldn't be better. We're just about to launch the new campaign we've been working on for the non-profit. Dr. Carmichael's daughter, having the time of her life celebrating a post-op success? It's perfect!" someone from the Zoom call chimed in. The name in his little square said Lawrence. He was looking at Lainey like he wanted to eat her for lunch. I immediately hated him.

They buzzed around me, a real enthusiasm orgy. Caplan grinned. Sturmond practically rubbed his liver-spotted hands together with glee. Everyone here was trying to spin this somehow, or monetize it. Everyone except me and Lainey, who had been conspicuously silent this whole time. She stared at her hands whenever I tried to make eye contact.

"Sorry...What's this?" Someone had shared a table on the screen that looked alarmingly like a schedule. A fully booked one, at that.

"Apologies, Dr. Reese, you're coming into this a bit late," one of the comms people tittered. "We've been working on this since yesterday. The key is to meet the media interest now, before other news crowds us out."

I'd already forgotten this girl's name, but I relegated her into the "Lawrence camp." Immediate no.

"These are all..." I peered at the screen up on the wall. "Media interviews? Caplan, I have a full slate of patient cases today, and Lainey is prepping for that bypass."

"You don't need to worry about this, Reese." Sturmond grinned. The fluorescent lights shone on his bald head, giving him the look of a sinister angel. "Dr. Carmichael will handle most of the interviews. It'll be a good showing from our best and brightest."

"I think I'm best suited to represent Cedar from inside the OR, where I'm using my training and education to serve patients." Lainey finally spoke up, jaw tense.

"Sweetie, you know we can't buy this type of publicity. For better or worse, you're my daughter. You're who people want to hear from. I mean, look at you. It seems like you love your work so much!" Dr. Carmichael's people all nodded enthusiastically as she spoke.

"I do love my work," Lainey gritted, though I doubted anyone else could see how frustrated she was. "As a surgeon. Not a publicist."

Everyone spoke over each other, trying to talk Lainey down. I only caught snippets like "just for a few days" and "back in action in no time." By the time the cacophony settled, it seemed like nothing Lainey had said made any difference. They began debating the interview schedule again.

Across from me, she curled up, arms crossed, staring at her lap.

"Dr. Carmichael is an integral part of this surgical team. You can't just remove her from her cases. Even temporarily." The PR people quieted, looking at each other. I wasn't sure if it was because she was Dr. Carmichael's daughter, or a woman, or what, but they seemed perfectly content to steamroll over her objections. Mine gave them pause.

"We have plenty of qualified residents, and fellows, who can take on Lainey's patients while she's away." Sturmond showed his teeth. So that was what he got out of all this; more OR time for his golden grandson.

"Reese, it's just a few days. We'll pull Lainey off her surgeries and make sure she still has time to check on patients in between interviews." Caplan tried to look soothing, but couldn't keep the smile off his face.

"I'd prefer not to transfer any of my surgeries right now. I'll make it work. But, I have to be candid here, I don't think this media campaign presents the right image for me." Lainey glared at the wood grain before her, weathering another eruption of denials and soothing words. "I'm not sure how this will look to my colleagues," she said in a raised voice, cutting them off. *That's my girl.*

"Interviews for a permanent position here are competitive. I don't like the optics of me doing all these media spots on Cedar's behalf right when something as big as my future at the organization is on the line."

"I think your future with the organization will be pretty secure by the time all this is done." Lawrence again, snickering. That fucker. Lainey finally looked up, searing him with her glare. He blanched and sat back from his camera.

"I know the way I got here was unorthodox." She glanced at Caplan, Sturmond, me. The ones who knew just how out of the ordinary it had been. "It's important to me to earn this next role on my own merit."

"Dr. Carmichael...Lainey, we accepted you into this fellowship program with zero hesitation. Your colleagues sing your praises. There's no doubt in my mind that a position here is yours, with or without this media blitz." Caplan patted his closed laptop as if it were the top of her head.

"But our organization also values team players, Ms. Carmichael. Your actions this week will tell us a lot about what we can expect from you in the future," Sturmond butted in.

"*Doctor* Carmichael." Lainey, her mother, and I corrected him all at once. He smirked without apologizing.

"What you can expect of me in the future is my full dedication to evidence-based, cardiothoracic surgery. Nothing more, nothing less." Lainey held his gaze. The half-smile on his face didn't budge.

***

"Holy shit." The door to Caplan's office closed behind me. I stared at the cheerful painting of daffodils in the hall and tried to wrap my head around what the fuck was happening. "Lainey, are you—"

She had already taken off, marching down the hall towards the elevators.

"Lainey, wait."

"I can't, Sam. If I slow down, I'll get mauled by a news anchor or something. I have to check my post-op patients, including Mrs. Singh, and start rounds with the residents before my eight back-to-back interviews that start in"—she glanced at her smartwatch—"forty-five minutes."

"Take a breath. It'll be alright."

"Ha! Easy for you to say. You're not the face of heart surgery for the next week," she growled, stabbing her finger at the elevator call button.

"It's just a few day—"

"That schedule had me booked for an interview in New York on Thursday. This is not just a few days. They're going to keep me out of the hospital for as long as media interest is there. And I'm going to miss out on OR time and get behind on my cases, just in time for these freaking attending interviews to really ramp up."

I held my tongue as we stepped into the elevator. I'd worked with her long enough to know anything I said right now would fall on deaf ears. But I wasn't just her colleague anymore. I reached for her the second the elevators closed.

"Sweetheart—"

"Cameras," she whispered, jerking out of my grasp. An ocean of industrial carpet opened up between us.

"Fuck the cameras, I need to know you're alright." But I stayed on my side of the elevator.

Teeth dug into her bottom lip. The same one I'd sunk my teeth into just two days ago. What the hell had happened? "I'm fine. I just need to ride this out and get to the other side. I can make it work." Her head bobbed. "We just can't be seen together like this."

"In an elevator?"

My weak attempt at a joke fell flat. "People saw us at dinner together on Saturday. What happens when they put two and two together?"

"We've worked with each other for years. No one will think twice if—"

"I can't risk it. Not right now. God, I want to puke. Just...just let me get through this, Sam."

The elevator doors opened, and she slid out. I stuck around long enough to hear Jones make a snide remark about how "well-timed" the video was, and then gloat about snagging her quad-bypass now that she was otherwise engaged with interviews.

As I made my way to the lockers to change (slowly, still interrupted every few steps by enthusiastic colleagues), I replayed her last words, over and over.

"Just let me get through this, Sam."

I couldn't help but think she meant something closer to, *"Just let me get through this without you, Sam."*

Chapter 26

Sam

"So, fame isn't all it's cracked up to be?"

I glared at Blake, taking a longer-than-necessary pull of my beer. Two days after the clusterfuck of a PR meeting and people were still cramming their phones in my face. I was a quiet guy. Private. I didn't love having someone stop me every two steps or yelling lyrics to *"Come and Get Your Love"* at me from across the street.

I assumed it was so much worse for Lainey, but I couldn't be sure. I hadn't seen her since she left me in the elevator. Our text messages and after-work phone calls were nonexistent.

"All the hype will die down soon." Blake did his best to sound optimistic. I'd been complaining to him about the ridiculousness of it all ever since we'd sat down. We'd gotten interrupted multiple times, turning down two selfie seekers and one guy who asked for my autograph, of all things.

I thought we'd be safer in a bar a few blocks from the medical district, surrounded by other doctors. But apparently, nowhere was safe.

"Not likely," I answered, slouched over our table. It was challenging to condense my 6'2" body onto a bar stool, but I was trying my damnedest. "Lainey's calendar is still full of interviews and she's supposed to be on her way to New York any minute now for some late night show thing."

Blake whistled. "I know it sucks, but I have to say, as someone heading up my department, I would do illegal things to get the kind of exposure Cedar's racking up."

Hence why all the madness had yet to die down. The Carmichael PR team was unstoppable, shamelessly using Lainey to plug a new cardiac care initiative for inner-city families. Meanwhile, Cedar was just as shamelessly riding their coattails.

Everywhere I looked, there was Lainey, talking about the importance of heart care or smiling at an interviewer while discussing her mother's foundation. The more articles that came out and media clips were generated, the more all of it snowballed a bit further out of control.

I had never realized a measly internet video could make such a splash, but the PR people were relentless. Between their new campaign, Carmichael's celebrity, and Lainey's beautiful face, suddenly it seemed like the whole country was thinking about heart surgery.

"And still no word from Lainey?"

"Nada. Which is the worst part." Another swig of beer didn't help mellow my agitation. This all might have been more manageable if she'd been around to commiserate with. Instead, I was on my own, trying to hide in the corner of a sports bar.

"I guess it's hard to talk to her when she's busy with the ladies of The View."

Had Lainey gone on The View? I hadn't caught that one. I needed to set up a fucking Google alert. According to Cooper, she was still keeping up with most of her patients, which I wasn't sure was physically possible, but who was I to question the Great Lainey Carmichael?

"Just let me get through this, Sam." I drained my beer, setting it down before moving on to the full pint glass sitting beside it. It paid to be prepared.

"They were doing a segment on good news, or something. She was great," Blake chimed in again, oblivious to how badly I wanted to bang my head against the table.

She *was* great at this stuff. Charming and smooth. She tied in some good plugs for Cedar and her mother's charity. In one of the morning show interviews today, she'd also mentioned that she and I were "great friends," which I'm sure was just because that's what someone told her to say, but it felt like one more nail in the coffin.

I'd admired Lainey from afar ever since we'd met, but over the last six weeks I'd gotten closer to her than I ever dreamed of. Even while she hesitated about committing fully to our relationship (who could blame her with her history?), she let me coax her out of her shell more and more as the days went on.

I'd always known she was charming, but she was also caring and thoughtful. She claimed she didn't do relationships, but she'd already adopted my family and friends as if they were her own. With every inch she gave me, I wanted a mile. And now I had nothing.

"Listen, man, if you're going to sulk this whole time, that's fine. I'll just watch the game."

I pinned Blake with another glare. Wasn't this supposed to be one of my best friends? Where was the support? I knew I should have gone to Molido's.

He shrugged off my angry look. "Tough love, buddy. You can sit here and mope all day, or you can grab your balls and call her. Talk to her about it."

"She basically told me to stay away from her, Blake. I don't think blowing up her phone was what she had in mind."

"Seems like she's getting put through the ringer even more than you are. Maybe she'd appreciate knowing you still have her back." He clapped me on the shoulder. "But what do I know? I've never gone viral before. I've also never dated quite this far out of my league. You're breathing rarefied air, over there."

"I just wish I knew where her head was at." Friday had been perfect. Saturday was a dream. All my hard work had paid off. All those lunches, quiet moments stolen in the hallways, and morning workouts had led to that one, perfect day, when I'd finally felt like I had every piece of her, not just the flashes she allowed other people to see. But then her cold shoulder after the PR meeting had pulled the rug out from under me.

I thought she'd felt it, too. That closeness. Intimacy that had nothing to do with sex. But maybe I'd been wrong.

"No time like the present to ask." Blake nodded towards the doors where Lainey made her way through the crowd to us. A few people stopped her to chat or take pictures. She obliged, but she was stiff, smile tight.

My feet hit the floor before I realized I'd slid off the stool.

"Aren't you supposed to be on a plane right now?" I asked when she finally made her way to our table. She shook off my offer of a stool, swiping my beer.

"No. No travel. I had to put my foot down. I'm running myself ragged over here." She chugged the IPA, downing about half of it before slamming it on the table. Foam sloshed over the side.

"We're going to need more beer," Blake muttered, trying to flag down a harried server. I was less concerned for my backup beer and more concerned about Lainey. Her usually riotous curls were sticking out from her surgical cap, which I wasn't sure she knew she was still wearing. Dark circles couldn't hide under the thick makeup rimming her eyes.

"You're not going to New York?" I couldn't help the hope rising in my chest. I was so damned happy to see her face in person, instead of on a screen.

"No New York. I couldn't..." She picked the beer up before putting it back down without drinking. "Caplan canceled all my clinical work for next week. Completely cleared my calendar without even consulting me."

"Definitely need more beer." Blake peered around the bar while I frowned down at Lainey.

"What do you mean, *all* your clinical work?" That couldn't be right. Cooper was slammed through August. No way would the department just release her from work right at the home stretch of her program.

"No surgeries, no rounds. I had to hand all my patients over to Jones. My time is apparently more valuable speaking to the media than it is in the OR."

"What the fuck?" Blake blurted. Lainey looked at him as if she'd just realized he was there.

"I. Know." She shook her head at him. "I tried to talk them out of it, but they steamrolled me. And Sturmond is over there spouting off his nonsense about me being a team player. He basically came out and said that if I did these interviews, I'd get a job. Can he even do that? You're the one in charge of the interviews."

I side-stepped the question. Now was most definitely not the time to get into my new role in the interviews. "That makes no sense. You need to go to Whitaker." I looked around for someone to give me a check. I could close out my tab now, walk over to Cedar, grab the fellowship director, and shake some sense into him myself.

"He was in the room, Reese!" My heart stuttered. *Reese*. She didn't seem to notice. "He said he supported the whole thing. Apparently, the hospital has been flooded with donors all week. The Gates Foundation called Caplan to talk about some sort of fellowship grant, or something. They said there's a chance I could be sidelined until the end of my program."

She buried her face in her hands. I wanted so badly to reach out and touch her, to wrap my arms around her, but I didn't dare.

Blake whistled. "That sucks. Seriously. At least there's one upside to working for a blacklisted program. The board doesn't dare tell us what to do. We're understaffed, as-is."

Lainey raised her head to look at him. I got a sick feeling when I saw the gears in her head turning. "For real?"

Blake nodded, still searching for a waiter. "Absolutely. They're so desperate to rebuild, we have nothing left to lose. They pretty much let us do whatever, as long as it's legal. If this happened at Mercy, you could totally tell them to fuck off."

She stared at him for another moment, eyes glazed yet focused at the same time. I could see where this was heading. I opened my mouth to say something, but she beat me to it. "And procedures? What about new or experimental surgeries?"

"You kidding? They can't get enough of them. They're hoping we can remake a name for ourselves by being more innovative. We're taking that LVAD that Cooper couldn't get approval on."

"Mercy is letting us do the LVAD?" she gasped, eyes lighting up like it was Christmas. Her excitement finally registered with Blake. He whirled on her like a shark smelling blood in the water.

"Just Cooper. It was Sam's idea, actually. We're calling it a training procedure so our team can watch. Can't do that with fellows. Now, if you were on staff with us, though..." He trailed off, dangling the bait. Lainey bit her lip, wavering for only a second before anger and resolve slid like a hard mask over her face.

"Are you interviewing? Can you get me in?"

Blake laughed so loudly that the patrons who'd lost interest in our table stared. "No interview necessary. Name your price."

"No, I want to do this the right way. All the right channels. I'm not saying I'm coming to Mercy, but I'll at least check it out."

They set up an interview then and there while I glared around for our missing server. You'd think going viral would at least help me get a beer. Blake pocketed his phone, beaming. He sobered up quickly when he saw my face.

"I'll go up for another round. This one's on me." He hoofed it to stand in line at the bar before I could respond. Like buying me a beer would make up for trying to poach Lainey.

"What?" She toyed with the empty glass on the table, finally sliding onto the stool I'd vacated for her. She looked somewhat calmer, now that she'd orchestrated a big fuck you to Cedar with this Mercy interview.

I shrugged, glancing over at the game. Cubs were up by two. Huh.

"You look like you want to murder someone. It's just an interview. I'm allowed to explore my options." She crossed her arms.

"It's well within your rights to interview with other institutions." I sounded like I was reading from an employee handbook. Funny how for the last few days, all I'd wanted was to talk to her, but here she was now and I couldn't bring myself to make eye contact.

"But? You're worried we won't see as much of each other if I work somewhere else?" In fact, yes, that thought had crossed my mind. I was glad to know it had crossed hers, too. Maybe there was hope for us, yet. "I'd probably get off most nights and weekends. And Mercy is just down the street. We could meet for lunch."

She wasn't wrong, but the source of my frustration wasn't that she was taking an interview at Mercy. "Too far away to worry about now." I reached for a coaster, sliding my knuckles across hers with the movement. "I'm sorry about the media stuff. It's ridiculous for them to sideline you."

She stared at her hand. I wondered if she could still feel the tingling rush from where our skin touched, like I could. "Thank you. Maybe...maybe it'll only be for another week? This will all die down just in time for the final attending interviews."

"Maybe." Hopefully. This video had effectively derailed all my plans—at least for the time being. The sooner it vanished into the social media ether, the better. If only the PR people would just give it a rest.

"Are you okay? You look...sad or something." Her pinky brushed mine. I sighed. Her thighs had been wrapped around my head for a full thirty minutes last weekend, and now I was settling for a centimeter's worth of contact. I was indeed *sad or something*.

"This has all been weird." Understatement of the year. What I wanted to say was that she felt like sand slipping through my fists, and I couldn't do anything about it. But that was too much to put on her when she was already dealing with losing her surgical roster. Not to mention, we weren't even technically dating.

Understanding and guilt washed over her face. She leaned closer, wrapping her hand around mine. Bold move, considering she'd practically leaped down an elevator shaft last time I tried to touch her. I opened my fingers to clasp hers.

"Sam, I'm so sorry. I've been so wrapped up in all this, I didn't stop to think how hard this must be on you, too. Obviously. God, I'm the worst. Are you alright?"

"I only had to give one or two quotes. You're the one doing the legwork."

"I am sure it's been hard on you, too. Especially if you've been accosted in the street as much as I have." I felt her peering up at me, but couldn't bring myself to look back. Now that she was in front of me, the hurt and confusion I'd been grappling with all week morphed into unshakable irritation. She had just left me high and dry for days, and now she wanted to come back like nothing had happened?

Her thumb stroked my knuckles. "Seriously, what's wrong? Is it just the publicity stuff? Are you mad I'm interviewing at Mercy?"

"No, that's not the problem." I cleared my throat, finally meeting her eyes. The way she looked at me reminded me of that first morning in the parking lot at R^3. Aware. Actually seeing me, instead of just looking. Maybe Blake was right, and I needed to be more open with her. I owed her my honesty.

"I wish we'd had some time to debrief when all this went down. You flew out of that meeting and pretty much ordered me not to talk to you." I cracked a smile, aiming for a joke. Her fingers froze on my forearm. "I thought we were on the same page, but now I'm not sure where we stand. I mean, I haven't heard from you since Sunday."

She removed her hand altogether, staring down at the table in front of her.

An uncharacteristic urge to fill the silence welled. "I know you have a lot more on your plate with this than I do—"

"I told you I was bad at this." She blinked up at me, eyes liquid. "I'm the worst, Jesus. You're right, I just...*left* you and acted like a complete moron. I wasn't...I'm only used to thinking about myself. It's inexcusable. Sam, I'm sorry." She sniffed.

"Do not cry, Honey, please." I didn't know if I could take it if she did. Her pain amplified mine. Made me feel even worse. "It's okay."

"It's not okay. I'm a self-centered idiot." She swiped her hand across her forehead, her eyes looking more watery by the second. "I didn't even think to ask about you in all this. I...I didn't think about *you*."

There was something about that statement that threw me back into uncomfortable oatmeal memories, but she looked so remorseful—beautiful and remorseful—that I reached over to cover her hand with mine. I paused, hovering over her fingers. "I'd like to touch you. Is that alright? Here?"

The question sent a single tear down her cheek. She swiped it away quickly, swallowing. "That you even have to ask..."

"You're in control here, Lainey. You always have been. You told me you were worried someone might see us together in public."

Her face tensed like she was tasting something bitter. "In the interview today, I told them we were friends. So hopefully...no one will think anything if they see us together."

Her hands were cold, despite the warm day outside. "So, you were thinking about me, after all."

"Only...only in the future sense. Like how I can just get this behind us so that we can go back to..."

"Dating," I supplied for her when she faltered. "I think we're past the trial period."

She snorted. "I guess. If you still even want me."

Oh, Sweetheart. Don't you see? "I do."

"Even though I ruined our amazing weekend and yelled at you in an elevator and haven't spoken to you for days? Crap, I'm the *worst*." The last bit was so quiet, as if she was whispering it to herself, before straightening up. "I can do better, Sam. I promise. Being in a relationship has to be like riding a bike, right?"

"You are a very quick study." My shoulders relaxed a few degrees at her hopeful expression.

"I am. I'm sorry. I just—between the interviews and my patients and my mom and now *this*. I'm not...used to having to think about other people. Which sounds horrible when I say it out loud. Especially to you."

"Why especially to me?" I wanted to hold her. Wrap my arms around her, kiss her hair, and wipe that wrecked, self-conscious pout off her face. I felt like I could breathe for the first time in days.

"You care about everyone. All the time. I must seem like a monster."

"I don't think you're a monster."

"I'll do better," she repeated, clenching her fingers in mine like we were shaking on it. "I promise. I'm sorry."

"If you apologize one more time, you're buying the next round."

She jumped to her feet. "I can do that! I can get the next!"

"I was joking, sit! Sit." I waited until she settled back on the stool. Her fingers rolled a coaster back and forth across the table as she glanced around us. We'd collected a few stares when she'd come in, but everyone had lost interest, going back to their drinks.

"So, we're good? Because I want us to be good. I want this, Sam."

"We're good, Honey." We sat in silence for a moment longer. Blake had just made his way to the front of the long line at the bar. The waitress was maybe lost forever. A thought occurred. "How'd you know I'd be here?"

"Hmm?"

"You came in here like you were looking for me. How'd you know I was here?"

"Ah." She scraped an old sticker off the table with her thumbnail. "I, uh, looked at your location. From your phone. You shared it with me, remember?"

"You looked at my location." It was probably stupid how happy that made me, but I'd spent the last few days worrying about how she felt about me and now she was right here apologizing and tracking my phone. I'd take it.

"I actually...kind of...look at your location a lot." More scraping. I bit my cheek to hide the grin that wanted to take over my face.

"Stalker?"

"It might be a problem." She looked at me, so seriously, so shamelessly, a laugh cracked out of me before I could wrangle it back down.

"Lainey." I leaned in close, catching a whiff of her clean vanilla scent for the first time in days. "I know your weekly schedule by heart."

"So, you're not going to call the cops on me? If we both stalk each other, it cancels out?" Her lips were pink, bitten, like she'd been chewing on them all day. I wanted to lick them.

"Something like that."

"I thought we weren't getting touchy-feely in public?" Blake set three beers down. I stepped away from her. I hadn't realized how close we'd gotten. Dangerous, tempting girl.

We managed to keep ourselves at a respectable distance, but Blake smirked every time Lainey or I brushed against the other, which we made excuses to do more often than was natural. She beat me back to my place from the bar and was pulling me out of the car before the garage door had even closed behind me.

Chapter 27

Lainey

Being banned from the OR was torture. For the next week, I was plagued by back-to-back Zoom interviews with various media personalities. Any time I thought the meetings were drying up, my mother's team hit me with another wave of calendar invites, another angle to discuss, another topic to comment on to bring myself, and the foundation, into the national spotlight.

The only good thing about the clinical hiatus was the copious amount of free time I had on my hands. Plenty of opportunities to hang around with a certain someone who I felt needed a bit more of my attention than I'd been giving.

I kept a wary eye on Sam whenever we were together, still shamed by how thoughtlessly I'd disregarded him when everything with the video had gone down. No matter how much I looked, I couldn't find any trace of ill feelings from him. Sam was his usual self: quiet, content, cuddly.

Initially, I came up with excuses to see him. The Wi-Fi was better at his house, so could I do my interviews from his home office during the day? On my way back from a downtown broadcast studio, I was starving and happened to pass by his favorite pizza place. Did he want to split one? After a few days, I realized he didn't need my excuses, so I stopped giving them.

He was always just happy to be with me, no matter what we did or how I ended up at his place. Somehow, this just sank the guilt-knife deeper. Despite our power dynamic on paper, Sam had let me call the shots on us since day one.

When I wasn't ready to date, we trialed. Before I'd said something, he hadn't texted me until I initiated. When I told him I needed space, I got it.

It was all a humbling reminder: it wasn't just me I had to think about anymore. Sam might let me set the pace, but he was an equal partner in this relationship. Thank God he hadn't been shy about telling me when he had a problem. It was nice to know that he wouldn't allow me to exploit his kindness, but I had to meet him halfway. As we spent more time together the following week, I made a promise to myself not to take him for granted.

His porch became my home base, and Sam and I lingered there as often as we could, chatting with Jas and Conner, or cozying up together after dinner. Tess came over for a girls' night take two, where we consumed almost as much wine as our first girls' outing.

I didn't remember how I'd filled my days before I had Sam and his family and Tess and Rija around. They rallied around me. Rija cussed up a storm when she recounted just how many surgeries Jones was leading. She assured me that the nursing staff had planned a revolt.

As the week wore on and the hype around the Dancing Doctors dissolved, we grew more confident that the viral video storm was blowing over. The PR teams were grasping at straws for interviews now, and those Zoom meetings were getting fewer and fewer. Sam even drove me to the gym the next Thursday night for a class, going out of his way to park in the *exact spot* my car had been parked that first night he'd put his mouth on me. Cheeky.

I was so busy teasing him about it, I didn't pay enough attention when I walked into the gym and almost smacked right into Katie McDaniels. Only Sam's arm around my middle stopped me from falling. He pulled me against him to steady me, letting go the second he registered who stood in front of us.

"Oh." Katie stared. We stared back, Sam's body radiating heat behind me. "I should have asked the name of your brother's gym, so this didn't happen." She lowered her voice. "I swear, I just looked up gyms around here, and this one had good reviews. One of them said sometimes there's kickboxing here. And that the owner will modify workouts for...." She trailed off, her fingers grazing her belly.

"Um. Mrs. McDaniels?" Will held out a credit card and a receipt, quirking his brow at us.

"It's *Doctor* McDaniels." Jasmine waddled from the back office. She and Will exchanged a look. In an instant, his features flattened. His charming customer-service smile disappeared. Jasmine leaned against the desk. "Good to see you again, doctor." Jas's smile conveyed only the bare minimum level of politeness.

Katie flushed as she glanced between all the Reeses, who were doing a heck of a job icing her out. Even Sam stood rigid, his usually easy going demeanor evaporating into the air.

"I really was just looking for a gym. I didn't know...I should go."

"No, it's fine." Katie stopped short at my words. Honestly, I had shocked myself. But looking around at all my allies made me feel magnanimous.

Jas was sucking her teeth. Across the gym, Tess's brow furrowed from the warm-up mats. Will probably didn't even know what the heck was going on and here he was, arms crossed, giving Katie the evil-eye. And Sam...Sam was helping me close a wound I'd thought had healed years ago.

It felt right to have his calm, quiet presence beside me. Correct and necessary in a way I'd never felt before. It felt strong. *I* felt strong.

Katie's betrayal would always sting, but standing here now, faced with a situation that would have featured in my worst nightmares just a few weeks ago, I realized I'd allowed her and Nate to dictate how I lived my life and what I thought I deserved for too long. Frankly, I was tired of defining myself and my worth based on their crappy actions.

The thought cracked something open in my mind. In an instant, the person in front of me wasn't Kate, the woman who'd cheated with my boyfriend for months. She was just Katie, seemingly overwhelmed and a little nervous.

"It's fine," I repeated. "You already paid. Will puts on a great class. You should stay." I eyed the Reeses around me. "Shouldn't she?"

They grudgingly mumbled an affirmative, which made me want to sweep them all up into a group hug. Katie still looked like she was mentally halfway out the door, hand gripping the strap of her bag. I felt an unexpected pang of empathy. There was a time when I was also new to this town with no clue who to trust. I was familiar with the feeling of being surrounded by potential enemies.

"Come on. I'll show you around."

Awkward wasn't a strong enough word to describe the next hour. I introduced Katie to Tess, whose smile turned rigid when she shook Katie's hand. Her eyes darted to mine, widening for a second when Katie turned away. I tried to look as reassuring as possible. This was fine. It was *fine*.

And it was. Katie kept to herself for most of the class, only asking Tess a few questions here and there. At my request, Will graciously agreed to work in a kickboxing warm up, modified for Katie's growing tummy.

Any time I found my attention drifting to where she was, a quick scan of the room reminded me I had friends here. She was the one intruding on my life; I didn't have to run scared. *I didn't have to be defined by her actions.* The thought was freeing. Revolutionary. Despite the strained, clumsy energy around our group, I was practically bouncing by the end of the hour.

"Good work, everyone. Carmichael, next time you take drugs before class, make sure to bring some for everyone." Will glared at me while I grinned.

"Seriously, can I have whatever you're having?" Jas grumbled, bouncing on a yoga ball behind the front desk. "I can't believe how chipper you are while *she's* here." She threw an evil-eye across the gym as Katie packed up her water bottle and towel.

"It's not that bad." I only hesitated a second before reaching out to rub Jasmine's shoulder. "You're a good friend, Jas."

"I know." She winked. "You are, too. Speaking of, as soon as this baby pops out, please tell me we can go to Molido and convince Tiago to make us some margaritas."

Sam leaned on the desk beside me, whistling. "Make sure you know what you're signing up for. He makes them strong. Lethal, even."

"I'm in. We'll get Tess in on it, too. I hope you're down for a good time," I told Jas, eyeing Sam. "Tequila makes me a little wild."

He took the bait, looking me up and down, hungry. "Very interested to see what wild looks like on you." I leaned into him without thinking about it, loving the way he wrapped his arm around me, stroking up and down my spine. Jas pretended to gag, and I was sure we looked like little emojis with hearts for eyes.

But I didn't care. That little voice screaming for me to slow this down had quieted to hardly a whisper. One I could usually silence by turning over in bed to cuddle under Sam's arm. He always let me in. His fingers would stroke the skin at the top of my thigh, or the curve of my butt, and it was like a mute button for my insecurities.

"Oh, um, sorry. I just wanted to say...um..." Katie trailed off when Sam drew back.

"I'm gonna go check on Conner," he muttered, walking away woodenly. I cursed myself for getting swept up in the moment and forgetting that someone from our hospital was here. We'd been so careful in public, but the gym felt like a sacred space. It lulled me into a false sense of security.

It didn't help we'd been spending so much time together at his house that I'd gotten used to how he touched me constantly. Gotten used to it and discovered how much I loved it. Like, ate it up. I felt like he couldn't get enough of me either. For someone who'd only had a few dalliances here and there for the last few years, I soaked up the attention, starved for it.

"I didn't mean to interrupt." She tracked where Sam was disappearing into the physical therapy half of the building, separated by frosted glass panels and a pony wall. Despite putting on my biggest big girl panties earlier tonight, seeing her watch him made me want to snap my fingers in front of her face, or grip her ear and wrench her eyes away. Instead, I pulled harder on my proverbial panties.

"Ah, you weren't. He's just...ah...a good friend."

"I can see that." Katie's eyes twinkled. I pointedly did not look at Jasmine, who I'm pretty sure was scowling.

"You wanted to tell me something?" I changed the subject, wary of engaging my ex-best friend in a discussion about the man I was quickly falling head over heels for. Our track record wasn't great there.

"I just wanted to say thank you. If I were you, I don't think I'd be able to be so, um, gracious." She chuckled, surveying the gym. "It's too bad. This place is pretty killer. But it's probably best if I don't come back. I'll tell Nate to steer clear, too."

The idea of seeing him around, or even both of them, wasn't great, but it didn't seem as horrible as it had a few weeks ago. I was even starting to make peace with the fact that I might have to work with Nate. It wouldn't be ideal, and I still didn't want them near my personal life, but Katie and I could do this. Civil. No tears.

"Anywhere else I need to avoid?" she asked. "I've been dying to try the coffee shop next door. Please don't tell me it's off-limits."

I nearly laughed out loud, trying to picture Tiago's reaction if he knew who Katie was and our history. We'd only hung out a few times, but I got the sense he'd ride into battle for me, if need be, just because of Sam. "The owner is Sam's best friend. So..."

Her face fell before she recovered with a self-deprecating laugh. "Wow, you're calling dibs on the good gym *and* the good coffee shop? Ice cold."

"I think I deserve them both, under the circumstances." I grinned, easing the sting of the barb that I couldn't help but throw her way. My big girl panties were only so big, after all.

"Of course. I obviously didn't mean...I mean, of course." She tucked a strand of hair behind her ear, fidgeting. "It's nice to see that you have this life here. I was worried about that when you left. These people love you, and I'm glad. You deserve it."

Her head tilted to the frosted glass where we could make out Sam's shadow as he talked with Conner. "It's not like that," I rushed. Some of my alarm must have shown on my face because Katie gave me a soft smile.

"It's okay. The heart wants what the heart wants. Trust me, I'm not a stranger to that," she drawled, dryly. "I just want you to be happy, Lainey. I'm glad you seemed to have found that here. Your secret's safe with me."

I replayed the conversation again and again that night, searching for some hint of malice or shiftiness. I came up with nothing.

Maybe she was being sincere, and didn't care that Sam and I were flouting hospital rules. But I didn't know how her husband would feel about all this, or if he'd be petty enough to slip that information to the right person at the right moment to edge me out of the interview process.

I kept my worries to myself. Sam would probably do something like go to HR to try and head off the threat, and I wasn't sure I was ready for something like that.

Things felt like they were too delicately balanced to risk it. Not right now, when I hadn't seen the inside of an OR in a week. So, we made chicken piccata and drank beer on his porch and I worried about it constantly in my brain, all night long. Even my Sam mute button didn't work.

I wanted to believe Katie, I really did, but they'd already screwed me over once to get what they wanted. Who's to say they wouldn't again?

Chapter 28

Lainey

Blake didn't waste any time. That Friday, after finishing the rest (and hopefully the last) of my media interviews and catching up on my patient notes from Sam's couch, I wandered the halls of Mercy while he gave me the song and dance.

I'd accepted his offer of an interview somewhat on a lark. My blood had been boiling, pushed too far for too long by Cedar's board. Taking an interview with a failing hospital seemed like the ultimate smack in the face for such a prestigious institution. What did it matter, I'd thought, when I wasn't going to end up at Mercy, anyway? If taking another interview made me feel in control of an uncontrollable situation, so be it. The trouble was, this failing hospital didn't seem to be failing so much.

The campus was nothing as flashy as Cedar's new digs. The yellowish linoleum floors had cracks here and there, and the gray walls had a few scuffs, but the halls felt homey and well-kept. Everywhere we went, people smiled. Patients, doctors, everyone. It wasn't that we were constantly scowling at Cedar, but all these friendly faces made me realize the Cedar staff ran around pretty harried and self-important most of the time. Blake gave me a rueful grin when I mentioned the contrast.

"The issues with the board were a big wake up call for everyone here. Good opportunity to reconsider our values. All our directors teamed up to develop a new value and mission statement. Our nursing leaders are spearheading our 'People First' campaign. The patients like it. It's a refreshing way to practice."

I'd seen signs about "people first" all over the hospital. I'm pretty sure there was even a billboard outside, promising to put patient and provider well-being over profits. Cedar did stuff like that all the time, but it always seemed like lip-service. This actually seemed, dare I say, legit.

The cardiac unit left a lot to be desired. The fallout of the board's corruption had hit them the hardest, and it showed, but I noticed that while there were abandoned beds here and there, medical staff were actively attending to the patients in occupied ones. I marveled at a young surgeon who seemed to be personally overseeing post-op procedures. At Cedar, we usually left that for the residents or the NPs.

"Dr. Hadley, meet Dr. Carmichael. Hadley's my right hand. This place would crumble without him."

"THE Dr. Carmichael?" The surgeon shook my hand after emerging from the patient's room. His dark fingers enveloped mine.

"Oh, please. THE Dr. Carmichael is my mother. Just Doctor is fine."

He laughed, shaking my hand slightly longer than was necessary. "I thought he was joking when he said he landed an interview with you. I've been following your research on hemodynamic optimization for LVADs for a while. Practically binged the article you wrote for *Circulation* last year with your preliminary findings."

"Hadley is scrubbing in with Cooper for the LVAD next week. Dr. Carmichael was supposed to assist on that case at Cedar."

"You're familiar with the patient?" Hadley practically waggled in his sneakers. "Do you mind me asking what your research suggests for longer-term synchronization with the device? She's an active woman. We want this to go as smoothly as possible for as long as it can."

He asked me smart questions, not that I expected any different. He was a heart surgeon, after all, just like me. Or perhaps I *had* expected something different. Maybe I'd drunk the Cedar Kool-Aid and imagined myself as superior.

It felt a bit odd to explore another program's inner workings after being at Cedar for so long. Weird and surprising yet equally shocking that I didn't totally hate what I saw. The ORs were outdated, but Blake assured me the team was working on several fundraisers to help support renovations over the next few years.

"It'll be helpful to get some high-profile cases for that. I mentioned it at the bar last week, but we're pushing to bring more innovation in-house. Better doctors, more curiosity, and bigger surgeries."

That, too, didn't seem like lip service. There was an energy about the place. A pleasant hum compared to the low-level buzz I was used to at Cedar. But even a nice hum wouldn't draw me away from my hospital, and Blake knew it.

After I breezed through a few softball interview questions in his office, he considered me from his patched leather chair. "Listen, I'm sure this is just a revenge interview or something, and it's going to break my heart when you say no, but I'd like you to meet a few more folks here. I can put together an offer in the meantime and just see what you think."

"That's nice, really, but—"

"I know, I know. You're killing it over at Cedar and this place probably looks dinky as hell in comparison. But I like what you and Cooper are doing over there. Everyone does. We could use a mind like yours on the team."

"If you really want to draw something up, I'll look. But Cedar's been the goal since med school." As soon as the words popped out of my mouth, I wasn't sure that was true anymore. I'd transferred my residency there simply because I knew it had been Nate's dream, and I was petty enough to grab it after what he'd done to me.

It didn't hurt that it was one of the top cardiac programs in the nation. Somewhere along the way, I'd convinced myself that if I couldn't have the life I wanted in Texas, at least I could have Cedar. But was that really true?

I walked back through Mercy's halls, taking in the cheerful artwork and smiling faces. The salary range Blake had just quoted rang in my ears.

"And that's really just a starting point," he'd assured me, no doubt mistaking the shock on my face for disappointment. "I'm sure I can talk the board up. We're throwing money at good surgeons these days. Invest in the people and the program will follow."

"People first," I'd muttered, still too shocked to respond to the outlandish figure.

I hadn't even asked about the salary at Cedar. I'd just assumed it would be better than what I was being paid now. Maybe that was my problem: I'd just *assumed* everything would get better once I moved through the ranks. Once I moved to Chicago or landed the fellowship or, or, or.

How much of my life had I been living on autopilot? Were there any parts of me that weren't shaped by what two stupid people had done together a few years ago? Had I just pointed myself in this direction, closed my eyes, and hoped for the best?

For the past few days, the thought I had at the gym has been coming back to me, and now it fluttered in my mind again. *I don't have to be defined by their actions.*

There was at least one thing in my life that hadn't been a reaction to the McDaniels. His face popped into my head and I changed lanes, diving headlights-first into brutal Friday evening traffic. I'd planned on staying at my place tonight, which Sam hadn't pressed.

I didn't relish the idea of leaving the porch and leather couch and *him* behind in favor of my somewhat lifeless apartment, but we'd spent every night together for a week. I assumed he needed a break.

The interview with Blake hadn't gone as planned, though. Now, a whole different lane of life opened up for me, an exit I never realized was an option before. It felt scary, shaking up the clear-cut path I'd laid out for myself.

In the wake of those smiling faces and the amazing offer, I didn't know what it meant for me, or Cedar. But at least I knew where I wanted to go right this second. Sam's condo and my happy-place-porch were calling my name.

*****

"When you said you were going to Conner's for dinner, I thought you meant something normal," I accused, my eyes darting around the kitchen.

Sam had been surprised, but happy, to see me. He'd whisked me across the courtyard to Conner and Jas's place to eat.

"This is normal."

This was not normal. Granted, I'd never been inside their home before, but I was very sure that the colorful streamers and balloons hanging from the light fixtures weren't every day decor.

"Sam? Why is your family having dinner here tonight?" He'd mentioned family dinner a few minutes ago, but I'd been too distracted sucking his face to pay too much attention.

Between the good but disorienting interview at Mercy and the unnerving realization that Sam was the first thing I'd really chosen for myself in years, I'd needed a little TLC. He'd been happy to oblige, but had drawn the line at hiking my skirt up like I'd asked.

"*Later*," he'd said, and I was too dazzled by his kisses to ask any further questions. I should have asked some freaking questions.

Now, I was standing in Conner and Jas's empty kitchen, a cacophony of voices and sounds filtering from the dining room. A twist of red paper streamers flapped lazily where someone had taped it across the mantel.

"Conner's birthday," Sam responded, digging around in a drawer for a pen. He scrawled something on the bottle he was holding, chucking the Sharpie back just as Jas rounded the corner.

"Hey, sketchballs. Party's in the dining room, stop creepin'. Sam and Lainey are here!" she shouted. Cheers drifted from the open doors to the other room. My heels dragged on the floor when Sam pushed me towards the sound.

"Samuel," I'd never used his full name before, but the night I unknowingly crashed a family party seemed like as good a time as any to start. "I cannot invite myself to Conner's birthday," I hissed as he propelled me forward.

"You didn't invite yourself. I invited you."

"I don't *do* birthdays. I don't even know Conner that well." Out of all the Reeses, he was the most foreign to me. We'd had a few interactions here and there, like over tacos and at the gym. Nothing that was I'm-coming-to-your-birthday-dinner-worthy.

"What do you mean, you don't *do* birthdays?"

I glared at him, ignoring how cute he sounded, mimicking my inflection back to me. "I didn't even bring a gift!"

"Didn't you?" With that cryptic remark, he gave one last push that slid me into the dining room, handing Conner the bottle in his hands. "Happy birthday, brother. For you."

"Thanks, Sammy. This is ni—holy shit!" His eyes widened, flickering from Sam to me. "This is too much."

"Don't drink it all at once." Sam clapped his brother on the back, moving to greet Eli and June, who were orchestrating some sort of dinosaur/truck battle at the end of the table.

"Thank you, Lainey. I'm glad you could make it." I snuck a peek at the bottle in his hand when Conner wrapped an arm around me. On the label, scrawled in Sam's almost illegible script, it said, "35 for 35. Happy Birthday, from Sam & Lainey"

I didn't know much about whiskey, but I got the feeling that a 35-year-old bottle was a pretty good one. I stared at that "& Lainey" a bit too long, its fresh black ink blending into the message I assumed Sam had penned earlier.

"I, uh, I'm sorry for just showing up like this. I know I wasn't exactly invited."

"Of course you're invited." Conner smiled down at me. "You're family."

I wasn't, but I sure felt like it the longer I sat at the table, swapping jokes and listening to stories about Conner's childhood. June and Jasmine had made enough food for an army. The table was loaded with lasagna, rolls, salad, and a horribly lumpy cake with enough neon blue frosting to be slightly off-putting.

Eli proudly informed us he'd helped decorate it. We all collectively spared a quick glance at each other before diving in, proclaiming how it was the most beautiful confection that had ever graced the planet.

Later, I attempted to make up for my unexpected presence by cleaning the kitchen with Sam and Will. Jas opened the screen door, and we watched Eli run around in the courtyard with an equally tireless June. Will and I chatted while Sam mostly listened in, adding his two cents when he felt like it.

The ringing of the doorbell sent Eli into a frenzy. He ran in from the yard yelling, "Genie's here! Genie's here!"

"Are we expecting someone else?" I watched as June followed, collecting her things from the patio table before she walked inside.

"Just my ride, dear. It was so lovely to see you." June deposited a kiss on both her sons' cheeks as an older man in a suit walked through the kitchen, carrying Eli on his shoulders.

"Happy birthday, Con. Hope it was a good one." The man handed Conner an Al Green record before shaking his hand.

"Hey, thanks, Gene. I appreciate it. You sure you can't stay for cake?"

"I demerated it!" Eli butt in, leaning over the man's head to stare upside-down into his eyes.

The older man, Gene, widened his eyes, hamming it up as he circled what was left of the cake, ooh-ing and aah-ing. He introduced himself to me as "June's fellow," then whisked June out the door without ingesting any Smurf-blue frosting. Smart man. Sam and I made our own retreat shortly after.

"I didn't know your mom had a *fellow*." I cuddled into Sam's shoulder as we walked across the courtyard. The night was warm. The scent of earth, grass, and gardenias tickled my nose.

He grunted. "He's a good guy. Been with my mom forever. Adores her, which I can't fault."

"Hmm. Why do you sound weird about that?"

He hauled me tighter when we walked up the few stairs to his back porch. The pads of his fingers rasped, raising goosebumps in their wake. "It's just a little weird when you watch a parent get romantic with someone. Mom deserves to be happy. I'm glad she's found a partner she loves." He gave me a pained look while he locked the door behind us. "He calls her 'blossom.'"

"Aw, because she's a gardener. That's cute."

"Maybe for someone who's not my mom. I don't know. I'm not into pet names."

I stopped in my tracks, cocking my head at him. "Could have fooled me."

"What do you mean?"

"I mean...there's Sweetheart..." I traced the swirls in his countertop, watching him start the dishwasher. "I like that one quite a bit. Sometimes Honey, when you're feeling extra sweet."

"Those are endearments, not pet names. It's not like blossom or muffin or—"

"Baby?" He snorted. "I have never in my life called a woman 'baby.'"

Chapter 29

Lainey

Was he joking? Surely he was. But as I studied him across the kitchen counter, the theory I'd been holding onto about Sam and sex solidified.

"You called me baby three times. Yesterday."

"No, I didn't." His denial was fast and absolute, like the slamming of the dishwasher door. "That term has always seemed too...possessive."

"You only call me baby when we're having sex." I enjoyed the blank look on his face more than I should have. Highly entertaining, the way his eyes darted back and forth like he was trying to replay our sexual encounters. "I don't mind it. It's kind of hot, honestly. Especially now that I know you're being *possessive*."

"It's hot." It was a question, but didn't sound like one. He either didn't believe that I enjoyed it or that he actually said it.

"Do you want me to show you?" My pulse quickened. His eyes went dark as he crept around the counter, wrapping me in those big, strong arms.

"You gonna start calling me 'baby?'" His words rasped against my ear.

The seductive slide of his palms around my waist woke something needy and sensual inside me. Heat simmered, and I drew a deep breath, trying to slow my rapidly increasing heart rate.

My teeth sank into my lip, coy, as I shook my head. "No. I've spent long enough calling you by your last name. Just 'Sam' does it for me these days."

"You called me Samuel earlier." His nose traced down the side of my face. "I *liked that.*" The evidence of just how much he'd liked it pushed against my belly. "Like a librarian. Like I've been bad."

I ran my hands up over his chest, loving the warmth under my fingers and hating the fact that he was still wearing a shirt. Why were either of us wearing anything? "Have you? Been bad?"

"I made my girlfriend crash my brother's birthday," he murmured, flicking the tip of his tongue over my pulse. My breath left me in a sigh, heat traveling lower and lower. I was already wet for him, and getting wetter by the minute. The sound of him calling me his girlfriend made my heart stutter.

"That's pretty bad. Maybe I'll forgive you if you call me baby."

I felt his smile, right before I felt his teeth nip the side of my neck. He didn't bite me every time we had sex, but I almost always had a mark or two on me somewhere. Who would have thought that my quiet, considerate attending was so into marking his territory? Who would have thought that I was so into it, too?

His hands cupped my face, thumb ghosting across my jaw. "Sweetheart. Honey. Lainey." Little kisses pressed to my mouth with every word. I wriggled in his arms. "There's no way."

Oh, yes, there was. No matter how effectively his brain disconnected from his vocal cords during sex, he'd remember calling me baby tonight. I'd make sure of that.

"We'll see."

I hated to leave his arms, but the look on his face when I sashayed across his living room and deposited my blouse on the stair railing was worth it. I could practically hear his gulp when he caught the skirt I slid off and kicked back at him. He followed, rapt, as I took the stairs slowly, giving him time to admire the view, a thin scrap of silk the only thing covering my butt.

"Please tell me you're planning to keep the heels on." He caressed my spine, feeling the bumps and curves there. He dragged the tip of his finger across the line of lace hugging my rear.

"Maybe." I leaned against the wall of his bedroom, watching him stalk me with hooded eyes. "Hold on." He froze the instant I spoke. I spread my fingers across his chest, smoothing the fabric covering his shoulders, lightly scoring my fingernails across his collar, where skin met cotton. He shuddered. His breaths fractured, stuttering in and out while I explored, keeping my touches light and playful.

"Take your clothes off, and get on the bed."

Buttons snapped. He nearly tripped over his pants, still peeling off a sock when he rolled onto the mattress, looking at me like I commanded his next breath. It was heady and hot and hilarious.

"A little eager?"

"Honey, you have no idea." He reached a hand out. "Come here."

"Hmm, Honey. Not baby, yet?" I purred, sliding across the room and ignoring his outstretched hand. "Sit back against the headboard."

It banged against the wall. Another funny moment, but all the power was going to my head. Instead of laughing at his impatient rush, I remembered what he'd said to me last week. That I was in control. He had no idea.

If I was really in control, I'd have listened to that panicked voice that still piped up every once in a while to warn me that falling so hard, so fast for a colleague was a bad idea. That I was sleeping with the man in charge of hiring me, and I loathed nepotism. That if it had been up to me, none of this would have happened.

But it had, thank God, because here he was, spread out for me, his hard-on bobbing for my attention, eyes begging me to do anything I wanted to him. I could, I realized, do nearly anything and he'd take it in stride. He exuded the quiet confidence that soothed my inner babbling.

Except in bed, where his mouth and his body competed for which could possess me most thoroughly. That's what I wanted. Right now.

"That looks uncomfortable." I crawled up the bed, gratified when he groaned my name, fisting his length and pumping it like he couldn't fully control himself. "Want some help?"

He hissed when I leaned forward to take his crown into my mouth, stroking. I swirled my tongue, relishing the slick, salty taste of him. He twitched, bumping into the roof of my mouth, saying my name again and again. No baby, yet. What would it take to get him to break? Surrender?

He liked the eye contact, thrusting a little harder into my mouth, grimacing like he was in pain. He hardened more under my stroking fingers.

"Take your bra off."

I took my time working my way back up his shaft, sliding him out of my mouth with a long lick. I fisted him, working up and down, bumping his length against my cheek. "Please?"

His immediate response of "please, Jesus, fuck" was so gratifying, I didn't even tease. The moment I sat up and opened the clasp, his eyes fell on my nipples. *This* made me feel in control. His face openly worshiped me in a way I wasn't sure I deserved, but liked too much to question. He wanted me, badly. Bad enough to obey every command, grant every wish. I could feel it in the rush of slickness between my legs, the tingle in the peaks of my breasts.

My fingers brushed there, tweaking the tight buds. Sam swallowed, quiet, eyes tracking every move I made. The only evidence of his excitement was the occasional twitch of his cock, but I wanted his words.

"Do you like this? Watching me?"

"Yes." His response vibrated between us, heavy with lust. Need.

I slipped a hand down my stomach, circling the tip of one finger at the top of my slit. His pupils dilated. "What would you like to watch me do?"

"Touch yourself."

"I am."

"More, baby."

I grinned, heat and triumph blazing through me. *"More, baby."*

He didn't register my teasing, instead grabbing his dick and squeezing like he was about to burst. "Touch yourself how you'd want my tongue on you. Show me how you want me to lick that sweet pussy."

I shuddered, my fingers delving into my folds like he was the one calling the shots. His rumble of satisfaction vibrated against my skin. My core quaked in response. Suddenly, I couldn't stand the inches between us. I crawled forward until I straddled his lap. My breasts pressed against his chest, his arm wrapped low around my hips to pull me closer. I hissed at the contact.

"Sam!"

"What do you need, baby?"

I choked out a laugh, repeating it back to him in broken, halting gasps. *"What do you need, baby?"*

"To see you get yourself off." He still didn't get it. He thought it was me saying those things to him, clueless about the words pouring out of his mouth. "To watch you break apart over me." He fisted my hair, craning my neck backwards to trail a line of stinging kisses down my neck. My hand reached down once more to tease my clit.

He spread his thighs, bumping my legs wider to get a better view. My thumb slicked over my center, the feeling magnified by his eyes on me. I moaned. "Oh, Honey, so good." He cupped my chin, devouring me with deep, devastating kisses that built up the fire in my belly before he ripped away from me, staring down at my hand once more.

"You want to pump those beautiful fingers inside your cunt, baby? Fuck yourself like you want me to?" I choked on air, slipping my index finger inside. His words were absolutely filthy, too much for me to repeat back to him. Not when I felt like there was lava flowing through my veins, burning me up from the inside out.

"That's not enough, Sweetheart," he murmured against my mouth, spearing his tongue inside again and again, setting a rhythm I matched with my fingers. "Give me another. Hell yes, that's it. You feel how you stretch? Like it's my cock inside you, baby."

"Feel h-how you...stretch?" I gasped, wrist twisting to hit that spot inside that always helped send me to the stars. Sam stilled, brow creasing at my words, unable to place them. I bit my lip, writhing against him, begging with my body for him to resume the pinching, grabbing torture on my breasts. "Like it's my cock inside you, b-baby..."

I quoted back, squeezing my eyes shut as a wave of pleasure rolled through me. Hearing his dirty words echoing around me in surround-sound only elevated my desire. I could barely force them past my throat, they were so wild. But this is what he thought about me, unfiltered. His need for me was completely base and beautiful and desperate, spilling out of his mouth with no thought.

His face cleared, eyes widening in comprehension when he replayed my words. "That's what I sound like?"

"Yes," I gasped, desire spilling onto my hand. He gripped my body, holding and stroking me like I was going to fly away.

"And you like that?"

I squeezed his neck with my free hand, kneading the flesh, feverish in my need to pull him closer. I wanted all of him on me. In me. "I love it. So much, Sam, you have n-no ide-e-a..." My voice caught, the inferno roaring in my ears. My fingers worked inside, reaching for that one spot I needed.

"So possessive, and you fucking love it. You love that you're *mine.*" I slowed, feeling his gaze burn across my body. It was possessive, and I *did* love it. It lit the fuse that I hadn't quite been able to start myself. I bit back a cry when he placed his hand over mine, moving my fingers in and out in a rhythm only he could master. "Look at you, baby, dripping for me."

"Sam," I groaned, waves of heat licked up my breasts, my neck. Something about the way he moved me to suit him, my hand obeying him, made me realize I wasn't in control anymore. I hadn't been for a long, long time.

"I love the way my name sounds in your mouth, Honey. Say it again while you play with yourself. Come all over me just so I can push up inside you and make you fall apart all over again."

"Fuck." I lunged, glimpsing the shock on his face an instant before I slammed my mouth onto his, clawing and grasping my way further onto his lap. I was going to die if he wasn't inside me right now. I fumbled beneath me, hearing his muttered curses when I gripped him, lined him up where I needed him.

He'd been right. I was dripping. I sank onto him fully in just two strokes, settling on his lap and taking him to the hilt, rising on my knees to envelop him again and again and again. Fingers dug into flesh. Our cries mingled together. His hard length hit that perfect spot inside me, sending me over the edge in seconds, stoking that fire even brighter.

"You ride me like a dream. So good."

Our mouths clashed, even while I struggled to breathe with the swirl of sensation tumbling around me. I was coming again. He gripped my body, hugging me tighter, anchoring me through the storm while he continued those steady, upward thrusts. His litany of dirty talk took everything to a new place. Higher and hotter, until his words started slurring, running together. He pounded into me, sloppy and irregular.

"Fuck, baby. Fuck me just like that. God damn, Lainey. You're so perfect. So fucking perfect, baby. I love it, I love…"

He bit my lip, hard, the sting distracting me for just a moment from what he'd been about to confess. And then it was over. Another wave of pleasure crested alongside the sting of my lip, and Sam pulsed inside me, hot and strong.

I collapsed on top of him, breathing hard, like him. Warm palms swept up and down my back, stroking while he came down from his own climax.

"You called me baby," I mumbled into his neck. He gripped my butt, squeezing.

"You said fuck. I think I win."

I swallowed, still panting, replaying his last words in my head. *"I love it, I love..." you*. I knew it. I knew it to the depth of my soul. That's what he'd been about to say. And he meant it. I knew that, too.

But I wasn't sure he remembered it, whether it was just one more muttered, mindless prayer to leave his lips mid-penetration. I wasn't sure if he was ready to say it yet. Most importantly, I wasn't sure if *I* was ready for him to say it yet. Asking him felt like I'd be poking the hornet's nest.

I stayed curled up against him long after our breath settled and he'd gently guided my feet out of the heels I'd completely forgotten about. I fell asleep curled up against him, the unspoken words swirling around us in the darkness.

Chapter 30

Lainey

Monday morning couldn't come fast enough.

I wasn't just antsy to get back to my normal clinical schedule. I also hoped getting back into my regular routine would help me decide how I felt about Sam's near-confession. For the last few days, he'd been acting like nothing was wrong. I tried my best to match his energy, but I was rattled.

It was one thing to feel myself sliding towards the big "L." Another entirely to hear it from him. As much as strapping myself into a serious, committed relationship with my coworker made me want to grab my heels and sprint in the opposite direction, the thought of doing it with Sam made me want to squeal and melt into a happy puddle. A conundrum. One that would have to wait till later.

I'd scheduled one final debrief with the PR teams and Caplan, and then I was back on the cardiac floor. If they tried to stop me, I'd bulldoze them all. I'd pushed for the earliest possible meeting time, impatient to start my normal rounds again. The hospital had that quiet, early-morning hush to it. I felt like I was breathing fresh air for the first time as I walked down the empty halls.

Caplan and Sturmond were already sitting at the conference table, huddled together and talking quietly. The presence of the latter made me do a double-take. The infuriating man had played a starring role in this media circus, nearly racking up as many interviews as me, riding the wave of interest my mother's team had generated.

The last time I'd talked with him was when he'd taken the lead on insisting, strong-arming, and bullying me into doling my patient load out to other doctors, including Jones. I'd thought that would be the last of him, for now. I hadn't invited him to this meeting, and his presence here set off alarm bells in my prefrontal cortex.

"Director Caplan. Doctor Sturmond." I was tempted to call him mister, instead of Doctor. He was one of those obnoxious people who demanded that everyone use his title, even strangers. I wondered if he made his wife call him Doctor. *Probably.*

Yet, I refrained. If my fate was hanging in the balance, he was more than likely holding at least one of the strings. I had to play nice if I wanted to scrub in, and I did. Badly. All week, it had felt like part of me was missing. I wasn't myself if I wasn't in the OR.

"Doctor Carmichael! I thought our meeting didn't start for another ten minutes?" The gold chain of Caplan's Rolex clinked when he checked it. Sturmond shifted in his chair, looking at me like I was a child who had wandered out of my room past bedtime. I had the distinct impression I wasn't welcome here, despite having a meeting scheduled in just a few minutes.

"I figured I'd pop in a little early." Ten minutes wasn't that early, was it? Caplan smiled stiffly.

"Well, I suppose we can dial in the comms team in a few. I doubt they're ready for us yet."

The whir of the air conditioning was the only sound as I set my laptop and tablet down. I straightened my blouse—my new uniform these days. I couldn't wait to get into some scrubs. Caplan scrolled through his phone while Sturmond sat back and studied me like I was an insect pinned to a board. I cleared my throat.

"The interviews have gone well, I think."

"Of course. You're a natural." Caplan smiled.

"I'm eager to get back to work today, though."

His smile faltered. Sturmond audibly snorted. My stomach dropped.

"That's what we were just discussing, actually. It may be in the hospital's best interest for you to continue promotional work for just a bit longer." Despite the gentleness of his words, Caplan sounded strained. The floor dropped out from under me. Surprise made me blunt.

"I thought the media campaign was ending?" I sounded pleading, even a little desperate. I hadn't had an interview since Friday morning, and hadn't heard from the PR team since then. Caplan shifted, gaze flickering off to the side. "Surely, it's better for me to use my training to serve our patients."

"Donations are up by eight percent since your little video got popular. It's in the patients' best interest for our program to be properly funded." Sturmond crossed his arms, a grin I didn't like stretching across his face. "You'll be working with the PR team to announce our new partnership with your mother's foundation. Besides, your fellowship is almost over, and your cases were all successfully handed off to other qualified doctors within our program. Think of it like a little vacation."

The way he said it somehow implied that those other doctors handling my patients were more qualified than me. I knew it wasn't true, but it was a punch in the gut, nonetheless. Rija and Tara had been quick to complain to me when a resident fumbled something with my patients, though I could hardly put any blame on my replacements. They were doing the best they could after my caseload was unceremoniously dumped in their laps.

A cell phone beeped on the table. The buzz of a pager followed immediately after. Caplan cursed, eyes darting between his two devices as he stood.

"Sorry, I need to take this. I'll be right back." He paused, looking from me to Sturmond, then back again. "Let's...ah...pause our conversation here and pick it up when I'm back in just a moment."

I glimpsed his face just before the door closed behind him. Guilt, apology, and warning all wrapped into one look. The closing of the door echoed around the room, sounding like the turning of a lock. Caplan was nervous about leaving me alone with big bully Sturmond. But he didn't realize that he'd also left Sturmond alone with me.

I folded my hands neatly on the table, casting a critical eye over the man. Big, but not in the naturally burly way Sam was. He was overweight. The veins along his nose and pudginess of his cheeks hinted at regular overindulgence with his nightly wine or whiskey or whatever. He had beady little eyes that reminded me of his stupid little grandson. He was currently assessing me in the same way, except he looked like the cat who ate the cream.

Satisfied. Like he was watching a trap spring.

I took a deep breath. "So convenient, don't you think? That your grandson was one of those 'qualified doctors' to handle my caseload? I bet those extra surgeries look great during attending interviews."

He might be ready to spring a trap, but he had no idea who he was dealing with. I was Rebecca Carmichael and Ross Davis's daughter, for God's sake. I was the future; he was the past, and I was done with feeling the pressure of his loafer heel on my neck.

"Bold of you to hint at nepotism, Doctor Carmichael." The way he emphasized my last name—my mother's name—set my teeth on edge. "My grandson earned his position at this organization before I headed up the quality board. Fair and square. Robert belongs here."

Sturmond had still been on a board at the time, moving through the ranks by spearheading fundraising for the new surgery center. But that wasn't his point. We both knew that between Jones and myself, only one of us had entered Cedar the traditional way.

I wouldn't be here without my mom on the sidelines, pulling strings. I tried to ignore the cold, squirming feeling in my chest that sprang up whenever I thought about how I'd abused my mother's fame to cement my position here.

But that was then, and this was now.

"I've completed more surgeries than any other member of my cohort, both in residency and throughout my fellowship. I've earned my place all by myself. Whether or not you bar me from the OR for the next three weeks, I will be an attending here."

A smile slithered across his pudgy cheeks, Grinch-like.

"Bold of you to discuss personal merit when you're fucking the hiring committee chair."

Ice cascaded down my spine. "Wh...what?" How could he know? No one here knew. There was no way. I swallowed. Perhaps he was just making assumptions and accusations. Informed, maybe, given our recent viral video and the camaraderie there, but still baseless.

"Let's not play games, Ms. Carmichael." *Doctor* Carmichael, I wanted to scream. But something about the way he narrowed his eyes, enjoying the view of my horror-stricken face, held my tongue. "Do you really think HR records are completely confidential? I have a direct line on everything that happens within this building. Everything. Were you upset when he submitted the paperwork?"

"I...I don't know what you're talking about." My mouth was dry. Why didn't I have any water? Why didn't I have any air?

"Play dumb all you like. I have a paper trail. Fascinating timing, that you began a relationship with him just before interviews started." He looked me up and down, like I was something disgusting stuck to his shoe. "Were you upset when he reported it? When he recused himself from the voting process? Gallant Doctor Reese. I'm sure you weren't expecting that."

"He what?" My head was spinning. I was hearing things. Or I wasn't properly processing what I was hearing.

"You didn't know?" Sturmond clicked his tongue. "Hell of a way to find out your boyfriend doesn't have the sway you thought he did. You've unnecessarily opened your legs for a mediocre doctor with minimal power. A shame."

He sipped his coffee, clearly having the time of his life with his little villain speech. Despite my pounding heart and racing thoughts, I prickled at the slight against Sam. "Doctor Reese is a talented surgeon and a gifted teacher. The resident and fellowship programs would fall apart without him."

A phlegmy chortle rattled from his chest. "Whatever you have to tell yourself to sleep at night. But we both know Reese could get hit by a bus tomorrow and everything would go right on turning, just the way it always has."

I gasped, his casually cruel assessment penetrating the haze of adrenaline and confusion. Blood roared, filling my ears with a pounding, rushing noise that blocked out everything else. I could feel my face heating. "How dare y—"

He spoke over me. "I'm the one who keeps this place running. You think it was easy? Hand-delivering the money and the proposals for your precious new hospital? You think all these shiny new toys just fell out of the sky?" He swept his hands around, gesturing to the room and the halls beyond. "This is my legacy,

Ms. Carmichael, and you are more useful to me in print than you are in the operating room."

He rose. I was standing, too. I hadn't realized it until now. My fingertips felt fuzzy. All of this felt fuzzy, like I was dreaming, or it was happening to someone else, but as Sturmond speared a finger towards me, I knew it was all too real.

"So that's what you'll do. Put on your makeup. Smile for the camera, and tell the world that you are fucking privileged to work for one of the best medical institutions in the country. Because you are." His hand fell, slapping on the table. He leaned against it, crowding my space, despite the expanse of polished wood between us. "And maybe, if you do it well and keep the money rolling in, you'll continue to work here."

"What are you even saying?"

"You know exactly what I'm saying." He settled his girth back in his chair. "Keep the interviews up, and the hiring committee won't need to find out about your little affair. Imagine how poor Reese's reputation would take a hit, fucking one of his precious fellows during the interview process. Gifted teacher, indeed. That would cut him out of the running for that program director position he's been after, for sure."

He lifted his brow at the irony. I felt sick. "You can't do—"

"I can do whatever the fuck I want. Don't think for one second I don't own this place. Robert will have a permanent role here. It's up to you to decide if you want one, too." His lids lowered, glowering at me. "Maybe that surgeon from Texas should round out the new hires. You're familiar with Doctor McDaniels, aren't

you, Ms. Carmichael? A lot of rumors flew around after you made
the sudden switch to Cedar. I wonder which is true? Was he really
fucking you both, and you were too self-absorbed to see it?"

It was a final blow I wasn't prepared for. I'd thought I had hidden my relationship with Sam. I thought I'd outrun the embarrassment of everything that had happened with Nate and Katie.
But this man was single-handedly deconstructing my carefully
crafted existence like a kid stomping on a sand castle.

Everything crumbled, my foundations washing away like grains
of sand.

Sturmond knew...*everything*. It made me wonder who else
knew why I'd ended up at Cedar. Did they know about Sam
and me, too? While I was strutting around the halls, convinced
I was at the top of the program, were they laughing behind my
back, assuming, like Sturmond, that I was only with Reese to give
myself another leg up? Using my influence to circumvent regular
proceedings? Again?

My throat tightened. No wonder he looked at me like I was a
worm. The complete picture of it all—my failed relationship, my
flagrant use of my mother's power to get into the program here,
my new romance with Sam—it all made me look like a twittering,
self-absorbed, opportunistic idiot.

And Sam...maybe he'd seen that. Maybe that was why he'd gone
to HR. I only understood about half of that, but I wasn't about
to ask Sturmond. He didn't need any more leverage.

I gathered my things with shaking hands. "I have to go," I said,
forcing the words around rising bile.

"You do that. I'll let the PR ladies know to send over the new interview requests."

I turned and fled. Maybe if I ran fast enough, I could outpace his smug grin and his small-minded assumptions. I collapsed into the elevators, a shuttering breath leaving my body. It sounded like a sob. Was I crying? I couldn't tell.

My reflection stared back at me, pale and flushed at the same time, looking terrified and shaken. I gulped, watching the numbers tick down. I'd hit the button for the cardiac floor out of habit, but when the doors opened, a surge of panic nearly took me down. Who here knew about Sam, too? What must they all think of me?

I jabbed the button again. Not fast enough.

"Lainey! Wait." Jones appeared, pressing the doors to stop them from closing. "I have to tell you...Shit. You've already seen my grandfather." His fingers raked through his hair. It already stood on end. "Fuck. I didn't mean for this to happen, I swear."

"W-hat?" I croaked. I'd left my brain somewhere back on the executive floor.

Jones flinched. "I was jealous. It was stupid. After the video came out, I told my grandfather how much time you and Reese were spending together. I said..." His face twisted. He squeezed his eyes shut.

"You said what?" I breathed. I couldn't trust my voice. I didn't understand anything.

"That I wouldn't be surprised if...you weren't..." He looked up again, pained. "Lainey, I was just venting. With all the media attention, I was worried you'd make me look bad during interviews. I didn't think he'd actually go after you like this."

"You told him about me and Reese?"

"It was just some stupid comment. I never thought he'd actually look into it. Or that it would be..." *true.*

My stomach lurched. "I have to go." My thoughts were racing too quickly for me to keep up with, swirling between Sam and Jones and Sturmond. I couldn't catch my breath, didn't want to risk looking weak like this in front of this man, my so-called colleague who had brought everything crashing down on my head.

"Lainey, I'm sorry."

I gulped against rising bile, refusing to acknowledge the pained remorse on his face. "You should be."

Jones stumbled back. The doors closed. I reminded myself to breathe as the elevators rose back up to the tenth floor.

Chapter 31

Sam

"I know I don't have to tell you this, but it happens to everyone." Caplan squeezed my shoulder. I appreciated his attempt, but it did little to alleviate the pit in my stomach.

I'd lost countless patients before. I had protocols for it now: Go home, take a scalding shower after pumping some iron in my garage, watch some mindless show or see if Jas and Conner were up for some company. Early to bed, then back at it again in the morning.

Like all specialties, cardiothoracic surgery had its ups and downs. A bypass was common practice for me now, but some patients had a harder time bouncing back than others. Some people's bodies just couldn't recover. I knew this, but it was hard to tell a family that a routine procedure had taken the life of their loved one.

"Listen, I know this isn't the best time for this, but I wanted to get to you before you heard it from someone else." At Caplan's grimace, I steeled myself for even more bad news.

My life had been going pretty well recently. In fact, it had been a fucking dream. I was with Lainey. My family was happy and mostly healthy. My work was going well, barring the intermittent drama with board oversight.

Maybe that's why today had been miserable.

Lainey had already been in the shower when I woke up, which threw me off kilter before my eyes had even opened. I was used to her lying around with me in the mornings, chatting or checking her phone or just laying there together. Later, over her tea, she'd been...fine, just like she had been this weekend. Nothing overtly wrong or off, just a little distant. I'd still gotten a kiss before we parted ways at her car, but it lacked any of the heat I'd grown used to when her lips were on mine.

Work had hit me like a freight train the second I stepped into the building. My patient in the ICU was rapidly deteriorating, not to mention three back-to-back stent procedures.

I'd come out of the third surgery to a nurse with sticky notes all over her binder. The patient in the ICU had passed away. My brother had called to let me know Jas was back in the hospital after a concerning check-up. On and on and on. One emergency after another.

Now, three hours past when I was supposed to leave, with a tension headache pounding between my eyes, I braced for more. Caplan looked like he'd swallowed something sour.

"We're naming Dr. Whitaker's replacement for program director this week. We've decided to go with Garcia."

I stared, head throbbing. Garcia. The man who'd never shown an interest in the residents past how much work he could shove off on them or which one he could take his anger out on during a bad day? Garcia, the doctor nearly as old as Whitaker?

"I know what you're thinking." *Unlikely.* "But he's old buddies with someone on the board, and he's losing his edge on the OR. This lets us keep him around and minimize his time with patients. It was a win-win."

The board. Why did it always come back to that, these days? I'd heard more grumblings over the past few weeks about it than I'd heard my entire tenure at Cedar.

"That's a bad call."

Caplan drew back, but I didn't have it in me to soften the blow. Not today. He waited, but I didn't explain any further. We both knew exactly how shitty this move was. For the residents, and the rest of us. With Garcia at the helm, they'd be hard-pressed to get a holistic experience, much less the support they'd need to get through some of the most stressful years of their lives. The quality of the residents' experiences trickled down to the rest of us, including patients.

Caplan cleared his throat. "I'm afraid my hands are tied on the matter."

I wasn't sure that they were. Maybe Caplan was between a rock and a hard place, but his job was to lead the fucking department. Not grab a trampoline when the board told him to jump. My silence must have said as much. He studied his shoes.

"There's an enormous amount of pressure in this position. Not every decision I make is popular."

"That'd be fine if it was really you deciding." I hiked my backpack onto my shoulder. I was over this conversation. This day. "Just don't be surprised when people get fed up when there's no one around to stick up for them."

***

The knots loosened from my shoulders when I saw Lainey's car parked by my house. I wondered how much better my protocols for losing a patient would be when she was around. In the shower with me, snuggled up watching a war documentary. Then early to bed with her wrapped around me. That was the kind of thing I could get used to.

She brightened up everything. It made me want to beg her to move in. Keep her forever. Was it too early to offer her a drawer? Half my closet? A ring?

I dropped my bag, feet scraping up the stairs. I was exhausted. And angry. And hungry.

"Sweetheart?" My voice barely carried across the first floor. Anything louder and my head was bound to pop off my neck. I made a beeline to the kitchen, throwing back two Tylenol and sticking my head under the sink. A glass was too much work right now. Out of the corner of my eye, I saw Lainey padding across the living room.

I turned to give her a tired smile. "Hi."

I knew something was wrong before she even opened her mouth. Something about that blank look on her face, the way she was standing there clutching a sheaf of papers, warned me. Too late.

"You reported our relationship to HR."

Oh. *Fuck.* My temples pulsed.

"Yes." There was no use denying it. I hadn't technically been keeping it a secret from her. More like waiting for the right time. And now it was catching up to me at the exact wrong time.

I wanted to be holding her and talking about ordering Mexican for dinner. Not fighting. But that's what this was gearing up to be. The tilt of her chin told me she was spoiling for it.

"Were you planning to tell me about it at any point?"

I paused, choosing my words carefully. The process was difficult, given how tight the invisible band around my skull had become.

"Don't stand there and *think* about what you want to say, Reese. Just say what's in your head!" The papers cracked as she swiped them through the air. *Jesus.*

"Of course I was going to tell you. I was waiting for the right time."

"Ooh, sure. The right time. Probably before Sturmond blindsided me with it when he accused me of sleeping with you to get the attending position."

"What?"

"Yeah, super swell meeting today. Because of your little stunt"—she waved the papers around again—"he knows we're together. He's threatening to expose us unless I keep up my media appearances. We'll be a laughingstock."

"How did he know?" I rubbed my eyebrows. I'd specifically asked Gina in HR to keep it quiet when I'd turned in the paperwork informing the organization of my relationship with Lainey. It had been too early to say anything publicly, but I couldn't keep doing whatever it was we were doing together when I was interviewing her.

"Apparently, his spy network is impressively large. How could you, Sam? You said we'd take this slow."

"We *are* taking things slow. I told you not to worry about the hospital finding out."

"Yeah, because *they already knew* about it. Does Caplan know? Who else, Sam?"

"It's a massive conflict of interest, Lainey. I'm biased as hell towards you. There's no way I could have kept going pretending like everything was fine while I interviewed other people for a job I want *you* to have."

"You should have told me! That's what normal people do!" Her face twisted. "It's called communication. I know it's a foreign concept for you."

"What is that supposed to mean?" My brain throbbed, vision going blurry. She was coming at me hard and everything seemed all wrong.

"It means you don't give me anything to work with! I never know what's in your head. I watch you filter every word that comes out of your mouth. It's ridiculous!"

"*I* don't give *you* anything? The only thing I've gotten from *you* is red lights. You've been against this, us, from the start." My palms dug into my eyes. Little fireworks exploded at the pressure on my lids. "Forgive me if I couldn't find the right time to tell you I was fulfilling a *moral obligation* to tell the hospital about us, when you made it very clear you didn't even want a relationship to begin with."

"You know why I had my reservations about this. And guess what?" She waved the papers through the air again. "I was right. Once again, my life is falling to pieces all because I picked the wrong guy."

"Now, hold on—"

"I told myself not to get too tangled up; not to mix work with my personal life. But you went ahead and did all the paperwork without me. You had no right to make this decision for me." The papers spun where she tossed them on the granite countertop. "Now, Stumond is breathing down my neck and both of our reputations are on the line. I'm already on thin ice because of how I became a resident here. Now, it just looks like I'm using someone else to get to where I want to go. Like I can't get there on my own."

"No, it will look fine." When it all blew over. No one would give us a second look when we were celebrating our tenth wedding anniversary. But I couldn't say that. Not without pushing her away even more. Not when she was looking at me like she wanted to fling a scalpel at my neck.

"It will not. You know, the ridiculous thing is that you're right. I *didn't* want this. I knew better." I watched the emotions play across her face. The anger, rage, now edged with resignation. The grim acceptance that flickered in her eyes spiked my heart rate. It didn't look like she was spoiling for a fight. It looked like she was giving up.

"Wait, Lainey. I know you're mad, just..." Her bag was sitting beside the front door. Fully packed. "What...what's happening here?" The band around my head contracted a bit more.

"I'm leaving."

"Hold on. Just...dammit, Lainey, wait. Let's talk about this."

"Oh, now you want to talk? It's too late." She grabbed the handle of her duffel. I took the corner around the island so fast, I banged my hip hard enough to bruise.

"Fuck. Listen, I know you're mad right now. But—" I reached for her, but she just kept backing away.

"Yeah, I'm mad...and disappointed. I thought I could trust you." Betrayal was written all over her face. I felt like the smallest piece of shit on the planet.

"Honey, you can—"

"Not when you go behind my back like this. I've done this once before, Sam. Losing my relationship, all my friends, my job? I'm not doing it again."

"Lainey, you can't leave—"

"That's the only thing I *can* do."

"I'm in love with you!" I blurted the words, pain and panic sending my brain into a fever pitch. Her chin quivered. Then she turned on her heel and left without another word.

***

Was four-thirty in the morning too early to call a woman after you broke her heart? Probably. Still, I stared at the screen of my phone, knee jiggling.

Five was possibly more acceptable. Lainey was an early riser. I watched another minute go by.

I'd stood frozen in my living room long after she left. She hadn't even slammed the door. All I'd had to mark the moment she walked out of my life was a jumbled pile of papers and the memory of her disappointed face.

But she couldn't just leave like that. It was one fight. We could fix this. She just needed some time to cool off.

At least, that's what I told myself last night, laying in bed, clutching my phone as sleep eluded me. Now, I wasn't so sure. For the hundredth time, I replayed the best hits from her tirade.

"Once again, my life is falling to pieces all because I picked the wrong guy."

"I didn't want this. I knew better."

"It's too late."

Four-thirty-five wasn't too early, was it?

"What's wrong?" Tiago yanked on the door handle, impatiently gesturing for me to unlock it. The door jerked open. "Is it Jas and the baby?"

"No." I pulled myself out of the car, feeling sore. My headache hadn't fully dissipated. My limbs were dead weight.

"Your mom? Will?"

"Everyone's fine, T."

"Well, what the fuck, Sammy? There's a reason you're sitting in front of the store at four a.m. looking like someone died. You'd better spit it out."

"Lainey left."

Jordan wrapped his arm around Tiago's waist, thumb stroking his side. They shared a glance more intimate than any caress. I looked away.

"Come in, *Amor*. I'll make you a cup."

Parking my ass between R^3 and Molido before the sun came up had been a strategic move. Lainey liked to work out the morning after a bad day, and Tiago was one of the best listeners I knew. I figured one of them would eventually show up and put me out of my misery.

While Jordan prepped the ovens and pulled out rack after rack of dough from the walk-in, Tiago cranked up the espresso machine. I helped him flip chairs off the tables and told him the whole story.

"It didn't occur to you to talk with her before you reported her?" His hands planted on his hips while he watched me.

"I didn't report *her*, I reported us."

He'd only turned on the bronze star lanterns clustered on the ceiling. I let the dim glow and increasingly powerful scent of coffee ease some of the tightness in my skull.

"I'm not sure there's much of a difference when you do it behind her back." Tiago clicked his tongue, not bothering to help me with the rest of the chairs.

"I didn't…" I rubbed gritty eyes, sagging to a seat. "It wasn't behind her back."

He rubbed my neck as he placed a Cubano and biscotti in front of me. "I know you were doing what you thought was best, *Hermano*, but consider this from her point of view."

"I am." I had been up all night thinking about all the ways I'd let her down. When I tried to figure out what I could have done differently, better, I kept coming up empty. "But you didn't see how skittish she was at the beginning. I had to hold her lightly or risk scaring her off. I'm in love with her, T."

"I know, Sweetie. That's why you should probably hold on even tighter." He sighed, wiping down cups for the day's service. "There's no use dwelling on it now. What are you going to do next?"

I glanced down at my phone. Four-fifty-one was late-ish, right? "Call her?"

"You want to run that by me again without sounding like you're asking permission?"

"I can't stop thinking about how hurt she looked last night. Like I'd failed her. I don't know if she even wants to speak to me right now."

"It's too late," she'd said. Fuck, maybe it was too late.

"She might not." He shrugged. I stared, waiting, but he offered nothing else.

"Then, what do I do? If she needs space—"

"Sammy, you tried holding her lightly. It backfired all over your pretty face. You need a trim, by the way." He stroked his own bare jaw where my beard had gotten scraggly. "So now you try something different."

I scowled into my coffee. "You say that like it's easy. What am I supposed to *do*, Tiago?"

"Call her," Jordan sang from behind the counter.

"Call her!" Tiago flung his towel down, drowning out Jordan's words. "Go to her apartment. Text her. Tell her you love her."

"Tried that. Still couldn't get her to stay."

"Hey, Eeyore!" Tiago snapped his fingers in front of my face. "You had a fight. People fight. They get mad and walk away. Is this girl the one?"

"She's the one." I knew it down to a cellular level.

"Then tell her that, again and again. Apologize. Find a way to be better. Hold on tighter, Sammy."

I swallowed past the lump in my throat. Tiago was right. I'd been too cautious, treating this relationship like it would disappear into thin air the second I made a wrong move. Now, though, there was nothing left to lose.

If I stayed silent, just let her walk out the door, she might never come back. And I'd never recover.

"Just don't stalk her, or anything." Jordan's rumble split through the heavy air in the cafe. Tiago scoffed.

"You stalked me and it worked out fine."

Jordan placed a kiss on Tiago's nose before disappearing into the back. "You were a special case."

They worked around me, prepping and stacking, letting me think.

At five-thirty, I tapped Lainey's contact information. Her Cedar headshot popped up. I'd wanted to replace her picture in my phone with the photo Jas had snapped of us a few days ago. The one on my porch, me hugging Lainey from behind. Both of us happy. But I hadn't wanted to risk someone at work seeing it.

I dialed. Waited. She didn't pick up.

Chapter 32

Lainey

Samuel Reese

I know you're upset, but please let me explain.

Call me when you have a minute, please.

Good morning. I miss you. Please answer my calls.

I hate coming to work knowing I won't see you there.

Update, if you were wondering: Leaving work is worse because I know you won't be home, either.

Me again. I'm sorry.

Please let me talk to you.

I'm about to call you. Please pick up.

> Your voicemail is full.

> Sorry for that, too.

> If I get a bottle of that white you like so much, would you come over?

> Bribery might seem beneath me, but I'm desperate.

I cringed when Sam's last message illuminated my phone. He'd sent a picture of his porch. Sun shining, his feet just edging into the bottom of the screen. It physically hurt to look at it.

A lot of things hurt these days.

I'd told Sam I was leaving to protect myself, because I couldn't go through it all again: losing my partner, my friends, and my job.

A horrible joke, seeing as I lost Sam, nearly all of my friends were related to him, and my job prospects were hanging on by a thread.

True to his slimy word, Sturmond had directed the PR people to book me for any media event they wanted. Apparently, I'd graciously agreed to continue on the media tour, acting as the spokesperson for the new program Cedar and my mother's foundation were collaborating on. The initial campaign had been such a rousing success, both organizations had decided that a long-term partnership was in everyone's best interests.

I took every interview from my apartment, avoiding the hospital as much as possible. I didn't have the strength to run into Sam, or Sturmond, or anyone else that might know about our relationship.

I was on the fence about telling Rija, too. I wasn't sure how much she knew, or if telling her would alter her perception of me, just like it did with Sturmond. Lainey, a spoiled little brat who just used others to get where she needed to go. I couldn't handle the disappointment or disgust on her face.

I'd been right before all this started up: mixing my personal and professional life was too messy.

After leaving Sam, my days took on a dull, repetitive haze. Wake up. Do my hair and makeup. Read through background documents for today's interviews. Get through all that. Eat something...maybe. Then fall back into bed.

I didn't even want to watch my trashy TV shows, not when they reminded me of sitting on Sam's couch with a glass of wine, filling him in on the back story of each character while he chopped vegetables. I couldn't bring myself to work on my LVAD research, which made me remember how Sam had gotten my patient in at Mercy and why she'd had to be referred there in the first place. I was bored and sad and alone.

It had been too easy, in hindsight, to get sucked back into friendships with other people. I hadn't realized how much I'd missed that over the last few years. But now, living in limbo, waiting for my third and final interview at Cedar and avoiding the outside world as much as possible, the need for someone else was like an ache. It followed me constantly, and there wasn't much I could do about it.

Tess was wrapped up in a huge, time-sensitive project at her company, and I'd been too much of a coward to text Jas. She was

Sam's sister-in-law and loyal to a fault. I couldn't put her in the middle of all this, not when I knew she'd probably pick his side. I missed them both.

Most of all, though, I missed Sam. My white-hot rage had cooled with time. Now, whenever I thought of him, I was just sad. Bitter, too.

I hated how I questioned everything now. Had he always had his own agenda? Moved on his own timeline, all the while telling me I was the one in charge? Had he planned to expose us—*me*—all along, regardless of my reservations about us being together?

Late at night, I convinced myself that these worst-case scenarios might be true. Maybe I hadn't known him as well as I thought. In the light of day, though, it was harder to convince myself he was a villain.

I missed the way he could make me laugh when I least expected it. How he listened to me. How he took me into account when he made plans. I missed the way he held me, like I was precious, but wouldn't break. The endearments. All of it.

The more I thought about it, the more I regretted how I'd handled our argument.

I'd been upset—rightfully so—to find out that Sam had disclosed our relationship to my employer without my knowledge or permission. But now that I'd had some distance from the whole thing, I kind of understood why.

Sam was nothing if not considerate. Of course he would do what he thought was best to create a fair environment for all the candidates. The paperwork was supposed to be confidential, if the notes on the forms HR had copied were anything to go off of. The only reason Gina had handed them over to me was because my name was on there, too.

Plus, I'd been so livid, I might have overstepped in our argument.

Sam was quiet, yes, but he was honest with me and everyone else around him. I'd accused him of not giving me enough, but the more I thought about it, the more I realized that he'd given me everything I asked for and more.

He'd taken it slow with me when I asked him to. Not only accepted me into his world, but softly introduced avenues to get to know his family and friends, as well: tacos with Jas and Conner, taking me to Molido, Conner's birthday. I realized it was his way of showing me how little I had to fear. He was putting all of himself on the table for me to see—his life, his family, his past. He offered it all up freely.

Was he right? Was I the one who had held too much back from him? The last few weeks had felt like a whirlwind to me, one compromise or surrender after another. But maybe it had felt like that because I was so woefully unused to sharing more than a single piece of myself with someone.

My parents got the award-winning, dutiful daughter. My colleagues got the dependable Doctor Carmichael. Before Sam, it had been a long time since I'd shared more than just scraps of who I was. Revealing the full picture felt raw and vulnerable.

But he'd been so wonderful about it all, taking everything I'd been willing to give him, even the ugly, selfish bits. Where that left me, I didn't know. Sad, mad, guilty, unsure.

Existing in a vacuum wasn't helping, either. Nearly a week after my fight with Sam, the most social interaction I'd had was with the DoorDash people and the perfectly coiffed reporters who conducted the Zoom interviews that filled my days once more.

Tess's only free time was when she could escape her office for a class at R^3. I wasn't sure if I'd even be welcome there (just one more piece of my life shattered in the wake of my breakup with Sam).

She'd told me several times that Will kept asking about me, but I couldn't risk it. On top of everything else, I couldn't handle it if I walked into that place and felt their judgment weighing on me. Still, I was going insane sitting inside my apartment ruminating all alone.

So, on Sunday night, I crouched behind the wheel of my car, waiting for her class to get out while I obsessively tracked Sam's location on my phone. He hadn't rescinded his sharing permission. I knew he probably had just forgotten about it, and it was possibly creepy for me to continue to spend so much time stalking him now that I'd left. Tonight, at least, I had a good excuse. I had to make sure he stayed put at the hospital. If his dot so much as blinked in the gym's direction, I'd hightail it outta here.

I was so focused on his pulsing blue circle, I missed the flash of copper outside my window. I jumped so high when June knocked on the glass, I nearly dropped the phone to the floorboard.

"You mind?"

"...Huh?" I rolled the window down, unsure if my leaping heart rate was because of the adrenaline from her sneak attack, or if it was because she was Sam's mom.

"You mind giving me a hand? Fucking gravel weighs about fifty pounds. I'm no spring chicken anymore." June nodded at the bags of pea gravel piled in the back of her Jeep.

"Ah. Um..." Was I so petty and antisocial that I was going to force this woman to carry twelve bags of gravel around by herself? Ugh. Manners were the worst. "Of course."

"I'm helping Tiago with the garden next door. I got tickled with the idea of a little pathway." She gestured to the gap she'd carved in the overgrown foliage behind R^3 and Molido's. Now that it was pruned, I could see straight through to the little patio back there—the colorful umbrellas and lanterns swinging. Exotic looking flowers and fresh mulch marked June's work.

"It's beautiful." Nothing like Sam's courtyard, with the wild roses and perfumed jasmine. This was a tropical world all its own, with spicy scents and red and orange flowers I didn't know the names of.

"Well, thank you, sweetie. That's nice of you to say."

I hefted a bag out of the trunk. "Just let me know where you want them."

"You're a lifesaver. Come dump them down by the deck." I followed her through the foliage, ducking every once in a while to avoid a low-hanging limb. It was cooler in the shade, and quieter. The noise from the street was muffled here. A little oasis.

"Isn't this nice? I like having a pathway here. The gym people can come straight over without sweating in the parking lot. Makes my heart happy to see my boys doing so well together. Two businesses, side-by-side."

"You must be proud." It didn't escape my notice that she readily referred to Santiago as one of "her boys." She beamed back at me.

"Of course I am. A heart surgeon and a handful of successful entrepreneurs? It's a mother's dream."

"I told, ah, Sam as much once." I nearly gulped his name back down my throat, but I forced it out. Even if it hurt.

"It's nice that they're stable, but I want them to be happy, too. Let's set the next one a little further down." She directed me back to the Jeep. We walked a few paces before she spoke again. "Sam's always been the one I needed to watch, you know."

"Oh?" I croaked. I didn't know what June knew about me and Sam. Surely she wouldn't be talking to me about him if she knew I'd ended things, right?

"So quiet, that one. Some people mistake it for weakness."

"It's not," I supplied, softly. I'd made that mistake before, too, thinking just because he didn't fill every silence that he was boring or lifeless. It couldn't be further from the truth. June nodded in approval.

"Good, you recognize it. It's not. He took on so much responsibility when the boys were growing up. Too much, I think. Maybe some of that was my fault. Put that one over in this corner and we'll grab another one."

"I'm sure you did your best." It seemed like the right thing to say in the moment. I dumped the bag, thinking I should probably let her know that Sam and I were no longer together. That would be the right, if not a little awkward, thing to do. I kept my mouth shut, though.

"I did, but it was hard." June shrugged off my comment. "Times were tough. I remember one year, I was short on cash for Will's birthday. I hated it, but if I had to choose between paying the bills and getting them a new toy, it wasn't really a choice. I'd gotten a few things from the thrift store for him. Some new shoes and used games. It was something, but I could tell he was disappointed. Broke my fucking heart, let me tell you. I thought we were both gonna cry." She chuckled, like she was fond of this memory.

"Well, Sam leaves the table and comes back with this horribly lumpy package, all wrapped up with newspaper he'd found from the recycling. It was his favorite monster truck. Someone from the church had given it to him a few months before for doing some work around their house. Picking up sticks and such. All the boys were just wild over it. It made sounds and lit up. It was a big deal. And Sam just handed it over to his brother. No muss, no fuss. I think I was prouder that day than when he graduated medical school."

I set another bag down where she pointed and wiped my brow. My heart clenched. That was just so...so...so *Sam*. "How old was he?"

"Oh, must have been about ten. I worked my ass off the next month. Saved up enough to buy him a replacement. Conner, too. I think they all still have them somewhere stored in the attic." We shared a smile, but her eyes grew serious. "That's the reason I've always worried about him. He gives too much of himself without thinking to ask for what he needs in return."

My smile melted off my face. Ah. This wasn't just friendly rambling and rock-hauling. This was some sort of maternal intervention.

"Oh, don't give me that look. I don't know exactly what's going on between you two. All I know is that my boy has been walking around for the last week like someone told him Santa wasn't real, or something." She reached out to place a hand on my arm, keeping me from grabbing the next bag from her trunk. "You're the first thing I think he's ever really wanted to keep for himself, Lainey."

A lump found its way into my throat. I swallowed it down. And again, when the first attempt wasn't successful.

"It's not my place to get in the middle of things, and Sammy would probably die if he knew I was talking to you." She peered up at me. "But he *is* quiet. I hope you see how much you mean to him. Even if he might not say it all the time." She shot me a dry look. "Though he should."

A weak laugh bubbled out of me. She squeezed my arm before letting go.

"Lainey? Sorry, I just got your texts." Tess emerged from R^3, ducking under the arm of a tall, insanely attractive man who held the door open for her. "You still want to talk?"

Her eyes widened, flicking from the man behind her and back to me. I couldn't read her face. It was hard to tell if she wanted me to save her or leave her alone with the Henry Cavill look-alike staring at her with rapt attention.

"You go have fun, dear. Thank you for listening to the musings of an old lady." June grabbed a bag of gravel and hefted it to her shoulder with ease. *Sneaky, sneaky, June.*

My chat with Tess was quick, mainly since her ex (the ignoring, birthday-forgetting ex who was suddenly here looking like a movie star and hanging on her every word!) followed her around like a puppy and I wasn't willing to get in the middle of whatever was going on there. Based on the surreptitious, hungry looks she was giving him, I didn't think she needed any borrowed relationship drama in her life. She had enough of her own.

She leaned into my car window after I ducked back into the front seat, ignoring Superman, where he leaned against the spiffy, new-model EV parked across the lot. "I'm sorry I don't have more time to talk. There's...a lot going on."

"No, it's okay." I snuck another look at him. "I *will* need a download on what's happening here as soon as that work project is done."

She groaned, resting her forehead against my car. "The project is with *him*. I can't shake him even if I wanted to."

"Do you? Want to?" I peeked around her to take another look. "I wouldn't shake him off if he was stuck to me…"

"Hey. We're here for your crisis, not mine. Focus." She sighed, tilting her head to look at me. "It sounds like you have a lot of thoughts about what's happened. Maybe instead of talking to me, you talk to Sam about it?"

"I'm still mad at him. And sad."

"You're allowed to be mad and sad. He did a stupid thing. Boys are stupid. I validate this." She held her palms out like she was trying to calm a raging beast inside my vehicle. "But it sounds like you said a lot of things in anger. Maybe now that you've gotten a little distance from it all, it would be nice to revisit things with a calmer head."

I slumped in my seat. "I miss him." It was a whispered confession while I watched June make yet another trek from her car, this time hauling one bag on each arm. "I miss him and I'm mad at him."

Tess's eyes flickered to the man across the parking lot. "Both things can be true at the same time, unfortunately."

We looked at each other for a moment, commiserating.

"Boys are stupid."

"Boys are stupid," she agreed.

I stayed up too late that night, tossing and turning and thinking about monster trucks and morals, and how good intentions can still have bad consequences. I thought about my work, my career, and the things I loved about it and hated about it. Sam, so much Sam. How much I wanted to be curled up on his porch, pouring all this out to him. He'd probably know what to say. And maybe we'd be able to work past it and move on.

The problem was, I was still terrified. He'd shattered my trust. Besides, how could I move forward with him now, when I was still reeling from things that happened years ago? Nate and Katie's faces flashed in my brain more than I wanted to admit. How many betrayals did I have to go through until I got the picture and left well enough alone?

Maybe I'd said some wrong things to him out of anger, but I'd been right about at least one thing: I couldn't do it again. Losing him, losing everything? I wasn't strong enough. And I hated myself for it.

I wanted to give him a monster truck, but I felt like my emotional bank was empty. He deserved someone who could give him everything he wanted without a second thought, and I had second, third, fourth, and fifth thoughts.

I laid awake for a long time, thinking about anger and fear. And how sometimes they feel the same.

Chapter 33

Lainey

Perched on the edge of an uncomfortable pleather chair, sporting my white coat and a pencil skirt, I waited to be called in for my third and final interview at Cedar. My foot jiggled while I stared down at my phone. My thumb compulsively toggled back and forth between two message threads.

One from Blake this morning:

Blake Dresden

> Good luck with the interview today. Just a reminder that this is still on the table.

He'd attached a PDF of the official offer from Mercy. I didn't have to click into it to visualize that big, fat salary and all the significant benefits they'd offered me.

I flipped back to the messages from Sam. I'd yet to respond to him, but the fact he kept sending them was a lifeline. However lost I was in my own feelings, topsy-turvy with the need to punch him and kiss him (perhaps simultaneously), his continued attempts to contact me felt steady. I liked seeing his name over and over on the screen. My call logs looked very similar.

I wanted to respond, to answer one of his calls. But what would I even say?

I'd been wracking my brain for the last few days and still didn't know where to start. And time was running out. He was on the other side of that door, and the most I'd come up with so far was "hi."

Down the hall, the elevator chimed and Nate McDaniels stepped out. As if this day wasn't weird enough. He faltered when he saw me, but continued ambling forward, ending up uncomfortably close as he seated himself in the other chair in the waiting area. Only a small end table and a bright pink plastic orchid separated us. He cleared his throat.

This was the first time I'd gotten a good look at Nate since I'd left Texas. I'd only had a second to glance at him at the gala before I'd bolted. I wish I could say he was balding or pudgy or something, but he wasn't. His curly brown hair was longer than it used to be, yet the style suited him. I wondered if it was Katie's doing. He'd dressed like me for the occasion—white coat and business attire. He clutched a leather folio in his lap.

He cleared his throat again, and I realized I was staring at him. He, at least, was making an effort to ignore my existence, like a good cheating ex should.

"What time is your interview?"

His cheeks flushed at my question as he checked his watch. "Ten. I know I'm early but...wanted to make a good impression, you know?"

My interview was at nine, which meant he was over an hour early. I blinked down at my phone. Well, that blew past a good impression and straight into desperate territory, if you asked me.

Then again, now that I thought about it, his extreme punctuality had always irked me when we'd been together. The man had no concept of flexibility or being fashionably late.

Katie had been that way, too, come to think of it. I couldn't count how many dinners or study sessions I'd shown up to on time, only to find both of them had already settled in, drinks in hand. Something about the recollection shamed me. Maybe they really had found each other. Those little idiosyncrasies meant a lot in a relationship.

Like, I loved how Sam had a passion for working out, but also enjoyed a good cocktail and over-ordered Mexican takeout. I liked the way he was content to sit back and listen while I spoke with other people. From what I could recall, Nate had a frustrating habit of interrupting or cutting me off. Often.

Sam made me feel heard without making me feel like I was dominating the conversation. I liked how confident he was. I didn't have to worry about him, even if he was quiet. He'd speak up if he had a problem.

Usually. I wish he'd spoken up before filing paperwork on my behalf.

And just like that, I oscillated more into the punching end of the spectrum than kissing.

A week of overthinking had brought me to the conclusion that he'd made the right move. I just wish I'd known about it. But if he'd told me while I was still on the fence about everything that he was submitting formal documentation of our relationship to my superiors, I'd have keeled over.

So…was I the problem? Him? I kept landing somewhere in the middle, and I didn't know what to do with that.

"How did you know Katie was worth the risk?" My question echoed in the eerily quiet hall. Nate looked physically shaken, staring at me without speaking. "I mean, it didn't seem like it at the time, but surely you had some concerns. Dumping Rebecca Carmichael's daughter? The lease? We were working on that research paper together that was going to get published…What made you decide it would be worth it, even if everything fell apart for you?"

He stared—mouth wide and fishlike—for a second before clearing his throat (for the third time, what the heck did he have a cold or something?) and straightening his tie.

"I…I'm sorry if it seemed like I made the decision lightly. I didn't…" He trailed off, staring at the blank wall in front of him. Thinking, or maybe just avoiding my eyes. I couldn't even believe I'd asked him, but it was suddenly imperative that I heard his answer. How did one know if risking their entire life was worth it for one person? Well, I was sitting next to someone who might have some insight into that.

"It just felt right." He finally looked at me, apologetic. "I know that's probably not the answer you want to hear, but she and I just…fit together. Everything was easy. It worked. You and I, we bickered, you know? And, I always felt like—oh."

I flapped my hands at him, waving off what seemed to be devolving into some years-overdue "it wasn't you, it was me" type speech. "I don't care about that part. We weren't right. You and

Katie are. Fine. Whatever." Flap, flap. I needed to get control of my wrists. "But what made you finally do it? Break everything off? Take the jump?"

"I, erm, well…" He coughed. Again. Jesus. "I've never loved someone the way I love Katie. Falling for her, it was like looking in my pocket and suddenly realizing there was a priceless diamond inside. She'd been right in front of me for so long, and I hadn't even known it. Once I saw it—saw *her*—I couldn't waste any more time."

His words struck a chord so deep, so profound, that my brain somehow erupted in a cacophony while falling quiet at the same time. Maybe this is what people felt like after something exploded near them. The noise. The lack of it. The panic. The calm.

Once he saw her…

"Lainey? Are you okay?"

"I…don't know."

We stared at each other for a long moment, his head slowly nodding as he looked at me. "I hope you are."

"Thank you," I whispered. He looked at his folio. I looked back at my phone.

After a few moments, the door in front of us swung open. Jones sauntered out, still saying something about golfing to the people inside. I hadn't given him much thought since he'd confessed the role he played in my exile. He'd done a crappy thing, but he wasn't really to blame for how everything was going down. It wasn't his fault his grandfather was evil. It was only his fault that he was a jealous little baby man, and I had no time for people like that in my life.

At this second, with him mere feet away from me, I still wasn't thinking about him. Or care. Because there was Sam.

I shot to my feet when I saw him, his face achingly familiar. My heart jumped to see it. He looked tired, smudges under his eyes and a weary expression. His lips tipped in a strained, sterile attempt at a smile.

"Dr. Carmichael. Come in."

Jones brushed past me, muttering something to me I didn't catch. The longer I looked at Sam, the more the uproar in my head settled. The silence rose to become a single voice. Urging me forward. Towards him.

Through the open door, I could see Sturmond and the rest of the quality board sitting along one side of the conference table, waiting. A hysterical laugh burst out of my throat.

"Dr. Carmichael?" Sam cocked his head towards the conference room, cool and collected as always. Only now that I knew him, I could see the strain on his face and how hard he was working to mask it. He was hurting like I was.

His brow furrowed, a crack in his façade. I'd been standing there for too long, caught like a spider in a web of past and present and future.

I felt everything all at once. The ache in my chest—I missed him. The eyes on me—Nate, and Jones, and the Board. The numb, floating feeling as all the little pieces in my head settled into place with a final click.

"I can't take this job. I'm in love with you."

My declaration lost some of its impact because I was still laughing. I was certain I sounded hysterical. Maybe I *was* hysterical, but that didn't change the truth: I was in love with Samuel Reese. I'd been in love with him for a long time. Perhaps all along. Maybe my heart had put on blinders with him because it knew the minute I opened my eyes and truly saw him, it would be all over for me.

Well, I saw him now. And it was all over.

"Lainey?" He reached for me, looking concerned. For good reason. He was watching the woman he loved throw her years-long dreams out the window. Poof. Gone. At least I thought—I hoped—I was the woman he loved.

"Say it back."

Sam huffed out a laugh. "I've been in love with you for years. I don't have anything to prove." His head turned. One of the board members shifted closer. They all watched us, eagle-eyed, except Sturmond, who was chortling about something. "Listen, I appreciate the gesture, but let's just get this interview over with, then we can talk—"

"It's not a gesture. I'm in love with you. And I can't work under a board that compromises clinical care and blackmails its staff." I speared a pointed look at Sturmond, whose mouth popped open. Whispers erupted around the conference table. I ignored them, giving my attention to Sam. "I'm taking that job at Mercy."

"Mercy?!" someone inside the room hissed. Sam must have seen the writing on the wall. He let the door close behind him.

"Just take a second to think about this." He smoothed his hand over my hair before settling it low on my back. He nudged me down the hallway. The weight that had pressed me down for weeks was gone. I felt like I could move again; breathe again. I wanted to prance around and throw glitter.

"You're right. We need to think about this. We're going to make some changes. Your garage is full of workout equipment."

"Obviously, your car takes priority over my weight rack."

Together, we sidestepped Nate, who was still glued to his chair, and Jones, whose eyes were bugging out of his head. Maybe his mouth was hanging open, too. I wasn't sure. My only concern was the quiet surgeon marching me down the hall.

"Lainey, I'm so sorry about—" he started, but I cut him off. We could do apologies later. I was tired of not being on the same page as him.

"And I want kids, but not right away."

Sam flicked his eyes sideways at me, hesitating, before he gave a short nod. "I'll give you three years. Or as soon as you get the Golden Heart. Whichever comes first."

I laughed again, practically floating when he steered me around a corner to another hallway, less infested with my ex and smarmy fellows. I didn't know which was crazier, talking about having Sam's kids, doing it in front of my dreaded ex, or his casual, convicted belief that I could win one of the most prestigious awards in our specialty.

"I want two kids."

A wince crossed his face as he slowed to a stop in the dead-end of the deserted hall. He looked almost apologetic when his hands skimmed down my arms. "I'm going to talk you up to three."

I considered it for a moment. Nodded. "Fine, but I'm not giving up my career, and our kids won't be raised by strangers, so we're going to have to work that out."

"Are you forgetting about Gammy June?"

"I love Gammy June." I sighed. Grasped his shirt. "I'm taking that job at Mercy."

"Sweetheart, I have an open offer at Mercy. If one of us needs to leave to save face, I'll go. They're giving Garcia the program director position. There's nothing keeping me here." His fingertips were rough against my jaw. Feeling him touch me again seemed to open up some floodgates I didn't realize I'd been squeezing closed.

"No," I choked out. Thumbs stroked my cheeks and there might have been tears there. I wasn't sure and didn't care. "Garcia's not going to do crap. They'll need you here more than ever, continuing to be the unofficial resident mom. I'll go to Mercy and take all the cases Cedar is too paranoid to approve."

Our foreheads were pressed together, and I loved everything about it. There was something comforting about pushing my face as close to his as I could get it. Almost as close as I could get, at least. I glanced down at his mouth.

"This is a big step. You sure about it?"

"Mercy's offering me three days off a week," I hummed, shifting closer. "It's a dream."

His mouth hooked to the side, deepening at one corner. I couldn't believe I'd lived without seeing that look for a full week. It revived something inside me that had withered up.

"I meant us," he whispered.

I took his face in my hands. His beard wasn't as neatly trimmed as he usually kept it, and it rasped against my palms. "You're my monster truck, Sam."

His brow furrowed. "I'm—my mom told you the fucking monster truck story? God dammit."

I laughed, rubbing my nose against his. I wanted to roll my whole body in him like catnip. "I love that story, Samuel Reese. And I love you. You're the gift I never saw coming and most definitely don't deserve. Even in my wildest dreams, I couldn't have imagined someone being as gentle and kind and patient with me as you have been, without asking for anything in return. Let me be your monster truck, too."

He sighed my name, tilting my head closer, pressing his lips against mine in the most chaste kiss in the history of the world.

I gripped his hair, pulling him back an inch. "But you. Can. Not. Keep stuff from me again." I punctuated each word with a kiss. He shook his head, tilting to get better access to my mouth.

"I swear. I'm sorry, Lainey. I'm so sorry. It's been killing me."

I sighed. "I think you did the right thing. I'm sorry I blew up at you."

"I'll forgive you if you forgive me."

I grinned, remembering a similar bargain we'd made with a punching bag between us weeks ago, before all this had started. "Deal." I kissed him again. "I love you."

I tasted his smile. Licked his lip to get some more. "I love you so fucking much, you have no idea."

"I might have some idea. Are you mad? About Mercy?"

"Honey, I'm not in a position to be mad about anything right now." He swallowed, eyes darting between mine. "As long as you're happy, I'm happy."

"We won't see each other as often if we're in separate hospitals." I'd been fretting about it ever since I'd gotten the offer from Mercy, before all the drama happened. "It's hard enough right now when we work together. What if..." I trailed off, struggling to articulate the sheer volume of what ifs I had rattling in my brain.

What if we grew apart? What if some other, prettier fellow came along and caught his eye? What if we never saw each other?

He kissed me like he could hear every fear multiplying in my brain.

"Baby." He smiled when I shivered at the term. "I've been waiting for you for years. I'm not going to let you go now."

It should have felt odd, standing in a hospital hallway, pressing myself up against my attending, planning our life together, and sealing my mouth against his. But it didn't. It felt right. Right like someone checking my tire pressure. Right like extra queso after a hard day. Right like the feeling I got when I thought about leaving this place behind.

So, I'd go to Mercy and Sam would stay here and keep watch over the residents, the way he was born to do. Jones would probably get the attending job, along with Nate. He and Katie could live their lives here, raise their babies, and be blissfully happy for all eternity. The thought still didn't sit 100% right with me, but I didn't dwell on it too long. I had my own happy ending to start living with the man in my arms, who I'd overlooked for too long.

"I'm sorry it took so long for me to catch up."

Epilogue - Lainey

Three Years later

"I can't believe you made me carry this across town."

I huffed out a laugh, opening the door to our house. I'd always loved Sam's place, but I liked it so much more now that it was *ours*.

The funky velvet furniture I'd picked out blended beautifully with his leather couch. We'd expanded the patio to add a pair of chaise lounges that were just about my favorite thing in the world. We often laid out there together watching Conner, Jas, and their three boys, Eli, Xander, and baby Rupert (Ru, for short) run around the courtyard.

"We had a limo," I answered, dumping my clutch on the kitchen countertop and grabbing a glass to fill with water. My husband needed it.

He, Conner, and Will had gotten a bit too into the wine while they were toasting my success. Sam took the glass, downing it in a few massive gulps, before setting my award next to my purse. The Golden Heart *was* heavy. I'd nearly dropped it when Cooper and I were giving our joint acceptance speech. We were one of the few surgeon pairs on record to be recognized by the American

Heart Association. But, if I did say so myself, our joint work on mechanical transplants was pretty revolutionary.

Once Cooper jumped ship and joined me at Mercy a mere two weeks after I'd left Cedar, everything had come together. We worked better than ever in a hospital that trusted us to do our jobs. Plus, I had to say, watching the egotistical surgeon fall in love with his truly incredible wife was one of the more hilarious things I'd ever witnessed.

"Limo, sure, but we *could have had a hotel*," Sam whispered, grabbing around my waist. He'd been making excuses to do so all night, utterly entranced by the expanse of skin my backless dress bared to his touch.

"But *here,* we can be as loud as we want," I whispered back, pressing my lips into his. He groaned.

"Good call," he muttered without taking his mouth from mine. I squeaked when he lifted me up, carrying me up the stairs to our bedroom. "So smart. Impressive, award-winning wife."

I bounced on the mattress where he dumped me. By the time I sat up, his bowtie was already halfway undone. I scrambled to assist with his shirt buttons, running my hands up the smooth skin we revealed.

"You know we had a deal, right?" He lowered me back down, grabbing handfuls of my silk dress to pull it up my body. I did, in fact, remember our deal. Hard to forget when he found an excuse to bring it up every month or so.

Three years or until I won the Golden Heart. That had been his timeline for kids. They'd just happened to coincide. When we'd found out Cooper and I had won, Sam hadn't stopped smiling for weeks. He'd started making many, not-so-subtle hints about making an appointment with my OBGYN. If he'd had his way, I'd have gotten my IUD out weeks ago.

Good thing I loved for my husband to have his way.

"Actually..." I gasped when his fingers found the crease between my legs. He uttered a ridiculous curse against my collarbone.

"You haven't been wearing underwear tonight?"

"Panty lines, Sam," I sighed. He groaned again, fingers working where I was already dampening. He sucked at my mouth, thrusting his tongue against mine. He tasted like champagne. "I have something to tell you about that, actually."

"About your panties? I want to hear it. Tell me while I eat you out."

I giggled so hard I snorted. Teeth exposed by his grin grazed the inside of my thigh. Oh, God, I needed to be quick about this. I could already feel the heat building between us, threatening to consume me.

"I just feel bad. You've done such a good job of keeping up your end of the bargain. Not keeping anything important from me. Me...I can't say the same."

I patted his cheek, enjoying the bewildered look that crossed his face.

"You're keeping something important from me?" he rumbled, my skirt rucked up around his chin. "More important than you going commando all night?"

I couldn't help the smile that took over my cheeks. "I've been keeping a secret. A kind of life-changing one. But I figured if you did it once, I got one chance, too."

"Lainey..." He raised up on his hands. I pouted when his weight left me. "What are you talking about?"

"You know, I couldn't have done this without you. You've been such a rock. Your support is one of the only reasons I got that award tonight."

His fingers stroked over my hairline. "Your gorgeous brain might have had something to do with it."

I ignored his mutterings, losing myself in the feel of his body above mine. "I thought you might deserve a little something, too; a thank you, so to speak."

He looked down at me, waiting. The slight line between his brows the only hint of his impatience. My stoic, quiet husband.

"I got my IUD taken out three weeks ago."

He blinked, looked down at my stomach, then back to my face. "We've had sex since three weeks ago."

"Yeah. Lots of it." I shimmied my hips.

"I....you...*unprotected sex*." He sounded so scandalized, he should have been clutching his pearls. I burst out laughing.

"Yeah, that's our favorite kind."

His fingers skimmed down my belly. "Regular reproductive functionality can be restored almost immediately after an IUD removal." A grin split his face. His fingers caressed, soft and reverent. "Honey, are you pregnant?"

My cheeks hurt from smiling so hard. "Maybe. Maybe not, but...I haven't gotten my period yet. Could be a good sign."

"Lainey." He lowered his head to my abdomen, my name sounding practically like a prayer. He grinned up at me, his eyes suspiciously misty. "You might be pregnant."

"I might be," I agreed, pulling him back up over me. I wanted to be eye to eye for this. "If I'm not..."

He stroked my hair from my face. "Then you're not. And we'll keep trying."

Our kisses were deep and sweet. The start of a brand new adventure together. His mouth quickly turned probing, burning.

"We should probably keep trying right now," I whispered. "Just in case."

"Good idea," he murmured against my mouth, fumbling with his zipper. "Smart, brilliant, award-winning, *pregnant* wife."

I swore I could feel his dick jump against my thigh at his declaration.

"*Possibly* pregnant."

"I'm going to do my best to turn that possibly into a definitely."

"You think you're up for it, Dr. Reese?"

"I know I am, baby."

Epilogue - Sam

"Aren't you hungover?"

My wife picked her way across the living room. Lainey. My wife. My *possibly pregnant wife*. My chest tightened.

Most days, I woke up feeling like I was in a dream. Lainey stole the covers, and slept like a starfish more often than not, but she was always willing to curl up against me when I prodded her back into a normal position. We drank coffee and tea together almost every morning. Met up with Blake and his wife, or Tess and her husband, or my family over the weekends. Took on home improvement projects together. Bickered every once in a while about stupid shit that we'd kiss and make up about later.

To anyone else, it was just a regular life. But I'd known from the minute I saw her that with Lainey, it would be special. I hadn't been wrong.

"Yes." I was very hungover, in fact. Last night, Will had gotten the bright idea of starting a toasting war. We'd polished off the complimentary bottles at our table at a shocking rate, raising glass after glass to the award winners. Mostly Lainey.

I couldn't help it. I was in the mood to celebrate my wife and her incredible achievements. I hadn't thought twice about her single half-glass of champagne. I wrote it off as nerves, or wanting to be sharp for her speech.

But I should have known better. It was something much, much more than that. Maybe.

I reached over to pull out the box from the bag on the counter. The one I'd gotten up at six a.m. to buy, and yes, I had been up last night Googling the store hours of our nearest pharmacy. Lainey sputtered a laugh, picking up the pregnancy test while I poured her a glass of tea from the pitcher I kept in the fridge.

Lemongrass, today. I'd probably break out the peppermint once this was gone, or maybe one of the blends my mother made for her. Something with ginger, for any morning sickness.

But Lainey didn't look sick. She looked radiant, like she always did. Hair in a messy bun, make-up free, and wearing one of my shirts. My favorite sight in the world.

"You're not messing around, huh?" She tapped the box that might hold the answer to the most important question of our lives.

"Nope."

She dropped it on the counter, looking unsure. "You're not mad about that, are you? I thought it would be a good surprise. But I know we didn't really talk about it first—mmph."

My arms wrapped around her before she could finish her sentence, lips claiming hers. "I love it. I want your babies so badly you have no clue."

"I have some clue. Watching you play with Ru makes my uterus tingle."

I tilted her head back, angling her so I could sink in, taking her mouth with mine. She sighed, looping her hands behind my neck, returning my kisses with lazy licks and smiles. Like she had all the time in the world to kiss her husband on a Saturday morning.

She did not. We had things to do.

"Lainey."

"Hmm?" She nipped across my jaw. I gripped her face, looking her in the eyes.

"Go pee on this stick."

Moments later, we leaned over the bathroom counter, staring at the little test she'd flipped upside-down. Her phone counted down a two-minute timer.

"Full transparency, I just got really freaked out." Her fingers drummed on the marble counter.

"Full transparency, I'm fucking terrified. But our kids will be incredible." I looked over at her, the sheen of tears shimmering in her eyes. "I want to meet them, don't you?"

A single tear fell, rolling down the cheek that curved into a beautiful smile. "Yeah, I do." I held her tight while I watched the timer tick down. If the test was negative, we'd try again. If that didn't work, we'd figure it out. Everything I wanted was already right here in my arms.

The shrill beep bounced off the tile. Lainey shut the alarm off and bit her lip, glancing at me when she flipped the test over.

My heart stopped as I stared at the two perfect pink lines we saw. Clear as day.

"Oh my God. Oh...my God. Ohmigod!"

I swept her into my arms, emotion clogging my throat. "You're pregnant."

"We're pregnant! Oh, my God."

She soaked happy tears into my shirt. I wiped a few off my cheeks myself. We swayed back and forth in the bathroom. Periodically, I peeked over her shoulder to look again at the test on the counter.

"Sam." She buried her face in my chest in the way that I loved. She fit under my chin like she was made to be there.

If I'd been gone for her before, I wanted to worship at her feet now. Pregnant. With my baby. I wanted to beat my chest and yell it from the roof.

I pressed my lips to her eyes, nose, cheeks...anything I could reach. My hands moved on their own, charting the familiar path down her body. Pulling the hem of my shirt up over her skin.

"Sam...Samuel, I can't," she snickered, batting my hand away.

"Intercourse is perfectly fine with a healthy pregnancy." I pinched a light bite on her neck. I hadn't marked her in a while. I was craving the sight of my teeth marks on her skin. Maybe her thighs. *God damn*, she was pregnant.

"I told Jas I'd watch the kids today while she runs errands. Conner's booked up all morning."

Just one more reason I loved my wife. When we'd first gotten together, she'd claimed she was broken, but it was the gift of a lifetime to see her flourish as she accepted my family as her own. She was as ingrained now as Jas was. My mom called Lainey her daughter. Santiago teased her mercilessly. And I got to come home to her every night and call her mine.

"When?"

"Seven-thirty."

"You have time." I captured her mouth with mine once more, smiling to hear her groan against me. Not surrender. Not yet. But close.

"I have to shower," she gasped.

"I can fuck you in the shower."

"Sam!" she laughed, pretending to be horrified. "Watch your language in front of the baby!"

I probably looked like a besotted fool, grinning down at her with stars in my eyes. I felt like a besotted fool but wouldn't have it any other way. "The baby."

She looked as sappy as I felt. I walked her backwards, twisting on the taps.

"Come on, Honey. If we hurry, we can do it twice before you go over there."

"Sir, you are forty years old. There's no way."

I nuzzled her neck as steam filled the room. "I think you underestimate my motivation."

She sucked in a breath. "Wait, Sam..."

"What, Lainey?" Anything. Anything she wanted.

"Does this mean I can call you Daddy now, too?"

I laughed. Squeezed her closer to me, but not too close. Not too hard. She was carrying precious cargo.

"Baby, you can call me anything you want, as long as it's not oatmeal."

Acknowledgements

Writing never happens in a vacuum, and there are a bajillion people who contributed, however big or small, to the making of this book. Here are a few of them:

Houston, my forever MMC. There were ten thousand times I wanted to give up, but you told me ten thousand and one times to keep going. Without you, this book would not exist. Thank you for always supporting me.

Rebecca, Jas and the rest of the Romantasy Crew. Thank you for sticking by me and always being down for one more sprint.

Jessica, my editor, you made the overwhelming slog of editing and publication seem easy, and for that I will be forever grateful.

Kim, a genuinely incredible human, who never batted an eyelash when I asked her crazy questions about OR logistics. You told me this was an okay book, so if it sucks, it's on you.

Gabriella, for believing in a perfect stranger and lending your time and knowledge to a fledgling debut author. Thank you.

About the author

Romance author Julia Fisher writes about smart, relatable characters, sizzling chemistry, and life-changing love stories. She lives in Atlanta with her family, too many pets and a massive TBR she'll never be able to work through.

Hearts on the Table is the first installment in the Occupational Hazards series, where all is fair in love and the workplace...as long as no one calls HR.

Head to JuliaFisherWrites.com to stay up to date on the latest in the series, including release dates, bonus chapters, freebies, and more!